*Moon Gaffney*

# Moon Gaffney

## BY HARRY SYLVESTER

Foreword by Sean C. Hadley

Angelico Press

For information, address:
Angelico Press, Ltd.
169 Monitor St.
Brooklyn, NY 11222
www.angelicopress.com

PB: 979-8-88677-078-0
Cloth: 979-8-88677-079-7

Book and cover design
by Michael Schrauzer

*For* JOHN C. CORT *and for* DOROTHY DAY;
*for* PHILIP BURNHAM *and for* EMERSON HYNES:
*all good Catholic radicals*

# MEET HARRY SYLVESTER

HARRY SYLVESTER'S writing career began in 1926, with his first published essay appearing in the Notre Dame *Scholastic*. That essay, an exercise in sports journalism which would be Sylvester's primary vocation for many years, put his skills on display. The elements which would shape his career into some of the most promising Catholic fiction in the twentieth century showed their earliest manifestations in the undergraduate Sylvester. For the next fifty-five years, Sylvester wrote journalistic pieces, short stories, novels, letters to the editor, radio scripts, and book reviews that covered a wide range of the human experience. Alongside these writing endeavors, the life of the author was likewise varied and tumultuous, with broken relationships and the pressure of constantly moving weighing heavily upon him. And Sylvester seemed keenly aware of how biography shapes a writer's legacy. In one of the only autobiographical pieces of writing Sylvester authored during his career, he explained: "The real landmarks in anyone's life lie within. A man's birthplace and travels are meaningful only in that they may have helped shape and mark him."[1] Though the external "landmarks" of a writer's life do not provide a secret code with which to unlock meaning, the shaping and marking which such experiences exert on an author should not be overlooked.

---

1  Stanley J. Kunitz, "Sylvester, Harry (January 19, 1908–)," in *Twentieth Century Authors, First Supplement: A Biographical Dictionary of Modern Literature*, ed. Stanley J. Kunitz (New York: The H. W. Wilson Company, 1979), 977.

A key element in understanding Sylvester's works comes from his contribution to Kunitz's *Dictionary*: "the Catholic Church has been the central theme of almost all of my serious writing, I cannot write of myself as a writer without making clear my relation to that Church, past and present."[2] Of course, the Catholic Church is larger than Sylvester's singular experiences. Thus, when trying to place his fiction in the lineage of American Catholic authors, it is important to articulate what this means. If all his "serious writing" is directly connected to the Catholic Church, how might this claim shape a reader's interpretation of his texts? What constitutes Sylvester's serious work as opposed to his unserious work? And how do these distinctions give the reader a better understanding of the Church and the moral tradition of literature that grew alongside it for two millennia? These questions are the proper starting point for understanding how Sylvester's writings serve as an historical witness, capturing the wholeness of the human experience. And one of the best ways to dig into such concerns is to pick up one of his novels. *Moon Gaffney* is a great starting point.

POWER MAY CORRUPT, BUT FAITH REDEEMS

Sylvester's fourth novel, *Moon Gaffney*, was originally titled *The Color of the Sky*. Though it took eleven years to write, edit, and publish, *Moon Gaffney* remains Sylvester's most well-known work today. In the character of Moon, Sylvester sought to connect his writing to an aspect of the public square that often lures poets into political movements. The relationship between the Church and the State drives the action of *Moon Gaffney*, though it is played out on an individual scale rather than writ large, inverting Plato's attempt to understand the individual by looking at the City. The topic lends itself to a kind of timeless relevance. While selling a decent amount, even hitting the *New York Times* bestsellers list for two weeks in July 1947, the numbers did not rise as high as

2  Kunitz, 997.

Sylvester had hoped.[3] Active efforts at suppression from Catholic groups like the Knights of Columbus, whom Sylvester had considered a friendly organization that he financially supported, ensured that attention to the book would remain focused on the more controversial aspects.[4]

The story of *Moon Gaffney* follows the titular character, Aloysius "Moon" Gaffney, a young Catholic in New York considering a life in politics. Moon is plagued by sexual sin and the wider social implications of Catholic teaching. Gaffney's rise to prominence brings him into contact and conflict with unions, journalists at *The Catholic Worker*, and the Irish upper class. Sylvester's characters in the novel learn through conversation, reminiscent of Willa Cather or Ernest Hemingway, who also drew from the Tradition in crafting their stories. As Moon grows by discussing life with the lawyer, James McGuffey, his friend Bart Schneider, and the liberal Catholic Father Malone, he questions whether his own pursuit of a political life is in keeping with Catholic teaching. These questions are answered through an accidental death, arguably made possible through Moon's own compromises. Sylvester brings the novel to a crescendo as Moon agrees to defend three black men in his first courtroom trial, bringing together the threads of racism, hatred, and fear which characterize so much of Moon's journey. While much the primary questions stay unanswered by the novel's close, Moon's journey from a power-hungry nominal Catholic to a lawyer defending the poor with his reinvigorated Catholic faith as the primary motivator.

*Moon Gaffney* continues Sylvester's argument that parish life offers the best insights into the Catholic experience. In what may have been a contrarian spirit, Sylvester typically found things to criticize on both the political left and right amongst his Catholic

3  Denver Lindley to Harry Sylvester, July 18, 1947, in Harry Sylvester Papers (Washington, DC: Georgetown University Libraries: Booth Family Center for Special Collections), https://findingaids.library.georgetown.edu/repositories/15/resources/10124.

4  Denver Lindley to Harry Sylvester, May 5, 1947, Harry Sylvester Papers.

brethren. But it was Sylvester's affirmation of Church teaching which enabled him to take an inward glance and find within the American Catholic Church practices at odds with the standards of Christian living.

Sean C. Hadley
Fayetteville, Arkansas
January 2024

OVER THE EVENING traffic of Canal Street a bell tolled. Mournful, evanescent and mobile, its sound hung in the air, renewing itself unurgently, shedding a kind of silver through the failing light. The policeman directing traffic at an intersection saw the red car approaching and halted traffic for it to make the turn. Then his raised left arm and extended right moved as though signaling, for the car held not some ordinary fire chief but Patrick Gaffney, a deputy fire commissioner. The left arm came to the side and the right arm broke in a salute acknowledged by the commissioner with a weary and unsmiling lift of his head. He was fearfully glad to be home.

The car moved a half block or so down a side street, its bell wearily tolling, just why not even the driver could have said. Stopping the car he alighted and opened the door for the commissioner in front of a house with a worn brownstone stoop.

"This thing rides like a donkey cart," the commissioner said. "Hereafter we use the Cadillac all the time."

"It has no bell on it, Commissioner," the driver said.

"I always forget that. Why couldn't we get a siren on it?"

"I guess we could."

"We never think of those things," Gaffney said. He had been thinking about Danaher, the next lower ranking commissioner to himself. This afternoon had been the second time Danaher had refused to come out of a burning building. Gaffney had had to go in and order the men to take Danaher out.

A door opened above them in the vestibule and a young man came down the steps in two bounds. Tallish, thick-chested and powerful, there was yet an unhealthy quality about the early jowls, the freckles showing clearly against the pale skin.

"So he's been out again, Mike," he said. "What are we going to do with him?"

"Enough of that crap," the commissioner said. "Should I be sitting on my tail in an office all day like you while my men are out on the job?"

"Oh, all right," his son said.

"Sure, Moon," the driver said, "I kept him near the car practically the whole time."

"I'm going to speak to his boss," Moon said.

"You'll get far doing that," the commissioner said. Moving toward the house, he turned once more to his driver. "Nine o'clock sharp, now, Mike. Don't be late."

"Okay, Commissioner."

As his father turned toward the house, Moon turned to Mike and held up all ten fingers. Mike nodded sardonically and got into the car. Pleased, Moon turned back to his father, putting lightly one hand on the old man's elbow as they mounted the stone steps. "You'll kill yourself," Moon said.

"Small loss."

"All right, so you'll kill Mom with worrying."

"That I don't believe. She's had forty years of it now, from the time I'd be up to my neck in it as an ordinary fireman."

"Neither one of you is young any more, though."

The commissioner made no answer as they ascended the stairs to the second floor. The stairs' dimness and their smell had reassured him for the greater part of life, although neither the smell nor the dimness formed part of his conscious thought. The house had four stories. For some time he had been able to afford a more fashionable part of the city, but this was the district of his rise and his affluence; and habit and his son's future had merged into and become indistinguishable from what had once been necessity. Nearing the retirement age, Gaffney, a deputy fire commissioner, had come not as far as he might, but as far, he found in mild amazement, as he cared to go.

They had made more than a virtue of necessity and the two floors they occupied had been done by an uptown decorator from Madison Avenue. Mrs. Gaffney had thought of having another stairway cut into the back so that they would not have to use the outer stairway with the fourth-floor tenants. But in time it proved easier and less disturbing to let the top floor remain unrented. Even without an inner stairway the two flats gave much the appearance of a duplex apartment and the contrast between the solid and harmonious interior and the shabby outside was always good and sometimes startling, impressing the poor and giving to others reassurance.

Moon opened the door from hall to dining room and held it so for his father. Mary, his sister, and their mother advanced upon the commissioner, having obviously composed themselves. "Are you all right, Patrick?" Mrs. Gaffney said, while Mary leaned to kiss her father's cheek.

"God," the commissioner said, "here I've been sitting by the curb spitting into a fire all afternoon and you ask me if I'm all right." Neither his scorn nor their concern was new in this house and they realized one more time that there simply was no more to be said.

Dropping the rubber coat from his shoulders into Mary's hands, the commissioner walked from the dining room through a bedroom and into the parlor looking out on the street. His wife and Moon followed him and as he sat down, Mrs. Gaffney said, "Your supper will be ready in a few minutes, Patrick. We put it on as soon as we heard the bell coming."

"Anyone call?" he said.

"Half a dozen people. I told them I didn't know when you'd be back."

"Did you speak to any of them?" he said, turning to Moon.

"Only Ryan. He didn't seem to have much on his mind. He said he'd probably stop by this evening."

"He makes me nervous," the commissioner said. "Fat and all that he is, he makes me nervous."

Mrs. Gaffney sat down beside her husband and took his hand. For several reasons Moon left the room. He had eaten with the rest of the family, and there now seemed no more to say to his father. Moon had about decided to go to the mission at their parish church tonight. All week his mother and sister had been after him to go, but there had been too many other things to do.

Two or three years previously, Moon had taken a degree at Fordham Law School in the Woolworth Building, but he had never practiced law. Without conscious pondering and while still an undergraduate at Manhattan College, he had made politics his career. During the three years in law school he had begun a kind of apprenticeship by acting as a confidential messenger and go-between for various politicians. His pay he had drawn from a vague appointive job at City Hall. And in turn he had begun to pay his own price: the big body was already a little soft from drinking and the irregular life required of it; it was no longer easy to tell his real humor from the false professional one he wore on the local streets or engaged in his work.

Although he dressed in the loose clothing he had learned to buy as an undergraduate, he still wore ties in the long, narrow knots favored by the other young men of the neighborhood. Now in his room on the upper of their two floors, Moon put on a dark gray suit and somber tie. Some daylight yet remained, and, as so often lately, he would not light a lamp in his room until darkness was entire in it. In the mirror he saw himself, faceless, a study in shades, a blackface comedian whose triangle of white shirt alone possessed brightness, a

[4]

darkness moving in the dark. He wondered pointlessly but no longer in annoyance why Mary taught at that junior high school with the nigger kids when she could teach any place she wanted to in the city. Perhaps it was her step on the stair that had roused her name in him, for she passed through his room on the way to her parents'. In the mirror she was another shape, tenuous like himself, and he knew she wore a dressing gown only by the wind of her passing. In the room's autumnal twilight she, too, wondered why Moon dressed so often in that dimness.

"Going to the club?" she said.

"Maybe later. Going to see Kavanagh first."

"Try to stay sober." She had not paused in her passage; her tone was flat, without rancor.

"I wish you'd stop that," Moon said. Her concern lately had annoyed him—all of them knowing no Irish family but had a drunken relative close in memory—yet tonight her remark brought him only a certain smugness, perhaps the first stir of conscious personal irony. Smiling into mirrored shades at this new pleasure, he did not know its name. He told himself he was going to the mission because they had shut up about it. Actually he went out of a vague concern and the surer knowledge it would be good politics to be seen at least once at the mission.

The tie arranged as he wanted it, he pulled vest and coat straight and snapped on the light. The mirror's solid figure pleased him, its dark suit, the brown hair curling once neatly from the white part. Tucking a linen handkerchief in his breast pocket, he beheld once more the perfection, ready for wedding or funeral. Of the two hats that lay on a small table, for just a moment he thought of wearing the black Homburg, then decided it wasn't quite the occasion or place and put carefully the gray, snap-brimmed one on his head. Neither were gloves called for. He opened the door into the outer hallway.

The odor of cabbage hung in it, persistent enough to be the place's aura and identity. Going quickly down the stairs, he was stayed by voices behind the doors of the lower flat and he wondered who was with his father. Probably local people, seeking preferment, he thought, descending to the street floor. Opening the inner door of the vestibule, he stood for a moment on the threshold of the outer one, never closed but in winter. Some yards to his right, the dwindling traffic of Canal Street went by and he smelled the odor of roasting sweet potatoes from an unseen Jewish peddler's cart. For an instant he hesitated, hardly knowing he wondered whether just possibly it was Congressman Foley closeted with his father, or Assemblyman Billy Ryan. Then, glancing at his watch and seeing he had but ten minutes before the mission began, he went down the stone steps and walked briskly northward.

People greeted him from stoops and shop doors, one greeting touching and often overlapping the next, as Italian, Jew, and Irish, child and adult, each made unconscious homage. It was, in its way, a remarkable tribute, and one hardly recognized as such by Moon. He was conscious of few enemies and the natural charity of his mother and sister was also in him, informing his relationship with these people, unconsciously utilized by himself, and in its turn utilizing him. Hardly at the threshold of being able to obtain political favors, it was not that which attracted people; nor anything so obvious as his nickel for a child or a word for its parents. There was in him a current or quality and at his age it could still color and give to even his professional manner a sincerity and depth of which while using it he was unaware. It extended to the Lenihan brothers, Patsy and Ed, where they lolled before a drugstore. although their horse faces, thick-featured, reminded anyone of what they were: bouncers for the local assembly district club by night, by day truckmen. Moon wondered why they were not at the mission.

Turning a corner, Moon saw the church as two things. Flats hid its structure, an unconscious service to aesthetics, so that there showed first only a scattering of small groups of people, then three long canvas signs fixed to the iron fence and to the façade over the triple doors. Closer, Moon looked for but could not see Kavanagh, and so inevitably read the signs, although the highest and widest one he had known for months, waking and, most puzzling, sometimes asleep. Its weathered red-and-blue lettering said: BINGO!—EVERY THURSDAY NIGHT AT 8—BINGO!

The signs on the fence were new, repeating each other's words and the older sign's coloring: MISSION FOR MEN—Oct. 1-7, 7:30 P.M.

Kavanagh touched Moon's shoulder. "What do you say?" He was a very tall young man, lean, angular, and, like Moon, carefully dressed. His face, pale and severe behind steel-rimmed glasses, was placid by an effort showing in the gathered and sensitive mouth.

"Save your money," Moon said. Then he saw Bart Schneider with Kavanagh and restraint came over him. He had met Schneider only once or twice before, but knew of him, a boyhood friend of Kavanagh's from Brooklyn, who had gone to school in the Middle West and, until a few weeks ago, had been working in Chicago as a correspondent for a New York paper. Dark and stocky, with regular features, Schneider had a brisk, open quality which caused Moon and others to distrust him. As they turned to enter the church, Schneider said, "They're sort of beating that bingo thing to death back here in the East, aren't they? Wonder what they do with the money."

"It's used for good purposes, all right," Moon said gravely. "In this church for paying off the mortgage." He put his hand in a holy water font. Beads of light scattered around his head and one of them fell upon, briefly staining, the tie of dark green silk. He had thought Schneider a Catholic, too. When all of them genuflected, Moon felt not reassured but puzzled.

They found seats together in one of the center pews. Five minutes later when the missionary came out upon the altar, the church was crowded. In dress and general appearance Moon and his companions were several cuts above the rest of the congregation, mostly laborers and office workers in Sunday clothes, with a scattering of boys from high school and college. Many of the local families, whose heads had good civil service jobs, lived in the neighborhood for the same reason the Gaffneys did, and were able to send one or more of their sons to college as day-hops. Indeed it was better, they reasoned, and not much more expensive than to have them idling around trying to find jobs.

The missionary knelt on the predella and led the men in the five Glorious Mysteries of the Rosary. His voice, strong, clear and assured, bounced back at them, seemingly from the altar, and the men responded in a hoarse, inarticulate murmur. Relief was in the rustle and clatter with which they settled back in their seats while the missionary made his way up to the high pulpit. Out of sight for a moment, he appeared in the pulpit suddenly, a heavy, florid man wearing thick-rimmed glasses. His lace surplice imparted a stylized and almost doll-like appearance to him. He blessed himself, the audience following him brokenly and rather as though a little weary of it by now.

In the quickly forthcoming silence for which archly he had waited, the priest began. "Tonight—tonight we will consider again and in full a subject upon which, other nights of this mission, we have merely touched. The great, one might say the besetting sin of our time, that sin which has sent more souls to Hell than any other—the everlasting sin of the flesh."

It was as though death, imminent and fearful, had entered visibly into the place; as though sin, somehow incarnate, danced terribly in the aisles. Many in the audience hung their heads, others made small, silent and uneasy gestures. Looks of distress appeared on the faces of the students. Only a few outwardly unregenerate souls faced the pulpit as if to say that although they were dirty and only the priest clean, still they would not be dismayed. Imperceptibly and indeed unconsciously the missionary touched his tongue to his lip.

"This sin," he continued, "is one which can send souls to Hell by a mere glance, a thought, a light touch. . . . More often, it is one in which the sinner is the direct occasion of someone else's sin. So that guilt is twofold, one might say. Each of the participants is guilty both for himself and his or her partner. Yet it is usually the man who is the aggressor and therefore has the greater responsibility. The lowest pit in Hell is reserved for him who first deflowered some pure virgin. We have the word of many people for this, including the great Eyetalian novelist, Dante Aliggeri. To say nothing of the writings of that great son of Ireland, Father Michael O'Shanahan, probably the greatest theologian Ireland has produced in this century. The lowest pit in Hell, let me say it again, for him who first deflowers some pure virgin."

That silence was still there when he paused; sick and deadly it hung in the air like an acrid incense. James Kavanagh had concealed part of his face with one hand; his eyes were closed in the bowed head. Schneider's face was grim, a puzzle to Moon. Turning from these two, Moon found himself bewildered and filled with pity. What the missionary said was not new to him; he agreed with it, in a sense it sustained him. Brave, bright, and interested he turned back to the pulpit, finding he had missed some of the words.

"It is up to us to guard our thoughts, words, and even trivial deeds and to be careful of our company if we are to avoid this filthiest and most heinous of sins. Some may argue that this is a very difficult thing. But if once we take thought of the terrible consequence or consequences of our act, it will no longer be difficult. Think, men, think of the dirt and degradation that are involved, and not only on the spiritual plane. . . . Think of virgins despoiled, of women led from the virtue of holy purity; think of the fairest flower of womanhood degraded and bespattered with dirt. And by whom? Why, by you! And then think, think of the terrible consequences.

"Would you in Hell wish to be further tormented by the pitiful plaints of your victims, their wails of anguish broken only by their voices raised to accuse their betrayers? Mankind *knows* no greater evil than the great sin of the flesh. Nor is anyone free of its temptations, neither princes nor presidents. Let me tell you a story by way of illustration."

Moon, for some reason, was not interested in the story. He had begun at last to feel the general pressure in himself and again let his glance and attention move. Schneider's face at the moment held Moon's glance, although he read in it only the most obvious component, scorn. Then anger, itself obscure and shapeless, deafened Moon for a time and during that time he sat there, hating Schneider. The clearest form his thought took was that Schneider should have more respect for a priest. When Moon could hear again, the priest was saying, ". . . nothing filthier. There is no virtue higher than the virtue of holy purity and no sin more heinous than that committed against holy purity. I give you this thought to take with you to your offices, your schools, your very homes, wherever there is temptation to sin against holy purity. Amen. A blessing I wish you all: In the Name of the Father and of the Son and of the Holy Ghost." Then, as an afterthought, "There will be no benediction tonight."

The congregation began to clatter from the pews. Moving slowly up the aisle in the crush toward the doors, Kavanagh felt his body come free again, although of what he could not have said. In the wide vestibule as they came to it, a priest stood, no older than themselves. His hands were in the pockets of his cassock as he stood surveying the men coming out. In half-shadow he stood, a faint, pleased look on his face. A few of the passing men noticed him and to their respectful greetings he returned a half-nod, almost of annoyance, as if disturbed in a pleasure. Seeing him, Moon groped for his name; usually good at names, he could never keep straight those of the three or four curates and assistants in the parish. "Evening, Father," he said.

"Ah, good evening, Moon," the young priest said, moved to animation and a separate pleasure by this word from the near-great. His head turning to watch the priest and give no offense, while at the same time he kept moving, Moon made a curious and ingenuous spectacle as he tried to avoid introducing Schneider and the nameless curate. His awkward, momentary helplessness was not lost on the curate. "Well," the priest said, jovially, "Father Minihan really gave it to you people tonight, didn't he?"

"I guess so," Moon said. It was no longer possible to face the priest without stopping or turning further. Moon looked ahead, seeing the two banks of tiny lights, white of the stars under the pointed arch, red of the cigarettes. He could hear both Kavanagh and Schneider breathe the new air as they came out of the vestibule's dirty marble. "I wonder why no benediction?" Kavanagh said.

"It's getting toward the end of the mission," Moon said. "He didn't want to make it too long."

"Or a sop for listening to his filthy sermon," Schneider said.

No one spoke as they turned east. Kavanagh might have sighed in the quietness.

"Why do you say that?" Moon asked. He spoke quietly, anger having left him: in the outer world of politicians and of picnics he had schooled himself to avoid anger. It might almost have been said he felt it only at home and in church.

"Because he's a liar for one thing and an obscurantist for

[11]

another," Schneider said. "The Church has always taught that the sins of the mind are more grave than the sins of the flesh. It's all through the New Testament. And he didn't distinguish once between fornication and adultery. Worse than that, he'll send half the people home thinking they and their wives are filthy."

"How do you figure that one out?" Moon said.

"Well, did he distinguish?"

When Moon hesitated, Kavanagh said, sullenly, "No, he didn't."

Now Moon sighed or rather exhaled in a kind of exasperation. He had not felt much one way or another about the sermon. It was dark and the street lights touched somberly, made grave their faces, each man's weariness separate and apart. When Moon still did not speak, Schneider went on. "It's people like him who are responsible for aberrations. Do you think any one of the kids there tonight went away thinking sex, *per se*, was anything but filthy? A fine way to begin married life."

"He didn't say that," Moon said.

"The hell he didn't," Kavanagh said.

"Just how did he?" Moon said. The pain, he recognized, was that of betrayal.

"A matter of emphasis," Schneider said, calmer. "The man hates sex because it's not allowed him. For some minds it's easier to abstain from a thing one hates. What he and the others like him forget is that if he—"

"You are the damnedest man for a Catholic I have ever seen," Moon interrupted. "What kind of a way is that to talk about a priest?"

In silence again, Schneider felt that uneasy awe and pity people like Moon always brought to him. In a flat tone, "I mean that if the salt have lost its savor wherewith shall it be salted?"

[ 12 ]

"Meaning what?" Moon said.

"Meaning I suppose that if the clergy or the doctors have become confused or somehow perverted, something ought to be done about it. Even if it's usually the wrong thing. Don't get me wrong. I'm not antichurch. Maybe I wish I had the guts to be anticlerical. But the obscurantists among the clergy during the last generation have about persuaded us it's a sin to be such. And if they're right an awful lot of people, including St. Bernard and Catherine of Siena, were sinful. I suppose the difference is that the saints spoke with such an authentic note that no one today could match it. Our ears are attuned to the clerical voice on the radio and somehow it alone seems authentic. A kind of unconscious technique of self-perpetuation."

Silence returning, changed again its tone, a bell variously muted, an expanding room; in this particular tone each man knew separately the burden of his own chastity. James Kavanagh said, "What about a drink?"

"All right by me," Moon said.

"Here's a joint," Schneider said.

"Not this one," Moon said. "I know another one." He chose his drinking and eating places in the district with meticulous care, depending indeed on the season, day and even hour. LaGatta's was the place for now. The regulars would be finishing a late dinner, and others coming in for a drink. And memory, sly, knew some of the uptown people had taken to coming there. He turned a corner and with quickening pace led the others west. Rosemary Danaher, he thought, honestly surprised. Twice now she had been at LaGatta's in recent weeks.

Two hours later, when a group including Rosemary entered the place, Moon was in a not uncharacteristic position. He and his chair were half-turned away from the table at which Schneider and Kavanagh sat moodily over their drinks, half-turned to the next table at which sat four minor politicians of the district, two Italians, a Jew, and an Irishman. Moon had begun to drink with these others while, more or less over his shoulder, he maintained a broken conversation with the two at his own table. As Rosemary and her friends entered, a sudden brief immobility seized him, as if stunned at being found so between worlds. It could hardly be said Moon recognized the situation, although he was aware of the faint sardonic grin on Schneider's face. There was only that hesitation, enforced and startling . . . then he was on his feet, burly, genial and alone, moving quickly to greet the newcomers as if LaGatta's were his own place.

Rosemary's eyes opened in a burlesque of surprise; she stopped moving and raised her arms as if to embrace Moon. "Why, Moon!" she said in a kind of amazement. Moon, too, had raised his arms, but stopped just short of touching her shoulders. The pale-haired young man with Rosemary waited patiently. The two other couples smiled. "Say, Moon," Rosemary said, still mock-urgent, "I hear you're going to be the next mayor. Folks—"

"Well, I'll tell you—" Moon began.

"Folks," Rosemary persisted, "meet the next mayor, Moon Gaffney." She introduced Moon to the others although he knew all of them more or less. Whitey Travis, with her, he knew least well. The two other men, Neal Hartigan and Peter Calahan, he saw occasionally at dances or political functions, and the girls with them, Ellen Doarn and Patricia Moore, Judge Augustine Moore's daughter.

Moon shepherded them to the table where Schneider and Kavanagh sat, against which Johnny LaGatta was already pushing another table. The newcomers' reluctance seemed to stem from Peter Calahan's disapproval. Large and dull, he knew relatively few emotions, and disapproval he had come to think a fashionable one. Moon was annoyed at Calahan's stiff, unbending manner, one Calahan thought military. Having got the two tables started, Moon returned to the district captains, for it would hardly do to leave them abruptly.

Schneider knew none of the group with Rosemary. Kavanagh knew slightly or had seen all of them before. Having less money than they, in college he had not associated with them, and even now a diffidence lay on him.

"Well, well," Rosemary said, getting their attention, lighting a cigarette. "Well, well," she repeated, "so this is Bart Schneider."

Schneider unexpectedly flushed. "Meaning what?"

"Aren't you journalism's white hope or Communism's or something?"

"Something."

"You don't miss a trick, do you, Rosemary?" Neal Hartigan said.

"She certainly doesn't," Kavanagh ventured. "Bart's been back in the city only three weeks and she has all the dope."

"What will you ladies have to drink?" Peter Calahan asked. He turned to the pretty girl with him. "You're not drinking tonight, are you, Ellen?"

"I don't think so," she said.

Everyone wanted Scotch and soda except Calahan who asked for Irish. He recommended it to all the others but they took the Scotch. Schneider said that Irish was a cold-weather drink and Hartigan agreed with him, but Calahan ignored them both. There was a good deal of chatter, led by Rosemary, and the lighting of cigarettes. Somewhere above them, just beyond their aura or radiance, the figure of LaGatta hovered darkly. And somewhere they heard Moon's voice booming: ". . . Kelly delivered his district, and it so happened that it was a hell of a tough time to deliver it with that Cloney affair breaking. . . ."

It gave their own talk a political tone—rare among them,

[15]

for although the families all owed much to politics, it was not a thing their generation often discussed. Now Rosemary was in a familiar element, without need for dissembling: her father, like Moon's, was a deputy fire commissioner. She led the discussion. Jackie Meagher would be mayor again, they agreed, but the Hall would have to clean house in some fashion. Most of them were very pious about this. "The Hall is no worse than its predecessors," Patricia Moore said with a faint smile.

"The Hall is the gathering place of Irish Catholic gentlemen," Peter Calahan said, "and as such is above doubt."

"Oh, come, come," Kavanagh said. He allowed himself a thin smile. It froze as he saw that Calahan had been entirely serious.

At the next table, the district captains were standing ready to depart, making vague and respectful gestures toward Kavanagh and Schneider, who gestured in return. From the door of the captains' departure, Moon returned to the larger table. Only Kavanagh could tell that Moon had had a lot to drink.

"Everything going all right?" Moon asked. He leaned solicitously over Rosemary in the burlesque of a headwaiter.

"Everything is fine, Alfonso," Rosemary said. "Except when does the floor show go on?"

"The floor show goes on any minute now," Moon said. "And if it doesn't, I will put on a show for you myself. Was the terrapin just the way you wanted it?"

"Just, Alfonso," she said.

Having made most of the others smile, Moon felt he could now sit down. LaGatta waited with a chair for him. His mind toyed gently with the thought of giving his imitation of Al Smith, but rejected it: it required standing on a table or chair, and that would not do here; nor now—with those present who might see it as sacrilege; in various corners, regulars and other captains yet remained.

Schneider was saying, ". . . there were thirty or forty of them. All of them around the bishop—"

"Let's have another round," Moon interrupted.

"We really ought to be going," Calahan said. He didn't like the way Schneider looked at Ellen, the way Schneider addressed himself to her when he spoke.

"The evening is but a pup," Moon said, "and tomorrow is Sunday. We can all go to the printer's Mass and sleep late." He put a heavy hand on Calahan's shoulder, and sat down.

"This round is on the house," LaGatta said, and hurried off. For some reason they were all looking at Moon, the solid figure bent forward from the waist so the fingers of one hand could play with a spoon near the center of the table. Moon was pleasantly aware of the others' fixed attention: it had happened before with various groups. Yet in this one he was separately conscious of but two people, Rosemary and Schneider. While they waited, none of them could have said for what, Moon thought he should phone Rosemary about going out some night, and that he didn't trust Schneider. Then, the moment calling for appropriate words, he said, "We figure to sweep the city again next fall." Lately he had taken to cigars and now felt the need for one in his teeth, but the taste for liquor was sharper.

"You mean you're already worrying about that?" Schneider said, not unpleasantly.

Seeing Moon's annoyance, Hartigan smiling said, "It's a twelve-month job, strictly," and the others laughed.

Ellen Doarn said, "My father—" but Rosemary talked faster. "They're going to run Moon for assembly, aren't they, Moon?"

He shrugged, his eyes widening appropriately and appropriately dropping. Peter Calahan stirred. "It's late, Ellen, and—"

LaGatta came, following a waiter with glasses, and Moon's voice boomed again over the other sounds. "You think we run the party like a clambake. We—"

[ 17 ]

"Sure," Schneider said. "That would be the way to run it. Strictly amateur, instead of—"

"Oh, stop that stuff," Kavanagh said. His face was drawn up in a kind of mock pain, his eyes harassed.

But why harassed? Schneider thought. Perhaps Kav felt now, in weariness, the earlier betrayal of Moon. Himself, he was alone, Schneider knew, but then it seemed he had been alone for a long time, a period to which he could hardly name a beginning any more surely than he might its end.

Patricia Moore said, "Father would agree with Mr. Schneider."

"Sure—" Moon began and then stopped. His head was inclined, the face held a light, sardonic smile. Almost, he had to bite his tongue. Moore was a federal judge and above the need for party politics, or nearly so. Then, with a sense of shock, Moon saw the others knew just what he had been thinking, without his having said it, and that Hartigan and Schneider knew it most clearly and Patricia and Calahan least, perhaps not at all.

Into the embarrassed quiet, Schneider said, "As a judge, Miss Moore, your father is able to take an objective view, one which the rest of us much envy."

So now *he* had said it, Moon thought, and without hurting anyone's feelings. And yet some of them, Moon saw, groped still for all Schneider's meaning. He might be a good man to help write speeches.

"Judge Moore was always such a man, Schneider," Calahan said. Like Moon, he had drunk more than any of the others.

"Glad to know it," Schneider said. "Anyone got a cigarette?"

Ellen Doarn held out a pack and he took one. Neal Hartigan lit it for him.

"I hope all you people are going to the St. Linus's dance," Ellen said. "It's for a very worthy charity and—"

"I'll go if you go with me," Schneider said. Everyone

[ 18 ]

laughed but Calahan, and Ellen colored slightly. "I've already got an engagement to go. But I know some girls who would like to go with you and Mr. Kavanagh."

"What makes you think we can't get our own girls?" Schneider said.

Ellen smiled but made no answer.

"She knows the kind of women you newspapermen go with," Moon said, "and she doesn't want them at a St. Linus's dance."

Even Calahan laughed this time. "You might have something there," Schneider said. Not enough of them, he thought. The bitterness, nameless yet not obscure, was never distant.

"I'm no newspaperman," Kavanagh said. "I'll go to your dance and I'll bring my own girl."

"All right," Ellen said. "You can get your tickets right now." She opened a gold mesh handbag.

Moon took a roll of bills from his pocket and slipped off two fives. "You got enough?" Schneider said to Kavanagh in an undertone. The tall man nodded.

"It's a dinner dance," Ellen explained. "That's why the tickets are fifteen dollars."

"But who am I going to take?" Schneider said. "All my girls are in Chicago."

"Oh, I was serious about getting you someone," Ellen said.

"And I just as serious about going with you," he said. The disturbance the words induced in the others seemed unreasonable to him. Calahan stirred but seemed unable to speak.

"But you see, I'm engaged," Ellen said. Calahan brightened and the others looked mildly surprised.

"Why, Ellen," Patricia said. In the little flurry of talk Schneider felt depressed. The clock in a near-by church struck a single note and Calahan rose and again urged them to go. Moon took them to the door, while Kavanagh and Schneider remained at the table. Returning, Moon saw Kavanagh's face in his hands out of sheer tiredness, and Schneider playing with the engraved invitation he had just bought. He had taken it out of the envelope, and made a small tent of it between the circles of wet on the table.

"Well, now," Moon said, "if this place bores you, we can go to another."

"Not me," Kavanagh said. "I'm going home. I'm out on my feet."

"Me, too," Schneider said. No one moved. "You don't suppose that Doarn girl's really engaged to that stuffed shirt?"

"Why not?" Moon said cheerfully. "If you had what he had, she'd be engaged to you, too."

"What's that?"

"About half the tea in China," Moon said.

"Oh, come, come," Kavanagh said. "His folks own a grocery chain. That's all."

"Well, good for them and good for her," Schneider said. He stood up, a blocky figure, feeling separately, like all men, his own particular wearinesses. He struck Kavanagh on the back. "Come on, James, pull yourself together."

Kavanagh also rose, an unfolding through layers of light. An old and nameless desperation was in Moon, perhaps the need for companionship in a darkness not yet named for him. "Look," he said, "we could go to Mass if you want to leave here. Then you wouldn't have to get up in the morning."

"Not me," Kavanagh said. "I'm out on my feet."

They gave Moon money and he paid the waiter. Outside, the air was moist and cool. In a taxi, Kav said he wanted to go to the nearest subway station. It was only a few blocks away and Kav got out and stood uncertainly in the street. "You coming along?" His face, uncaring for anything but his own weariness, looked sullen and meager.

"No," Schneider said. "I'll go with Moon. You get home all right?"

"I'm not drunk." The tall man turned away into many shadows and the subway swallowed him gradually.

Moon gave the driver the name of a church in the twenties. Neither he nor Schneider spoke as the cab wheeled through empty streets. The church lights were dim or filtered through stained glass, and through more shadows people moved toward the forever triple doors, in clothes shabby or those of their profession, firemen, and conductors.

The Mass had just begun. They knelt in a rear pew and Moon pulled out his rosary beads. Somewhere near them a woman in cheap evening clothes giggled and said something about whisky sours. A man's handkerchief covered her head. She was, Moon saw in mild surprise, with Assemblyman Ryan's party.

Schneider's hands felt the need of a missal, and he tried to remember the Ordinary of the Mass: "I will go up unto the altar of God— To God Who giveth joy to my youth. Judge me, O God, and distinguish my cause against an ungodly nation." He gasped at new and too prideful meanings his mind gave the words, and still other words distracted him. "If the salt have lost its savor . . ." Yet he was not less self-righteous than they, he thought, remembering the cheap women in Chicago, the distortion of facts, very slight . . . the hate, the despair, his jeers at people simpler than himself. And what were the Collects for today: something to beat his brains out, as usual?

2

THE DANAHERS lived on Park Avenue. Arthur Danaher had grown up in this assembly district but farther to the east, on the other side of Lexington Avenue. Unlike the Gaffneys, the Danahers could move into a better neighborhood while still remaining in the district of their influence. Moon was aware of this as he stood in the foyer of the apartment house that was the Danahers' home. The doorman's appraising glance had irritated Moon, and irritation was the principal if not his sole source of new awareness or growth. His father ranked Arthur Danaher; Moon was even reasonably sure that they had more money than the Danahers; yet the doorman had not liked his appearance. Moon wondered whether, if his own family lived in a fashionable equivalent of this place, it would transform him or his appearance in some subtle way so that the doorman would not look at him as though he did not belong here.

In the foyer mirrors he saw himself. Dark gray, rather snug, the topcoat was fashionable, he was sure; and there were the carefully creased trousers, the black Homburg held in the hand. Gloves, too, were suitably dark. There remained for doubt only the tie and he wondered about that knot. The fingers of one hand moved to it, there was an unrealized idea of loosening and widening it—when the doorman came from the house phone and said that Miss Danaher was in.

In the elevator his lack of sureness gained his attention. There had been enough other girls, he thought, for this to be no novelty. They had not lived in this particular neighborhood, yet some of them had been more closely related to his political future. Leora Ryan, for example. The name raised in him the image of her heavy body and roundish face; the tiny features and the constant talk of Uncle Billy. The contrast with Rosemary added a fresh layer to Moon's discontent.

On the fourteenth floor, he wondered if the man in the elevator was going to wait for the Danaher door to open, and was relieved when the elevator closed before the apartment door opened. A Negro maid let him in. There was no one in the living room and this reminded Moon he had looked forward to seeing the commissioner as well as his daughter. Bookshelves filled one large corner, wide sets of Kipling and Dr. Eliot. But there was a thick scattering of what Moon recognized as religious authors, their books sturdily classified in diocesan weeklies as "fine Catholic novels," their names, surely synonymous with genius, just familiar enough to cause him unease: Lucille Papin Borden, Owen Francis Dudley, Frank Spearman. There were, he noticed, the unease increasing, two or three books on fire fighting; his father had none that Moon knew of. The rest of the room he found larger but not more grand than his mother's living room: the overstuffed and brocaded furniture, the heavy rugs, the literal barrier of expensive furnishings along each wall.

Turning to the windows in relief, he remembered how the city viewed from above by night always pleased him, perhaps because he rarely saw it so. It added nameless pleasures to another he did not like to name: that someday he could be mayor of its magnificence. It was, he knew intuitively, not a common thought among the men he worked with, even those farther advanced than himself; it was not even a safe thought, he knew.

The Danahers came into the room in a body, mother, father and only child. "So nice to see you, Aloysius," Mrs. Danaher said, as her husband shook hands with Moon. She was a large, firm woman, wearing a mauve evening gown. Her husband was in a Tuxedo, so that Moon's mind automatically ran over the possibilities of their destination; he could think of no politically important affair for tonight.

In speech he found himself awkward and stammering. There was that humorous and by now professional quirk to the mouth, the widened eyes, something very close to conscious naïveté; he could not be unaware of the disparity between his age and his advancement. And yet here and now the words came unsurely. "Why, I'm fine, Mrs. Danaher. How—"

"And the commissioner?" she went on.

"Oh, he's the same as ever. He—"

"We were just on our way to the theater," Mrs. Danaher

[ 23 ]

said. "I'm sure you won't mind. We were rather surprised to learn you were coming, Aloysius. Rosemary never tells us about these things. Don't you like the place, though?"

"It's the best view in New York," Moon said. "I think when the commissioner retires, we'll come up this way ourselves."

Mrs. Danaher smiled in a peculiar manner that did not include her eyes. "We'll have to go now, Aloysius," she said. "You'll give our regards to your mother and the commissioner, won't you? I mention it now because you probably won't be here when we come back."

"And mine to your mother, young man," Commissioner Danaher said. "I see your father too often to have to send him my regards." Both he and Moon laughed. Mrs. Danaher had already gone out of the room and the commissioner followed her through the door the maid held open. Rosemary was over by the window lighting a cigarette. The door's closing signaled or renewed in Moon the various tensions. His lips were dry.

"Well, Aloysius," Rosemary said, turning on him, "how did you manage to tear yourself away from the boys in the back room?"

"Why," he began, his hands moving in a heavy burlesque of explanation, "it was this way—" They both laughed inordinately. That streak in Moon of the conscious clown set up in Rosemary an answering current, a kind of despair recognized since her undergraduate days, but not as such.

"Sit down," she said. Sitting down herself, she patted the place next to her. "I want to see what makes you tick."

Moon sat down carefully. His smile had become the fixed and lugubrious one of the clown. He wondered if Rosemary would offer him a drink. "That," he said, "is a remark that could be taken in a number of ways."

"Why, Moon!" she said. Her eyes blinked in the mockery of innocence, the imitation of surprise.

He sighed and fumbled for a cigarette, forgetting he no

longer smoked them, then for the cigar in his breast pocket. So here was a fellow clown; he felt a sense of relief; it was odd he had never before seen her as such. Wondering what *her* reason was, he was forced to consider for the first time his own. But there was only a wall.

She said, the mockery now touching her horror, "You're not going to smoke a *cigar,* are you?"

"Oh, all right," he said. "Give me one of your coffin nails."

"Why, you're right out of the eighteen nineties, Moon."

He held her hand with the match to light the cigarette in his lips. "That's what comes of being in politics." Letting go of the hand, he leaned forward, affecting to gather himself around the cigarette as did lesser men. Somewhere in the silence a door closed firmly. "Ghosts," he said.

"Just the maid leaving," Rosemary told him. "Niggers give me the creeps, though. I've been after mother to get a white maid."

Moon had been about to say something, its nature unknown until his lips should open—when Rosemary went on. "You know, we have to be careful about them. . . ." She wasn't looking at him; her head was nodding fixedly and he found it hard to tell whether she was still clowning. This ambiguity confused him, as did most values not sharply colored, and consciously he changed the subject.

"Who you going to the St. Linus's dance with?"

"Oh, I have to go with Whitey Travis. I've gone with him every year." Her shoulders moved, registering not so much distaste as resignation.

"You don't act as if you were crazy about it."

"I'm not exactly. I guess I'm just sort of used to Whitey and he'd be disappointed, I guess." She sat there still looking straight ahead.

Moon found this not easy to reply to. The only ambiguity he understood and moved freely in was that of political talk.

Heat against his fingers reminded him he had not smoked the cigarette. He took a single drag and rubbed it out. "I don't know who I'll take," he said. "You know—"

"Oh, you just play the field, Moon. We all know you could just put the numbers in a hat and—"

He felt the smile crease into his unwilling face. "You know Leora Ryan?"

Rosemary half-closed one eye thoughtfully. "I think so. Billy Ryan's niece or something."

"That's it," he said. He thought that Rosemary really ought to appreciate what a risk it was for him to take her to the dance instead of Leora. "This Travis," he said. "I don't know much about him."

"Oh, he's in the brokerage business. I knew him in college."

"Where'd he go?"

"Yale. You probably know his father's firm: Lockheed, Travis and Carr?"

Moon shook his head; his fingers moved to the cigar in the breast pocket, perhaps as a kind of touchstone. Moon felt more curious than resentful. There was somehow nothing more to be said on the subject.

"You want a drink, Moon?"

"I wouldn't mind." Her tone had made him hesitate.

"What do you want, rye, Scotch?"

"Rye." He added lamely, "No hurry."

She believed him apparently, for she sat and waited a little time, uncomfortably poised on the edge of the sofa. "Is Ryan really going to run for Congress?"

Moon nodded. "I think so."

"I thought it was definite."

"I guess it is," he said. How to tell her, to tell anyone, that Billy Ryan couldn't decide whether there was more in Washington at ten thousand a year or in the district at fifteen hun-

[ 2 6 ]

dred. Why, Ryan hardly knew it himself! The thought pleased Moon.

"Then that means they'll really run you for assembly?"

He nodded. The possibilities, even the satisfactions of his position were so old now in his mind that her reference to them raised no more than a flicker of pleasure. "It looks that way."

"Gee, can I touch you?"

"Well, I usually charge a small fee—but seeing as it's you—"

She laughed and went for the drinks. Moon stood up and again moved toward the window. He felt freer for some reason; perhaps because his relation with Rosemary was already so easy; perhaps because he could now, with clear conscience, ask Leora to the dance. Enpatterned, the lights of the city held his sight, dazed him with an enchantment; yet were hardly a thing conscious in him, his own sad reflection of Augustine's *City of God*.

Rosemary had returned to the room. When he did not turn or show any awareness of her presence, she yelled, "hey," and Moon quickly turned. For some reason she had not put down the tray with the glasses and a plate of crackers on it.

"Quick like that," he said, ashamed of something, and hurried over to her. His fingers touched and covered hers, which slipped quickly from under the heavier ones. The tray had so little weight that, holding it, he felt ridiculous. Putting it down he took one of the glasses, suspending it delicately by his finger tips and sat beside her. He leaned back in a kind of relief. The drink was weak but he said it was all right when she asked him.

"Say," she said, "who is this Schneider?"

"I don't know. He's no friend of mine. Kav knows him."

"Reason I asked—they say he's a Communist." She leaned back, limp and satisfied.

Moon shrugged. "I don't know. He went to Mass with me

[ 27 ]

the other morning after we left you people. But—" He shrugged again.

Reference to the Mass silenced Rosemary for a moment. "I know. But the Communists all are doing that now. The ones with Irish names go to Mass so that people will see them and they can bore from within."

Moon nodded. "They pulled that down at our church. But what would Schneider want to fool me for?"

Now Rosemary shrugged, her lower lip caught between her teeth. Her vague distrust of Schneider—it was hardly a dislike—was similar to that she felt for Negroes. Both Peter Calahan and Whitey had heard about his being a Communist.

"Old Father Malone down in our district," Moon said, "he ran into what you were talking about during that longshore-men's strike." He drank, finishing the glass. "Some of the Commies in the union were trying to take over during the strike, because a lot of the members thought Brosnan, the president of the union, was playing ball with the companies. And the Commies had a pretty good chance of pulling it off, except that they were Commies and most of the union was Irish. So they started sending two or three Commies with Irish names to Mass." Moon hesitated. "I don't know whether Father Malone was tipped off or what. Some of them said he recognized one who'd been an altar boy at St. Ambrose-by-the-River. Any-how, when he was leaving the altar to go to the pulpit for the sermon, he saw the two men down near the front of the church and he went to the altar rail and told them to get out of his church, that he knew who they were and why they were there."

"Good for him," Rosemary said.

"Still," Moon went on, "it was a hell of a thing to do at Mass. Actually, you can't order anyone out of a church. Canon law or something."

"But if he knew who they were and why they were there—why, what else could he do?"

Moon nodded for some reason. He guessed she was right; his admiration for her took on another layer. There was no other girl with whom he could talk on such terms, no other so intelligent.

"They got out, too, I bet, didn't they?" she went on.

Moon leaned back. "Well, it was a funny thing. I wasn't there but I talked to a fellow who was. And he said one of them went out like a rat—and the other one went out crying."

"Huh, imagine that," Rosemary said. "You want another drink, Moon?"

"I wouldn't mind."

This time, while she was out, he looked at the books again. He ought to read more. He wondered about that Commie crying and tried to laugh but felt silly; there was nothing he could think of to explain it.

When he heard Rosemary returning he went to the door to meet her. "Why, Moon," she said, "we'll make a gentleman of you yet."

Knowing how she kidded practically all the time, Moon grinned back, again taking the tray. This time on the sofa there seemed less to talk about. Moon put his arm up on the sofa back, above Rosemary's shoulder. After a suitable interval he let the arm touch her shoulders. Rosemary looked slantwise at him and said, "Why, Moon!" then deftly moved his arm.

"What's the matter?"

"Why, Moon, this is only the first time you've been here."

"Oh, all right." That was reasonable enough. He wondered about Travis and Rosemary knowing him so long. It was funny about him, Moon thought; the image of Leora or Kavanagh or Neal Hartigan, Moon could always make in his mind, but he could not make one of Travis. Uneasily, he wondered what Rosemary could see in Travis; it must be money. "Are you engaged or something?"

She was contemplating her hands, long and carefully treated. "Why, no. What makes you think that?"

"Well, you been going with this Travis since you were in college."

"Oh, Whitey," she said. "He's just like a kind of cousin. I suppose I *could* marry Whitey. His father's awfully strict with him about money, though."

Moon frowned over the apparent *non sequitur;* Rosemary was just too quick for him. "You've got to get married sometime."

"Oh, I will," she said. She had leaned back against the sofa again and this time closed her eyes. Moon had leaned forward; as he talked he could not see her.

"I thought you were maybe in one of those long-time Irish engagements," he said. "They're the damnedest things—"

"Say, aren't they, though." Rosemary was bright again. Springing up, as it were, to life, she was now leaning forward with Moon. Animation lit her face, her speech lilted. "The Irish are really the darnedest people." Something amused her a good deal and she laughed merrily, stopping only to light a cigarette.

Moon's face creased again in that fixed and unwilling smile. He would concede it was amusing; many others beside Rosemary found it so, and he supposed it must be for some reason or other. Personally, he thought, he would not like a long engagement. The thought made him feel guilty and in the guilt he lost again the possible reason for the length of the engagements.

"I had an aunt once," Rosemary said, leaning back and picking a fleck of tobacco from her tongue. "She was engaged for eight years and when he died they still hadn't announced the wedding." She found it very amusing.

Moon laughed, too, not to displease her. "I have an uncle,"

he said. "He got engaged to a girl in 1918 when he was going over to France. And, honest, he's still engaged to her."

"Years and years," Rosemary said. Her head went back in merry laughter.

They were still laughing when the phone rang. It was in another room and Moon could hear the rise and fall of Rosemary's voice but few of the words. Something about the St. Linus's dance. His disappointment about it was gone. Laughter always made him feel good. He lit another cigarette.

"That was Ellen Doarn," Rosemary said, seated again beside Moon. "Isn't she lucky, though?"

"I wouldn't know," Moon said. "Tell me about it." He leaned against the sofa, his head going far back. Ease from the laughter was good in him.

"Why, she's engaged to Peter Calahan. Isn't that wonderful?"

"I guess it could be, but I really wouldn't know."

"But you know who he is, don't you?"

"I saw him stiff at enough dances to know."

"Oh, he's no worse than a lot of others," Rosemary said. Moon tried to remember if Travis, too, was a drunk, but could not remember anything about the man. "Anyhow," Rosemary went on, "Ellen's engaged to him and everyone thinks it's wonderful." Her voice had dropped to a curious breathless note that could have meant almost anything, both retreat and defiance and even a kind of nothingness. To someone more knowing than Moon, the voice might also have been a warning.

"Why do you think it's so wonderful?" Moon turned his head to her as he spoke and was startled to see how definite was her annoyance.

"Now, look, Moon," she said. "If you think I'm going to let myself be cross-questioned about my friends, you're crazy. I—"

"What friends? I wasn't cross-questioning. I—"

"Oh, skip it." She smiled, perhaps because some hint of the ridiculous came to her.

"I didn't know Calahan was such a friend," Moon said. "If—"

"Well, Ellen is." She looked straight ahead.

"But I didn't say anything about Ellen. I asked why everyone thought it was so wonderful she was going to marry Calahan."

"Moon, I'm not going to discuss it." Rosemary got up and went to the window. She lit a cigarette and stood looking out across the city, her back to Moon.

Moon thought he had better go. Moving over to Rosemary he said, "Look," to her back, "if I've done anything to offend you, I—"

But she turned, smiling, bright, and patted his cheek. "Oh, don't be silly, Moon. Let's forget the whole thing. Come on, sit down. I'll get you another drink." She pulled him along by one arm.

"I ought to be going," he said. It was ten forty-five. Uneasily, he wondered if the Danahers would be worried finding him there when they came home. . . .

"I have to see some of them down at the club," he said. It was as valid an excuse as he could make for Rosemary.

"All right," she said, nodding her head. "All right. Leaving me for a bunch of the boys in the back room." Moon felt better now that she had begun to clown again: one shoulder hunched, the corresponding hand at a right angle to its wrist. "I suppose you're going to see what they'll have, eh? The boys in the back room, eh?"

Laughter was relief. She could certainly be all right when she wanted to be. Having made him laugh, for some reason she didn't press him to stay. "Give my best to the commissioner," she said at the door.

[ 32 ]

"And *you* tell the commissioner I'm sorry I couldn't stay until he got back," Moon returned gallantly.

Moon gone, Rosemary returned to the sofa. She felt both tired and restless and wondered about Whitey. She just wished his father would give him enough money, instead of making Whitey go through all the motions of working his way up in the business. If Whitey wanted to get married so bad, he could just keep after his father. She could wait; it was no trouble at all for her to wait, she thought with satisfaction; she told herself again that she was glad she wasn't like men.

A little after eleven the phone rang again. It was Mrs. Danaher. She wanted first to know whether Moon had gone yet. Then she told Rosemary that they had met the mayor and a party and would be late returning. Mrs. Danaher also thought that Rosemary ought to go to bed.

Not immediately after her mother called, but between five or ten minutes later, Rosemary decided to phone Whitey. It was a relief to find him at home, although she did not relate cause and effect. She asked him if he wanted to come over for a while, there was no one home. They talked in the quiet, clipped speech of people who know each other well, and who have long before accepted as inevitable the restraints placed upon them. Whitey lived around the corner in an elaborate private house, and he was probably, Rosemary knew, speaking from the phone extension in the living room and with some of his family near by. He said he would be right over.

While Rosemary rubbed powder on her face in her room and wondered if she already had enough scent on her dress, she also wondered if Whitey might ever get impatient and go with someone else. But he certainly couldn't marry anyone at all, the way things were with his father, unless some fool girl would marry him on that fifty a week he was getting. Still, none of the girls either of them knew would be likely to do that.

[33]

She ran a few steps when the doorbell sounded, then caught herself and slowed down. After she had let Whitey in, they stood for some time, kissing and not speaking.

There was more light in the living room and in it she thought Whitey looked worn, the eyes tired and not focusing quickly. When they sat on the sofa, Rosemary was a little disturbed that Whitey didn't immediately put his arm around her. She moved up close to him in a series of quick, repeated motions and leaned her head on his shoulder. He put his arm around her and kissed her on the lips but only turning his head. When he raised his lips, Rosemary asked him how things had been at the office that day.

"About the same," he said. "Things are slow." He told her about the market. She didn't listen and after a little silence, she said, "I certainly wish your father would let us get married."

"I wish he would, too," Whitey said. "Sometimes I think he doesn't want us to get married."

"But why?" Rosemary felt weak. "He's always been as nice as pie to me when I visit your house." She wondered if Whitey noticed the change in her voice.

"I don't know. . . . He likes you all right, but I don't think he likes the idea of my marrying a Catholic."

"Oh, that's silly," Rosemary said, looking down. She quieted her fear by telling herself no, not for anything would she ever leave the Church. . . .

"I know," Whitey said. "It doesn't cut any ice with me." After a pause he said, "To me that's just one more reason for getting married now."

Rosemary's hesitation was not studied. "But, darling," she said, "how can we?" She raised her head from Whitey's shoulder and looked at his wearily turned face. Her own face showed concern, an anguish for the greater part real, the mouth slightly open, the eyes ready for tears.

Whitey turned his head away in complex embarrassment. "A lot of other people are living on fifty dollars a week," he said, indistinctly.

"But, darling, you couldn't have *anything*. You couldn't have a servant, or a car, and you'd have to live in some other part of the city. And I don't know what we'd do about children."

"I don't either."

They sat there like that for almost a minute, Whitey looking down and in front of him, Rosemary looking at her love. Although she was convinced only of her own concern for their dilemma, some part of her, hawklike, watched his face for change. But as so often before, nothing happened, neither acquiescence nor rejection.

"I don't know why you just couldn't go to your father," Rosemary said, "and tell him how little more it would take. On even a hundred a week we could live near here in some small apartment."

"You ought to know my father by now."

There was nothing to be said to that, she knew. They had been to this place so often, both of them knew exactly what came next, the precise way and moment for the tension to break. So that when Whitey turned to her, Rosemary, dry-eyed, was ready for their embrace. It lasted some time and was not terminated until Whitey fumbled for one of her breasts. Rosemary sprung away as though she had been jabbed with a needle. "Whitey—what do you think I am!" She almost wept. "That's the second time!"

"Oh, all right," he said. "I'm sorry." He sat, facing her, one leg flexed and drawn up on the sofa, an elbow on the sofa back, the corresponding hand loosely covering his eyes.

Rosemary experienced a new kind of panic: she wondered if she had begun to look cheap or what. Slumped heavily against the sofa back, she hardly thought of Whitey at all. Then she

[35]

began to wonder if he could possibly know how tired she felt. Whitey spoke and she said, "What?"

"I think I'd better go along," he said. "Got to go to the office tomorrow."

After a pause, Rosemary said, "I didn't mean to hurt your feelings. I just don't want to cheapen our—our relation. And besides, we both know it's wrong."

Whitey stood up and moved a few steps toward the hall. In it, by the door they embraced again but without passion. Rosemary's lips felt cold and seemed to have lost their fullness. He felt pretty dopey, Whitey thought. Hell of a time to be up with tomorrow a working day.

After Whitey had gone, Rosemary went into her bedroom. The little clock on her dressing table said one and she wondered about Mama and Papa not being home. She was so tired she decided to skip cold-creaming her face. But not too tired to say her prayers, she told herself. So she knelt by the side of the bed and asked God to bless Mama and Papa, and for Papa to buy her that new black caracul coat she wanted. Then Rosemary got into bed and pulled up the covers and was asleep in no time.

3

TWICE A MONTH the ladies of St. Linus's Hospital Auxiliary met for what was euphemistically called The Sewing, patently a making of bandages, bed linen and other articles for the hospital. There was about their collective effort, for most of the ladies, some of the quiet and almost unperceived satisfaction many people derive from atavisms like pruning trees or plucking a fowl. Few of them sewed at home; in the long, dim room at the hospital they salved conscience, satisfied ego and learned a good deal about their neighbor. For some reason not quite clear to them, they also had a certain amount of what their retiring president, Mrs. Danaher, called "cultural activity." Mostly, this was an occasional speaker, one every third or fourth meeting. Muscular ladies who spoke on first aid, missionaries who had climbed a mountain, teachers who had once seen the hidden convent in Mexico City: all had given of their pearls to the Auxiliary.

Today, the poster Ellen Doarn had lettered, announced J. Martin Murphy, art and literary critic. Mr. Murphy would lecture on "Catholic Art and Literature." The wording for the poster was Mrs. Danaher's. While lettering it, Ellen had not thought of Mr. Murphy's cultural versatility so much as the reason for a kind of unpleasant amusement or scorn among young men when his name was mentioned. She herself had no feeling about Mr. Murphy, as she thought of him. Once or twice she had danced with him at formal dances and had found him dull, a man in his early thirties, plumpish, the smile grave and superior but easily broken into a toothy and humorless grin. It was odd that she had never thought of that smile before. Peter, too, sometimes broke into that pointless and fatuous grin, she remembered. The thought made for a certain queasiness in her body. Since this, too, had never happened before, she dismissed both thoughts from her mind. Peter, she told herself, was a very considerate and devoted young man.

J. Martin Murphy would not arrive before four-thirty, after the sewing had been in progress for two hours. It might almost have been said that he was a kind of carrot dangled before the ladies' noses. Meantime, they sat in three or four circles and sewed and talked. The circles were rough divisions by age or interest. Rosemary, Ellen, Patricia Moore, Marie McGuffey and other young women were in one; there was what could have been called a political group about Mrs. Danaher; and a third talked mostly about work actually related to the hospital. Words, occasionally a whole sentence or phrase from one circle fell upon the ears of those in another and sometimes distracted it or changed abruptly or gradually the tenor of the group's talk.

The current charity for which the Auxiliary worked and held its dances was the new maternity wing of the hospital. There was always the business of the sewing, of baskets for the poor, of being—a few of the younger women—lay assistants in the maternity clinic; but these activities, of themselves matter for virtue, rarely gave the women any conscious satisfaction. That was reserved for such solid tangibles as dances and bridges, affairs not only giving occasion for display but resulting in the gain of good, hard cash. So zealous were they for this house that the wing had been started the previous year by the hospital in the serene knowledge that the Auxiliary would raise funds for interest and payments on principal in its usually sturdy and inevitable fashion. And now the building of the wing had progressed to a stage where there were talk and rumor of what its charges and personnel would be.

This was the topic in the middle circle, the one between Mrs. Danaher's and the young women. The wing was to be named after the late Cardinal Geraghty, a great advocate of large families—"I care not whither they bay in country or city," he had been fond of saying—and now Mrs. Ratigan said for perhaps the fiftieth time that year that it was certainly an appropriate thing to name the wing after His Eminence.

"It's something they should have thought of long before they did," Mrs. O'Reilly said. "I named one of my boys for him, the least anyone could do."

Other women had also named sons for the late cardinal, and there was much nodding, with Mrs. O'Reilly's distinction now diluted, and various others wishing they had thought to name a boy for the cardinal.

"Mayor Meagher often said the same. If he had a child, it would be named after the cardinal."

[38]

In the little pause this created, some of the ladies actually thought they shouldn't say it. Others thought it their duty to say it and one of them did. "I don't see how Mayor Meagher could have a son when he isn't living with his wife." Gasps followed from the uninitiated.

"That I simply don't believe," one woman said, heartened by the gasps.

"Whether it's believed or not, he's not."

"But I see her with him at Mass at the Cathedral."

"A lot of people do."

"She's paid to go there with him." Again the gasps.

"That, I flatly don't believe."

"Nevertheless, Mrs. O'Reilly, I know."

"Then it must be her fault. She's not a Catholic."

There was, of course, no answer to that one, but someone said, "It could be."

"All right, now, if it's her fault, why so much talk about this other woman?"

A kind of Babel broke out for a few seconds. "I don't believe it, I don't believe it," one woman kept saying, stitching and shaking her head, trying simultaneously to deny and ignore.

"It couldn't be so. I know—"

Then they all stopped, for Mrs. O'Reilly was close to tears. "It couldn't be so," she said, tearing the words from her as she stitched with slow, ponderous care. "It couldn't be so. Our Jackie could never do such a thing. With my very eyes I saw the cardinal put his arms around him on a platform that day in Central Park. 'Tis a terrible thing when a group of Catholic women have to talk so about—about a Catholic statesman. I—" She dropped her head again, shaking it and stitching now faster.

"The best thing would be just to drop the subject," said Mrs. Danaher, who had felt it necessary to come over to this

[ 39 ]

group. Not all the ladies were anxious to follow this sensible suggestion, but the nun who exercised a kind of mild supervision over the sewing made her appearance in the room. One might have made a fairly accurate guess as to what each circle was discussing by the way its voice was raised, lowered or silenced. Marie McGuffey giggled and held up the baby clothes she was sewing. "I guess you don't mind me sewing on these here for myself, do you, Sister? I'm expecting my second, already."

"Not at all, Marie," the nun said.

"Well, anyway," Mrs. Ratigan said, "what we *were* discussing was the new maternity wing. I hear they're going to charge twelve dollars a day, same as at the Pavilion uptown."

"I have it as fact that it will be nothing of the kind. It will be sixteen dollars a day and not a penny less." The speaker's voice had risen and induced silence in the other circles.

But who, Ellen wondered, could pay it. Themselves, perhaps, but hardly those who came to the clinic downstairs. The thought embarrassed her, part of some shapeless heresy.

"Sister Frances," someone said, "is that what they're going to charge for the new wing, sixteen dollars?"

There was no pause in the nun's passage toward the sewing machines. Only her face turned, a faint, tolerant smile on it. "Why, yes," she said.

"And why not?" one of the political circle asked. "Why shouldn't the maternity wing be of the best class? It's named after the great enemy of birth control."

There was no answer to this, either; although the phrase "birth control" induced other and more fearful silences among them. Most of them practiced birth control of one sort or another (Mrs. Danaher, for example, simply refused to sleep with her husband) and these were naturally not comfortable discussing it. In the silence the nun finally reached the sewing machines. As usual, she noted, the bad sewers had the ma-

[40]

chines. Still, she supposed it was better for them to be at the machines; most of them could do no more than turn a hem on a sheet. With her arrival there, the talk rose again in the room, louder and more general.

"Edna Robson," Rosemary said, "is going to have a baby. At last."

"Oh, good," Patricia said.

"I don't know," Rosemary said, stitching slowly and thoughtfully. "Everyone knows what her husband's been doing the last few years."

"He's been going with other women," Marie said, "but I don't know what that has to do with Edna's having a baby. I think it's nice she's going to have one."

"Well—" Rosemary said, and both hesitated—the lips pursed —and savored the moment. "I happen to know—" Pause and stitching. "From a very confidential source—someone in the medical department of civil service—Joe Robson has syphilis." The group gasp sealed Rosemary's pleasure.

"That's awful," Patricia said. "But I don't believe it."

"I don't, either," Ellen said, "but if he has—"

"I know!" Rosemary said, pronouncing each word separately. She raised her head, widening her eyes; the eyes still wide, she lowered her head again, inducing a suitable silence.

"If you do know," Ellen said, also pausing between phrases, "if it's really so, someone ought to tell the doctor. I mean the doctor that's going to deliver the baby. It—"

"Oh, no!" Patricia said. "My heavens, it would kill old Mrs. Robson and the judge to know that about young Joe. I don't believe it, but if it is so—"

"Well, I do know," Rosemary said, "and they ought to do something. I mean—"

"Naturally," Ellen said. She had become a little sick; just why, she did not know; perhaps her love of children. Reluctantly the words came, torn by a compulsion strange to her.

"The doctors have to be careful when a baby has that kind of heredity. The baby's eyes have to be washed with some sort of germicide—or something. Perhaps do something for Edna. I don't know exactly."

Her manner—an accentuation of her often hesitant way—impressed them more than what she said.

"But what a thing for young Catholic women to be talking about," Marie McGuffey said. Her manner and tone, at once bright and severe, was in the best diocesan weekly or sodality tradition.

"And I still think more harm would be done by telling people than not," Patricia said. "Judge Robson is a wonderful old man. Just the other day, Father was saying—"

People rose to greet the advent of J. Martin Murphy in the rear of the room and Patricia stopped talking. The ladies began to fold their lengths of muslin, of linen, and there was a general motion and rising, an anticipatory quiver in the graying light. Circles of chairs became rows, machines were closed, the last patch of winter sun lessened perceptibly on the wall. Ellen stood up, feeling the unease leave her body. Across choirs of matrons, Mr. Murphy beamed at her, beamed at Rosemary, beamed at all the girls. She smiled thinly and by a window lit a cigarette. Smoking was not approved here and usually she tried to keep custom. But sixteen dollars was all some of them had in an entire week, she thought. Not that women from the clinic could be expected to take rooms in the new wing. The idea of bearing children was less attractive than usual, and this change freshly disturbing. Or was it the thought of having children by Peter that seemed less attractive? It was difficult to say. As usual in such moments, she rubbed out the cigarette (or lit one) and turned from the window. Rosemary was patting a chair beside her, all the ladies were in their seats, and Mrs. Danaher, about to introduce the speaker, was looking at Ellen. Just before sitting down, Ellen noticed others had come in, part-time workers from the clinic below, and with them a few young men to squire some of the girls home. She recognized Mary Gaffney, whom she knew slightly from the clinic, Moon, and James Kavanagh.

"As you all know," Mrs. Danaher began, "for indeed we have been anticipating it for some time, we have with us today probably our leading Catholic critic. Or anyhow, our leading Catholic lay critic," she qualified into the patter of applause. "It was only after much urging and arranging that we were able to persuade our speaker to come here. His various duties such as that of secretary of the St. Dymphna Book Club and Editor in Chief of *Catholic Art and Painting* give him a very full schedule, to say nothing of his critical articles in such publications as *Our Sunday Visitor* and *The Catholic World.* . . ."

The Catholic Boiled, Ellen thought, but there didn't seem much point to the thought.

"And so," Mrs. Danaher was finishing, "it gives me great pleasure to present to you Mr. J. Martin Murphy."

The applause, multiplied by the confines of the room, was very satisfying to J. Martin. As he rose, he noticed that the nun left the room and two of the young men in the back turned to each other as though debating whether to go out and have a smoke. J. Martin wished they would: men disturbed him in various ways, and Moon particularly. Moon always called him Joseph and the Joseph part of his life was one J. Martin would just as soon forget, with his aunt's three-room flat in a walk-up and the boys at St. Patrick's Prep calling him sissy.

"As we all know," he began, lisping slightly, "we live in a time of the most abominable paganism. The main current of American art and literature is infected with this virus. We see it in the magazines, the books, the moving pictures. You are all aware of its existence. My purpose here today is to discuss the Catholic opposition to this paganism, the strong, virile, realistic Catholic countermovement in the arts." He paused for breath. "Some of you are perhaps unaware that such a movement has begun. You know that here or there is some fine Catholic novel by Lucille Papin Borden or Frank Spearman. Or that there is an exhibition of the marvelous paintings of J. Montmorency Delaney, with their so wistful cherubim and their saints to rival those of El Greco. But you do not know, perhaps, that there are organized groups and publications to promote this movement in Catholic Art. Not so much to tell you what to read as to keep you informed, for the sad fact is that the secular press, in a kind of conspiracy, either ignores or misrepresents Catholic literature in this country.

"So, while I am hardly here to tell you about the St. Dymphna Book Club, I feel that in discussing some of our recent selections, you will get an insight into the main stream of Catholic literature in this country. And then, time permitting, I will discuss Catholic painting in this country.

"First, this last month's selection, a novel by Edith Hooper Hannigan, entitled *Only Angels Sing*. In a sense, Miss Hannigan is a discovery of ours. For many years, this obscure little woman wrote and wrote, but her work was of such a spiritual nature, of such a truly spiritual nature, that naturally no secular publisher would touch it. And she was too humble to submit it to a Catholic publisher, thinking her spirituality of perhaps not a sufficiently high order. Then a friend or associate of ours—perhaps I might take the liberty of calling him a scout?—" J. Martin paused to smile while some of the audience tittered. "This friend called her work to our attention. Perhaps I would be revealing too much to say that this friend is a member of the hierarchy? Perhaps some of you would think I was guilty of *lèse-majesté* in calling him a scout?" He paused for reassurance, his eyebrows raised, his smile winsome, and his audience generously gave him what he asked, their smiles faint, fair, and fleeting.

"I would hesitate, also, to tell you that Miss Hannigan is a relative, a cousin of our—agent, for that, too, might be revelatory. But I or rather we—myself and my associates—were so struck by the resemblance to Emily Dickinson. The similarity in the ways they were discovered. . . . But to get on with the description of the book. It concerns an English family wintering in Italy about a generation ago or perhaps two. While Miss Hannigan has never been to Italy, she has a wide acquaintance with the English. One of her grandparents was born in Wales although most of her heritage is naturally Irish. But anyhow, this English family is naturally not a Catholic one. In spite of the Chesterton and Belloc influence, very few English families are. This family, in fact, might be best described as anti-Catholic. Nevertheless, they are attracted to Italy by its beautiful churches, the pomp and ceremony of Rome. And, of course, the lovely climate and the orange blossoms. The father is a successful businessman, naturally very intelligent, but almost completely without spirituality. The mother is a woman who, while devoted to her family, is inclined, to put it gently, to sniff at the things of the Church." J. Martin paused to indicate, by delicate movements of head, hand and shoulder, how incomprehensible this was to him.

"Nevertheless, she permits her daughter to visit the various churches of the Eternal City. It is in her description of these churches that Miss Hannigan excels. In fact, they might be called the high light of the book. For example, she refers to St. Peter's as a kind of Carnegie Hall, only larger and lit by candlelight. The child, the daughter of this English family— her name is Rosalind—naturally cannot be subjected to so much spirituality without being affected by it. Before the parents are aware, before they can do anything about it, behold,

[45]

the damage has been done—the child insists on becoming a Catholic.

"Naturally, her parents are horrified. I will not go into detail here. Suffice to say they do everything in their power to dissuade her, but to no avail. Reluctantly, they consent to their daughter being received into the Church. And by a bishop at that. As you know, in Rome there are many bishops.

"But do not think for a moment that this fine book ends here. Ah, no. Do not think so. Time goes on and the child, Rosalind, falls ill, perhaps worn by her continual efforts to convert her parents. The doctors cannot diagnose the child's illness. She sinks lower and lower. The parents despair. The saintly monsignor who converted the child—although it was a bishop who baptized her—comes in to administer the last rites to her. Although she has been in a coma, she revives when the monsignor bends over her. He leans to catch her words. His face lights up. He gets up and tells the grieving parents: 'Your daughter says that if you embrace the Faith, she will recover.' Pause. "It is indeed a desperate decision for the parents. Prejudice is very strong in them. But they see there is no alternative. They consent to embrace the Faith. Not with joy, it is true, but reluctantly. Yet almost immediately joy comes to them, for the child begins to recover. Perceptibly, before their very eyes!"

Again J. Martin paused, as much for breath as to survey the effect on his audience. As he drank from a glass of water, he noticed that the men were no longer in the back of the room, but several of the older women were watching him in a real wonder, their mouths slightly open. Two of the younger women had their mouths open in yawns and suddenly J. Martin hated them. He put the glass down and began again. It was now quite dim in the room but no one thought to put the lights on. Into the dimness J. Martin spoke, almost grate-

[46]

fully, with new pleasure, as if some formerly jarring part of the environment had now been made appropriate.

"This," he said, "this is the sort of thing, the sort of book we are giving our readers, the kind of thought we are promulgating. However, there are other sorts, too. Nonfiction for those of a more serious bent, and spiritual books for those so inclined. I will not dwell on these at any length, but merely indicate two of our recent selections. The hour grows late. One, a survey of the European scene by a prominent Midwestern bishop, featuring the territorial claims of Germany and Italy along with graphic descriptions of the fighting in Ethiopia and entitled *Fighting the Red Beast*. The other, one of our little dividend books, is by a prominent Irish cleric, Father Patrick McGoon, and is entitled *The Virtue of Holy Purity*. These books and their titles speak for themselves. I need not go into their contents. They are characteristic of the sort of thing we do. Some of you might perhaps wish to come down to our offices on Barclay Street and browse around. We should indeed be happy to have you. There we could explain more fully the nature of the arrangements we make." J. Martin went on a little longer, stopping when a bell rang softly in the corridor. Fully half his audience crowded up to meet him. Mrs. O'Reilly apologized two or three times for not having subscribed to their wonderful club before now. Mrs. Danaher said she hadn't received *that* dividend and she would most certainly like to have it for herself and Rosemary.

Rosemary and Ellen escaped toward the door. Moon had reappeared, with Kavanagh close by, curiously less apparent than Moon. Mary Gaffney seemed to be with Kavanagh.

"Yoicks," Rosemary said. "I forgot I'd told Moon to meet me here."

"Apparently *he* hasn't," Ellen said.

"I know, but Mother's going to be worried if she thinks I'm seeing him so much."

[47]

"But why?"

The question upset Rosemary; she had not expected it from Ellen. Then anger dissolved in fright. What had ever led her to say such a thing? Rosemary wondered. She hurried just a little, so that in greeting the Gaffneys she could forget to answer Ellen.

"Why, old Moon," she said, patting his cheek before turning to greet his sister. "How are you, Mary? Still wrestling with the Ginnies downstairs? My lord," she went on, giving her hand to Kavanagh, "I told Mother, I wouldn't mind working there, if it wasn't for the *garlic!* How do you ever manage to stand it, Mary?"

"Oh, we wear masks," Mary said. "One of those surgical masks," she added, when she saw Rosemary believed her.

"A clothespin would be more likely," Ellen said.

"Let's get a drink," Kavanagh said. "You must all need one after listening to J. Martin. What did he talk on this time— —Holy Purity?"

"Now, you leave our Martin alone," Rosemary said. They were all moving into the corridor.

"I wouldn't touch him with a pole," Moon said. "We went out and had a drink. If I'd known he was going to be here, I wouldn't have showed up so soon."

"Not even for me?" Rosemary said.

"Well, maybe for you."

"There they go again," Kavanagh said.

"How is your friend Schneider?" Ellen said to make conversation.

"Bad as ever. He's got a new thing now. This *Catholic Worker.*"

"I've heard of it. You don't mean he's given up his job for that?"

"Not Bart. He likes drinking too well to be without a job. He's got what might be called a lay interest in it. I think it salves his conscience to give them five dollars now and then or pass out the coffee cups on their bread line."

The wet air's broken darkness mottled them harshly as animals in a country strange to their coloration. "I really have to go uptown," Ellen said. "I'll be late for dinner." She usually helped her mother with the younger children.

"Come on," Kavanagh said. "LaGatta's is just around the corner. Besides, there's someone there I want you to meet."

"I can't imagine who," Ellen said.

"Kav has a new girl," Mary said. "He likes to get another girl's opinion on her. Kav is a very careful person."

"Come, come, now," Kavanagh said. "No heavy analysis."

Ahead of them they could hear Moon and Rosemary clowning again, loud enough to attract glances from passers-by. Ellen felt deeply uneasy. LaGatta's showed just ahead, a block of light projected thinly on the dark air. Ellen tried to know the nature of her disturbance before they reached the light, but something would not move in her, some darkness intervened.

Outside the door, Kavanagh and the two girls could hear Moon already booming within. "That man," his sister said. Through partly misted glass, Kavanagh saw Kate Bannon sitting alone at a table and his heart lifted. But it was not she Moon was greeting, for he did not know her; Schneider was sitting at another table with a young man none of them knew, and Moon and Rosemary had paused just inside the doorway. "Oh, if I'd known he was going to be here, I wouldn't have come," Rosemary said.

"Who?" Kavanagh said, as they came in the doorway.

"Bart Schneider. He—"

"I didn't know he'd be here, myself," Kavanagh said. "What have you got against him?"

"He's a radical," Rosemary said. "He believes in the socialization of women."

[49]

Kavanagh turned and looked at her. Blinking, she held one hand over her heart. "Oh, *Mr.* Kavanagh! Don't look at me so!"

"Rosemary," he said, "why don't you grow up?"

Already LaGatta was pushing tables together and Kavanagh had gone over to Kate Bannon. Moon, always at the mercy of a gregarious nature, had brought Schneider and the other man over. The stranger's name was Ed Galvin. In his wide face the features were broad yet clearly marked below a mop of thick, curly hair. The worn clothes seemed to go with his air of quiet belligerence, yet his gaze met none of theirs directly.

"Apparently," Schneider said to Ellen, "this is the only place I can ever get to see you."

"Where else would you expect to see me?"

"I don't know. In church, perhaps."

"I didn't think you went."

"Oh, now and then." He held her chair for her, then sat next to her. There was nothing she could do about it, she knew; the unease she had known outside was with her again, and although she knew its nature no more clearly, she did know that now Schneider or his closeness related to it. She remembered other times.

Moon alone remained on his feet, ordering drinks for everyone. Kav sat close to Kate Bannon and obviously held her hand under the table, while Rosemary made small, obliquely disapproving gestures. She noticed how fresh Kate's complexion was stung by the cold. Mary Gaffney asked Galvin if she hadn't seen him before.

"I don't know," he said. "I get around." She noticed he smoked continually and his fingers trembled when he rubbed out a cigarette or lit one.

"Are you in newspaper work with Bart?"

He smiled. "I'm in newspaper work, all right, but not with Bart."

"Who are you with?"

"I help edit *The Catholic Worker*."

"Oh, that," she said.

Galvin smiled again, the bitterness on two levels, real and feigned. "You'd better be careful. Your friends will—"

"I heard the cardinal or the chancery office was going to suppress it."

"I guess they would if it were possible," he said, without satisfaction. "Trouble is, we don't really come under their jurisdiction. There are no clerics or religious on our staff. The chancery office can't exercise its censorship over us." He paused, added, "Deo gratias," and smiled.

"I see," Mary said.

Schneider leaned across the table to whisper loudly, "It's sometimes known as the A.C.A.C. or Anticlerical Athletic Club."

Most of the others laughed. "That's not fair, though," Galvin said. "At least to my associates. We have a number of priests interested in the movement."

"I don't think that's anything to laugh at," Rosemary was finally able to say.

"What's that?" Galvin said. They faced each other across the table.

"That name he said. That nickname, criticizing God's holy clergy."

"No one was criticizing the clergy, Rosemary," Kavanagh said. "There's enough of it done, but it just so happened this wasn't one of the times."

"Why, that name—?" Rosemary said.

"The name was a joke," Schneider said. He did not look at her as he spoke, nor at anyone. "Not a very good one, to be sure, but nevertheless a joke. You're losing your sense of humor."

"I think the rest of you are losing your minds," Rosemary said.

"I'm no anticlerical," Moon said. He had been wishing in his unaccustomed silence, that Galvin and Schneider were not here. It was too late to save the moment. The others did not know it; he alone knew it, he told himself without conscious pride; but he made the effort to save. "How about everyone staying for dinner?" he said.

"I have to get home," Ellen said. "I'm late now." She wondered if Peter had called; or rather she wondered if he had been much disturbed at not finding her home.

"Me, too," Rosemary said. About to leave the remainder of her drink, she decided it would be too obvious a mark of her displeasure, and finished it quickly.

"If you drink like that," Schneider said so quietly only she heard it, "people will try to take advantage of you in taxicabs."

She started to glare at him, then decided it was better to ignore such a remark.

"Wait, I'll take you home," Moon said. He came over to help her into the caracul coat.

"It's not necessary, Moon," she said, with a kind of brisk and pious dignity. "It's early. Good-by, everyone," she said, brightly. Ellen, too, said good-by and followed her friend out the door.

"I work in the Brooklyn chancery office," Kate Bannon said, "but I didn't see anything wrong in what we said."

"Well—" Moon said and in amazement found the words would not come. Turning, he looked for the waiter, and saw the others were silent, too, and that no one looked at another. Ed Galvin stared at a point on the floor and Mary watched his face. For the first time she saw the terrible, fixed weariness in

[ 5 2 ]

it, and her heart became a swollen thing in her breast. No matter what he was, she told herself, amazed, she would hold him to her against the night, against anything.

4

TEN O'CLOCK and Moon, Schneider, and Galvin were still there. The others had gone, Kavanagh because he wanted to talk alone to Kate, and Mary because she was tired. There were almost no politicians in the place tonight and Moon talked steadily with the other two. Galvin, Moon discovered, was a nephew of Judge Francis Galvin. When this first came out in their talk, Moon experienced the singular spiritual lift a new and possibly valuable connection always brought to him. Yet as the talk went along and became increasingly more frank after the two girls had left, this characteristic exhilaration of Moon's departed or rather became something else, souring on itself: an irritation and a bewilderment. For Galvin was full of horror stories. Smoking almost continually, he drank little, perhaps one to Schneider's two and Moon's three. Moon was disposed to like Galvin more than Schneider. He felt that Galvin was not so much a liar as one given to exaggeration, one of those whom misfortune, hunger or injury had given what Moon thought of, in a phrase borrowed from the diocesan weeklies, as a "warped point of view." This charity Moon had for Galvin and not for Schneider was an amazing thing, depending as it did almost solely on a name and the already lost hope that Judge Galvin might someday be helpful to himself.

"Then there was the young missionary came in to see us last month," Galvin said. "You talk about lay people being confused," he said to Schneider. "You should have talked to him. Confusion maybe isn't the word. He'd been giving a mis-

[ 5 3 ]

sion in St. Louis the month before and he apparently hadn't been much good for anything since. His order had sent him East on a business trip to help him get over it, I guess."

"All right, come to the point, Edward," Schneider said.

Galvin's voice rose slightly from its monotone. "He'd said one of the Masses on a Sunday in this church in St. Louis and he was in the sacristy unvesting and one of the local curates was there, too, and this missionary had just taken off his chasuble when in comes one of these flannel-mouthed ushers, one of these boys that's always anxious to impress the pastor with what a holy pious soul he is, always taking good care of the parish, and Father this and Father that and look what a good boy am I. Anyhow, this usher comes into the sacristy just bursting with joy. 'Oh, Father,' he says to the curate, 'I don't know what we're coming to. One of those niggers came up and got in with the white people going to Communion instead of waiting like he should. So I very firmly took him by the arm around to the end of the line.' 'Good for you,' the curate said, 'but why didn't you give him a bat alongside the head to teach him manners along with it?'"

Schneider was laughing quietly in an unpleasant manner, and Galvin almost smiled. It was the smile that bothered Moon the most, yet even he noticed the similarity between the two at the moment. "That, frankly, I don't believe," Moon said.

Galvin shrugged; he was used to that. "The man had no reason to lie to me. Unless you think I'm lying to you."

"Not at all," Moon said. "It's just that the story has passed through so many hands that it's probably been exaggerated or distorted in the telling. Now—"

"How many hands?" Schneider said. "Only Ed's. He got it from the priest that saw it happen, that heard it happen."

Moon looked fixedly at his glass. "But the man may have

[54]

been under a strain that made him exaggerate or see the thing distorted some way. I—"

"Look," Galvin said. "Even allowing for some exaggeration, which in this case I doubt, the cumulative effect of so many stories like that is what can't help making an impression. Not spectacularly, but in a quiet way, it's an indication that something has gone wrong in the Church."

Moon was already shaking his head, shaking away all doubts, all doubters.

"Some people might call it dry rot," Schneider said. "Others, more violent, might even say the Church stank. Teresa of Avila did once," he added, seeing Moon's scornful glance. "Still others, the *New Republic,* for example, might say that there existed a grave dichotomy between Catholic thought and Catholic practice."

"Very clever," Moon said, "very clever." He noticed Galvin laughing at what Schneider had said. Noticed, too, that all their glasses were empty. Summoned the waiter; ordered the drinks. Summoned order, too: for all their lives, but especially his own. "Look," he said. "Some of these things have happened. I wouldn't doubt it. In any large organization—why, look at us in The Hall. We have people we can't always control—" He had to stop, for both Schneider and Galvin were laughing too hard.

"You look at the Hall," Galvin said. "I got sick of looking at it. My uncle was head once."

"I know," Moon said. He found himself smiling for some reason unknown to him, perhaps as a buffer. What hurt most in the entire moment, what alone possessed venom and a sting, was just that fact of Galvin's uncle being prominent in The Hall. Some betrayal was involved, some door opened on a new darkness. He gathered himself. "What I was saying," he went on, keeping the faint, slow smile on his face, "what I was saying when you bums interrupted me—was that in any large organization the human element plays a very large part. And what you say may be very true or pretty true, but not to any extent in the East here. You mention St. Louis and Bart said something about Chicago, but Catholicism is relatively newer there. Here in the East we have a Catholicism that is sound and full of—"

"Full of cold tea and holy water," Schneider said.

"I named one city tonight," Galvin said. "It happened to be in the Middle West. But every other incident I mentioned happened in the East. And the only city I know of where the Church is in worse shape than it is in New York is Boston."

"I deny that," Moon said. His voice rose for the first time. "Father Malone says that next to Ireland there is no finer type of Catholicism in the whole world than in New York City."

"Which Malone?" Galvin said. "That old turkey over on the water front? He doesn't know the right time. He was anti-labor for years until one of his own parishioners became head of the dock union."

Moon looked at Galvin before answering. "There isn't much of anything you like about the Church, is there?"

"I wouldn't say that." Galvin didn't take the cigarette from his mouth. "I like everything about the Church except the people who run it or try to run it."

"Anticlerical, see?" Schneider said, and Moon remembered Schneider didn't hold liquor well. "I told you before. The A.C.A.C."

"What do you say to that?" Moon asked Galvin.

Again Galvin moved his shoulders. "I don't know. There's several definitions of the term. Personally, I wouldn't say I was so much anticlerical as anticlericalism."

"Quibbling," Moon said. "In any event, a very negative attitude." He felt quieter and perhaps because of Schneider's approach to drunkenness, himself consciously approached in manner the judicial.

[56]

There was a little silence before Galvin again spoke. "Anyhow, we were talking about the Church here. Look at it. Look what's been happening right around here."

"What?" Moon said.

Galvin glanced away before answering, as if to gather and winnow memory; he weighed the effect of what he had to say on Moon. "It's probably not news to you that the diocese owns slum property all over this part of Manhattan?"

Now Moon shrugged. "I know that. A lot of people do. The diocese can't help what gets willed to it when people die, can it? As a matter of fact, the diocese happens to be starting a slum-clearance project now. I happen to know that for a fact," he went on, pressing home in spite of Galvin's waving a hand at him and smiling the sour and crooked smile.

"Hurrah for the diocese," Schneider said. "Hurrah for the archdiocese. Hurray—"

"That's what I'm talking about," Galvin said. "They want to level the tenements to put up lofts on the property and they've given the tenants thirty days to get out."

Moon wet his lips, groped once for Galvin's meaning and seized it. "That isn't much time, is it?" he said. "Are you sure about that?"

"Sure I'm sure," Galvin said. "They come down to the Worker and tell us about it. You know how easy it is for people with that kind of an income to get a place? And in winter?"

"It's not easy," Moon said. "This outfit, Kerrigan and Brannigan, that handles that sort of thing for the diocese, just aren't—well, no matter . . . but I'm sure that if someone went directly to the chancery office and laid the case on the table—"

"Such talk, such talk," Schneider muttered, "and all about a chancery too."

Galvin sneered. "You try getting into the chancery office, Moon, if you're anything less than a Knight of St. Gregory or an assemblyman."

[57]

"Suppose you know an assemblyman? Suppose you tell an assemblyman what to do?" Moon felt the little flicker of power. It was not newly come by, but the knowledge of, the conscious pleasure deriving from it was. So that what would have been his usual resentment became effortlessly something else.

Galvin's sneer did not leave him. "Who? Bo-Bo Ryan? That—"

"I never heard him called that before," Moon said. He paused to belch and found that Galvin's name for Ryan pleased even himself.

"As a matter of fact," Galvin said, "a committee of the tenants tried to get into the chancery office and were given an appointment for three weeks from now, about the time they're due to get out."

Moon kept shaking his head. "What I'm trying to say is that I'll get you an appointment there. I'll call Ryan. Hell, I'll go with you myself!"

"Hear, hear," Schneider said. His voice was muffled in his hands, covering his face.

"Only one thing," Moon said. "I'd like to be sure that what you say is entirely true. I don't want to be in the position of telling one story and finding another one is so."

"Come on over to the Worker with me now," Galvin said. "Probably some of the tenants will be around. Ask them yourself."

Moon's hesitation was a strange and ambiguous thing. He kept thinking that maybe the reason the chancery had given the committee the run-around was because someone from *The Catholic Worker* was on or with the committee. But that was without point, he knew, for the conclusion he was trying to reach. He must be pretty drunk.

In that silence or hesitation which even Moon found strange, Galvin remained tense and waiting, waiting with surprising patience, with quietness even. Like Moon he was a little shocked when Schneider spoke next and at what he said. "Moon's afraid he'll be seen going into the place. Like a whorehouse."

"Shut up," Moon said. "I'll go with you," he told Galvin. "Right now."

"Good," Galvin said. "Anyway, it's too dark for you to be seen."

Anger flared and died again in Moon. He saw that Galvin smiled. They stood up and put on their coats. Schneider put ten dollars on the table to pay for the check, which was over twenty, but Galvin did nothing, so that Moon wondered why and resented it. Galvin ought at least to make an excuse, Moon thought.

Outside, it was cold. They stood for a moment, breathing deeply, then Schneider started off in the wrong direction while Moon stood still in scorn. Galvin got hold of Schneider and turned him, and the three of them went east toward Mott Street, moving through many shades of darkness, of half-light, stung by the cold to an increasingly hurried pace. Almost no one was on the street.

"Whose idea was this?" Schneider said.

"Your communist friend here thought of it all by himself," Moon said. The air balanced the liquor in him: for the moment his humor was there. "He wants to kill a bishop and he figures now is the best time. On the altar would give too much scandal to the faithful."

"Rather than give them scandal, them we will dandle," Schneider said.

Hatless, Galvin's head and face showed clear in any street light. He was half-grinning again. "That's one thing the Commies have us on, Moon. They can kill someone they don't like, but we have to wait for him to die. A definite inferiority in technique."

[59]

Turning into Mott Street, Schneider said, "Best Chinese whorehouse in New York on this block."

"You seem to know all about it," Moon said. They were still walking fast.

"Hearsay only," Schneider said. "Trouble is, I can't do business with whores. Tried to once in Chicago. Nothing happened. Tried again in Brooklyn. Still nothing. Just sat around talking to the madam. Only nice girls. Nice girls the only ones I want and you can't have them."

"I don't know what you're talking about," Moon said. "Do you, Ed?"

"Leave him alone," Galvin said.

A man coming out of a doorway between two stores almost bumped into them. Whirling abruptly away from them he walked in the opposite direction. "Familiar face, familiar place," Schneider mumbled as they strode. There was the shock again in Moon. The man had looked like Whitey Travis. Yet it couldn't have been Whitey, Moon knew: Rosemary wouldn't be attracted by a man who would go to a whorehouse. He found himself wanting to speak of the resemblance. Instead, he heard himself say, "I don't believe there's any houses operating down here or many anywhere else in the city. Not with a Catholic mayor."

"Just here and there," Schneider said.

"There's none down here, are there, Ed?" Moon asked.

"One or two. Got to expect that in this kind of a neighborhood."

"Then why have you got your place here?" Moon said. "No wonder the chancery doesn't like you."

"Where do you want us to have it, Park Avenue?"

"Sure," Schneider said. "The Jebbies will give you space in their basement on Eighty-fourth Street."

They crossed another street and now Galvin preceded them a little. "Here we are," he said. The building was like that from which the man had hurriedly emerged two blocks back, a doorway between two store fronts. One of the stores was blank with darkness, the other showed a faint radiance on plain table and chair. Moon noticed as they turned into the doorway that the radiance came from a vigil light in the store. The light burned in front of a small statue, probably one of the saints, he guessed, for it was neither Christ nor Virgin.

Inside the doorway they found a hall dimly lit by a small kerosene lamp. A flight of stairs on the left led up into more dimness and the hall itself led back to another door, dimly seen. Following Galvin toward this door, Moon sniffed the stale cooking odors and was reminded of his own home . . . yet his unease would not depart: on many levels it persisted, spurious and unreconciled, something that had indeed begun a long time ago and in another country.

This door opened on what might have been called a small courtyard. Cobbled, it lay among four walls, the two high ones formed by the backs of tenements, the low ones by indeterminate masses of old brick. The courtyard was windless like the hall and only slightly colder. Crossing it, Schneider tripped once and saved himself only by grabbing Moon's thick chesterfield. Galvin held open the door across the courtyard and the two half fell through it.

There was a little more light and some warmth here. Both came from a small room on their right. People were in it, books, two tables, some chairs and a small, round-bellied stove. The light fell across the hallway into another, dark room, showing a good-sized hand printing press, the first thing Moon and Schneider saw as they stumbled through the doorway. A voice was reading in the lighted room. Moon and Schneider turned toward it or the light and stood a moment with Galvin, listening. *"He who does not bellow the truth when he knows the truth makes himself the accomplice of liars and forgers."* By craning his neck, Moon could see a gray-haired woman

[ 6 1 ]

reading to a group of four or five people. She stopped on that sentence and said, "Come in," turning her thin body toward them. "Hello, Bart. Who's with you?"

"Galvin and a politician," Schneider said. "He's come to get a few votes."

"If it was the right time of year, I'd believe you," the woman said. Moon, they could see, was embarrassed. He stood, wide-eyed, in the light, his hat held before him in both hands, his lips working slightly. Schneider introduced him to the others. They took their overcoats off and sat down. "Go right on reading," Moon said. "Don't let us interrupt you." He half-regretted coming here and half-hoped Galvin might somehow forget to hold him to his promise.

"Oh, no," the woman said. "We've been reading for too long. You're not really a politician, are you, Mr. Gaffney?"

"I'll tell you," Moon said. "I'm a lawyer, and in New York it's the same thing."

She smiled and the others he had newly met did not even that. They would be hard to please, he thought. Or was please the word? He became fully conscious of his tension and wondered at it. Surely not the evidence of their poverty disturbed him: he saw *that* every day, in and out of his work. What then? Could it be their apparent lack of sympathy for him here, right next door to his own district? Or was it something foolish, something incongruous such as these people reading one to another by night, instead of being in bed or at work?

"Would you like some coffee?" the woman said.

"Why, yes," Moon said, then regretted it, freshly disturbed, perhaps over accepting food from people poorer than himself.

"I'll make it, Dorothy," a dark girl said. She was obviously a Latin, probably an Italian, since the neighborhood was full of them. As she brushed by Moon, he found a curious antinomy in himself: his mind leaned back from her, but not his body. Her own accidentally brushed his. It was accidental, too:

[62]

the thin face, with its aquiline nose and clear skin, acknowledged nothing.

"You want a job?" someone was saying across the room.

Startled, Moon realized the words were addressed to himself. "Who, me?" Seeing that something had finally lightened those around him, Moon kept on. "I got a job. Thanks just the same." Looking more closely at the man who had addressed him, Moon saw he was perhaps a year or two older than himself, somewhat better dressed than the others there, the face placid, almost fixed, the features regular and even, what might have been called stylized, a conventional sort of American good looks. Moon thought that most women would like that face. Certainly Rosemary would. That fixed quality, though, he himself did not like. It usually went with someone who was a nut. He could tell a nut by his eyes, Moon knew. Looking closer at these eyes, Moon saw that they were not those of a nut and grew again unsure.

"I mean a good job," the man said. Finally, Moon separated his name from those of the others: Linford Thomas. Hardly a Catholic name, Moon considered. . . .

"Depends," Moon said. "How's the pay?"

"See," someone said. "Like all lawyers."

"That's right," Moon said. "You'd have been disappointed if I said anything else."

Schneider laughed, aimlessly. The gray-haired woman said, "That should teach the rest of you charity."

"The pay's pretty good," Thomas went on. "You can even go on practicing the law."

"Tell me more," Moon said. He had never practiced. His law degree had been taken in the almost fully conscious knowledge that it was a convention best for all young politicians to fulfill, if someday they might want to be first a magistrate.

"There's a union that needs a lawyer," Thomas said. "They'll pay you three, four thousand a year."

"Labor lawyer, Moon," Schneider said. "There's your chance."

"I have commitments," Moon said. "But I'll tell you what I'll do. I'll get you someone. I'll get you a good lawyer, Catholic and everything. Jim McGuffey."

"A substitute sacrifice," Dorothy said.

"No," Schneider said. "You do my friend wrong. He came here tonight to help out the poor and downtrodden and here they rise up and bite the hand that feeds them."

"God knows we're downtrodden enough," Dorothy said. "That cop was in again today, Bart, patting his revolver and telling us that when the time comes he won't hesitate to use it on us filthy Communists. An Irishman, too, Moon."

Moon considered that out of the half-mists in which he moved. There was something wrong but he could not have given it a name. "I'll have him broken," he said. "I'll have him sent to Staten Island." It was doubtful that he could, he knew, yet the words of power came pleasantly on his tongue.

"No one wants you to do that, Moon," Dorothy said. "And even if you did, what good would it do the thousands of others like him in New York? I don't mean policemen, either, Moon," she added, reading his face.

"I don't know exactly what you're talking about," he said. In the closed room tiredness grew and with the drink at last made his tongue thick.

"Let's stick to the point," Schneider said. "Moon came here because he said he wanted to make an appointment for those tenants to get in to see the chancery office. He wanted to talk to some of the tenants if there were any here tonight."

"Unfortunately, there aren't any," Dorothy said. "You probably didn't believe the story, Moon. Neither did we, until Ed went up there with them."

Moon nodded, yawning heavily. "I believe you. First thing in the morning, I'll phone Ryan."

[64]

Galvin and the Italian girl came back with a pot of coffee and some chipped cups. In a corner of the room was a narrow cot covered with a torn spread. Moon stood up and walked over to it. Weariness to him was a cloak, a refuge. There was an enemy and there was a place kept by friends to sustain him against that enemy. But which was which, Moon did not know. Lying down on the cot, he turned to the wall. Something sustained or would sustain him, either sleep would from these people, or these people from some other and more shapeless antagonist.

\* \* \*

It was dark when he woke but he knew exactly where he was. Someone had thrown his overcoat across him and, turning, he could see the thin red chinks of the stove. He was very thirsty. Sitting up, he swung his feet to the floor and sat on the couch's edge for a few minutes. Not given to staying away from his home at night, even when he had been drinking heavily, Moon was puzzled at his doing so tonight. Memory gave no answer; he simply hadn't been drunk. And reason seemed more ineffectual than memory.

As his eyes grew accustomed to the light, he saw someone sleeping on the floor, a blanket under, another overcoat across the figure. Standing up, he saw that it was Schneider. The face lay in a bar of thin, red light. A peculiar weariness informed its features, something that took its character from within rather than from the body; and Moon had the disturbing feeling that Schneider had fallen in a fight. . . .

He couldn't find any water. There was a toilet in the hall, but no washbowl with it. His thirst, as always after drinking, was intense. Outside in the courtyard, it was windless and cold. Entering the other hallway across the yard, he almost stumbled over two people sleeping. Puzzled, he struck a match and saw they were ordinary tramps. There were perhaps a dozen of them in the hallway. Even in the cold he could smell them.

A flicker of his automatic scorn for such people passed in him, and he opened a door on his right. It led into the room where the vigil light burned. The light still burned and he went closer to it. The statuette was that of a Negro. Faint, raised letters, the same pale color as the base, could just be distinguished. Leaning closer, he almost spelled the words out. "Blessed Martin de Porres," Moon said. "Christ, a nigger saint!"

More bewildered than shocked, he crossed the yard again to the room in which he had been sleeping. His feelings were mixed. It could not have been said that he was a hater or even a fearer of Negroes. Some of his sister's charity was in him, too; watered down, but there. What he felt in their presence was a dislike, a queasiness. Yet twice he had delivered speeches to Negro gatherings and obviously impressed them. So his bewilderment now was not so much over white people venerating a Negro saint—as he thought of Blessed Martin—but that such a person or category should, in fact, exist.

He was no longer sleepy. From the hallway he could see Schneider still sleeping and he could smell coffee being made. The smell seemed to come from above and Moon ascended the stairs. There were two doors on the next landing and he knocked on the one behind which the noises of a kitchen could be heard. A woman's voice said to come in. Inside, there was an old coal range with a very large two-handed pot on it, of the kind used at camps or outdoor gatherings. The Italian girl and a large, dull-looking blonde woman were tending it. "You're up early," the girl said.

"I was thirsty. Got any water?"

"I'll get you some. Want some coffee, too?"

"I wouldn't mind—if you have enough. I guess you have, though, with that reservoir there. I didn't know you had that many people in the house."

[66]

"It's for the bread line." She handed him a cup of cold water. "Didn't you know?"

He shook his head as he drank. "There's some bums sleeping in the hall."

"That's the beginning of it."

He considered that, yet without surprise. Somehow, he had always had a formless disapproval of bread lines. The Christmas baskets distributed by the club were something else again, operating on more than one level, all of the levels tangible. There was no feeling now, except one of faint concern over women tending a bread line. "Doesn't Galvin help or some of the other men?"

"Usually," she said. "We're short of men now, though. Lin Thomas doesn't live here now that he has to travel for his union. And Galvin would probably be up now if you hadn't made him drink all night."

"A man has to have some recreation," Moon said. "Matter of fact, he hardly drank at all." He noticed the blonde woman glaring at him. "How about some of that coffee?"

"I guess it's almost ready." She went over to the stove and stirred the coffee with a long wooden spoon. The blonde woman went out of the room and Moon said, "Your friend doesn't like me. What's the matter?"

"Oh, Elizabeth is a simple soul. She thinks in a straight line. She believed me about your getting Galvin drunk."

"Maybe if she's that simple, you ought to have her where she could be taken care of."

"No-o," the girl said, without heat. "That's the idea. We don't want her in an institution. She just isn't that bad. But she has no relatives and if we—" She stopped talking as Elizabeth returned, a woolen stocking cap on and a worn leather jacket over her dress.

"I guess it's ready," the girl said. She slipped into a coat and approached the stove.

[67]

"Hell, you can't lift that," Moon said. He went in front of her and with Elizabeth lifted the great pot down. It was even heavier than he thought, but when he wanted to rest it on the floor, Elizabeth kept right on going through the doorway and down the stairs, Moon laboring along behind her.

There was already a line in the courtyard, extending into the hallway opposite. In the thin light the men huddled into their rags. Their only movement was a slight, shifting one from foot to foot, giving the line, along with the rags, a not unstylized quality. Since no one appeared to help Elizabeth, Moon began handing her cups from a basket on top of a small coal shed. The cold bit into him and he returned to the room to get his overcoat. Schneider still slept and Moon thought of waking him, but decided not to; somehow he knew or sensed that Schneider asleep, more than most perhaps, was spared certain things that Schneider awake was not.

Outside again, he saw the Italian girl had appeared with a basket of stale sliced bread, and was standing next to Elizabeth, distributing it. "I thought you'd gone," she said.

"Just to get my coat. Anyhow, where would I go this time of day?" No bars were open, he thought, with irony, not even the club. He began handing the cups to Elizabeth. The line swayed past them, the men wolfing the bread almost before they had turned away. There was enough light now to see their eyes, pained, blank or sullen. One of them that glanced at his coat enviously, Moon wanted to hit. Yet after a time he was aware of some change in himself, not love of people nor even kindness, but an abatement, the partial loss of an ancient and cloudy antagonism.

The line was a good deal longer than Moon thought it might be. Another basket of bread had been brought by the Italian girl and the coffee was almost gone. Dorothy had appeared beside Moon, a missal in her hand. "I suppose," she said, "I might better have stayed here and helped."

[68]

"Say," Moon said, "we did fine. We're almost out of coffee, though."

"It's too bad," she said. "That's all we had for today."

"I suppose you have to save some for tomorrow."

"Why, no. There isn't any to save. Maybe a few spoonfuls upstairs for our own breakfast."

"Then how are you going to get any more for tomorrow?"

"Oh, we always have."

"This is one way of running down a few votes, isn't it, Moon?" Schneider had appeared in back of them, grinning, almost cheerful, the unshaven beard dark against the pale face.

"That," Moon said to Dorothy, "is the characteristic remark of a low mind. As a matter of fact, I let you sleep," he added, turning to Schneider, "in the hope that you wouldn't bother us."

"Now, if some of the boys from the district saw you here," Schneider said, "what else could they think?"

"Far from getting votes," Moon said, "I have been hoping no one would recognize me."

"Yes, so many of the boys in the line have voting addresses," Schneider said, almost inaudibly.

"No coffee." Elizabeth spoke for the first time.

Moon glanced at the line; it went back through the building and turned into the street. "What'll we do?" he said.

"There isn't very much we can do," Dorothy said. "We'll just let the line finish the bread."

"I got money," Moon said. In the clearing light his head, hatless, moved and turned with a certain ease and even nobility: he was taking over now, organizing, doing one of the things he possessed talent for.

Dorothy shook her head. "It would take another hour for the stores to open. They wouldn't wait. . . . If you wanted to for tomorrow—"

"Sure," he said. His voice was the hearty and confident one

that most people thought of as characteristic, yet he felt a peculiar futility. And because futility was not common with him, he was moved to try to know why it came to him now. He saw that the lack of coffee and the consequent uselessness of handing out more cups were only the outward manifestation of the futility, the symbol by which it had been communicated to him. The real futility lay in circumstance, in a set, in sets of circumstance. With a kind of inward gasp he saw how complex, how various, how concatenated they were, saw almost the multiplicity of levels on which they operated—and still gasping, in his mind turned away.

With Schneider, he followed Dorothy up to the kitchen. Galvin and three or four others were there. "Put you to work, Moon?" Galvin said. Unlike Schneider, sleep had not healed him.

"More or less. What time you want to go to the chancery?"

"You mean we have a choice?"

"Ryan could get us into there within an hour of when we wanted to go," Moon said. "I'd bet on it," he added.

"Don't you and Bart have to go to work?"

"I don't go until noon," Schneider said.

"And I not at all if I don't want to," Moon said. Something, perhaps the warmth, made him expansive. "I'll call Ryan at his house as soon as its eight o'clock."

They ate a breakfast of oatmeal, bread, and coffee with condensed milk in it. Galvin took Moon next door to a stationery store owned by a Jew named Spiegel and Moon phoned Assemblyman Ryan. Two of the Ryan virtues were early rising and complete availability to his constituency at almost any hour. More pleased than not to have Commissioner Gaffney's son request a favor of him, the assemblyman didn't even ask Moon what he wanted at the chancery or who might be going with him. He merely asked Moon to call him back between nine and nine-thirty.

At ten o'clock Moon, Galvin, Schneider, and a short, middle-aged Italian named Giuseppe Buonaventura left for the chancery, where Ryan had secured them an appointment for ten-thirty. Buonaventura was dressed in his best clothes. He had a handle-bar mustache and, although intelligent, like many southern Europeans he had never lost a heavy accent. Buonaventura, Schneider speculated, if he had stayed in Italy, would have been at one time a member of the Christian Democratic Party. If he had remained in the Church. If he had left the Church, he would have been a Socialist. In either event, he would have been clubbed sooner or later by the Blackshirts and would have shut up or pretended to join them. Or perhaps would have freely joined them. . . . One never knew, Schneider conceded to the more ruthless part of his mind. He wondered what he himself might do under those circumstances, and supposed it would depend on whether one had a family or not. A somber thought.

Buonaventura was quite cheerful. He had explained to Moon how things had been with the chancery, and Moon had said he was sure there had been a misunderstanding, the chancery just didn't understand, and he personally would make it clear. Galvin had been quiet and Moon wondered if it was the drinking the previous night that had made Galvin talk so much then. Going uptown in the subway, Galvin talked politics with Moon and Schneider tried to understand the Italian over the roaring of the train. There was that unease in Moon, although this did not manifest itself to him until they were up out of the subway and walking across town to the chancery. Schneider noticed Moon's silence and even read it correctly but for once decided to say nothing. At the foot of the stone steps leading up to the chancery office, the group paused as if there were a definite reluctance in each of them to lead.

"What are you waiting for, Moon?" Schneider said.

"I'm not waiting. You're the ones that are waiting."

"Then go ahead. It's your appointment."

But it was Galvin who went up the steps first and Schneider and Giuseppe last. A porter, a layman with a black tie, led them into a waiting room. In less than five minutes he returned and said that Monsignor would see Mr. Gaffney. When the others also rose to accompany Moon, the porter seemed dismayed, but preceded them down a short hall and showed them into another room.

This room contained an expensive desk, some chairs, files and a small, dignified crucifix hung on the wall, its corpus stiff and, but for the limp head, unfelt. There were two windows behind the desk and from them a flood of gray light illumined the room and at once outlined and illumined its sole occupant, a lean priest with an almost expressionless face. If the face showed anything, it was a kind of vague, not quite polite surprise. In the warm room he had chosen to wear a silk soutane, picked out in the purple of a monsignor. He did not rise to greet them.

"I'm Aloysius Gaffney, Monsignor," Moon said. He leaned to respectfully take the narrow hand extended, knuckles up.

"Oh, yes, Mr. Gaffney," the man said. "I had no idea you would come attended. Mr. Ryan mentioned no one else."

Moon could not put his finger on what it was he disliked about the monsignor's words and was not sure he knew just what the man meant. "I'm sorry about that," he said, remembering that somehow he hadn't mentioned to Ryan the others or his own purpose in coming here. "I thought perhaps he had."

The monsignor shook his head delicately and without speaking; there remained nothing for Moon to do but introduce the others.

"And the purpose of your visit?" the monsignor said.

There was a hesitation among them, as if each of the three

[ 7 2 ]

knew that properly only the Italian was entitled to speak. When Moon remained silent, Galvin said, "It's about that slum clearance in the property of the archdiocese downtown."

"And you wish to know?"

"Well, actually we don't wish to know anything," Galvin said. "The representatives of the archdiocese have given the tenants thirty days' notice to get out. Now that's a pretty short time for people of their means to find other places and particularly at this time of year."

"And what is it you wish of this office?"

Behind him, Galvin heard someone sigh and guessed it to be Schneider. He found that he himself was grinning, a peculiar, ghastly, defensive and idiotic grin. He became aware, too, of his nerves and his incredible tiredness; and of that new feeling he had noticed lately and whose name he knew for the first time to be emptiness: as if God were no longer in him. "Why, the obvious thing," he heard himself say. "An extension of time." When the monsignor said nothing, but only continued to look at him, Galvin said, "Perhaps you are not familiar with the case?"

"Oh, quite," the monsignor said. "I'm quite familiar with it. In fact, for *your* information, Mr. Galvin, we have set a hearing on the matter for some two weeks or so from now."

"Day-a before thrown out," Giuseppe said.

"Eh?" said the monsignor.

"He says," Schneider said, speaking each word too clearly, "that the day for the hearing, so-called, is the day before the thirty-day notice terminates. Not much time in case they receive an unfavorable answer. Understand?"

After a moment in which an angel, but no one else, might have seen a darkening of the monsignor's skin, he said, "Your position here, Mr. Schneider, seems anomalous. Or are you also one of the tenants?" He glanced at Schneider's expensive coat.

[ 7 3 ]

"Oh, I just came along as a kind of interested bystander. But if you're worried, I'm also a newspaperman."

The monsignor turned to Moon. "Mr. Gaffney, I must say that I feel you and perhaps Mr. Ryan have betrayed us here somewhat. This is nothing the press should be bothered—"

"Don't worry," Schneider said. "I'm not here professionally. I'd have let you know."

"And you're not a Catholic?" the monsignor said.

"Alas, yes," Schneider said. "But we're sort of drifting away from the subject, if you don't mind my saying so."

"And you perhaps do not mind my telling you," the monsignor said, "that this is none of your business."

"I could debate that," Schneider said. "But if it will make you happier, I'll get out." He turned and left the room.

His victory having restored some of his confidence, the monsignor turned on his other tormentors. "And just what is it you wish, gentlemen? The time is short."

"It is, indeed," Galvin said. Moon noticed that Galvin panted slightly and himself wished he had never come here. "Look, if these tenants wanted to go to court, the court would allow them ninety days' grace. That's what all the magistrates' courts are allowing now in similar cases. Yet all these tenants are asking for is sixty days. And quite apart from that, there's the matter of Christian charity."

Almost but not quite the monsignor smiled. "Mr. Galvin," he said gently, as though talking to a naughty child, "this is not a matter of charity but of business. As such, we leave it in the hands of our business representatives and will abide by the decision they have made. And if you think for one moment," he added, his tone changing, "that any of the faithful would dare go to court as plaintiffs involving the diocese—"

"You seem to be aware," Galvin said, "that most of the tenants are Catholic. . . . But a few of them are not. Some Jews."

[ 74 ]

"Ah, they," the monsignor said. "Perhaps we would have to expect that from them."

Galvin was now swaying perceptibly. "Anti-Semitic, too."

One no longer needed angels' eyes to see the priest flush. "Mr. Galvin, I'll have you know that I have friends on both sides of that controversy."

"Which is almost the most completely meaningless remark I have ever heard." Galvin talked with his lips barely open as if something, perhaps vomit, would come out if he opened them wider.

"Mr. Gaffney," the priest said, "I would say that however good your intention may have been regarding this meeting, it was ill-advised."

"Yes, Monsignor," Moon said. His hat, the Homburg, was held before him in both hands.

"And now, gentlemen, I bid you good day."

As Moon and Galvin turned to go they found that Giuseppe was still facing the monsignor and that the Italian was weeping, the tears running down into his ridiculous mustaches. Like Moon he clung to his hat, pressing it against him with both hands. "My fad'—" he said. "My fad'. In Italia. In Italia he say a long time ago, dat da peep like-a you, they mak-a shit out-a the Church." And still weeping, he let them take him, one by either arm, and lead him from the room.

5

IN THAT DIM PART of his mind where most of Moon's decisions were made, what had happened at the chancery office had but one tangible and conscious effect: he asked Leora Ryan to go to the Auxiliary dance with him. Yet as days passed and there was no even indirect evidence of the assemblyman's displeasure, Moon felt a little cheated. It was not that he could have asked Rosemary instead, although there were other girls he could have asked. It was something to which Moon could not give a name nor indeed realize; something known by its effect rather than any direct knowledge of itself, like God or electricity: this time bred of having done something unwillingly and out of fear.

On the afternoon before the dance, Moon sat at his desk in the Municipal Building and consciously made gestures toward order. Important functions of any sort were spiritual landmarks in his life, not unlike the equinoxes in the life of a primitive tribe, and before each he usually tried to order his affairs, or at least to tend to things for weeks or months untended. Today, he had dictated a few letters, made some phone calls, ordered a corsage for Leora; sent a check in his mother's name to an order of missionaries; called two district captains to figuratively pat their backs; phoned Kavanagh to make sure that he, too, was going; given his gray-haired stenographer, Miss Clancy, two free tickets to a show, and now sat back to feel satisfaction.

There remained on a pad before him a number to be called and the name that went with the number, a name he had had some small difficulty in identifying, had perhaps been even reluctant to identify, that of Linford Thomas. All other names and numbers had been dealt with. Moon decided to call this one, too, perhaps more to make a clean sweep of his desk than for any other reason. A rough voice answered his call and told him it didn't know whether Thomas was around or not. While Moon waited, he could hear noises at the other end and guessed they came from some sort of hiring hall. When Thomas's voice did come to him it was clear, gentle, almost apologetic. He had wondered if Moon remembered him.

"Sure," Moon said. "How's everything down your way?"

"I don't get down to Mott Street as much as I'd like to,"

Thomas said. "Not with this new job. What I called you about was that lawyer you were going to get for us here."

"Oh, yes," Moon said. "I'm going to see that fellow tonight. You could even speak to him yourself if you wanted to. You wouldn't be going to the St. Linus's dance tonight, would you?"

Thomas said no, he wouldn't be going, the voice again almost apologetic. Maybe Moon could have this lawyer call the union offices tomorrow, though?

That's just what he would have him do, Moon said. Name was McGuffey.

Thomas was properly grateful. But he didn't hang up. He wondered if Moon had heard about Galvin. Galvin was going to have some kind of a breakdown, they were afraid.

That was too bad, all right, Moon said. But almost anyone would be apt to have a breakdown living down there and eating that kind of food.

Thomas supposed that had something to do with it. Then he said something that stayed with and disturbed Moon for a long time afterward. Thomas said that they were all grateful to Moon and that it was good to find a politician who was also a Christian and that they would all pray for him. Moon couldn't think of anything to say to that and while he was silent Thomas hung up.

Moon felt a complex satisfaction. He was surprised at having forgotten this piece of patronage laid in his lap. Perhaps he had forgotten because it was somehow associated with the unfortunate visit to the chancery and the risks that had, he now saw, attended it. Yet it was so substantial a bit of patronage that neither he nor anyone else in politics could afford to ignore it, and the vague association with the affair of the chancery office was not enough explanation. Of course, being a labor lawyer was hardly a fashionable or even a respectable profession among the people he knew; still there were those who had got their start that way. And three thousand was

pretty good pay, especially in these times. Moon was just a
little troubled that Thomas and his union had had difficulty
in getting a lawyer. And from that thought Moon's mind
effortlessly strayed to a consideration of whether the job might
not more profitably be offered to someone other than James
McGuffey. His first impulsive thought of McGuffey had been
a generous one: their families had known each other for years,
and although McGuffey had gone West to college, to Notre
Dame, he had later attended Fordham Law School with Moon.
And about a year and a half ago, McGuffey had married a
Brooklyn girl whom Moon hardly knew, although he knew
her family. They already had one baby. McGuffey, then, as
Moon saw it, was doing his duty, and everyone knew how
hard it was for young lawyers to get along. Still, whether Mc-
Guffey would ever be really useful to him was doubtful, Moon
knew. There were others, even closer to home or to the club.
James Kavanagh, if he did not live in Brooklyn, where he was
of little direct value politically. Neal Hartigan, but Neal was
definitely associated with uptown and Park Avenue in everyone's mind. Mike Terry, in Moon's own district—but here
Moon's mind finally perceived the true hazard: the job might
prove embarrassing in one fashion or another and even if one
of these others would take it, they could hold any embarrassment against Moon, at least anything that would hurt them
politically. And, actually, none of them except Kav and Mc-
Guffey needed the money.

The job would do all right for McGuffey, Moon decided.
If he didn't like it he could leave it and no harm done. Mc-
Guffey had no serious interest in political advancement but
he always helped out during the campaigns with some street
speaking. Besides, although Moon did not recognize this consciously, there was a resilient and impervious quality in Mc-
Guffey that resisted disappointments and frustrations. Mc-

[ 7 8 ]

Guffey had been a good prep-school quarterback and had gone to Notre Dame to play football, but had been too small.

Moon and Leora arrived early at the dance. It was a habit of Moon's to arrive early at social gatherings; that way he had plenty of time to see everyone that should be seen, and nobody would think he was trying to be fashionably late or fashionably anything else. Moon looked very well in tails and white tie; they made him appear slimmer and brought out in his broad, definite face and brown hair with a single wave in it, the appearance of a certain natural and rude nobility. Leora was proud of him. She had noticed a certain slackening in his attention lately. Not that there was ever anything serious between herself and Moon, but she did enjoy his attention, particularly since almost no one else gave her any. She was, she knew, a little plump for most tastes. Moon had phoned when she had given up hope of going with anyone. Of course she could have gone with her uncle, as she did to other affairs, but in a sense that was admission of inadequacy or defeat and, in her own way, even Leora knew it.

So now, pleased and proud, in dress of white satin, with Moon she paused at the entrance to the ballroom and surveyed the scene of possible triumph. Perhaps a dozen couples were dancing and as many more were around the edges of the room. Leora looked for girls she knew and Moon for men. Only Moon was successful: James McGuffey and his wife, Marie, were among those dancing. There were, Moon often told himself, various ways of doing a thing and he favored the indirect approach. He danced with Leora until he could speak a word to McGuffey.

Marie saw Moon first, which was the way he had wanted it. The four of them became almost motionless in a corner of the room, yet they never quite stopped dancing, as though compelled by some invisible force to conform in all outward things. Marie had a stiffly pretty face, Moon noticed again. Its longish chin alone kept it from beauty and indeed had kept it from a good many other things, yet Jim McGuffey was only one of several young men who would have been glad to marry her. But he had had apparently the best prospects and so Marie had married him.

She knew who Moon was, of course, and although she had seen him only two or three times before, was more glad than not for Jim to be on familiar terms with him. Her father was a clerk of the courts in Brooklyn and it had given them a certain position which she and her mother had always felt they must maintain. Leora, Marie knew less well.

"And how has the barrister been treating you?" Moon said to Marie.

"About as well as can be expected," she said. "I'm so busy with the baby and he's so busy with his work that I really don't see too much of him."

"Well, it's a nice thought, anyway," McGuffey said. "There isn't that much work. If you're going to try to make me look good, Marie, you oughtn't to try it on another lawyer."

They all laughed but Marie, who smiled with her mouth. Just then the orchestra stopped playing, although the laughter carried over in the brief life span Marie allowed it. Over her head, Moon saw Kav and his girl entering the room and raised an arm in greeting.

"I tell you, Jim," Moon said, "I got something I think might interest you. Maybe we could talk someplace a little later."

"Why not now? I'll do business on a street corner. Any place."

"I got to see Kav for a minute, but I'll see you at my table in a little while." Walking toward Kav and Kate Bannon, Moon found that he had been reluctant to discuss the job in front of Marie. She made him uneasy, even apart from his anticipation of her disapproval.

"Talking to Brooklyn society, Moon?" Kate Bannon said.

"Who, the McGuffeys? Why, they live on the edge of my district."

"Say," Kate said, "Marie Hennessey will always live in Brooklyn, no matter where her home is. Hello, Leora, how's your uncle?"

"Uncle Billy's just fine. He'll probably be here tonight."

"I should think wild horses couldn't keep him away," Kate said.

"What's that?" Leora said.

"How's business, James?" Moon said.

Kavanagh shrugged loosely. In his borrowed tail coat he looked seven feet tall. "You know the one about what the lawyer said? He'd had a fifteen-dollar case that week, a ten-dollar case and two small cases."

All of them laughed, even Leora, who didn't quite see the point. She could never understand all this shop talk among lawyers. Who were they, anyhow? Her Uncle Billy had them coming to him all the time and he'd only gone to grammar school.

"Let's sit down and have a drink," Moon said. He steered them to a table he had paid a waiter to reserve and saw the McGuffeys start, perhaps a minute later, for the same table. Saw Judge Moore come in with wife, daughter Patricia, and Neal Hartigan; figured that probably meant something; turning saw Ellen Doarn and Peter Calahan, saw for the first time, in the moment of turning, their separate uncertainties; and turning still, turned away, as always, from knowledge to where the waiter, gargoyle-faced, bent slightly to him.

While Moon ordered, speaking under the music, he heard with some part of him Kate begin on Marie. "Why, Marie, fancy seeing you here among the *hoi polloi*. . . ."

McGuffey had eased in between Moon and Kav while Marie had seated herself beside the two young women. Moon waved

[ 8 1 ]

for Peter Calahan and Ellen to come over. Ellen seemed disposed to, but Peter turned firmly away toward Judge Moore's party across the room. The big lush, Moon thought.

"What's on your mind?" McGuffey said under the noise.

Moon puffed once on his cigar, almost consciously aware of the pleasure the moment of hesitation gave him. While he wondered about speaking in front of Kav, the tall man got up and moved over with the girls. "I got a pretty good proposition for you," Moon said.

"What, trying to spring some white slavers?"

"Now, what kind of talk is that?" Moon said.

"Well, that's about the sort of deal most young lawyers are being offered," McGuffey said. "When they offer you anything."

"This one isn't too bad," Moon said and puffed again on the cigar. "You want to be a labor lawyer?"

"I knew it," McGuffey said. "I knew it good. And I suppose you'll have next a few retainer fees from whorehouses?"

"What kind of talk is that from a good Notre Dame man?" Moon said.

"All right, all right. Tell me more."

"There isn't too much more I can tell you," Moon said. "I don't even know the name of the union. I'll tell you the name of the man to contact and give you his phone number." He looked at McGuffey now, and saw the way he had drawn his lips up and across his teeth. "Any money in it?" McGuffey said.

"About three thousand a year."

"About three what?" McGuffey said. "Why, for three grand I'd bring suit against the cardinal. Why didn't you say so in the first place? I thought it was something to be done for maybe fifty bucks retainer or a bag of oats."

Moon enjoyed McGuffey's sudden change, although something about McGuffey's words was what Moon could think of

[ 82 ]

only as unpleasant. "I'll tell you again," he said, "I don't know too much about what you'll have to do. You call this fellow, Linford Thomas, tomorrow and tell him you're the man I'm sending to him."

"All right," McGuffey said, "I'll do that. And thanks, Moon, thanks a lot. A lifesaver, too. We're going to have another baby."

"I'd never have known it," Moon said.

"Oh, it won't be before spring."

There was something more to be said but their joint silence formed and became evident under the music, the chatter, and Leora saying, "There's Uncle now. Like I was saying—"

At last Moon said, "What's Marie going to think about this?"

McGuffey straightened from his crouch and faced the table, raising his head slightly. "To give you a plain answer, not much."

"I was afraid of that," Moon said.

"On the other hand," McGuffey said, crouching again and wagging his head, "Marie doesn't have too much interest in my work and there's no particular need for her to know everything about this. Not that she's indifferent or anything, but she devotes a lot of time to the baby and—"

"I see your point," Moon said. "After all, it's not in her— in her sphere."

"Actually," McGuffey said, "it's not Marie so much as her folks that I'm worried about. That father of hers, my God, man, does he hate Communism or anything like it. You know him?"

"I see him now and then at some rally," Moon said. "He's an awful flannel-mouth but—"

Someone slapped Moon on the shoulder. "Hard at it?" Schneider said. "Why don't you give it a rest, just for tonight?"

Moon had not seen him since the morning at the chancery

[83]

and now drew in his lips and waved Schneider off. "I can't get away from you," Moon said; then seeing the girl with Schneider, rose and saw that McGuffey and Kav were up before him. Apparently she was a foreigner and no one understood her name. Only Kate Bannon recognized her as a dancer from the ballet playing in New York, and told the other girls. Meantime, the girl stood, assured, dark, talking to the men.

Marie said to the girls, "She's a nice one to be coming to the Auxiliary dance."

"Why?" Kate said.

"A Red here," Marie said. "The cardinal would have a fit if he heard."

"Red, my elbow," Kate said. "You ought to grow up." She stood up and touched Kav's elbow. "Dance me out of this sodality meeting."

"Why, a pleasure," he said.

Moon had asked the girl to dance and Schneider was left to move onto the floor with Leora. In the middle of the floor, she said, "I hear your friend is a dancer."

Schneider nodded.

"And a Communist?"

"A what?"

"A Red. She's from Russia, isn't she?"

He shook his head, swallowing. "No. She's from Rio de Janeiro. The niece of a bishop there."

"Aw, now," Leora said, "you must be joking. Marie McGuffey says she's a Red from Russia. From the Russian ballet."

"And who is Marie McGuffey?"

"Jim McGuffey's wife."

Schneider nodded weakly. "I heard he'd married an awful dummy, the last time I went to an alumni meeting, but I didn't know she was that bad."

"And what would you be doing at an alumni meeting with Jim McGuffey?"

[84]

"We went to the same school."

"What!" Leora said. "You went to Notre Dame!"

"Why, yes. I—" Gratefully, he relinquished her to Neal Hartigan's tap on his shoulder, and started across the room to where Ellen Doarn danced with Calahan. Before he reached them, a patter of clapping began near the doorway and couples broke apart to join the clapping, many of them retiring, as it were, dutifully to the sides, so that down the long ballroom could be seen under the arched doorway, the former governor of the state, Alfred E. Smith, smiling, pleased, of all who had come his way clear-cleanly only he.

The orchestra squawked to a stop, the floor cleared entirely; Moon felt a joyous lump rise in his throat; breaking from Kate, James Kavanagh said, "Love me?" saw her nod; Schneider yelled, "Hurray"; and to the strains of *The Sidewalks of New York* the great man and his lady waltzed once, solo, around the wide room. The place roared with yells, clapping, the sound of rung glasses and their repeated and conglomerate echoes. Above its dying surge, Schneider yelled to Moon, "Sometimes I think it pays to be an honest man," and Moon looked at him in a kind of surprise. Between the two of them, the dancer, Concepción Escobar, said, "Bart, who is this man?"

"Sweet," Schneider said, "he is the only honest politician in New York. The only one it has ever known. Everybody is always so surprised they forget to hate him."

"Signals!" McGuffey yelled in Schneider's ear.

"Ball!" Schneider yelled back and McGuffey dived for a derby hat that had fallen to the floor.

"Your friend?" Concepción said.

"Crazy," Schneider said. "A special quality his college endowed him with, the capacity for eternal mental youth." He put an arm around her and she moved easily up to him. It was, he thought, like dancing with a spirit . . . then catching himself, he almost grinned. There was nothing spiritlike

[85]

about that firm and supple waist. Seeing Leora dancing with her uncle, he said to Concepción, "What does your uncle say about your dancing?"

"That I left the Church the moment I stepped on the stage."

"Do you think so, yourself?"

She looked down. "I hope not. You know about the Juggler in the old story?"

He shook his head for some reason.

"He could do nothing but his juggling, so that he did before Our Lady."

He nodded, choking slightly.

"So-o," Concepción went on, "when I go out in the ballet."

"You're a good girl, Concepción," he said. It occurred to him that he had asked her here tonight—he had met her only once before—perhaps in the hope that she was not a good girl. About the people of the ballet he knew very little; he supposed that they were something like the people of the stage and them he had never liked. It was not so much that they were sick—it was, he knew, a sick time—as that they wallowed in their sickness. And supposing Concepción was not what was called a good girl? What was he going to do about it? His own chastity was, indeed, a strange thing, shadowed, unwilling and, he often felt, vain. There was, he had come to think, no sanction for chastity but a religious one, and all talk of figurative cleanness, of greater strength from it, of more wholeness, was also vain and even vicious. A man or a woman should be chaste for God alone and not because some Irish Jansenist of a priest thought sexual intercourse was filthy. It was, he supposed, easier for a certain type of mind to abstain from a thing thought of as evil rather than good; yet someone, somewhere should know which was the more acceptable sacrifice.

Neal Hartigan wanted to dance with Concepción and Schneider relinquished her to him. Hartigan's face seemed

[86]

fatuous, he thought; Hartigan always knew which side his bread was buttered on: he would marry Patricia Moore for money and preferment and Patricia would marry him, knowing all about it. Glancing up, Schneider saw J. Martin Murphy entering the room, standing for a moment where lately Al Smith had stood. A young man was with J. Martin—it seemed he was always with young men—and suddenly Schneider hated them. So bitter was his feeling that he was moved to know its sources. And in a continuation of the meditation begun with Concepción, he saw J. Martin not so much as the intellectual end product of the clerical schools as their symbolic product, subject to all false restraints, to all specious and convenient misunderstandings; to all half-truths, to truth watered or etiolated; to ecclesiastical caprice and priestly confusion; mawkish, mock-serene, forever fatuous; smiling and fearful; gilded, gelded, and glad; your true spiritual androgyne, the intellectual capon.

"Why, Mr. Schneider," J. Martin said, "fancy seeing you here among the gentry."

"I'll gladly kick your tail for you, Martin."

"Ha ha," J. Martin said. "You know Mr. Burke Riley."

"I don't know," Schneider said.

"Why, yes," Riley said. "I was at Notre Dame with you, old man. Before I transferred to Georgetown."

Actually he did remember Burke Riley, a precious youngster, even as a freshman, much given to conferences, clubs and the like.

"I say," Burke Riley went on, "isn't that Judge Moore's daughter? I'd much like to meet her, old man."

Schneider looked at him. "Where did you acquire the accent, old man?"

"What's that, old man?" Burke Riley said, inclining an ear, his face slightly pained, surprised at such treachery.

Schneider walked away. And who was to be charitable to

[ 8 7 ]

the J. Martins and the Burke Rileys? he thought. It seemed that there was only one answer, a saint. And yet there were many not saints who liked and accepted the two and their kind. He wondered uneasily if he were becoming a misanthrope; the thought worried him more than his now conscious anticlericalism. For some reason he thought of Linford Thomas.

The music paused again and he turned to look for Concepción, but almost ran into Ellen and Calahan with Rosemary and Whitey. "Why, fancy seeing you here, Bart," Rosemary said.

"I know," he said. "It won't be for long." He felt the wry twinge as always when he saw Ellen with Calahan. It seemed that she ought to know better. The Calahan money went with the Calahan drunkenness, yet Schneider felt she should know better. Perhaps, he thought in something like an inward gasp, it *was* a matter of charity with her. God knows, all of them had twisted and perverted the Church's teaching in everything else.

"Is it true, Bart," Rosemary was saying, "you have a girl with you from the Russian ballet?"

"Sure, why not? Have to bring a little sex into the gathering."

Whitey smiled feebly and Ellen, too, while Rosemary opened her mouth but amazingly could not speak. Calahan looked bitterly at Schneider.

"That's just what I was thinking," Rosemary said. "I mean in another way. I mean, after all why did you? This isn't the sort of place for—"

Already, seeing Concepción approaching on Moon's arm, Schneider regretted what he had said. His attempt to leave those he was with was too late; it was an opportunity such as Moon delighted in, and seeing Schneider start away from the group, Moon forced Concepción into a run and the two of them skidded up in time for Moon to grab Schneider's arm, turn him and stand between Schneider and the girl facing the other two couples, not unlike a master of ceremonies, which happened to be one of Moon's secret admirations.

"My friends," he began in his sonorous imitation of Al Smith, "let us look at the record." Then remembering the great man was actually there in the flesh, Moon clapped both hands over his mouth.

"Why, Moon!" Rosemary said. Like all her mock rebukes, this one was three parts grave, and in the moment she knew for the first time that her control over Moon was actually more assured than that over Whitey. Perhaps Moon in the moment was also more aware, for he turned to Concepción and said, "These are some of the quaint inhabitants of our city, Concepción, and I'd like them to meet you."

Schneider reflected that Moon was probably as drunk as Calahan, yet it was impossible to dislike Moon, even in his drunkenness. And he wondered if what possessed Moon was actually, too, a kind of charity.

"I think I saw you the other night, Miss Escobar," Ellen was saying. "In the dances from Prince Igor. You were the Polish girl, weren't you? It was really delightful—"

"I didn't know you'd gone to any ballet," Peter said, turning to her. "Who did you go with?"

"Oh, Peter, grow up," Rosemary said.

From opposite sides advanced upon them Judge Augustine Moore, accompanied by daughter, Patricia, and Assemblyman Billy Ryan, accompanied by niece, Leora. Judge Moore reached them first. "Miss Escobar, it is indeed a pleasure. Many a time, when Mrs. Moore and I have attended the ballet—"

"Hullo, folks," said Billy Ryan. "This is quite a gathering. Hullo, Miss Escobar. I'm Billy Ryan, assemblyman, 97th district. How are you? Heard all about you. This is my niece, Leora."

Somewhere McGuffey again yelled: "Ball!"—the orchestra

[ 89 ]

sounded and Schneider turned to Concepción. It was, he could still marvel, as turning to a place of refuge. Moon, heeding the stern voice of duty, turned to Leora, and Rosemary snuggled up to her Whitey. Ellen, feeling Peter's heavy yet actually incurious hands fall upon her, wondered whether if she also took a drink it would help her to stand Peter's breath.

"Dear girl," Peter gurgled. "You shouldn't have to mingle with such people. Filthy Reds. They believe in the socialization of women. That's why Schneider—" He stumbled and for an instant his weight came on Ellen so that she nearly fell. It seemed to mean something, yet her mind when it tried to grasp meaning, turned away as always. Everyone, she told herself once more, had said that once they were married, Peter would be all right. His mother, his aunts, Father Rhatigan, the priest in the Jersey town where the Calahans lived, all had assured or reassured her. It was, she thought for the first time, rather odd that the subject came up so often. She, herself, had never mentioned it to anyone but her mother. And she wondered in just what way the transformation would be engendered in Peter. Sexually, she supposed—Rosemary had hinted at difficulties with Whitey—and yet Ellen couldn't see how *that* would make any real difference.

"Hello, Peter, hello, Ellen," J. Martin Murphy said. "With your permission, Peter, I'll cut in. Ha ha. Looking wonderful, Peter, old man."

"Peter is certainly a fine person," J. Martin said as he danced with Ellen. "You don't know how glad we all are to know about your engagement."

"Well, it's not exactly formal or announced yet."

"Yes, but we know, you rascals. I'd get engaged myself, but I haven't abandoned yet the idea of perhaps having a real vocation."

"I see," Ellen said.

"I have Auntie to think about, too," J. Martin went on.

[90]

"Actually, nothing would do her more good than to have me enter the seminary. Yet I feel she would be lonely. And then there is my work, the cause of Catholic literature. Although I am reasonably sure I would be allowed to pursue that, in time. That is, after ordination."

Ellen's disturbance increased, although not her knowledge of it. Twice J. Martin had been denied admission to the seminary for reasons both he and his aunt properly thought vague. A few people knew of this, and although Ellen was not one of them, for some reason she felt a change of subject called for. "Who's the young man dancing with Patricia?"

"Why, that's Burke Riley. A charming person. He's in finance. You know Knobby Brannigan?"

"That crippled boy they make so much fuss over? I think he's out in the foyer tonight."

"Exactly," J. Martin said. "We helped—I and Burke—the chauffeur bring him here tonight. Well, Burke is in Knobby's father's organization. Personal loans, you know."

"Oh, yes," Ellen said.

"I'm surprised you don't know Burke," J. Martin went on. "He was at Georgetown with Peter. He's been working out of town, in Pittsburgh until recently. He just received a promotion."

"I thought he looked familiar."

Schneider cut in on them. Ellen felt her usual disturbance in his presence, one quite apart from what she felt with J. Martin. "What did the white hope of Catholic literature have to say?"

"Not a great deal," Ellen said. "In a way, I feel sorry for him."

Schneider slowly let her away from him until he could see her face. It was very beautiful, he thought; something began to twist in him. "You're more than ordinarily charitable," he said. When she glanced away, he hesitated, then decided to go

[ 9 1 ]

on. "Sometimes people are betrayed as much by their strength as their weakness."

"I wouldn't say that was a very new or profound remark."

He nodded, pleased with her. "Like Teddy Roosevelt, I'm known for the emphasis I place on the obvious. But what I was going to say was that there's charity and the perversion of charity."

She colored, although Schneider did not know why until she said, "If you mean why those people snigger at poor Martin—"

He shook his head. "No, I wasn't thinking about him."

"Actually, Martin has tried twice to get into the seminary—"

His face twisted in on itself. "I'd heard . . . First the clergy bitches him up and then they turn him down. . . ." Seeing McGuffey heading toward them, he had indulged his frankness, aware of impending severance and departure, and now swung away from Ellen as McGuffey touched him. "To the side lines," McGuffey said.

Walking toward the edge of the dance floor, Schneider wondered idly how it came to be that years away from the football field and its pain, McGuffey could still think in its terms. With little effort he could himself: it was easy to think of himself moving toward the bench from a scrimmage with the varsity: too easy. He supposed McGuffey would have done better to marry someone like Ellen instead of the chisel-chin he had married. It was the Church's insistence on order that would keep McGuffey with Marie the rest of his life. Order was the cake and McGuffey one of the broken eggs. His own despair, he supposed, was because always there would be people like Marie to take eight or nine kinds of advantage of words spoken on a hillside a long time ago.

Glancing up, he saw Moon was with Marie McGuffey and kidding her about something; that Burke Riley was dancing with Patricia Moore again or still, and Hartigan was with

Leora. Judge Moore danced ponderously with Concepción. Some drunks in a corner sang: "Ole No'ra Dame will win over all," and more drunks in another corner were trying to compete by singing the Fordham Ram.

Moving toward Concepción and the judge, Schneider told himself the time had come to depart. Some mood, somber and majestic, completely disproportionate to the occasion, was on him and he knew exactly the pleasure he took from it without knowing its complex origin. Hate, he knew in the moment, was his own besetting sin; as once he had thought it to be lust; now he hated no one here unless it was Burke Riley; and yet he hardly knew the man.

He touched the rounded judicial shoulder. "Ah, young man," Judge Moore said, "I thought you would be arriving. You are a very lucky young man, indeed."

"Why, thank you, sir, thank you." It pleased him to conform, his irony faint though conscious, as for a little while he made the required gestures, fitted word, deed and thought into the ungalling pattern. Dancing with Concepción, he even nodded piously to the two priests standing, discreetly shadowed, near a potted tree. It was, he noted, a palm.

He didn't want to speak, only for a while feel the lithe turn of her body. Its lightness seemed to include his own, to carry him with it, for a time release from thought and all real or fancied responsibility. Gratitude was in him and that in turn made him wonder what would become of Concepción, and so returned him to thought. . . . For the first time he noted consciously in her face the full lips and delicately flared nostrils. He wondered if, like many Brazilians, she had a strain of Negro blood. His amusement over the effect such a revelation would have on Rosemary and the others was brief. For a moment more giddy than he could remember he felt that, although not loving Concepción, he did not care whether she had Negro blood. Yet a dissatisfaction remained . . . grew

[93]

with ghastly swiftness, a genie spreading from its bottle, and stood overshadowing him: he had to know. He did not trust himself or his intention. That distrust, that constant and oblique doubt of his own intention, was the secret of his growth, the sole catalytic of his maturity; and now it acted in him again, more subtle than his fear. "Listen," he said, his voice husky. "Will you be angry if I ask you something?"

"I don't think so." She smiled and he saw that she already knew.

For an instant he wondered if it would help to first lie and say he loved her. "Tell me—you're part Negro?"

She smiled again. "I thought you knew. Maybe an eighth. Maybe a sixteenth. I don't know. I don't think it matters for you."

He nodded. "There was a time when it would have. But now, I think you're lovely."

"Oh, I believe you—about it not mattering. But what would Judge Moore think?"

"You know, I don't think he'd mind. But that girl over there—" he nodded toward Rosemary clinging to Whitey— "she'd scream."

They laughed and the ease and lightness was with him again, as he had never known it before. He thought pointlessly of Blessed Martin at the Worker and he thought of Linford Thomas for the second or third time that evening and looking up he saw Thomas standing to one side of the doorway where separately tonight had stood Al Smith and J. Martin and for an instant all of them.

Thomas was not in evening clothes. He wore a topcoat buttoned to his chin and his face seemed at once placid, free, and almost severe. He beckoned with his head to Schneider and Concepción and they walked over to him. "What goes?" Schneider said.

"Sorry to bother you," Thomas said, "but Galvin's sick in the hospital."

"That's fine. What do you want me to do?"

"Well—" Thomas almost smiled—"you're about the only one we know with any money and he needs a blood transfusion."

"The others you know must be poor, indeed." He felt both flattered and displeased, and like others before him in similar moments, turned to look for Moon, now dancing with gray-haired Mrs. Moore. "Wait a minute," he said and left Concepción and Thomas together, forgetting they did not know each other. He put his hand on Moon's arm. "Excuse me, Mrs. Moore," he said as she turned, thinking he was cutting in. "Say, Moon, Galvin's in the hospital."

"Good place for him," Moon said. "One more session with that guy and I'd be ruined."

Mrs. Moore laughed, not knowing. "All right," Schneider said. "I know how you feel. I just thought I'd tell you. I'm going down there with Thomas."

"Go ahead," Moon said and put a careful arm around Mrs. Moore's waist, making it the excuse for his turning away.

Thomas and Schneider were waiting for Concepción to get her wrap when Moon came stalking out of the ballroom. "You guys will ruin me yet," he said. (It occurred to Schneider that actually they might.) "Leora can go home with her uncle, she says." While Thomas held his coat for him, Moon said, "You're not going to let these dopes take you on a wild-goose chase, are you, Concepción?"

"I don't mind." Her accent was stronger.

"I'm going to drop her at her hotel," Schneider said. "It's on the way downtown."

"No, I want to go," she said.

"You have rehearsal and a show tomorrow."

"I'll sleep late."

In the cab they made a silence in which Schneider knew

[95]

fully the nature of his own disquiet. There was about his relationship to Concepción, whom of course he did not love, something delicate and precarious. Both of them were aware of his concession. And who was he, as male, not to take advantage of that, or she to let him? Yet it was an advantage he did not want to press, that fragile balance not to disturb. In abeyance it filled the cab, engendered in him the disquiet each of the others perceived and differently read. Seeing its effect upon them, he deliberately let the oldest of his dream images rise in him: astride Sancho Panza's mule he was charging the windmill, charging, charging. . . .

In the ward at Bellevue there was a single figure in the night light by Galvin's bed and Moon was shocked to find it was that of his sister. She had just got there and once she had told him that, Moon found there simply wasn't any more to say.

Galvin was conscious. Wide-eyed, he seemed bewildered and perhaps frightened. A weary intern was impressed by their evening clothes and a nurse obviously resented them. It was this way, he thought, the intern told them, malnutrition, anemia and a certain amount of what he supposed you could call shock. Something resembling a breakdown. A blood transfusion would help but there was the matter of money. Furthermore it was needed now and there were no professional donors near by.

"Why, hell, I'll give him blood," Moon said.

"Not tonight you won't, brother," the intern said. "He'd be higher than a kite on a pint of your blood."

Thomas's blood had already been typed and even as they talked a second nurse came in to say that Mary's wouldn't do, either. Schneider and Concepción offered theirs and the little group sat almost silently around the bed and waited.

As Schneider had morbidly expected, only Concepción's would do. "Perhaps Mr. Galvin would not like my blood?" she said, gently.

[96]

"Why not?" the intern said.

"Because I am part Negro."

"Well, I'll be goddamned," Moon said.

"Christ," Galvin said, "a pleasure." And both the nurse and Mary gasped.

They sat around the bed while the transfusion was made, Moon with his head in his hands and his sister weeping quietly. Schneider moved and turned and went outside repeatedly to smoke. Only Thomas remained quiet. Once Mary raised her head to say, "And him Irish. Oh, my God." And then wept again, but now because she knew she was a fool.

When it was over Moon went home with Mary and Schneider took Concepción to a good restaurant and made her eat a steak. He was somber during the meal and could not speak. In the cab going to her hotel, he kissed her and again almost wept. Wanting to say that he loved her, even now he couldn't, realizing that part of his anxiety went back to the days of his football, remembering that she was expected to dance the day after losing blood. He left her in the lobby, shaking his head because the words wouldn't come, and went out to walk in the frosty streets. Perhaps Thomas could help him, he thought, help them all, but, dazed, Schneider couldn't remember where they had left the man.

6

LIKE HIS MOTHER, Peter Calahan had come to feel that marriage to Ellen would be a touchstone, something to transmute inertia and drinking into the gold of accomplishment and recognition, although in what way he was not sure. Of course, there were other ways, too, and on this particular Sunday in January, Peter could hardly wait for Ellen's arrival to tell her the news. Largely as a result of his father's most recent campaign contribution of twenty-five thousand dollars, Peter was going to be made an honorary deputy police commissioner. There was no pay and little work attached to the position, but it would give Peter a special license for his car and the privilege of carrying a pistol.

Besides their estate in New Jersey the Calahans kept a good-sized house in the city. Both houses were open all year, staffed by various pensioners, although the family lived in the Jersey house summers and the city house by winter. Usually the family would go to the country house for Thanksgiving and the holidays, and often during the summer Peter would have friends in to the city house for some drinking while the family was away. Being an only child, he had been subject to various pressures all his life. There was his mother's constant regret that he had done so poorly in school. And there was still often expressed regret that he would not go into the family concern, but Peter had learned at Georgetown to detest the grocery business. It was the equivalent of going into trade and he was damned if he would do that. So at twenty-seven he had never worked nor done anything of a useful nature. The large monthly allowance went he rarely knew where. And while he often thought of going into brokerage with Whitey, there was nothing to really encourage him to do so; Whitey himself was still in a subordinate position.

Ellen was late in arriving, so that Peter had taken to answering the doorbell himself, and he had already ushered in Rosemary and Whitey, two cousins and latest, Patricia Moore and Burke Riley. Peter had come to like Burke Riley a good deal and couldn't understand how they hadn't been better friends at Georgetown. It was the two or three years Burke had spent out of town that made him realize it, Peter had already told Burke. There was something about Burke that made a person feel good, an ability to say exactly the right thing. Peter had even come to wonder how he had managed to get along without Burke. It had been Burke's idea for Peter to ask his father about the deputy commissionership and even more recently Burke had said he didn't see why the two of them shouldn't go into the personal loan business together. Hard times like these, Burke said, were best for the personal loan business; and since all business had an element of risk in it, they really couldn't pick a better time to start in loans. With his experience and Peter's money, Burke said, they ought to do well, starting, of course, in a small way. Peter had not mentioned this to anyone as yet. He didn't want to bother his father so soon again, and he felt his mother and Ellen mightn't be interested.

When Ellen arrived about five o'clock, Peter was busy talking with his friends in one of the double parlors and he didn't answer the doorbell this time. His mother, father, and some relatives were in the other parlor. As Ellen appeared in the doorway of the room in which Peter sat, the others with him saw her before Peter did, a slender girl, almost thin, much of her beauty in the exquisite modeling of the facial bones. Turning, Peter saw her and was annoyed. "You're late, Ellen," he said. He stood up and kissed her impersonally. "And mother did so want you to meet Cousin Frederick. He's gone now."

"I'm sorry," Ellen said. "The children keep us so busy at home."

"You'll have your own soon," Burke Riley said. The others laughed politely and, looking at Burke, Ellen saw an odd expression in his eyes, almost as though he felt she were a rival. But that, she knew, was ridiculous and she put the thought away with other thoughts revolving around Peter. Then, Peter's arm about her shoulders, she let him seat her in a chair next to his own. She said she didn't want anything to drink and Burke Riley resumed the conversation where it had been when she entered the room. "I was telling them, Ellen," he said, the look now gone, "what a fine person Knobby Brannigan is. I've had opportunity to watch Knobby for many years, in prep school and in college and now again while I'm in his father's organization. And the fortitude he has displayed and the charity are really exemplary things. This past Christmas he took his father's car, his biggest car, and the chauffeur, and loaded the back with baskets and went all around one of the slum districts, distributing them."

In the murmur of approval, one of the cousins, perhaps jealous of Burke, said, "And what might your position be in the Brannigan organization, Mr. Riley?"

"Why, I have several titles," Burke said. "The one I like best is that of Assistant to the President, the president being Sir Maurice, himself." Seeing a peculiar and uncomprehending look come into their eyes, he added, "Mr. Brannigan is a Knight of St. Gregory, you know."

"Naturally," said the cousin.

"Actually," Burke added, "I feel much as though I am a squire, to take care of Sir Maurice as in olden times." When the silence told him that this had been a little rich for their tastes, he said, "But we were talking about Knobby. Actually—" his voice dropping—"I probably shouldn't say this, because they don't want it known yet—but his father's sending him to Lourdes in the spring. Just as soon as they can be sure of a smooth passage on the high seas."

"Isn't that wonderful," Rosemary said. "And he's just the type that would get good results and all there. I mean, probably a miracle would be worked for him." It would be nice to go there with Knobby, she thought effortlessly. She didn't know whether she'd even mind too much being married to Knobby: his father had more money than Peter's, perhaps as much as Whitey's; and besides there probably wouldn't be any children.

"His father wants me to go with him," Burke said. "And I suppose I will. I'll continue to get my pay, of course—" he grinned delicately—"and be doing a work of charity besides. But I really don't know. I have other interests here." Now, almost smiling, his glance flicked over to Patricia.

"It's a chance *I* wouldn't miss," Rosemary said. "I mean going to Lourdes and Europe and all. And that wonderful Spanish Catholicism. Don't you think so, Ellen?"

"Why, yes," Ellen said.

"Maybe we could all go together," Peter said. "I mean on a kind of honeymoon. Ellen and I are going to be married after Lent. And Whitey and Rosemary ought to be getting married about the same time."

"That's all right with me," Whitey said. Rosemary said nothing, but she thought that maybe at Lourdes, Whitey would even be converted.

"I wouldn't mind getting married, myself," Burke Riley said, and the others laughed pleasantly.

"Did any of you hear that awful story going around?" Patricia said. "About that girl Bart Schneider took to the Auxiliary dance? I mean, they say she's part Negro. And everyone danced with her, even Papa."

"I heard it," Rosemary said, "but I didn't believe it. And yet I'd believe anything about him."

"The man," Burke Riley said, "is a thoroughgoing rotter. Now at Georgetown, we would have known how to treat anyone doing a thing like that."

"But I heard she was a Communist," Ellen said. "A Russian. I didn't think there were any Russian Negroes."

"Well, I'll tell you all one thing," Rosemary said. "I'd far rather have had a Communist there than a Negro. Imagine if word had got out and people in general knew about it. What would they think of the Auxiliary? Where did you hear it, Patricia?"

"Oh, at The Sewing. You weren't there last time, were you?

I forget just who did say it. Everyone was talking about it. Mrs. O'Reilly actually cried."

"She didn't look like a Negro," Ellen said. "I mean—"

"Now, darling," Peter said, "what would you know about it? Every year thousands of Negroes cross the color line and no one is ever the wiser. There ought to be some sort of law."

"I can hardly bear to think about it," Rosemary said. "Imagine marrying someone like that and having a *black* child! Ugh!"

"Say," Whitey said, "if you're implying that—"

Everyone laughed and Peter rang for more drinks.

"Anyhow," Burke Riley said, "we're getting off the track. Was or was not that girl with Schneider a Negress? If she was, something ought to be done about it." He spoke with great decision so that a little silence came over the room. Whitey said, "But just what? I mean, what could be done?"

"That's right," Rosemary said. "Something should be done, but what?"

"Well, at least someone could write him a stiff letter," Burke said. "I'd be glad to do it myself, but I think it would be better if someone like the president of the Auxiliary did it. Or the chaplain. That would make it official. And the chaplain being a man, could really *make it* a stiff letter."

"Say, that's an idea," Rosemary said. "Do you suppose Father O'Driscoll would do it for us?"

"I don't see why not," Patricia said. "He'll do almost anything," she added gravely. "I remember him from when he was chaplain at Mount Murphy."

"So do we all, for that matter," Rosemary said.

"That's the same O'Driscoll used to be chaplain at the Athletic Club," Peter said. "I know him."

Rosemary had begun to laugh. "Oh, we remember him from the Mount, all right."

"But what's the joke?" Burke Riley said. "If it's that good, we all ought to know about it."

"Oh, we couldn't possibly tell you," Rosemary said. Both Ellen and Patricia had colored. The joke was that at Mount Murphy, when seniors who were about to be married went to Father O'Driscoll for advice, particularly about the 'rhythm,' Father O'Driscoll always told them exactly the reverse of what was true about the fertile period, and of course the girls always had a baby before they had been married a year. It became quite a joke in certain circles, although at first it was told only by Father O'Driscoll himself, with great slaps on the thigh, to appreciative and strictly ecclesiastical audiences. Of course, there was the corollary story, too, that Mother Thomas More had had Father O'Driscoll eased out of his position at the Mount for that very reason. Ellen herself had never been able to see the joke, but had attributed this to some lack in herself. Somehow she always remembered a classmate named Monica Brady who had had two children in her first two years of married life, both by Caesarean section. Monica had known that was the only way she could ever have children, but in spite of this, had married. Now, she lived in continual dread of a third child; there wasn't much hope for a woman having her third Caesarean.

Naturally, this wasn't anything the girls could discuss freely before the men, who, seeing how things were, gallantly allowed the subject to be changed, or rather returned to the original topic. "I'm sure, anyway, that he's your man to write the letter," Burke said. "I couldn't think of a better one."

"I agree," Peter Calahan said.

"But what would he say?" Ellen asked. "After all, no one knows for certain the girl is a Negro. She certainly doesn't look like one."

"I think Ellen may have something there," Calahan said, and Burke pouted judiciously, then nodded.

"But it was all anyone could talk about at The Sewing," Rosemary said. "I wasn't there, but Patricia was, weren't you, Patricia?"

"Yes. But no one knew for sure. I don't know just who it was first mentioned it."

"Well, anyhow," Rosemary said, "I think he's a perfectly filthy person and should be barred from all future dances we have anything to do with. If that girl wasn't a Negress she must have been a Communist, and even if she was neither she's nothing but a professional dancer and we just don't want those kind of people at our affairs. So there."

"Well put," Burke Riley said. "Well put."

"And furthermore," Rosemary went on, "this Negro business is a lot more serious than we'd been led to believe in college. I tell you it's something for white *men* particularly to be worried about." She nodded several times, not knowing exactly what it was she was speaking of.

An Irish servingmaid had been standing for some moments in the doorway, a lace cap askew on her gray hair. "Ah, Annie," Calahan said, "there you are. Please bring all these good people an Irish and soda."

"Yis, Misther Peter," the woman said. "I thought you would like to know that Commissioner Gaffney and his son are in the other parlor with your father."

"I would, Annie, I would, indeed. I'll go right in with them." Peter's heart lifted. The Gaffney visit could mean nothing less than solid confirmation of his appointment. It had been through Commissioner Gaffney and the local assemblyman that his father had worked. And, of course, through Mayor Jackie Meagher, too. Peter rose quickly, seeing as he turned, the round open mouth of Rosemary.

"That's another thing," Rosemary said as Peter was leaving the room. "I don't know what's coming on us. Moon Gaffney's sister, Mary, the one that works in the baby clinic at the hospital, is going to marry a Communist. A friend of Schneider's."

"Come, come," Whitey said. "Everyone is a Communist."

"Now, listen, Whitey," Rosemary said. *"I* know. He's one of those people down at that *Catholic Worker* and everyone knows that's just a Communist front organization."

"But I know two priests that go down there," Ellen said. "They wouldn't if it were a Communist front group."

"Oh, I think some of these young priests don't know the score," Rosemary said. "Why, everyone knows this Galvin is a turncoat. His uncle is Judge Galvin and the old man has forbidden his nephew to come into his sight."

"Now, really," Burke said. "And his cousin at Georgetown was an excellent chap. A real Hoya. Knobby and I knew him well. He played on the golf team. Name was Ranford Galvin."

"That may be," Rosemary said, "but it just goes to show what queer times we're living in. You never know what your own family might be doing."

Peter Calahan showed again in the doorway, Moon Gaffney now by his side, the two of them in a contrast that made everyone separately uneasy, but Ellen especially. "Ladies and gentlemen," Moon began, rubbing his hands.

"Well, if it isn't the next mayor," Rosemary said.

"Say," Moon said, "how would you like to be the first lady fire commissioner? That is, after I'm elected."

"Why, I'd love it," she said. "And there certainly couldn't be any objection with the tradition right in both families."

"That's the way I figured," Moon said. "Hello, Patricia, how's the judge these days?"

Annie appeared with the drinks and after passing around the room, stood before Moon and Peter with one glass remaining on the tray. "Go ahead," Moon said.

"Oh, no, old man," Peter said. "I can get another."

"All right," Moon said. He took the glass and raised it. "Well, folks, here goes. Fire and fall back." He drank deeply,

[105]

feeling the need rise flooding to meet the taste, his first drink today.

"Very clever," Burke Riley said. "I'll have to remember that."

Moon sat down on the far side of Ellen Doarn. Unease bit deep; of all here, only Ellen reassured him. For the men present he had little use: Whitey, of course, was a kind of rival; and Burke Riley, as Moon had put it to Kavanagh, he considered a one hundred per cent phony; Peter was a lush. Both Moon and the commissioner felt bad about securing the appointment for Peter, but twenty-five thousand a year from Peter's father was nothing to risk losing. As Mayor Meagher had put it two days previously to the Gaffneys: "You can't go on screwing people like that without giving them a kiss now and then." And Moon had felt embarrassed at such talk with his father present.

"Say, Moon," Rosemary said, "is that true about your sister being engaged to this Ed Galvin? I mean—"

Moon waved a violent hand at her. "Don't *talk* to me about it. If Mary wants to lose her mind, what do I care."

"It's true, then?"

"I wouldn't know," Moon said. "I hardly know the guy and about the only time I see Mary is now and then for breakfast."

"Ah, for one of those political sinecures that permits of late rising," Burke Riley said.

Moon glanced at him as at an idiot encountered, then turned away and went on talking to Rosemary. "I just don't know, I tell you. Mary's crazy enough to do anything. She teaches at a nigger school, washes Yid and Dago babies twice a week, and now starts going with a guy that's a complete radical."

"See," Rosemary told the gathering, "I told you Ed Galvin was a Communist."

[106]

"Who, Galvin?" Moon said. "No, he isn't. He's not a Commie. A radical, yes. I saw him—"

"But, Moon, old man," Peter said. "The two words are synonymous."

"Of course," Rosemary said.

"Well, I'm not going to argue about it," Moon said. "It's not important." He turned to Ellen. "What are you blushing for, Ellen?"

She had felt the color come into her face at the reference to the baby clinic; she herself had abandoned The Sewing for it two weeks back. "I didn't know I was."

"Oh, but you are, darling," Peter said, and everyone but Moon and Whitey laughed for some reason.

"How about another drink?" Moon said. "I been on the wagon all day."

"That's another clever one," Burke Riley said. "He's been on the wagon all day."

While Annie was getting Moon and Peter another drink, a second maid came in to say that Mr. Travis was wanted on the phone. As Whitey left them, Moon said that that reminded him he had asked Jim Kavanagh and his girl to meet him here. He hoped Peter didn't mind. Later on, he was going out to dinner with Kav and the girl.

"Not at all, old man," Peter said. "Glad to have any of your friends here."

Whitey returned and said he had to leave. He looked at Rosemary. "You don't mind if I stay, darling," Rosemary said. "It's awfully comfortable here."

As Whitey was departing, James Kavanagh and Kate Bannon came up the brownstone steps. They had not passed the vestibule before Commissioner Gaffney appeared in it on his way out, squired by the solid figure of John Calahan, and beyond them Moon and Peter, and still further beyond and in yellow light, the figures of the two maids dashing about under lace caps. There were greetings, standings-aside, easings-by. John Calahan and Patrick Gaffney assured each other of undying friendship although they had not met more than six times previously. Moon greeted Kate and James and told his father he would not leave with him. Generously, his father offered the departmental car for Moon's use and formally Moon declined it to his father's relief.

Mike Boland stood patiently at the foot of the brownstone steps; in the half-dark, the broken shadows, and with something he hardly recognized as another relief, the commissioner turned toward him, from the complex to the simple, from revealing light to easeful dark. As a kind of afterthought, Moon ran down the steps and with Mike helped his father into the car. "Christ," the commissioner said, "you'd think I was an old man." Moon stood there until the long, dark car had eased away, the wind ruffling his hair, and most of the others waited on the stoop, watching him.

Inside again, the yellow light seemed brighter, the warmth more luxurious. His father gone, Moon felt expansive; awareness of his position here was heightened: he was an honored guest, one to whom the family was obligated. It was no great feat for him to unconsciously take over in Peter's own home. And with Whitey gone it would have been a stickler indeed who insisted that Rosemary was not now with Moon. And yet some restraint had come to the room. It was evident that neither Burke Riley nor Rosemary liked the presence of James and Kate. Without entirely knowing its cause, Moon tried to break down the restraint. He told dialect stories, he told them what Mayor Meagher had said the last time he had seen him, he even told them something he shouldn't yet have spoken of, that Billy Ryan would definitely run for Congress.

"Then that means you'll run for Assembly," Rosemary said. "Why, that's wonderful, Moon."

"I say, that's remarkable, old chap," Burke Riley said. "I mean at your age and all."

"His slogan is all ready," Kate Bannon said. "Moon Gaffney, the working girl's friend."

There was some uncertain laughter and Moon asked her what she meant by that.

"Well, you've taken to showing up at *The Catholic Worker*, I hear."

"Oh, that," Moon said to gain time. "As a matter of fact, I have gone there once—" he had been there twice—"and that was with Kav's pal, Schneider, to see about feeding some people or something."

"It's nothing to be ashamed of," Kate Bannon said. "If we—"

"Say, Moon," Rosemary interrupted deliberately, "we were talking about this girl Schneider brought to the dance."

"Which dance was that?" Moon said.

"Oh, come now. The Auxiliary dance."

"That's a long time ago for me," Moon said. "You mean that dancer?"

"I knew you'd remember her," Rosemary said.

"What about her?"

"There's a story," Rosemary said, "that she's part Negro."

"That's the damnedest thing I ever heard of," Moon said. "She's from South America. Her uncle is an archbishop or something down there."

"Oh," Patricia began. "Why—"

"Why," Rosemary said, loudest of all in the room's confusion; "that's awful. I mean no one seems to know anything about her. I mean that it's—"

"What's so awful about knowing nothing about her?" Kavanagh asked.

"Oh, now I say, old man," Burke said, but stopped when he saw the way Rosemary was looking at Kavanagh.

[109]

"If you must know," Rosemary said, "we're pretty careful who we let into our dances."

"My lord," Kavanagh said, "I saw some of the worst shysters in New York there."

Ellen and Kate smiled and Peter finished the drink in his hand. He wished they would go.

"Name one," Rosemary said. "Go ahead, I dare you to name one."

"They're too well known to need to name them."

"That's a rather broad statement," Burke Riley said. "My own feeling was that the very finest people in Catholic society were there."

"Catholic what?" Kate said.

After only a slight hesitation, Burke said, "Families famous in the annals of Georgetown and the other great Catholic colleges."

Moon said, "I, personally, am starving. I have a table reserved down at LaGatta's, Rosemary. How about eating with us. All of you, for that matter." He waved an expansive hand.

"Thanks, old man," Peter said. "But we expect some other people here tonight. Our pastor from Jersey, Father Rhatigan, and others. We always have a lot of the clergy visiting us." He laughed.

"Rosemary?" Moon turned back to her.

She hesitated, even while they watched her. Kavanagh and his girl were nothing to leave the Calahans for. Yet, if she stayed, she would be without a man. She thought she could risk that for once. "I'd love to, Moon," she said, "but I'm pretty tired and I'm going home in a little while."

"Imagine you going home early, Rosemary," Moon said. "What are people going to say?"

"Oh, that I'm an exemplary little girl. Unlike the children of another fire commissioner I know."

"All right," Moon said. "All right. It's got so a man can't take a drink without everyone thinking he's a stew-bum."

"Exactly, Moon, old man," Peter said. "Exactly."

Moon turned to the hall to get his hat. When he and his friends had gone, Burke Riley said, "I must say that I feel better. There are certain people that oppress me by their very presence. Although I suppose, Peter, that since you are dabbling in politics, a certain amount of that sort of company is unavoidable."

"That's about it," Peter said, "although I find Moon agreeable. At least, he's not pretentious."

"Exactly," Burke said. He turned to Patricia. "I suppose your father encounters much the same difficulties at home, Patsy?"

"Well, not so much now, since Papa's got so high. He feels he can't see, well, just everybody. People would always be asking for things."

"Naturally," Peter said.

"Say, even with us," Rosemary said, "Dad has to practically barricade himself in at times."

Mrs. Calahan entered the room and Burke sprang to attention. She was a heavy, placid woman, a great favorite of the cardinal's, for his charities were always an object of her concern and her contributions to them ran regularly into five figures a year. After greeting the others, she gave Ellen her cheek to kiss. "Well," she said, addressing the room, turning from Burke at attention to Rosemary. "Well, I suppose you all know the news?"

"You mean about Ellen and Peter's engagement?" Patricia said.

"That's news, to be sure," Mrs. Calahan said. "But everyone knows that by now. I mean the new news, about Peter's appointment."

"Why, no." Rosemary wriggled to the edge of her chair. "No. Do tell us."

"Peter is a deputy police commissioner now," Mrs. Calahan said. "Isn't that wonderful!"

"Oh," Patricia said, "that is wonderful. Congratulations, Peter."

"I'm so glad, Peter," Ellen said. Maybe it would pull Peter together, she thought, then felt that was a kind of treason and quickly put the thought away.

"Why, Peter," Rosemary said. "That puts you right up there with my dad. I think that's wonderful."

Now Burke Riley had sprung again and in the middle of the room his slim, erect figure and blond, curly hair were in contrast to Peter's taller, heavier body as they shook hands. "Peter, old man, that's just wonderful. I'm glad to see they know ability when they see it." Peter stood there, allowing Burke to pump his hand; the grin on his face was close to a simper: all he wanted them to know was that he was going to be modest about it; ability and all, he was going to be modest about it. . . .

"And I think we should all drink a toast," Mrs. Calahan said, but before she could turn to the bellpull, one of the maids announced Father Rhatigan. And who should be with Father Rhatigan but his good friend, Father O'Driscoll, the same who was chaplain of the Auxiliary. So naturally, it became a very pleasant and uplifting gathering, what with the whisky for joy and the priests to give tone and unconscious assurance to all there that, knowing God's holy clergy so well, *ergo*, they could not but be saved. Indeed, that they already were saved. . . .

And the aunts and the uncles poured in from other rooms, up from the basement and down from upstairs, and in came the maids with a roast turkey and a clove-studded ham and all the fixings.

Congratulations for Peter were resumed and Father O'Driscoll cornered Mrs. Calahan near the serving table, while Father Rhatigan, who was younger and had an eye for the future finances of his Jersey parish, pulled a chair up alongside Ellen. "I can't tell you, Ellen," he began, "how much joy it brought me to learn of your engagement to Peter."

"Thank you, Father," she said. It was the first time she had really felt right about the engagement: she had had to wait for the priestly approval.

"Peter," Father Rhatigan went on, "is the sort of person whose abilities are potential. I mean he has the talent to do fine things, but it's just never come out. I'm sure that with you for a wife, Ellen, Peter will do great things, something in the tradition of the family. There's nothing like a wife and a family of children to bring out the best in a man."

Ellen smiled. She delighted in children, so much so that she often wondered if certain of Peter's characteristics might indelibly stamp those she would bear him. . . .

"What we need," Father Rhatigan said, "are more marriages such as I am sure yours will be. It is an amazing thing, the small number of children most Catholic marriages produce in this country. One might almost be tempted to think—but no matter. What I mean to say is that we rely on marriages such as yours and Peter's to show the way, to give example. Marriages such as those Patricia Moore and Irish of the better class might make.

"I suppose you will be married in St. Patrick's," he went on. "Naturally, I would like the marriage to take place in Jersey at my parish, but a wedding of two such principals could hardly occur in New York other than in St. Pat's. Have you set a date?"

"Not exactly," Ellen said. "Sometime after Lent."

"Yes, yes. There's hardly enough time before Lent. But I do hope you and Peter will decide to spend a good deal of time

[113]

in Jersey. Nothing could please me more than to have a group or colony, if you will, of young Catholic married couples from the better families, as my parishioners. It would help in so many ways. I tell you, we have a financial problem, especially in the winter with most of the native families not contributing very much, I must say."

"Yes," Ellen said.

More friends of Peter's had come in. Georgie Waters, a short, dapper youth who had gone to Georgetown with Peter, arrived with J. Martin Murphy. And a dark boy, a Spaniard named Armando Orvieto. Orvieto seemed mildly bewildered and in a way amused by the others. There were general shiftings and rearrangings of the group and Ellen saw Father O'Driscoll elbowing his way toward her. She felt rather flattered, for he had ignored her during the two years she had been at Mount Murphy and on his occasional appearance at Auxiliary meetings. "Well, well," he began, before he had reached her. "Well, well, this is indeed a surprise and I might add, a pleasure, Ellen." He shook hands with her. "To find you here and to learn of your engagement. Why, I said to myself, imagine little Ellen Doarn engaged to a Calahan. I knew her at Mount Murphy and no one would have thought so then. A future parishioner of yours, Father," he said, turning to his confrere with rising eyebrows.

"That's what I hope," Father Rhatigan said. "I was just saying—"

"I said to myself," Father O'Driscoll went on, "this is a wonderful coincidence. Two people I've known so long and so well, getting engaged without my knowing a word about it. But we'll remedy that, we'll remedy that. Mrs. Calahan just said that she wants me to marry the two of you."

"Oh, that would be nice, Father," Ellen said.

"I said to myself—" Father O'Driscoll began again, only to have Rosemary and the Orvieto boy break in on them. He had

[114]

also said to himself what he had said almost every time he had heard of a girl from Mount Murphy getting married—that they'd learn, all right. They all had it coming to them if they were going to indulge themselves, and she no less than any of the others for all her thinness. He often wondered how fine young Catholic girls could so willingly and at times hurriedly fling themselves to some man. Well, they would pay the price for it. And he had often enough seen to it that they had paid it early, with those flittering girls at the Mount coming to him and saying Jackie and I or Joey and I want to get married and we want children but you know how times are and we'd like to wait a year or two and what about this business of the rhythm, Father, and could you perhaps tell us about it? He'd told them, all right. Many a time he and the others had had a good laugh over it.

"Father," Rosemary was saying, "this *is* a coincidence. We were talking about you just a little while ago. Before the crowd got here. We had some work for you to do, but it turned out you didn't have to."

"What was that, what was that?" said Father O'Driscoll in his merry way, with his fair and famous humorous quirk.

"Why, it seems as though we thought one of the men who came to the Auxiliary dance brought a girl with him who was part Negro, and—"

"That's an outrage," Father Rhatigan said.

"Exactly what I said, Father," Burke Riley said. "I said that at Georgetown we'd have known how to deal with such a person."

"We'd of thrown the so-and-so in the Potomac with a stone around his neck," Georgie Waters said, and the others all laughed; Georgie was a card, all right: so little and so tough.

"But anyway," Rosemary went on, "it turned out it wasn't so. But at the time when we thought it was so, we thought someone ought to write this boy a good, stiff letter. And since

[115]

you were about the only man connected with the Auxiliary in any official capacity, Father, we thought that you might be the one to do it." Her eyebrows, delicate, delicately questioned him.

"Might?" Father O'Driscoll said. "Might? Why, my dear young woman, it would have been a pleasure. I'd have written him such a letter as would have curled his hair."

They all laughed again at that. Although Father O'Driscoll gave a humorous emphasis to almost everything he said, anyone could have told that he was serious this time, all right.

The maids in lace caps had finished with their dashing and the buffet supper was ready. In the midst of the laughter from the group around the priests, Mrs. Calahan clapped her hands for silence. "Now," she said, "I'll ask Father O'Driscoll to say grace. If you'd be so good, Father, you being older than Father Rhatigan and all."

"First a toast," J. Martin Murphy said. "To Peter and Ellen—"

"But now," one of the cousins said, "I don't know whether a toast should come before grace or not."

Nor did anyone else . . . but Father O'Driscoll, who operated on the principle that the clergy came first in everything, raised his hand and blessed the gathering, intoning in a sonorous voice over the bowed heads: "Bless us, O Lord, and these Thy gifts which we are about to receive from Thy bounty through Christ Our Lord. Amen."

Kate and James had left LaGatta's early to return to Brooklyn. But Moon sat at the table and found after a time that the quietness and being alone pleased him. He didn't even feel much like drinking, but then he almost never did drink alone.

Lately, he had begun to develop what some might have called a neurosis, others a conscience. Nervous strain was not a thing he thought of himself as being subject to, and yet even

[116]

a constitution such as Moon's could hardly endure without some ill effect the almost constant drinking, cajoling, dissembling, arranging, lying. But what bothered and puzzled him was new: certain more or less recent happenings would recur quite vividly in memory and especially when he was tired. Then some emotion, regret or perhaps even grief or anguish, would rise swiftly in him and he would find that his face had contorted in what looked not so much like the emotion he felt, as something else, perhaps fear.

There were three scenes which came most vividly to him: the faces in the bread line that morning of half-light; Galvin's face on the hospital cot; and a less recent scene, the face of a man, a minor politician named Joe Kiley, the time Moon had been delegated to tell him that the organization would not give Kiley the money to cover a good-sized deficit in his books. . . .

Finding that these and other faces tended to return in this moment, Moon thought of Kate and James. He liked them, he told himself; probably he liked them better than anyone he knew. Kav was lucky, getting a girl like Kate. This last thought occurred idly and even conventionally to Moon, yet it did not depart as had the others. So that he was moved, almost as against his will, to wonder why he thought of James as lucky and not of, say, Whitey Travis as lucky. Apart from being pretty and well made, there was nothing particularly desirable about Kate. Her family had, if anything, less money than Kav's. She worked as a secretary in the Brooklyn chancery, and her pay wasn't even enough for her and Kav to risk getting married on while Kav tried to make a go of the law. In a way, Moon wished he had given Kav the job with the Union. Moon had heard indirectly that McGuffey seemed to be doing all right there, and he had no qualifications that Kav lacked. Or had he? There was that adaptability, that imperviousness that Moon realized only now had had much to do with his deciding

[117]

on McGuffey. Neither one of them was a screwball like Galvin or Schneider; they were just a couple of young lawyers looking for any kind of legitimate work. Although, Moon conceded, being a lawyer for a union came pretty close to the edge of not being legitimate. He supposed that in a way it was the difference between Kate and Marie McGuffey that made him think the job might better have been given to Kav. More than tolerating such work for Kav, Moon had the impression—not undisturbing to him—that Kate would welcome it. That was a queer story she had told about the letters that came into the chancery office in Brooklyn after the first of the sermons the bishop had ordered on the labor encyclicals. There had been dozens of letters demanding to know in effect what the hell right a priest had to tell them what *they* should pay their help. No one seemed to know how the bishop felt about this reaction to his innovation—the latest labor encyclical was, after all, only thirty or forty years old—but the young priests attached to the chancery as secretaries had been divided. One of them felt it was no more than the bishop had coming to him for dabbling in such matters, like that fool bishop in Chicago. The other two young priests had been puzzled and grieved. One of them, Father McTiernan, had said that it was only what they could have expected after three generations of their parishioners' listening to sermons detailing three and only three major sins: fornication, eating meat on Friday, and missing Mass on Sunday. What he hadn't been prepared for was the violence of the reaction.

Moon himself wondered about that. Underpaying your help, he knew, wasn't a mortal sin like sleeping with a woman, and he could understand people getting upset about being told what they could or could not pay their help. But the letters had been angry and bitterly complaining ones. One man, who owned a factory in Williamsburg, had written that he was going to complain to Rome. Of course, anyone like that was a damn fool, Moon knew. It was like Billy Ryan when he spoke at the Holy Name communion breakfast, saying they all ought to boycott Madison Square Garden because the Commies had had a meeting there. Sometimes, he thought, Ryan could be an awful flannel-mouth.

Moon wondered if next fall, when he ran for Assembly, the Commies would run anyone against him as they had against Ryan, and would they bring up the labor issue; not because they stood a chance, but to embarrass himself? He would take a stand, Moon decided, he would come out for labor. He would not be like Ryan screaming: "I defy any man to prove that I, Billy Ryan, have ever done anything, by word or deed, to harm the laboring man and his family." Nor had Ryan ever done anything to help him, Moon thought. Except to get any good Democrat on the relief rolls. But there again, Moon suspected, Ryan had acted so promptly only because the Commies themselves had been using the relief rolls to play politics. Yet they had nothing to really fear from the Commies in their district: the idea didn't seem to appeal much to the Italians; the Commies were mostly, in this district, Jews or Irish turncoats. Ryan had been primed, Moon was certain, more by Father Malone in his church at the other end of the district, than by fear or any desire for justice or charity. Malone was always jabbering about the Commies and Bingo, often in the same sermon. Who was it had called him Bingo Bobby? Galvin or Kav? Lately, Father Malone had taken to talking about what he called "great men" in Italy and Germany who knew exactly how to deal with Communists. Ah, they did indeed, Father Malone said, and although he didn't supply detail, there was a relish about the way he said it.

But if underpaying your help wasn't a moral issue, Moon wondered, what were people like Galvin and Linford Thomas so coked up about? To say nothing of a sensible priest like this McTiernan seemed to be? A man had to make a living,

[ 1 1 9 ]

but saying it was a mortal sin to underpay your help was certainly laying it on thick. That was the risk anyone took, Moon knew, who wasn't smart enough to get a civil service job. Again and again he had seen young lawyers who had been brilliant in class with him, meaching around, in seedy clothing, unmarried, always together in some cheap bar because they couldn't afford to take a girl out. And seeing them he had been glad for his own job, although it paid only twenty-four hundred a year.

So Moon justified himself . . . yet again knew no peace. And some level of him knew that this time drink would not help. He put on his coat and went out into the street. The air seemed wetter and less cold, quieting against his face. For a moment he lingered aimlessly in the bar of light from La-Gatta's, then began to walk without haste toward the east. He hoped no one who knew him would see him and think he was going to a whorehouse. And he wondered about Whitey that time; whether someone oughtn't to tell Rosemary about that. A letter or something. He sighed on the wet air and decided not to: after all, he didn't know for sure that it had been Whitey.

And walking, Moon wondered about his sister and Galvin. Even he knew the superficial nature of his own dismay: actually, Galvin was a solid character; screwball or not, you had to hand it to him for the way he had stood up to the monsignor that day in the chancery with the rest of them weeping or routed or silent. Moon didn't like the idea of his sister paying for Galvin at the rest home in Jersey, but he supposed someone had to, and if Mary was so anxious to marry Galvin, Moon guessed it was all right. Of course, there were still a lot of things he didn't like about Galvin: it still gave Moon the creeps the way Galvin had been so damned happy to have blood from that girl that night. That goddam Schneider, Moon thought, it would be just like him to be kidding all of them about the girl's Negro blood. She didn't look it, certainly. Yet it was she who had mentioned it that night, not Schneider. Still, Schneider could have put her up to it, although that was hardly a time for kidding. He saw them all as separate and apart from himself; so separate and so apart that he felt in dismay either they were Catholics or he was, but not both of them. . . .

There was apparently no healing for him tonight. As he turned into Mott Street his pace imperceptibly slowed; he gnawed at his lip and his face contorted again as in memory he saw Kiley's face, blank, down-pulled and pallid, the pores darkly showing. . . . Yet how ever to make recompense to these people? Kiley had left the city; and the failure to help him had not even been his own, Moon knew. . . .

He had almost reached the place. Glancing around in the broken darkness, for all the world as if he were entering a whorehouse, he turned into the store front where the vigil light still burned before the black saint.

## 7

IN THE SMALL ROOM where he had first met them, the people of the Worker sat as though they had not moved, Dorothy, Thomas, the Italian girl, all the faces were familiar except that of a young priest. Moon found that he had wanted to see Thomas most. This puzzled Moon and on a vaguer level disturbed him. For Thomas himself was a leavening element in the life of anyone who knew him, and it was not so much the measure of any growth in Moon that he should know this as of the possibility of that growth.

Moon found the group quiet and what he could think of only as depressed. They seemed pleased that he was there, but after he was seated there was a disquieting silence in which only the Italian girl spoke to say they had missed him with the coffee.

"Why, just call me any morning," Moon said. "I'll be glad to whip over here. Chances are, I won't have been to bed yet." It pleased him inordinately that he could make them, too, smile, equally with the boys at the club. . . .

"I suppose you've heard about your friend McGuffey?" Thomas said.

"Not a word. What goes with him?"

Thomas glanced quickly around the room. "I think we had an idea that was why you came here. To tell us off, or specifically, to tell me off."

"I don't know what you're talking about," Moon said. "What's happened to McGuffey?"

"To put first things first—" Thomas looked at the floor while his fingers pressed and turned a crumpled ball of paper—"his wife has left him."

"She what?" Moon said. His emphasis and exaggeration were conventional; actually, he felt no way at all.

"She has gone home to Mama," one of the men said.

"But why?" As he spoke, Moon knew why, with depth and great clarity. "Jim doesn't drink any to speak of. And he's making good money. He—" Thomas's face made Moon stop talking; it was as if, without lack of charity, Thomas was amused. Thomas not only knew about McGuffey, but knew that he, Moon, knew.

"We thought you might know, Moon," Dorothy said. "She left him because she found he was working for a labor union."

"Well," Moon said and pausing found that not only was the truth in him but that it must come out. "Well, I'll tell you, I was afraid of that at the time. McGuffey was afraid of that himself. But he figured it might be a while before Marie knew about it."

"Strictly," Thomas said, "she didn't find out about it. She

knew all along, although she didn't like it any too well. She liked the money and she hoped her folks wouldn't find out."

"How did they?" Moon said.

Now all of them seemed to feel that delicate amusement. "Don't you read the papers, Moon?" someone said.

"Usually, but I must have missed out on this one."

"My union," Thomas said, "has been having a jurisdictional dispute with Brosnan's union." His voice sounded weary for the first time. "And McGuffey has been representing us in court. About a week ago, the thing got into the papers and, of course, McGuffey's name was mentioned and his father-in-law saw it."

"That flannel-mouth," Moon said. "You know there was a story for a while that he was the only court clerk in the history of the city that couldn't read or write." They were amused again, he saw, but would not be distracted.

"If George Hennessey and the others like him," the priest said, "were merely uneducated, it wouldn't be so bad."

"You know the Hennesseys, then?" Moon said.

As the priest nodded, Moon looked closely at him for the first time and saw that he was young and very tired. "They're in the same parish I happen to be a curate in. It's one reason I'm here tonight."

Moon nodded and put his face in his hands, a gesture he didn't usually allow himself in public. His feelings were a compound, concern for McGuffey and satisfaction that he himself had been right, along with things less definite, such as guilt over having given McGuffey the job and scorn for Marie. "That wouldn't be Bernie Brosnan's union, would it?" he finally said.

"Whose else?" Thomas said. "Among other things, about the only union in the city that might be said to have ecclesiastical support."

[ 1 2 3 ]

Moon looked quickly up. "He's been fighting the Commies, that's why."

They all spoke now at once and the thin man in a corner loudest of all. "Sure, everyone Brosnan doesn't like is a Commie. We're Commies. Lin's a Commie. Father Shanahan here is a Commie."

"Yes, but now look," Moon said. "That's the result of the Commies' obscurantist tactics. They bitch—pardon me—gum everything up."

"Only a fool can't see through what you call their obscurantism," the priest said. "The most terrible obscurantism of the time is in the Church."

Only later did Moon know the extent of his shock at the priest's remark. Now, as always, Moon covered the unpleasantness, slurred the edges. "I can't say I know exactly what you're talking about . . . but anyhow, we're getting away from the subject. What are we going to do about McGuffey?"

"What, indeed?" Dorothy said. "How about you having a talk with his wife or her family?"

"Who, me?" Moon said. "Why, I'd think Father Shanahan could do better for that kind of thing, right in the parish and all." Even as he spoke Moon saw the priest color.

"Moon," he said, "I think you say the wrong thing by instinct."

"I'm sorry, Father, if I have. I didn't know—"

"It's all right," the priest said. "You couldn't have known." Now he put his hands to his face and moved them tiredly over it, to Moon's embarrassment. "In the first place," the priest said, "I am fairly new in the parish. And in the second place, my pastor, Monsignor Clancy, has already requested my removal to another parish. . . . I am, he says, a radical, a Jew-lover, a complete fool." In the silence there was no movement, only the sense of movement. "A disgrace to the Irish race. Of course," he went on, his voice lifting and changing, "he attributes much of my recalcitrance to having been born in this country, to being what he calls an Irish-American. If I were real Irish like him, born in Ireland, I would not have such outlandish ideas. Like *The Brooklyn Trumpet* and the *Irish Rose* he distinguishes sharply between those who are Irish and those who are merely Irish-American. It is not so much having to live in his constant aura of rage, spite, and disapproval, nor his anti-Jewish sermons. It is the idea, which he reinforces every day, that such a man can be a priest and every morning call down into his fingers the body of Our Lord Jesus Christ." He shook his head, unable to go on, and the thin man and the Italian girl took him outside.

Moon was greatly confused. Horror was inextricably confounded with his emotion of pity and sympathy. Only Thomas seemed unmoved. Dorothy wept quietly and bitterly. "The bishop of Brooklyn," Thomas said, "has become a very progressive man. In addition to his belated interest in the papal encyclicals on labor he has recently appointed a committee to investigate the high incidence of insanity among the priests of his diocese."

Because there was nothing else to do or say, because never in memory had he been so completely confused and helpless, Moon said feebly, "All right, what do you want me to do about McGuffey?"

"If there is anything to do," Thomas said, "I would think you were the man not only to do it, but to decide what it is."

"You certainly have a good opinion of me," Moon said. Yet the flattery stimulated him and pride, like a secretion from some ductless gland paralyzed for a time by fright, began to flow in him again. "I'll go see McGuffey first. It's too late tonight, but—"

"What makes you think it's too late?" Thomas said. "You don't think he's asleep, do you?"

They had a way, Moon realized, of mentioning outright matters that others ignored or were actually unaware of. At the club for example, there might be talk about a man and his wife in bed but hardly that a man had been unable to sleep because his wife was not there. "Why, I hadn't thought about it," Moon said.

"I think it would help if you went to see him as soon as possible, Moon," Dorothy said quietly.

"We could phone him first," Moon said.

"I don't think he always answers the phone," Thomas said.

"We'll just have to take a chance on finding him in," Moon said.

"We have to take a chance on a lot of things," someone said.

Thomas stood up. "All right, let's go." Moon, also getting to his feet, found that there was a heaviness in him, as though his body were reluctant.

Finding himself with Thomas in the dark street, Moon felt as if he were being compelled to do something he did not want to do; yet when he tried to think of what it might be, he could not; certainly, he knew, he was glad to do anything he could for Jim McGuffey.

They walked to Canal Street and got into a cab. Going across town Moon found that as rarely happened he had nothing to say. The facts of McGuffey's small tragedy were all in mind, marshaled, fixed, clear, yet to Moon somehow without meaning. The closest to meaning he could come was to think Marie must be an awful dope. But then, he consoled himself, he had always thought she was a dope.

The three-story-and-basement house the cab stopped before had been converted into apartments. There were not many like it that far downtown. McGuffey's name was over the middle one of the three mailboxes, but when they pushed the button and waited, there was no response. The second time they listened but could hear no sound any place inside. Moon absently tried the inner door of the vestibule. It opened and they passed into the dimness beyond it. Moon sniffed; he had acquired the unconscious habit of comparing the smells of what the city ordinance euphemistically called multiple dwellings; there were the odors of cooking, stale or new, in such flats as those of his own home, and there were the odorless halls of such places as that of the Danahers. This place also smelled, but of nothing organic or alive; the smell was acrid, as of, say, the lacquer applied to cheap metalwork.

They went up the narrow stairs, noisy imitation marble, iron and plastic treads. Thomas went first and on the second floor paused. The single door must be that of the McGuffeys, Moon knew. They were aware of the silence their own lack of motion had brought to the place, and Moon became freshly disturbed. He wondered if McGuffey could have done something desperate. Of course, Moon consoled himself, the Irish rarely commit suicide. Still, there were all those cops suicide and a lot of them Irish and nobody knowing just why they did it.

Thomas pushed the button on the lintel and they listened. "He's probably out," Moon said.

"I guess so." Thomas pushed it again and this time they heard movement inside the apartment. When the door opened they could see McGuffey standing against a background of virtual darkness. In the anxious face hope faded as they watched. He wore trousers, a white shirt, vest, and house slippers. His hair was uncombed and the heavy beard showed blue through his skin. His eyes stared, then focused, then were almost hid by the eyelids crinkling to give the appearance of welcome. "For God's sake, look who's here. Come on in. I fell asleep on the sofa."

"Sorry to be coming around at this time, Jim," Moon said.

"One time's as good as another," McGuffey said. "What you doing up so late, Lin? I thought you always said your compline and went to bed early?"

Thomas said something Moon didn't quite catch because McGuffey closed the door behind them just then.

McGuffey switched on a light just as Moon, going along the little hall, stumbled over something. Glancing down in darkness, in light Moon saw it was a shoe. Then, looking up, he saw the place. In the small living room, clothing hung or was thrown on almost every piece of furniture. Trays of cigarette butts had spilled over on the tables and chair arms, and their ash had spread, adding to the film of dust that lay everywhere. Shoes, a pair of suspenders, three upright highball glasses and a scattering of children's blocks were on the rug; a picture of the Sacred Heart hung askew on the wall. Two floor lamps with large, pink shades had each apparently but one bulb, for their light was dim. Thomas sat on the littered sofa, while Moon, more slowly, seated himself on one of the overstuffed chairs after removing a coat tossed on it.

"What'll you guys have to drink?" McGuffey said. "Sorry the place looks like this, Moon. Marie ran out on me last week."

"That's what I heard," Moon said. "What's the matter with that girl?"

"What are you going to drink?" McGuffey persisted.

"Nothing for me right now," Thomas said.

"I think I'll skip it, too," Moon said.

"Well, I'm going to have one," McGuffey said. He picked up a glass from the floor and poured about two inches of bourbon into it, tasted it, and then sat forward, his elbows on his thighs, the glass in his hands suspended between his knees.

Moon looked downward and wet his lips. He wished he hadn't come here, yet his mind could be surprised at the wish.

"Moon didn't know about Marie until a little while ago," Thomas said. "But he thought we ought to come over now and see what could be done about it."

"Done about it? Done about it?" McGuffey moved his head

[ 128 ]

and upper body in a kind of purposeful swaying, but without looking at either of them. "I ought to go over to Brooklyn and run my shoe up the ass of that goddam old man of her's." When no one spoke, he went on more quietly. "Of course, in a way, Moon, both you and I knew something like this might happen."

"I know," Moon said quickly. For some reason, he felt relieved. "I remember we talked about it at the dance that night."

"But I was hot for the dough," McGuffey said, still looking at the floor.

There was nothing to say to that, Moon knew; he told himself that he also had been hot for something then, but what it was he didn't remember.

In their silence, Thomas said, "That may be, Jim, but the fact is that you've done a good job while you've been with us."

McGuffey waved a hand at him without raising his head. "What the hell, a lawyer does a good job for anyone that pays him the dough."

"I don't know," Thomas said. "I think maybe I meant something else—sincerity."

These words seemed to distress McGuffey, so that Moon felt it necessary to change the subject or at least mention another aspect of it. "That's good, though," Moon said. "I mean, here you never did any labor work before and just in a matter of weeks you're doing fine."

"Oh, I'm doing wonderful," McGuffey said. He drank again. Each silence brought an increase of tension to the room, and now Moon had the odd notion that actually the tension could not affect Thomas, but that freely Thomas allowed it to, a kind of willing participation by Thomas in something to which, unlike other men, he was not subject. It was an idea whose unreality was apparent, Moon thought, and he felt ashamed that it should arise in himself.

[ 129 ]

All their gestures had become random, mock-violent and sharply defined, a kind of pantomime of shared grief or its counterfeit. Now, even Thomas flung his body from the waist forward. "Nothing is wonderful if it breaks up a family," he said.

"Break," McGuffey said. "For fifteen cents I'd break her old man's head."

"It's a hell of a strain to work under," Moon said. "I couldn't do it."

"That's the remarkable thing," Thomas said. "He has worked and it's been damned good work." Bent forward, he looked at the floor.

"I kept working," McGuffey said, "because the only other thing to do was to get drunk. And Christ knows there's been enough rummies in my family."

"We have Brosnan worried," Thomas said. "He knows he has to let a vote be taken. So now what he's been trying to do is to keep us from distributing information about it. We've had two people hurt, and Jim wants to do something about that legally, but the way the rest of us feel is that the kind of men involved, the ones who will vote, are not apt to take kindly to legality."

"I was talking to Joe the boy reporter about it today," McGuffey said. "He—"

"Who?" Moon said.

"Schneider," McGuffey said. "Your pal, Schneider. He—"

"He's no pal of mine," Moon said. "If—"

"Schneider is no one's pal," McGuffey said. "He's too busy chasing that dancer around. Much better than a pal, I'd think," he muttered, "much more appropriate."

"I could tell you plenty about her, too," Moon said, then bit his tongue.

"We're getting off the subject," Thomas said.

"Anyhow, Schneider thinks as Lin does," McGuffey said.

"He's put something about it already in his sheet. And maybe that's the way to do it instead of dragging it into court."

"The best thing you could do," Moon said, "is to keep clear of that guy. He ruins anything he touches."

"I think you're wrong," Thomas said. "He's about average for a certain type of educated Catholic. But that's beside this point we're always getting away from. Maybe we'd better come right out with it. I think the principal reason we came here, Jim, is because Moon wants to do what he can about you and Marie."

McGuffey didn't speak for a moment. Moon wished Thomas hadn't put it quite that way. "I don't know just what he *can* do," McGuffey said slowly. "I've talked to Marie on the phone. The old man doesn't want me to go over there. For that matter, I'm afraid to go over. I wouldn't like to get started on him. . . . Sometimes, I think he's still sore because Marie lost her virginity when she married me . . . but that's neither here nor there. There's no use pretending I don't want Marie back here, and she can come back any time she wants to and on any conditions that suit her."

"Then what's stopping her?" Moon said.

"She wants me to give up this job and I don't know but what I'll oblige her. The thing is that I can't do it right now with this goddam business about jurisdiction and voting coming up."

Moon thought that oughtn't to stop him. "And how long is that likely to go on?" he said.

"Weeks," Thomas said. "Maybe months. Brosnan is well entrenched. He—" Thomas stopped, then went on—"I don't know but it would be better for Jim to give up the job. First things first."

Moon had been thinking how McGuffey must be awful damned hot for his wife and that in a way McGuffey ought to be ashamed of everything being so obvious. Especially if it was a question of just waiting a few months. Hearing Thomas, Moon said, "That would be about the simplest solution."

"Well, I'm not going to do that," McGuffey said. "I'm conceding enough as it is. I have no particular use for the union, but I'm damned if I'll let her and her old man have everything their own way."

"Anyhow," Thomas said, "I imagine Moon will be glad to go over and talk to them if you want."

"I'll go," Moon said. "But I won't be glad to go. I don't like George Hennessey any better than Jim does."

"That wouldn't do any good," McGuffey said.

"Moon could at least explain that we weren't Commies or anything like that, you were working with," Thomas said.

"I'd explain it," Moon said, "but I hope I wouldn't have to try to prove it. I don't know a union today that hasn't got some of them in it." He glanced at Thomas.

"I know one," Thomas said. "Brosnan's. There are others, too, but—"

"But yours isn't one of them," Moon said.

Thomas looked fixedly at the line where wall met floor. "No new union is completely free of them. Sometimes they get in as something else; sometimes we take them in knowing exactly what they are. The Commies are twenty years ahead of any other group in this country in the matter of organizing technique. No new union could afford to ignore their ability. It was either work with them or tolerate unions like Brosnan's."

"What did Brosnan's union ever do that was so bad that the Commies didn't also do?" Moon said.

"Superficially, nothing," Thomas said. "I suppose, actually, the thing is that a union like Brosnan's, about ninety per cent Catholic, resorts to the same tactics that the Commies employ. But there's a difference. I don't know a single Commie leader that's out for personal advancement in the way Brosnan is."

"All union leaders are the same," Moon said. "At least Brosnan isn't immoral like the Commies."

"By immorality meaning sex," Thomas said. "You ought to know better. You don't really think any longer that it's worse to commit fornication than to maim or to steal?"

Moon remembered with a sense of mild shock that this was one of the things he had been thinking about before coming to the Worker tonight. But before he could answer, McGuffey said, "You're talking to one union leader that isn't the same, Moon." He had poured himself another drink.

"Meaning you, I suppose?" Moon said, with that smile.

"No, meaning Lin." McGuffey drank and looked at the floor.

"Well, yes, of course—" Moon began, but Thomas interrupted him. "Anyhow, what we want to know, Moon, is whether or not you'll go to see Marie and her folks."

"Why, certainly I'll go," Moon said. "What do you think I came over here for."

"All I can say," McGuffey said, "is that it will be quite a gathering when you and Hennessey get together." He began to curse his father-in-law again, bitterly and aimlessly. Thomas stood up. "How about going out for something to eat?"

"I don't want anything to eat."

"Come on," Moon said. "It'll do you good."

"Oh," McGuffey said, "you want to do me good, now? The do-gooder done good to."

"What?" Moon said.

"Nothing," McGuffey said, rising. "You're as bad as Schneider."

"So I come here to see how you are," Moon said, "and I get insulted."

McGuffey took a tie from a chair back and tied it with care, looking in a mirror. "Schneider's all right," he said. "He just never got over being fifth-string quarterback at school."

[133]

"He never got over something," Moon said.

"And I," McGuffey said, putting on a suit coat, "never got over being fourth-string quarterback. Let's go."

"Why, once, Moon," Thomas said, "I heard you say you were going to get Schneider to write your speeches for you when you ran for mayor."

"I must have been drunk."

"Naturally," McGuffey said. "Naturally."

"Look who's talking," Moon said.

McGuffey followed them out onto the stair landing and pulled the door closed after him. The spring lock clicked and McGuffey reached into a pocket for something and then placed it under the small rubber mat before the door.

"What are you leaving the key there for?" Moon said.

"Can't tell but maybe Marie will show up," McGuffey said. The tone of his voice told nothing, and both Moon and Thomas grew alarmed. It was, they knew, about midnight. And for once, their thought coincided: either McGuffey had a girl coming tonight or there was something wrong with McGuffey. And both of them knew McGuffey had no girl coming. Descending the stairs' sickening odor, neither Moon nor Thomas could say a thing.

8

DRESSING, as always in half-light, Moon was aware of the precautions he had taken, although not entirely of their reason. He had contrived a piece of political business as his excuse for visiting the Hennesseys, and now found that beside his lies to them, he must also lie to his family. Leaving the downstairs apartment, Moon paused at the door and looked at his parents. His mother's fingers moved over a lace doily she was making and his father was in one of his rare static moments, sitting back in a Morris chair, without expression or movement, the fingers, the face possessing a translucent quality which Moon remembered seeing in other, older people but never before in him. Something caught in Moon, and something else almost came clear but Moon, as usual, wouldn't let it. "Anything you want me to say to George Hennessey?"

Nothing moved but the commissioner's mouth. "Oh, give the man my regards." When Moon waited or paused, silent, the commissioner added, "There isn't a great deal you can say to a man like Hennessey."

Moon moistened his lips. "I wanted to talk to him about getting a drayman's job for Gorevin's cousin. He's a family man."

The commissioner neither moved nor spoke for a moment. "I knew there were some temporary draymen's jobs over there, but I'd thought of Patsy Lenihan for one of them. He's been let out by his brewery. But no mind. If that poor omadhaun of a cousin of Gorevin's needs work, get it for him if you can."

"My best to Mrs. Hennessey," Moon's mother said, without looking up. "Somehow, we just don't see them very often. I don't think I've been to Brooklyn this year."

Outside the building, Moon paused on the stoop and looked at his father's departmental Cadillac. The family kept an old car in a garage, one which was used when they went to Atlantic Highlands for the summer. But for tonight, Moon had borrowed the Cadillac with its low number plate and departmental shield. Mike Boland had hopefully offered to drive it, but Moon told him he'd be up too late. Moon had also called James Kavanagh and arranged to meet him and Kate at nine o'clock in the St. George Hotel. That way, neither conscience nor any possible insistence the Hennesseys might make could force Moon to stay later than eight forty-five at their home. Kavanagh had said that Schneider might be along but Moon thought that this time Schneider might be the lesser evil.

[135]

Getting into the front seat of the car a little gingerly, Moon eased it through traffic to Brooklyn Bridge, crossing it to miss the traffic of Fulton Street and Flatbush Avenue extension, then wound his way through Columbia Heights until he came to a cross street that took him to Park Slope.

The Hennesseys lived in a limestone house two long blocks from Prospect Park. Like its neighbors, the house had no front yard or lawn, but a little sunken areaway on which opened the grilled iron door leading into the basement where kitchen and dining room were. Neat, palish and substantial, it represented what Mrs. Hennessey wanted people to think of her. Moon parked the car before the house, slammed the door a little harder than was necessary, noticed with satisfaction that under the street lamps the car outshone any other in sight, then walked up the front stoop. Marie answered his ring promptly and Moon was puzzled at the warmth of her greeting, the equal of what he might have expected had they both been single. "Say, it's good to see you, Moon," she said, as she took his coat and hat. "You ought to come over here more often. The folks would be glad to see you. They're always talking about you."

"Well, you know how it is," Moon said. "They run me ragged in the district." Wary, his mind reached for motive in her. "Besides, if I'm seen in Brooklyn too much, people would think I was slipping."

"None of that now," Marie said. "If it wasn't for the Brooklyn Irish, where would the Party be?"

In the neat, crowded living room, with its picture of the Sacred Heart, its picture of the Boy and the Rabbit, the ormolu clock, Moon marveled at the difference in Marie here and Marie at a dance. And at almost the exact moment Moon entered, George Hennessey also came into the room through the draperies of a large doorway that led back into darkness. "Why, Moon Gaffney," he said, "it's good to see you."

"Hello, George," Moon said. "It's always a pleasure to come here."

Hennessey took Moon's hand and elbow in his own two hands and pressed Moon's firmly: nothing so obvious as a pumping. Moon sat down and Marie, who had followed him into the room, sat on a chair near him. Hennessey, whose chair Moon had unwittingly taken, sat on the sofa across from them.

Marie seemed to glow, Moon thought. He had always had an idea there was something vaguely unhealthy about pregnancy, but he could see nothing in Marie but good health. Her skin had a fine, high coloring, her breasts seemed fuller than he remembered them and in general there was an air of vivacity and beneficence about her that he could not recall her ever having had before. For the first time, he understood some of McGuffey's strain.

"You really don't get over this way much, do you, Moon?" Hennessey said. "Just the other day I was saying to Mrs. Hennessey that we could stand to see you and your daddy more often."

"The commissioner isn't getting any younger," Moon said. "And he keeps answering alarms with the trucks, which he has no business doing unless it's something really big. Sometimes he gets pretty tired and for two or three days he doesn't go out of the house."

Hennessey was nodding before Moon had finished and smiling knowingly. His blue eyes, behind heavy glasses, seemed to widen and become at once pleased and avid. "That's the Irish for you," he said, when Moon had finished. "They die with their boots on." He nodded again once to fix and establish the idea, and Moon felt a glow, as much transmitted by Hennessey as coming up in himself.

"Well, Dad's always been pretty conscientious about his work," Moon said. "He—"

"Do you know an Irishman who isn't?" Hennessey said, with a fair, humorous quirk.

Moon knew at least a dozen who weren't and his face took on a sardonic quality which would have fascinated some but which Hennessey ignored. "Now that you mention it," Moon said, "I don't."

"What'll you have to drink?" Hennessey said, leaning forward. "Irish, rye, Scotch or brandy?"

"I don't care. Whatever you're having."

"I'm having Irish," Hennessey said.

"That's all right with me," Moon said.

Marie had stood up. "I'll get it, Papa."

"All right, Marie. That's a good girl."

She smiled at Moon as she left and he grew ashamed and bitter at the effect of that smile. There was a meaningless instant of anger, confusion, red and concern, from which Moon emerged to hear Hennessey saying: ". . . about the job for Gorevin's cousin, we could take care of it. Only we—and it's a big only—only we would want to be sure it wouldn't come out of our regular patronage."

"Oh, don't worry about that," Moon said quickly. He had actually forgotten his ostensible reason for coming here; and now that it was already dealt with he felt both relief and concern. "It's hardly that important. It's only that the man has a family and, well, you know how times are."

Hennessey seemed to harden for a moment of knowledge or near-knowledge, then was himself again, all doubts about Moon resolved. He wished that Marie had married Moon instead of that jackass of a McGuffey. And he was glad Moon wasn't going to bring *that* up.

Marie returned with a tray. "Mother will be down in a few minutes, Moon. She wanted me to tell you."

"I'm glad you did," Moon said. "I was beginning to get worried. You don't think I came all the way over here just to see you and your father?" He turned to wink broadly at Hennessey, who smiled with his mouth. It was peculiar, Moon thought, how little you knew of Hennessey's eyes behind those glasses.

While Hennessey poured the drinks, Marie came and sat next to Moon again. The ormolu clock, he noticed, pointed to eight, and a kind of panic grew in him. He wondered if he couldn't let the whole business about McGuffey slip. After all, he couldn't hope to accomplish much here. Why, just the way Marie and her father were, the separate ways, was enough to tell any sensible person.

Marie was wearing scent and whenever she leaned closer to Moon to speak, he could smell it. More in curiosity than annoyance, he wondered why she wore it here, why now. Then he found himself wondering if he should ask her to come along to meet Kavanagh. Certainly no one, not even Hennessey, could object to anything as well chaperoned as that would be. His fresh new alarm at that thought he countered by thinking that it would be a good deal easier to talk to Marie about Jim in almost any other place than her parents' home. He paused, as it seemed to him, on the verge of a precipice. It was again the measure of a growth that he saw many of the things that were in him at this moment, even the two or three kinds of fear. He opened his mouth to speak, not knowing exactly what was going to come out of it, saw that it was precisely the wrong moment as Hennessey started toward them, two fresh drinks in his hands, and in a true horror, Moon heard himself say, "I saw Jim last night."

The smile froze, then dissolved on Marie's face, her eyes dropped in some feeling which Moon could not name. Her father paused, as in mid-air, his mouth twisted, one corner caught between his teeth, the eyes round, large and now fanatical through the glasses. When he spoke it was, considering his appearance, with surprising quietness. "I'd hoped that name would not come up tonight," Hennessey said. He moved toward them and handed each a highball glass, looking carefully between them. Turning, he dusted his hands together as if ridding them of something unpleasant as he walked back to the sofa. "But since it has," he went on, turning to face them as he sat down, "it has. And I suppose some things had best be made known—and others made clear."

"I'm sorry if I've accidentally—" Moon said.

Hennessey raised his hand. "No apologies, now, Moon. No apologies. It's a perfectly natural thing, in a way, that his name should come up. And I'm sure you couldn't have known altogether how we feel. As if we had for a time harbored an enemy, not only of ourselves but of Holy Mother the Church."

Moon stirred. "That's putting it a little strong, isn't it, George? I mean—"

"And why is it putting it strong, might I ask? Has he not been working for a union and are not most unions run by Communists and are not all Communists sworn enemies of God and of Holy Mother the Church?"

It was a hard one to answer, Moon knew. "You certainly don't think Jim has become a Communist, do you?"

"Worse," Hennessey said. "Their paid servant. That's what he has become. Signed, sealed and delivered." The man's chin had come out so that anyone could see where Marie had got hers, and there was just the hint of a brogue in his voice although he had been born in Brooklyn.

Moon leaned forward and settled his elbows on his knees. It seemed that in no way could he even for a moment rid himself of Marie's physical presence. What he considered a weakness seemed to inform everything he did or said, clouding his mind, fretting his body and perhaps worst of all making doubtful his intention. "Look," he said. "I, myself, know one of the officials of that particular union and I know that he happens to be a devout Catholic."

Hennessey drew his body erect and the wintry shadow of a smile appeared on his face. "Moon Gaffney," he said, "I wouldn't have believed it. Here you are, brought up in the hard school of politics and now falling for that stuff. Let me ask you a question. If there are Catholics in the union James McGuffey is serving, why are they engaged in controversy with another union, most of whose members and whose great leader I know personally to be the very finest of Catholics?"

"That's not much of an argument," Moon said. "There are Catholics who are Republicans, too, aren't there, and—"

"Damned few," Hennessey said. "But perhaps I am still not clear. There are facts, not the sort one finds in the controlled secular press, but contained in honest, God-fearing, Church-serving papers like *The Brooklyn Trumpet*. And no longer back than last Saturday they had the facts on this union James McGuffey serves; that its leadership is almost entirely Jew Communists. Ah, let me tell you, Moon Gaffney, until and unless we meet the Jew problem as it should be met, the existence of Holy Mother the Church, of our own very lives, will be threatened."

Moon stirred again. It was a not uncommon topic among a certain kind of Irishman he met every day, and it disturbed him, or perhaps it was the frequency and rage with which it was discussed that did. He remembered his father speaking of what flannel-mouthed fools some Irish were, for the old man felt that if a persecution started the Irish would follow the Jews as its object.

"It is a definitely proven fact," Hennessey was saying, his voice hoarser, "that it is the Jews who are the great trouble-makers on every level, high and low, in international finance and in the ranks of labor. They—"

"Look," Moon said, "let's go back to Jim. I don't think he knew what he was getting in for when he took the job. And to a certain extent I was responsible for him taking it. And—"

"*No* one knew it, then, Moon." Marie spoke for the first time since her husband's name had been mentioned. "And don't think for a moment that anyone blames you." She was, he saw, uncertain and the feeling for her increased. "I left James only because he refused to leave the job after he found out what kind of people he was working for. And I didn't leave him in anger, but as my Christian duty."

She paused and her father added, "Exactly."

"And I'm perfectly willing to go back to James as soon as he does his duty and leaves the union," she went on. As she spoke the uncertainty gradually left her.

"That's a lot of money to ask any young lawyer to give up in these times," Moon said.

"It's dirty money," Hennessey said. "As dirty as though stolen. And if James McGuffey can't support his family except by that kind of money, Marie *should* come back here."

"Oh, he was doing all right," Marie said. "As well as any lawyer his age in these times. He just wanted that extra money." This defense silenced for a moment even her father. When Hennessey did speak again, it was in a relatively more quiet way, one he himself thought of as reasonable. "Let me ask you something, Moon," he said. "Is there any reason why James McGuffey shouldn't take a decent civil service job as his betters before him? Even if he is a lawyer? You're a lawyer, and you're not above taking such a job. And that's the thing that any young man, particularly one with a family, should do."

"Well, I don't know," Moon said. "It—"

"But not James McGuffey," Hennessey said. "Oh, no. He has to be better than anyone else. Independent. And where does his independence get him? The employee, the tool of Jew Communists."

Moon said, "That's not entirely true. In your diocesan paper—"

"Our diocesan paper!" Hennessey leaped to his feet. "That ignorant little sheet, run by young twirps of priests like that McTiernan. You don't call that a newspaper, do you? So far as myself and the rest of the Brooklyn Irish are concerned, *The Trumpet* is our only *Catholic* newspaper in this diocese."

"Now, George—" Moon smiled. "That's going pretty strong, calling your own diocesan paper non-Catholic."

"And strong, is it? I'm too strong, am I?" He remained erect, his head and neck out. "If you'd read the nonsense in it, the pure, vicious nonsense. Stuff that came to them from some Communist front organization. The same sort of thing Roosevelt has started to do. Ah, if ever a man betrayed his supporters, betrayed good Irish hearts, he's the one. With his filthy Jew advisers and his liberal backslappers. You know how the Church feels toward liberalism?" He had begun to pace and now paused to stoop slightly toward Moon. The ormolu clock struck once. Moon knew without looking that it was eight-thirty and his unease increased, grew more complex, permeated all levels of his existence. He took advantage of Hennessey's pause to say there might be something to that, but since he had to leave in a few minutes, he did want to say a little more about Jim.

"And what more exactly is there to say?" Hennessey said. Before Moon could answer, Mrs. Hennessey entered the room. She wore a dinner dress, perhaps because of Moon's visit, and her gray hair was neatly marcelled over a face that still retained prettiness. Moon stood up as she advanced on him.

"Oh, now, don't bother, Moon," she said. "Sit down." She shook hands. "Your folks are well?" She turned and seated herself. Her coming had relieved some of the room's tension. Hennessey reseated himself on the sofa next to her, his head bowed as in exhaustion. Mrs. Hennessey, though, faced Moon with a bright and almost cheerful smile. "I don't suppose for a minute, Moon," she said, "that you could think I didn't hear what was going on, with George here bellowing and what not. And you might as well know that I feel just the same as George and Marie do. She came and talked it over with us before taking this step and she not only had our advice and consent, but we welcome her here as a step to keep James McGuffey from going bad."

"Look," Moon said; "I didn't come over here to talk about Jim. But since it came up, I'd like to say something before I leave."

"My Lord, man," Hennessey said. "You talk about leaving and you just got here. Here, give your glass to Marie and I'll—"

"I have to meet some people at the St. George," Moon said. "But to get back to Jim, all I want to do is to assure you that he'll quit this union in a matter of days, and that he very much wants Marie back."

"I should think he would," Mrs. Hennessey said.

"And why in a matter of days?" Hennessey said. "If a man is living in mortal sin, he should go to confession immediately, not in a matter of days."

"I suppose it's a question of obligation," Moon said, without conviction.

"Obligation!" Hennessey was back where he had been before his wife joined them.

"In a sense," Moon said. "I mean, after all there are perfectly moral and good men who defend criminals in court and—"

"A different question entirely," Hennessey said. "The criminals at least are not attacking the Church."

"I'm glad you used that parallel, Moon," Mrs. Hennessey said.

"That wasn't what I meant," Moon said. "All I meant was that a lawyer more or less has an obligation to see a case through."

"A case?" Hennessey said. "But he's on salary or retainer with them. It's not a question—"

"This time it is a case," Moon said. "Jim wants to wait until this jurisdictional business is settled and then he'll quit the union."

There was a moment of silence before Mrs. Hennessey spoke. "And of course he expects Marie to wait here until he's good and ready to give up this work?"

This remark confused Moon; no answer to it seemed possible. While he groped, Mrs. Hennessey said, "I think it's the height of arrogance for James McGuffey to go on, doing what he's doing, taking his own good time, and expecting Marie will be ready here whenever he gets ready."

"I don't know exactly," Moon said. "I had an idea that that was the condition under which she would return. I'll tell you this," he blurted. "Jim is not what I would call a well man."

"What do you mean?" Marie said. Wondering why he had said it—for he had never thought this of McGuffey—Moon turned to see that her face had become a ridiculous mask of sorrow, concern, and suspicion. Before Moon could make an answer, Hennessey said, "Exactly. No person of sound mind would at the same time work for Communists and consider himself to be in the communion of the Church."

A sense of weariness oppressed Moon, a sense of what someone else might have called futility. It was a quarter to nine and he told himself that he must go. Perhaps his condition or some obvious part of it was manifest even to the Hennesseys, for Hennessey went on with, for him, surprising quietness. "It is really the damnedest thing, Moon. He is not only working for a union and for Communists, but actually at the moment he is fighting against one of the very few unions that are headed by good, honest Catholics."

Moon stood up. "I've got to go. Got to be down at the St. George by nine. I'm sorry we sort of got sidetracked this way."

[145]

"Now, no apologies, Moon," Hennessey said. "It's good for certain things to have an airing. What do you have to be going for so early?"

Glancing casually from Mrs. Hennessey to her husband, Moon saw with a sense of shock that Hennessey had taken pleasure from what had happened and was still taking it.

"I'm sorry your visit was marred by this, Moon," Mrs. Hennessey said, also rising. "Particularly when you visit us so seldom."

"Oh, that's all right." While he put on his overcoat they chatted but McGuffey's name was not mentioned. At the doorway that led from living room to hall, Hennessey and his wife said good-by to Moon: they wanted him to come see them more often, to come again, soon; Marie, too, they told him, would be glad to see him.

Indeed, Marie went with him into the lighted hallway and opened the vestibule door for him. The scent on her was strong again, so that bitterness was renewed in him. Smiling and almost tender, she said, "There's nothing really wrong with Jim, is there?"

He supposed, after an instant's reflection, that there really wasn't, and told her so. Reassured, she gave him her hand, longish, smooth-skinned: the contact informed and increased his feeling. Shortly he said good night and turning to the outer door went in relief down the steps. In the little distance between his car and the door he thought of what some men would call Marie. He wondered if her parents could be called the same. And yet it was not that gross, he knew; he wondered if what they felt was regret that Marie had not married someone like himself, and if their way now was simply a manner of expressing that regret. This was very close to charity, although he could scarcely know it; and he wondered, more naturally, if they could possibly know the effect of certain things upon

[146]

himself. He decided that they could not, and that he alone was gross.

Driving downtown, the sense of failure was strong in him and he could not understand its strength. Failure was not uncommon in his life: he stood in the same relation to it that a soldier does to death: administering it often, knowing that sometime he would receive it. In the heated cubicle of the car as he drove he knew finally wherein the strength of tonight's failure resided: any anguish or dilution of anguish for McGuffey, for political fences broken, for the sad confusion of his own race, went, seemed never to have been . . . and there remained in him only the feeling for Marie and the obscurity and bitterness of its origin.

It was a relief to Moon that only Kavanagh and Kate were at the hotel. Schneider would meet them later, Kav said.

"With his colored gal?" Moon said.

"I wouldn't know," Kav said.

Kate smiled. "She's leaving for Europe in a day or two. I think Bart feels rather bad about it."

Moon looked at her. "You, too?" His face was mock-humorous, his manner mock-reprimanding.

"Me, too, what?" Kate said.

What, exactly? he thought and tried to say it. "This business of it not making any difference what she is?"

"I don't think it does," Kate said. "It mightn't be something I'd personally like, but—"

"All right," Moon said. "Let's get out of here. I need a drink."

"How did you make out at Hennessey's?" Kav said when they were in the street.

Walking, Moon waved a hand at him. "How do you think I made out?"

"I can guess," Kav said. "We just wanted to hear it from your own silver tongue."

[147]

"From me," Moon said, "you will hear nothing." He felt strongly tonight the entity that Kate and James were and how completely outside it he was.

"All right," Kav said. "See if we care. We've been fighting between ourselves, so what happens to you and the McGuffeys doesn't bother us much."

"What were you fighting about?" Moon said.

"Oh, James is being silly again," Kate said.

"Sure and I'm silly's brother," Kav said. He turned them toward a small bar with bare tables. At the door, Moon balked. "What are we going into a dump like this for?"

"This is where Bart's supposed to meet us."

"All the more reason not to go in," Moon said.

"What have you got against him?" Kate said, as Moon held her chair for her.

"Everything he does makes trouble for someone," Moon said.

"As for example?" Kav said.

Before Moon could answer, the waiter came and they ordered highballs. Moon found that the break had been helpful: pressed, he could think only of the night in the ward at Bellevue and even if he wanted to, he doubted that he could explain exactly how he felt about what had happened there. "I mean," he said, after the waiter had gone, "he's always after the Church or the Irish or somebody."

"He's half Irish himself."

"It's nothing they'll ever congratulate themselves on."

"Anyhow, you were going to tell us about Marie Hennessey," Kate said.

Some part of Moon's spirit winced: this pain was new, varitextured and dismaying. For some reason he recalled books that, reading in college, he had been amused at: certain parts of the *Morte d'Arthur, Tristram, The Return of the Native.* He simply—with the good brothers at the college to help—

hadn't believed that anyone could become that intense about any woman, let alone someone else's wife.

"There is very little to tell about Marie," he said. It was necessary to compose himself before he could speak with his usual glibness, and he wondered in quick-passing alarm if James and Kate could read what was happening in him. "Anyone who goes to the Hennessey house deals with George and his wife. Marie sits there like a bump on a log and likes it."

"So?—" Kav said.

"So I got no place. . . . I was a damned fool for going there in the first place. You can't get a word in edgewise with George Hennessey. And so far as I can make out, they think Marie is some kind of weapon or something to help them or the *Trumpet* promote militant Catholicism."

Kav shook his head. His long, placid face was belied by the eyes. "You talk like Schneider."

"They're pretty awful," Kate said. Like Kav, she seemed preoccupied.

"On the other hand, you can't blame them," Moon said. "Here's McGuffey working for the Commies—"

"There's fewer Commies in that outfit than in most unions," Kav said.

"I can see," Moon said, "that I should have given you the job instead of McGuffey."

"What do you mean?" Kav said. "What did you have to do with it?"

In the moment before he had to answer, Moon reflected bitterly that he was certainly doing well tonight. "I thought you knew," he said. "This fellow, Thomas, asked me to get him a lawyer, so I thought of McGuffey." He noticed that both the others were disturbed and he quickly added, "I mean he was married and had a kid and so on and I thought—

[149]

Oh, hell, I suppose it would have been better to have given it to you."

Kav, Moon saw in something like horror, could not speak. "Oh, heavens, James, come on, now," Kate said. When Kav hid his face in his hands, Kate turned to Moon. "I'm sorry that had to come up now. It's what we were talking about when you met us."

"What was?" Moon said, knowing exactly how much his stupidity was feigned.

"Getting married," Kate said. Moon had the feeling that she had known the degree of his faking but had chosen to ignore it. Oddly, he felt sorrow.

"So what were you fighting about?"

"About getting married." She, too, turned her face from Moon.

"I thought that was all settled," Moon said.

"Sure," Kav said, not taking his hands from his face. "Everything's settled."

"It is settled," Kate said. She hesitated over something. "I want to get married now, but James won't."

"That's it," Kav said, taking his hands from his face. "Make me sound like Joe the boy gelding or something."

Kate flushed deeply. "That's not what I mean and anyone would know it except—"

"All right," Moon said. "So why don't you get married?"

"Because we haven't got the money, you dope," Kav said.

"We have, too," Kate said. "Between what he makes and my job."

"And how long can you stay on that job if you start to have a baby?" Kav said. "We'll wind up living in a hall room or somebody's basement."

"You see," Kate said, turning to Moon, "he has absolutely no faith in providence." She came close to smiling, yet neither of the men could think of anything to say.

"Sure, and what is all this pious gibberish going on here?" said a heavily faked Irish brogue. Looking up, they saw Schneider and the girl. Kav and Kate greeted them while Moon made elaborate gestures of hiding himself by wrapping his arms around his neck and head.

Schneider put a hand lightly on Moon's arm. "It's all right, chum. You can show that face. There are no children around." Moon slowly uncovered to the laughter. "For weeks now I have been trying to keep away from you," he said. "But it is no use." He rose slowly and slowly allowed the famous grin to crease his face as he greeted the girl. "How do you stand him, Concepción? Nobody else can."

"Oh, I stand him well," she said. Kav held a chair for her and she made her sitting down the excuse for not looking at Moon, for—Moon noticed—not looking at any of them. Himself finally seated, he thought that she didn't seem as good-looking as at the dance. And with reluctance he admitted that she did not look like a Negro. The thought that Schneider and even she herself could be kidding all of them disturbed Moon, and once it had begun in him, it grew complex, filling him and becoming one with Marie in him. After five minutes of leaning over his empty glass while the thing formed, became manifest and began to ferment, he decided it was not pleasant, and just as he began to wonder if people like Kav and Schneider and McGuffey felt that way often, he decided that it would be better to raise his head. He was both relieved and annoyed that no one seemed to have noticed him. Kav had changed and was alert again, almost cheerful. He was talking and had been, part of Moon remembered, for several minutes, telling Concepción and Schneider about the Hennesseys. Now these two seemed to stand in the same relation to each other as had Kav and Kate. Moon noticed the similarity—as so many subtleties this evening—and before his mind

[151]

could stop itself, concluded that they, too, were in love, knew even the degree of their unhappiness.

"So," Kav was saying, "the best thing might be to go down and picket old man Hennessey's house. But that would be ineffective at night and by day everyone would be working but Bart. Or we could go there tonight and throw eggs at the house. Except it might wake the baby."

"Honestly," Kate said, "you can take the boy away from old Ireland but you can't take old Ireland away from the boy."

"What do you mean?" Schneider said. "It's another Irishman's house he wants to egg."

"That's it exactly," Kate said. "A symbol of Irish history. Anyhow, you're no better than James for all your talk."

"Are you only finding that out?" Schneider said. "Concepción's known it for weeks now and she's about to give me up."

"Someone should have warned her," Moon said. "It's always—"

"You leave my friend alone," Concepción said. She smiled at the center of the table. Her blue beret, the dark, belted wool dress seemed to indicate a severity none of them had thought her possessing. Only lately had she known how definitely the ballet had been an escape from the warped Catholicism of her own country . . . and now to find its parallel here and to become involved with one of its victims, was, she thought, a kind of punishment for running away. The idea of leaving the Church had occurred often to her, but there seemed no other place to go. Her humility had never let her think she could move alone in that region of the spirit. There remained to her, she sometimes thought, of her girlhood's Catholicism only her chastity, and Schneider, she knew without too much emotion, could destroy that if he cared to; she had been puzzled that he had not.

She became aware that her own musing silence had brought

its counterpart to the table, one in which even Moon forbore to call for drinks for the empty glasses. She raised her head and looked at Kav. "Why don't you and Kate get married?" she said.

"Why," he said, making his hesitation elaborate by lighting a cigarette, "we were thinking of that."

Moon shook his head and muttered in an undertone. Schneider, noticing the confusion, half-guessed its cause. His own urgencies were renewed, some lightness came over him, yet all he could think of to say was, "Let's go egg Hennessey's house."

"Look," Moon said, touching lightly Concepción's arm, "if you're going to say things like that, why don't you marry Bart?"

"Exactly," Schneider said. "That's the idea, but she will have none of me." He was amused by the silence he had made among them. He wondered, too, what they would think if they knew the truth.

Since no one else seemed able to speak, Concepción said, "We can't interfere with each other's art, you know. And being Catholics, we can't go along just not married." She smiled faintly, so they would be sure not to take her seriously.

By great effort Moon summoned his faculties, his talents, ordered more drinks, made the gestures of expansion, but could not expand, could not even talk freely.

"We have to go after this round," Kav said.

"Go where?" Schneider said. "I will settle for nothing less than the egging of Hennessey's."

"Home," Kav said. "To our little separate beds."

Coloring in the silence, Kate had the unpleasant feeling that James was not well. . . . Schneider opened his mouth to speak, but was silent, thinking of the often heavy price these people paid for their chastity, of how his own had been an athletic feat, not more nor less, something to be endured and

[153]

clung to, like the last quarter in a mile race or the side of a mountain.

Moon's voice, rising gradually and booming, broke Schneider's thought. His mouth, he felt, had a peculiar fixed quality as so often lately, and he saw Concepción looking at him, again with pity. . . . Self-pity and self-hatred both came to him: desire to be alone with her curdled within him: whatever he felt for her had almost no outlet, deteriorated when he touched her into something whose common name he could not bear to think of now.

They had all, he noticed, about finished the drinks in front of them; he raised his own untouched one and drained it, rose and asked what they were waiting for.

It was still early and Moon said that if Schneider and Concepción would come with him while he took the others home, he would drive them to Manhattan. Getting into the car, Schneider and the girl sat in the back, leaving room there for only one other. "Come on," Moon said. "Somebody's got to ride with the chauffeur."

"I'll ride with the chauffeur," Kate said and got in next to Moon.

"And I'm supposed to ride where?" Kav said.

"It won't be so crowded in the back," Moon said. The big car did hold only two comfortably in the front.

Kav hesitated, then got in the back. None of them talked much as Moon drove through the narrow streets of the Heights. Schneider said, "I won't settle for anything less than egging Hennessey's."

"We have no eggs," Kate said.

"Will you settle for driving by the place?" Moon asked.

"Sure, you could spit on it," said Kav in a peculiar voice.

"It's right on the way home," Kate said. "Anything to soothe Bart."

[154]

In the returning silence, Schneider looked at Concepción and saw that she leaned back, her eyes closed, the occasional street lights making her face seem older, picking out each mark and feature. With her head back like that he was reminded of the joyous way it came back, moving from side to side, when she was the Polish girl in the Prince Igor ballet. And he was struck, of course, by the different moods the same gesture accompanied in her. He decided not to put his arm around her shoulders. . . .

"Here it is," Moon said, stopping the car. They turned, gazing through the car windows at the lightless house as though they were children and it the gingerbread one on a stage. "It smells bad," Schneider said. "Let's get out of here."

But the car remained still a moment longer. In that moment and without speaking, Kav got out of the car, closing the door after him, and walking away from them. At first they thought he was going up to the Hennessey house and Kate drew in her breath to speak to him, but he walked past the house and kept on going down the long slope that led away from the park and toward downtown Brooklyn. Kate made a meaningless exclamation and Schneider, rolling down a window, yelled after their friend.

"He's drunk," Moon said and let the clutch in. When the car was abreast of Kav, Kate said, "James, will you stop acting silly and get back into the car."

But Kav kept on walking and in the broken light they could see his set face. He walked fast, his long legs carrying him downhill and Moon shifted the car into second. Through the window Schneider said, "Stop acting like a screwball, will you, and get back in here."

"I wouldn't ride with any of you," Kav said. "The hell with you."

Driving, Moon had to look ahead, and he found this a refuge as much as a necessity. Some relation, vague, complex and dark, existed between Marie and Kate in his mind, but he could not give it a name or know its nature.

"All right," Kate said. "Moon, let me out."

Obediently, he stopped the car and Kate got out. Even in the moment it took her to do so, Kav got yards ahead of them and she had to run, awkward in high heels, to catch him.

Moon let the car drift down to them and Schneider called to where Kate plucked at Kav's arm. She turned her head partly to them. "It's all right—" her tone preoccupied, impatient—"we're almost home."

Moon let the car into second again and they moved away from the two. Glancing back, Schneider saw that Kate had managed to stop her lover on a corner and was standing there, her hands on his wrists, looking up at him. The wind moved their coats, but in the thin light of a street lamp the two had the dark, immobile quality of figures in an etching.

Schneider turned back to Concepción. She wept, quietly and briefly. He put his arm around her and she let her head roll back onto his shoulder. No one spoke and Moon tooled the big car across Brooklyn Bridge. There were lights everywhere, strings, towers and banks of them against the dark; but those on the bridge were dim and moved over their faces in a kind of rhythm. Somewhere below them a tug whistled and for a few moments in the center of the bridge they all, even Moon, had a sense of being suspended, not so much in air as in a mood or medium they might never know again.

As they came off the bridge, the cop posted under the elevated at the Manhattan end saluted the marked car, and it was easy for Moon to take the salute for himself. It broke the mood and heartened him. Behind him, he heard Schneider say, "Concepción, that's what comes of being a good, not to say obedient politician," but Moon chose to ignore the words. He turned right and stepped on it as the car swung into Lafayette Street. "Where do you want to go?" he asked them.

"Concepción's living with some girls in the Village," Schneider said. "You could drop us off around Washington Square. You want something to eat?"

"I don't think so," Moon said. "I'm pretty tired."

"I should think you would be."

Moon thought there was an odd note in Schneider's tone, something he should resent; but the more he thought about it, the less it seemed so. Schneider's remark had been without tone, had been like a closed door.

Moon let them out under the arch in Washington Square. He could think of nothing worth saying, was indeed impressed by his own gravity and formless concern. As with James and Kate, he drove away, leaving them in the shadow of the arch, less clearly seen than the two he had left in Brooklyn.

They, in turn, after a moment of hesitation also moved, westward, through varying shadows until they came to the place where Concepción had lived during the greater part of the season in New York. It was a house that reminded Schneider of McGuffey's, but shabbier and in better taste.

"Come on in," she said. "The girls will want to say good-by to you."

Weary, he climbed the narrow stairs after her. Her legs, sturdy, very beautiful, reminded him one more interminable time of the ironies he shared with her.

In the apartment a single lamp burned with a note pinned to its shade. He stood, feeling his topcoat as a burden, while she read the note. "They're down at the restaurant," she said, without looking at him. "They want us to meet them there."

"Maybe we'd better go," he said. It seemed that his hesitation, the slight thickening of his tongue as he spoke, was what saved him from calling himself, as Kav earlier, a gelding.

She didn't answer him, but stood at an angle to him so that he could see less than half her face. The beret still covered her hair. Moving slightly, he saw that her upper lip was caught

[157]

between her teeth. He let his coat slip onto a chair, went over to her, turned and kissed her. Defiance did what passion had already failed many times to do: yet the defiance was not of God he knew with that terrible, cold and implacable part of his mind.

His own clumsiness did not surprise him so much as hers. The head turned sidewise while he looked down at it—as in the dance, as in the car—was turned now in pain. And yet he knew that sometime it might be turned so again in joy. His own lack of pleasure now was not unexpected: in time he could think it appropriate to the pain in her. And in that same time afterward there was a great happiness in him that he could still think of her with love.

9

McGUFFEY found there were things to worry him these days other than the condition of his marriage. About the union, McGuffey did not much care: its service had broken his marriage and caused him an anguish deeper than any he had ever thought to experience, and his only reason for remaining with it in these last few days was, he recognized, a defiance of the Hennesseys. He had managed to reach Marie on the phone and she had agreed to return to him when he quit. So it was with relief and a kind of joy that McGuffey looked to being free of this particular work.

His feeling about Linford Thomas was something else. A first opinion of Thomas as a sort of great-hearted fool and large-eyed idealist had changed, so that although he could not give it a name, McGuffey had reached the knowledge that whatever Thomas was, it was not a fool. Indeed, his inability to classify Thomas had made McGuffey uneasy, and he had frequently the disturbing feeling that although on the level most men inhabited Thomas was unsure and habitually needed care, on some other level—one inhabited by no one else McGuffey knew, not even the priests at school—Thomas moved free and as a kind of mediator. The nearest McGuffey's mind had come to giving shape to these thoughts was to think privately that Thomas was a hell of a person to be an executive in a labor union.

By now it was evident to most of those who held office in it, that the union would lose the jurisdictional election. Brosnan was too well known and was not unintelligent: he had sensed the unwillingness of the new union to take incidents of violence into court, and had accordingly used violence in an effective and even subtle fashion: there had been no mass usage of it, no goon squads, but individual pickets or a man distributing leaflets would be set upon by two of Brosnan's men—he knew that more than two could attract attention and usually got in each other's way—and knocked down or run off a dock. Once an automobile had accidentally jumped the sidewalk and charged into a group from Thomas's union. McGuffey, whose humor often functioned at the wrong time, had suggested they send no one down to the dock area who couldn't swim.

So, on a bleak morning toward the end of winter, with the election and his release only a few days off, McGuffey continued to make the required gestures of his office. There was some paper work, there was the necessity for showing clearly in writing his disposition of certain small funds—for the two Communists among the union's seven officials made no effort to conceal their dislike for McGuffey now that he was leaving; there was the need to placate Miss Marko, his secretary, as best he could, for she was unable to understand that it was possible for him to be pleased with her without also sleeping with her; and, because Thomas had not been in the office, a

[159]

phone call had been diverted to McGuffey and he now had an engagement for lunch with Schneider.

At a quarter to twelve McGuffey left his office and took a cab across town to the bar where Schneider was to meet him. On the way he wondered about Schneider. They had been classmates at school although not what could be called friends, and McGuffey had always unconsciously thought of himself as being Schneider's superior, for in the hierarchy of the quarterbacks at their school, he had been fourth-string quarterback and Schneider fifth. Of course he knew that it was his size that had kept him from ranking higher, and suddenly he knew that with Schneider, who was somewhat bigger than himself, it had been lack of sleep. It was odd, McGuffey thought, that none of them had considered that while at school, its relation to Schneider's failure; and more odd that he himself should think of it now, five or six years after the event. Perhaps, he thought uncomfortably, his own recent sleeplessness had something to do with his belated knowledge of Schneider.

And where Schneider had got his notions, McGuffey could not guess. Certainly not at their school, although he remembered now hearing somewhere that Schneider had taken graduate work at the University of Chicago while working in the city. Actually, Schneider's ideas did not differ greatly from Thomas's; considering this, McGuffey was moved to consider also why he resented in Schneider ideas he more or less accepted in Thomas. Was it because in Thomas he saw a purity of intention lacking in Schneider? seeing Thomas as the intellectually honest man making sacrifices for his ideals, and Schneider as the fashionable imitation of a proletarian? Or was it that he simply grew fretful over someone like Schneider, with more or less the same background as his own, becoming dedicated to ideas that he, McGuffey, acceded to slowly and unwillingly? McGuffey had a feeling of inferiority about his education in Catholic schools, so that even if Thomas had not had the quality McGuffey thought of him as having, because of Thomas's education in a non-Catholic college, McGuffey would not have resented his ideas as he did those of Schneider.

McGuffey had resolved nothing by the time the cab had brought him to the bar. There was in him only a somber pleasure in the recognition of what he thought might be an approach to maturity and a new and almost unconscious respect for Schneider. But that, McGuffey knew, was probably because he had heard Schneider was vocal about the Hennesseys.

Schneider was already at the bar, staring vaguely out over a half-finished glass of beer. He had taken off his hat but not his topcoat and the face seemed bonier and more ascetic than McGuffey remembered it at school. This puzzled him, for if Schneider had been, as so many of them, an ascetic at school, McGuffey knew he no longer was. Indeed, McGuffey suspected Schneider of sleeping with that dancer.

"Hello, speedy," he said.

"Good afternoon, Buster," Schneider said. "What goes in your racket?"

"Look who's talking." McGuffey colored at the name, one given him in irony at school because of his size in comparison with his toughness.

They stopped talking. A kind of ennui was there, generated upon sight of each other: the sense of defeat so long present and now renewed by the election already lost, had been in them unrecognized and now came forth at this meeting and fixed each man in silence as in glass.

McGuffey ordered beer and found when it came that he had lost his taste for it. It was possible to talk, they discovered, by addressing each other in the mirror behind the bar. "Things don't look so good?" Schneider said.

McGuffey shook his head and tasted the beer. "They really don't. How's your girl?"

[ 161 ]

"All right, I guess. On her way to Europe. Already there, I guess."

Again that silence and this time McGuffey was grateful for it: his question, he knew, had not been from charity and he knew Schneider could beat his brains out: almost anything Schneider wanted to ask about Marie could beat his brains out. After a while he said, "You want to eat?"

"I'm not hungry. Why don't we walk over to the docks and see what passes there. We'll get an appetite, anyway."

"Got your brass knucks?"

Schneider almost smiled. "I don't think there'll be any more rough stuff. They know they've got you people whipped. Let's go."

Outside it had begun to rain, a heavy drizzle against which each man leaned. It was only a few blocks to that section where most of the activity had centered. As they approached, a thin stream of workingmen walked against them, going to near-by cheap restaurants for the lunch hour. By the time they had reached a broad, open wharf they had passed most of the men and could see the brown expanse of wood and beyond it the dark waters of the harbor.

The wharf was not quite empty. In the fine, billowing rain there were three figures on it. One figure was slight in its dark coat, and seemed tall until the other two approached it, when its hands moved to extend slips of paper to them. One of the larger figures passed behind the slight one, seized its arms and held them while the second bulky figure began to hit the slight one in the face with the short, heavy blows of the professional in violence. The held figure wilted and when its arms were released, fell on its back but turned and slowly rose and began to speak to the other two. This time both of them hit the third man and seizing him began to drag him struggling to the wharf edge.

Schneider had begun to shake imperceptibly. McGuffey was

[ 1 6 2 ]

running and was yards ahead before Schneider got started. The sound of their feet on cobbles changed to a short, booming note as the wharf came under them. It was Thomas the two men were dragging toward the edge and when Schneider first saw it, his anger, formless and dispersed, gathered into a rage that McGuffey had more quickly possessed. Schneider's knees lifted—he had always run faster than McGuffey at school—but it couldn't change the distance between them. Closer to the three figures, through rain Schneider saw that although Thomas dragged against his assailants, he neither struck back nor showed fear. This for some reason added to Schneider's anguish. He heard McGuffey scream cursing, knew from the slight curve in McGuffey's run exactly what McGuffey was going to do, and felt two separate fears: one of the new physical danger, another of the effect of rage on McGuffey's judgment. . . .

Schneider yelled formlessly, perhaps in warning—he could never remember later—saw the curving run begin to come back on itself, saw McGuffey's body leave the ground in what at school they had called a dive-and-roll block—saw the body, parallel to the wharf, at right angles to the men, cut knifelike across their knees, the knees break, the bodies crumple, the hands flung in gestures that could have been those of despair . . . before all three fell from sight, leaving only Thomas balanced on one knee; then he, too, from the pull of a last, despairing hand, fell soundlessly below the edge of the wharf.

Schneider stopped running. The rain gathered in his eyebrows and dripped into his eyes. Partially blinded, he stood in yet another frustration, looking down into water the color of crank-case oil, seeing the dull flash of hands in it, the terrible slow turning of bodies in heavy clothing and—all of them—out of their element. In the scene, obscure and brokenly visible, he saw but one thing clearly: where McGuffey had already wedged himself and one of the strangers between two pieces of piling and while one hand held the man's hair, the other, fisted, methodically smashed the man's face so that the head went each time against the wood. . . .

Then Schneider did something he never fully accounted for. Knowing clearly that the thing to do was to get the others out of there, he paused only long enough to take off his two coats, then dived headlong into the darkness. . . . Yet some order, some design was clear in him, for he came up behind the other stranger, who he had seen could not swim, and seizing the man by head and throat, held him under water.

. So, timeless, they moved for a space, McGuffey in a kind of joy as he hit and saw the knuckles cut, the blood run, the fear and terror of the other face. "Christ, man," the face said once, "don't."

Schneider existed now more formlessly than McGuffey. In the winter harbor water he felt no cold, but went below it with his opponent and rising, carefully breathed and as carefully held the man from the air. There was a rhythm to it, a placidity far more terrible than McGuffey's rage, for Schneider had not seen the face of the man he was trying to kill. He had lost anger: blood cooled by water, like lizard or snake he tried to kill without rage.

Yet in that water their adrenals began to fail them . . . and the breathing hurt McGuffey's throat, bubbled through Schneider's lips. McGuffey slipped clear of the piling, felt his opponent limp in his hands, but could not know yet that he had broken the man's leg with that first savage blow on the dock. Weakness came on McGuffey like a veil and he knew he was going to drown, letting go of the other man. Schneider had ceased to think in such terms . . . yet both heard the same voice. "In Christ's name, stop. You'll be murderers." And each of them, drowning with his enemy, knew it for Thomas speaking and was filled with a sorrow more terrible than anything yet felt in those moments, as though for the first time

[164]

they had knowledge of the full nature of sin; and so in that water were sustained: without knowing why. Somehow, near them, too, their enemies appeared, also sustained, seen—although not Thomas, they remembered later—and again time was without dimension and they remembered, each of them, his own sorrow.

Figures showed in the rain above them and there was a dull shouting. Schneider returned to clearer sight and saw the way a leg dangled just before it went out of sight beyond the wharf edge. He himself was the second the dock hands, the cops standing on the supports between the piling, dragged up and handed above. Then came the second enemy, then Thomas, and last McGuffey, with bleeding hands . . . and all of them lay on the dock in the rain, the shouting and the cold. There was nothing unusual about it.

Those in authority did nothing different from what others like them had done in other centuries: the two enemies were taken to a hospital uptown with which their union had a contract; and McGuffey and Schneider, when they were properly identified, were taken to St. Linus's Hospital where the Auxiliary had met that day for The Sewing. Thomas, they took to the prison ward at Bellevue, and charged with disturbing the peace, and assault and battery.

There was nothing seriously wrong with either McGuffey or Schneider. The doctors could see that. The two of them were put in the same semiprivate room at the hospital and given a sedative. McGuffey's fingers needed bandaging; somehow three of them had got cut to the bone.

McGuffey woke first in the late afternoon to find his wife there, weeping. It was the first time he had seen her in several weeks, so that at first he did not notice some of the other young women, Rosemary, Ellen Doarn, Mary Gaffney and one or two others. Mary and Ellen wore their nurse's aid uniforms. McGuffey said, "Where's the priest? Am I dying or is Schneider?"

Just before Marie flung herself upon him, McGuffey saw Mary smile; then Marie was kissing him, her tears warm on his face. In this moment McGuffey found he no longer loved his wife. Passion had departed there in the water and had not yet returned. Absent, he discovered with it also his love was gone, although lying in the dimness made by her face, he could remember times when, passion gone, his love had remained. Now there was neither . . . and later he would grow alarmed about this, wondering if it would be so for the rest of their life . . . but for the moment he just lay there and let Marie weep on him.

"I'm coming home," she sobbed. "I'm coming home tomorrow."

"All right," he said, "all right." His tone, part of him realized, was that used when placating a fool. And wondering why he used that tone, he recalled that whatever else he had thought Marie in the past he had never thought her a fool. Now, it seemed to him, without logic, he must consider her a fool and in their life treat her as such. Much of this feeling would depart from him with time, yet lying there on the hospital cot, he could not know that it would depart, so that the knowledge of his wife's being a fool was very strong in McGuffey, was, indeed, the most terrible of the things he had undergone that day.

"But what happened?" She raised her head and dabbed at her eyes.

"Oh, hell," her husband said. "Let's not go into that." His mind, he found, turned away from what had happened.

Schneider was awake and McGuffey turned to look at him. The eyes seemed bright in the bony face and Schneider had apparently said something in his forced and uneasy humor that had made the young women near his bed smile. "If you're going to go around in that kind of uniform," Schneider was saying to Ellen, "you've got to expect certain things. How about a kiss?"

To their mild surprise she bent and kissed him. His arm reaching to embrace her was slow and she was straightened again before he could get it from under the cover.

"And I thought he needed a priest," McGuffey said.

"I need a lot of things right now," Schneider said, "and a priest is only one of them."

The young women had gathered near his bed, perhaps because his mood seemed even stranger than McGuffey's, perhaps to leave Marie alone with her husband. Yet now she, too, moved to the other side of her husband's bed and turned to face Schneider, so that only Mary Gaffney remained near McGuffey. Mary was all right, McGuffey thought, none of Moon's hot air and promoting. Still, in a way she was as much a damn fool as Schneider, although in her it irritated him less than in the man. "I hear you're getting married," he said.

She nodded, her face changing. "Ed's better and he'll be back in the city in a few weeks."

"When are you going to get married?"

"I don't know exactly. Sometime after he comes back."

He recognized a familiar note, one common in their people, in their time: another of those interminable Irish engagements with friends always asking when the marriage was to be, and the principals always having the best excuses in the world: for Auntie to die, or for Sister to have her baby, so she could be matron of honor; for Eddie's promotion or for Agnes's firm to be in not quite such pressing need of her services: when all the time none of them had the money to raise a family in New York City. And always there were those of them, he knew, who never got married, whose engagements went on forever: why, no one knew. McGuffey had heard Schneider, drinking, say why, but McGuffey had his doubts.

[ 167 ]

Seeing Mary still there, McGuffey said, "Well, let this whole thing be a lesson to you."

She could not quite smile. "What whole thing?"

Trying to shrug, he found that weakness still enclosed him like a garment. "You mean you don't know?"

"No one seems to know much about what happened to you and Bart."

"But everyone knows plenty about Marie and me." His tongue thickened.

Mary colored. "But what has that got to do with this?"

"Plenty," McGuffey said. "Plenty. That's what I'm talking about. Let this be a lesson to you. The Irish aren't supposed to marry. Clergy frowns on marriage. Anyhow, at best tolerates it as necessary evil."

McGuffey saw that Marie, catching some of the conversation, had turned back to them, and so closed his eyes and let himself sleep.

Schneider remained awake. . . . Like McGuffey, sensing his special position as vague and injured hero, he had been baiting Rosemary and asking her why she still held out on Whitey, until he had driven her from the room. Patricia Moore and the others of the Auxiliary had found they must return to The Sewing. There remained in the room only Marie and Mary and Ellen in their role of nurse's aides.

"If they'll let me out of this place tonight, Ellen," Schneider said, "how about going dancing?"

"Of course," she said. "If they do."

"You know they won't," he said. "At least not tonight. So how about when I do get out?"

"I'm engaged," she said.

"Oh, yes," he said, looking straight ahead. "That guy." He was disturbed that the knowledge of her engagement should give him pain when he loved only Concepción.

"What's wrong with him?" Ellen said.

[168]

"Nothing, I guess."

"At least he doesn't go around getting into drunken brawls."

"No. No brawls," he said. "A great blessing." Turning his head, he saw she was leaving the room, and that precise and ironic function of his mind over which he had no control, estimated she had left his side just too soon to hear the last three words. He wondered if not brawling *could* make up for going to bed with a drunk?

A true weariness came over him. In gathering darkness he saw Marie, dry-eyed and composed, pass from the room, saw Mary for a moment hover between himself and McGuffey, her face strangely working, before she, too, turned in a kind of haste toward the door. Whether she switched off the room's light he never knew, but went himself into a shadow whose distortions never ceased, where the Church's silver-edged words were blunted by a brogue, and God spoke with the voice of an Irish Catholic priest.

10

ABOUT ONCE A MONTH, Judge Augustine Moore held a gathering at his home, or rather, two gatherings were simultaneously held there, one of Patricia's friends and another smaller one of various politicians the judge had known and collaborated with in the time before his judgeship. People from the Hall were always present, often two generations of them. At times, the mayor or the president of the board of aldermen would be there and on rarer occasions the governor.

One of them would not be there today and His absence was the cause for Moon Gaffney's being late for the gathering. A Bermuda boat was sailing that afternoon with Him aboard, and Moon, in his principal unofficial duty as confidential messenger for the Hall, had been given an envelope to deliver aboard ship.

[169]

The day was a gray, heavy one toward the end of March and a damp unpleasant wind blew off the harbor. The official car Moon drove was waved onto the dock and he tooled it carefully between the crates and bales, smelling gratefully the spices, feeling the heavy coat, the car gathered around him as a kind of armor. . . . Going from car to gangplank he shivered, wondering if his drinking had anything to do with the way he felt the cold. At the foot of the gangplank he came upon a hurrying figure, whose ruddy and genial face was none other than Father O'Driscoll's, whom Moon had not seen since an afternoon at the Hall a month ago.

"Why, Moon Gaffney!" the priest said. "I might have known you would be here. How are you and how is the commissioner?"

Tipping his hat and shaking hands simultaneously, Moon felt some of Father O'Driscoll's warmth might be related to the knowledge all insiders by now possessed that he himself would be an assemblyman come November.

Together they went up the gangplank and Moon hesitated at its head because the priest did. "The purser's office is down this way," the priest said. "I have so many friends sailing on these boats that I know exactly where it is. We can get His stateroom number there."

"I've got it," Moon said. "It's sixty-seven."

"That's right this way," Father O'Driscoll said, and off he went, Moon a pace behind and beginning to feel foolish. It wasn't generally known that He was sailing and Moon had been charged with the need for keeping quiet. Yet here was Father O'Driscoll barging around the decks and anyone who wanted to could blame Moon for having brought him. Still, there was nothing to do right now but follow where the priest led. Moon's disturbance increased as, coming within sight of the stateroom, he saw no one near its closed door but Gus Browning, a kind of bodyguard, chosen because he was not a

Catholic. For the first time in Moon's memory Gus did not seem to know what to do.

"Hello, Gus," Moon said. "How's everything?"

"All right," Gus said. "Seeing someone off?"

"Why, Him, Gus," Father O'Driscoll said. "The Boss." He half-laughed, half-smiled.

"What's that?" Gus said.

"Isn't He here?" Father O'Driscoll asked, plaintively. "I mean—"

"Why, not yet," Gus said.

"But it's within fifteen minutes of sailing time," Father O'Driscoll said.

"Well, I'll tell you," Gus said firmly and not altogether pleasantly. "It's like this. He ain't feeling so well."

"Yes?" Father O'Driscoll said.

"Well, that's all," Gus said. "He can't see no one."

"Oh," said Father O'Driscoll.

"I've got something for Him," Moon said in an undertone he foolishly hoped the priest would not hear.

"I know," Gus said. "You can leave it with me."

Moon's lips came in and he shook his head a little. "No dice. I'm supposed to give it to Him personally."

Gus hesitated. "All right, wait a minute." He spoke surlily and turned, carefully opening the door to sixty-seven no more than was necessary to admit himself, but both Moon and Father O'Driscoll could see there was no one in the room, although another doorway opened from it to sixty-eight. Almost, Moon thought, there was a whiff of scent, from one of the women passing on the deck. Then the door closed in their faces and they were left foolish in the cold.

"My own feeling," said Father O'Driscoll, "is that He has not been well. This whole thing merely confirms it."

"I wouldn't know," Moon said.

The door opened again. "He says for Moon to go on in and

[171]

leave it on the table," Gus said. "He says to tell you, Father, that He'd like to see you when He gets back next week. He ain't feeling so good."

Moon didn't hear the reply as he closed the cabin door after him. There was no one in the room and he could still smell the scent from the woman who had passed on the deck. Taking the Manila envelope from his inside pocket, he turned it over. The secretary had sealed it with only the tip of the flap, and Moon felt compulsion to open it. He put it down on the table, then hesitated before turning to the closed doorway that led to sixty-eight. When he tapped gently on it, His cheerful voice said hello.

"This is Gaffney, Chief. I have that for you."

"Okay, fine, Moon," He said through the door. "Just leave it there on the table. And thank you very much. So long."

"Okay," Moon said. "So long." Still he hesitated, made an unnecessary stumble to convey the impression of movement. Then he picked up the envelope and pulled the flap loose. It came open easily, leaving hardly a trace of glue where it had been fastened to the envelope. There were two thin objects inside, one a packet of new hundred-dollar bills, the other a small, transparent envelope inside which Moon could see a deck of condoms.

Starting to wet the flap again, Moon hesitated, then used his finger instead of his tongue, returning the envelope to the table. He closed the door firmly after him as he went onto the deck.

"Everything okay?" Gus said.

"Everything's fine," Moon said. He began to walk along the deck, Father O'Driscoll now a pace behind him, chattering away. It was nothing to be shocked about, Moon kept telling himself: he had heard enough stories about Him not to be surprised, though he had never believed them. But the shock or sense of shock remained, and with it a shadowy, unpleasant feeling to which Moon could not give a name nor even be sure it existed.

It was not until they were on the dock again that Moon heard the priest's talking as words. "And now I suppose you're on your way to Judge Moore's like myself?"

"Yes," Moon said. "Glad I'll have company going up."

Most of the drive uptown the priest talked about Him. "Oh, I know he takes a drink now and then, but what Irish gentleman doesn't? And if he takes a drink too many, well, what of it? If you and I were under the strain of his office, we would probably do the same, eh, Moon?" He jogged Moon's elbow when the younger man did not respond.

"Naturally," Moon said.

"And this talk of crooked politics and so on—all I have to say to that is that the use of certain funds for certain purposes has become so common and widespread that one might go so far as to say it had become sanctioned by custom. My whole point of contention in defending Him—and no week goes by that I don't do so—is that he leads for the most part an exemplary Catholic life. No Sunday goes by but what he is at Mass in the Cathedral with his wife. They appear together at Mass, so that no scandal may be given. And if the whole truth might be known, the thing, the difference between them would resolve itself down to her being a non-Catholic. Ah, Moon, there is nothing worse than a mixed marriage with its—"

Moon stopped listening. Not until he was turning into Sutton Place where the Moores lived did he hear Father O'Driscoll again. "My whole point in defending Him is to make it clear that in spite of a drink here and a few dollars there, he leads an exemplary Catholic life. I say that those of his predecessors who had the reputation of being clean in politics always had women in their lives and anyone knows which is the graver sin, or rather the grave sin. Besides—" he jogged

[ 173 ]

Moon's elbow again as the car stopped—"it's mostly Jew money. Jew bankers' money." His laugh was a kind of giggle.

Stepping from the car, Moon noticed it was getting dark. "I bet the house is mobbed," he said. "Patricia's friends practically drive the judge's out of the place."

"Sure and why not," Father O'Driscoll said. "First things first." With his hat off in the elevator, his upper lip drawn down to accentuate his quaint mixture of worldly wisdom and true piety, he looked not unlike a pale educated baboon.

They stepped out on the tenth floor. Since the judge's apartment occupied the entire floor, the door leading into it had been left ajar. There were two living rooms, opening one on the other and both overlooking the East River. Theoretically the judge presided in one room and Patricia in the other, but the two groups had by now so intermingled and in turn divided into smaller groups, which mulatto servants fed and served with drinks from silver trays, that one room could hardly be distinguished from the other.

There was a somewhat forced quality to the gaiety, given it by those of her friends who knew that the announcement of Patricia's engagement to Burke Riley had been postponed for some reason known only to the judge. Moon stayed talking to Patricia while Father O'Driscoll, despite the distractions of trays of drinks and calls from friends, made his way unerringly to the inner room where the judge presided with pinch-bottle Scotch and Corona Corona cigars. It was a stately and not uncharacteristic gathering, Congressman Clancy from Brooklyn, a borough president, a magistrate and two assemblymen including, to the priest's surprise, Billy Ryan. But then, he thought quickly, that was because Ryan would run for Congress this fall. Still, it was a long way uptown for Ryan.

"You are all we needed, Father," the judge said, rising, "to make our gathering truly representative. How are you and what delayed you? Affairs of state at the chancery, no doubt."

[174]

At once basking and beaming, Father O'Driscoll said, "The best of reasons, Judge, the best of reasons. I was down seeing that great man, his honor, off to Bermuda. He—"

He stopped talking, aware of the peculiar silence he had induced. "That is—" he began again.

"Why, I had no idea He was going to be away," Billy Ryan said.

"Nor I," said the borough president.

"Well, now," Father O'Driscoll said, "I didn't mean to be revealing anything. And in fact would hardly have thought I was, for he asked, when I told him where I was going this afternoon, to be remembered to all you gentlemen. That is—"

"I'd heard he was sick abed," the other assemblyman said. "For three days I've been trying to see him."

"It could be the doctor ordered him away for a few days," Billy Ryan said.

"I will say," Judge Moore said, "that He has not impressed me as being a well man on the few occasions I've seen him this past year. It seems to me he might very well have been ordered on a vacation.

"Especially at this time of year," Billy Ryan said. "Were many down to see him off, Father?"

"Why, why," Father O'Driscoll said, "why, no. In fact, there was but young Gaffney and myself."

There was a silence which might have been alarming to anyone but Father O'Driscoll, then the second assemblyman said, "Did he impress you as being a well man, Father?"

"Well, now, to tell the truth, I didn't actually see him. I talked to him through the door. It was young Gaffney that saw him. I will say this, though, that he *sounded* all right."

That silence returned again, so that even Father O'Driscoll began to feel uncomfortable. "Perhaps we should ask Moon how He was," the borough president said.

"A good idea," said Judge Moore. "Where is Moon? Doubtless talking to my daughter." He smiled uneasily. It would have been difficult for him to explain just why he had asked Patricia to postpone her announcement of the engagement. The old excuse that she might be married for her money no longer seemed valid: he had realized for some time that Patricia would be married for that alone.

"I'll run Moon down," Billy Ryan said. He waddled toward the other room. In its crowd he had trouble finding Moon but at last saw him talking to Rosemary and a dark young man Ryan did not know. "Why, Mister Ryan," Rosemary said. "What a pleasure. You know Moon, and—"

"I baptized him," Billy said. "Anyhow, I was there when they baptized him."

"And this is Armando Orvieto, a friend of mine."

"Pleased to know you," Billy said. He wondered what a fine Irish girl like Rosemary was doing with a Ginny like that. Not wanting to appear abrupt, Billy talked with them a little while and during that time Peter Calahan and Burke Riley came over to them and Billy became involved in greeting Peter. But finally he was able to tell Moon that the judge wanted to speak with him.

First pleased, Moon quickly grew alarmed. It was as though some part or function of his being warned him of danger before his mind knew the nature or cause of the alarm. Excusing himself, he went to the bedroom that served as cloakroom and there, as he put on his coat, found he was also angry and that the anger was directed toward Father O'Driscoll. But that in turn increased his fear, for he knew that it was bad luck to be in any way displeased with a priest. He went downstairs and out into the air, shaking so that he had to sit awhile in the car before driving. But still he didn't know his mind: there was only that instinct to flee.

While the judge and his friends waited for Moon to join them, the party of Patricia's friends began to break up. Peter

[176]

Calahan, Burke Riley, and J. Martin Murphy went off together to have some supper. Ellen had had to stay home today
because of the illness of one of her younger brothers, so Peter
had come alone to the gathering. Rosemary left with the
Orvieto boy. She had been keeping Whitey in the doghouse
lately, as she thought of it, because Whitey didn't seem to want
to press his father for that raise.

Rosemary had seen the Orvieto boy at parties a few times
but had been out with him only once, and then with others.
Now, as they walked westward, she felt very pleased with herself for some reason. She not only felt she was showing Whitey
but she began to think how nice it would be maybe to get married to a distinguished-looking foreigner like Armando, a real
Spanish Catholic, and maybe even go to live part of each year
in Spain and have your own private chapel and all. Of course,
those Spaniards did seem to have large families, and the idea
of her having a large family was very disturbing to Rosemary;
of having any family at all. "Where would you like to go?"
Armando said.

"Oh, just any place," Rosemary said. "Some place quiet,
huh?"

"Why, certainly," Armando said, his voice rising. He had
the most delightful accent, Rosemary thought, just enough to
be distinguished but not enough to make anyone think he was
a real greasy foreigner.

"Although really," she said after they had entered a cab,
"I ate so much at Patricia's that I'm not hungry."

"Whatever you say, Rosemary," Armando said.

"I don't know what to do," she said, uncertain. "We could
go to my house, if you wanted."

"All right," he said, "but perhaps you would prefer to ride
around some first."

"Oh, that would be nice," Rosemary said. "I love to see the
Hudson from the Drive."

Armando directed the driver to go up the Drive and then turning back to Rosemary he put his arm around her. Rosemary thought that was kind of rushing things, but decided she would let Armando kiss her. When he did a moment later, Rosemary was freshly shocked to find that he had also put a hand on her knee, something neither Whitey nor anyone else had ever dared to do.

"I wish you wouldn't," she said.

But neither her own hands nor her words seemed to make any difference to Armando. Rosemary was afraid to say anything too loud on account of the driver, and Armando seemed to sense this. Also, he knew just where all her clothing was fastened, and all of her protests and muffled cries seemed to just make him worse. Realizing he couldn't actually seduce Rosemary in the cab, he did what he could, finishing with Rosemary weeping and her pants in Armando's pocket. When the cab finally stopped before her apartment, Rosemary's maidenhead was still intact but her fine warm feeling for Spain was gone. She told Armando she never wanted to see him again, and turning away from him in the lobby, she was both angered and puzzled that nothing she said seemed to affect him other than to make him vaguely amused.

Calahan, Burke Riley, and J. Martin went from the party to a little place that Burke knew about. It had booths and, since only J. Martin was hungry, they sat there drinking.

"All I have to say," Burke said, "is that if the judge thinks I am marrying Patricia for her money, he is completely wrong. If it were a question of money, there are any number of other girls I could marry."

"Quite right," J. Martin said. "And some of the *very* best marriages are made that way. Myself, I feel it is a better basis for marriage than something as ephemeral as sex."

"Yes, but you miss my point, old man," Burke said. "I am *not* marrying Patricia for her money."

"Oh, I know," J. Martin said. "I was just remarking in passing."

"It's difficult, though," Peter said. "I mean I had to be sure Ellen was not marrying me for mine. I think the judge will be convinced. I really don't see why he—"

"Why," Burke said, "I could go into business for myself, Martin. I could go into the family loan business with Peter next week and with his funds and my experience, there would be nothing to it. Furthermore, I am making almost a hundred a week in the business now and it isn't as if we would have to use Patricia's money to live on. At least not much of it."

"You know, I think I will go into that with you," Peter said. "The family is anxious to have me in business and I am damned if I will go into theirs. I would much prefer to be the silent partner in anything I went into."

Burke's face brightened, his head came up in a kind of reverence. "You don't mean that, old man! Say, that's a go! Isn't that wonderful, Martin? You heard old Peter, here?" He half-rose and grasped Peter's hand and pumped it.

"It certainly is wonderful," J. Martin said. "I mean to think I should be here on such an occasion. Perhaps I should go into it with you. Ha ha, that would be a good one, to combine finance with literature."

They ordered more drinks and J. Martin another sandwich.

"I know the business like the back of my hand," Burke said. "Before I'd graduated, Knobby's father, Sir Maurice, came to me and offered me a position. But don't think for a moment that I had a sinecure or preference. I came up the hard way the same as anyone else. It perhaps did not take me so long, but I came up step by step all the way, in the matter of having to get rough on the phone or even in person. I tell you the business of making collections is not always an easy one."

[179]

"I was wondering about that," Peter said.

"Now, don't misunderstand me, Peter, old man," Burke said, putting an easing hand on his friend's wrist. "Don't get the idea that because collections are difficult, we don't make them. We make well over ninety-five per cent of all collections."

"I rather thought so," J. Martin said, while Peter nodded, reassured.

Burke was moved to indulge in confidences. A smile wreathed his fine-boned face; he wagged his head even as other and more vulgar men. "I must say that I've had quite some experiences, though, with collections."

"Who would you say you had the most trouble with?" J. Martin said. "I mean with what class of people."

Burke cocked his head judiciously. "I really think that the Poles around Pittsburgh are the worst. They are the most stubborn people. You'd think if people were so anxious to borrow money, they'd be glad to pay it back to the party that was good enough to loan it to them. But not those Polacks. Why, I remember one woman—I had to go to her house with two of our men before we could get any results. Of course, we went during the day when her husband was away, because he was a perfect so-and-so, too. But, anyway, there she stood, screaming at us from the porch so that the whole block could hear her, three or four children all around her, crying, and another actually nursing there in public. For all the world just like a family of animals. And she called us just about everything. Names you wouldn't have thought a woman knew. And all because we came to collect a perfectly just debt. Finally, I couldn't stand it any longer and I told our men, I said, go up there on that porch and see if you can at least make her shut up. So they went up and, more or less accidentally, of course—" here Burke raised his eyebrows and almost smiled—"stepped on the toes of some of the children. Well,

[180]

you know, it was the most amazing thing. That woman broke down and began to whimper, and not only that, she went inside and came out with five dollars, which ten minutes before she had disclaimed having."

He paused, perhaps for breath. A kind of fleeting pleasure emanated from him, a soft and delicate delight. His long-lashed eyelids fluttered two or three times, the smile slow, secret and fleeting. Peter, fairly drunk, grinned inanely, while J. Martin smiled, too, in his own fashion. J. Martin cleared his throat of the saliva and said: "That's amazing. I mean it really is."

"Of course," Burke said, "there were times when we did have to get rough, too. I mean really rough. I remember a case just outside of Pittsburgh. It was in a district where a judge, as a kind of grandstand play, was unsympathetic to any cases we took into court. So we had abandoned making any loans in that district. But a man to whom we had previously made a loan while he was living in the city, moved out to that particular district."

"Knowing exactly what he was doing, of course," J. Martin said.

"Exactly," Burke said. "Well, anyway, he refused to pay us, and we knew it was almost useless taking him into court out there, about all we'd get out of it was a lot of publicity, if anything. So we went out there one evening just about the time he'd be coming home for supper. I had the same two boys with me as when I went to the Polish woman's. This fellow lived in a house on the edge of town, and we parked the car a couple of blocks away and waited for him under some trees in the dark. By and by he comes along swinging his lunch pail and whistling just as if he owned the world. We didn't say a word—no use giving ourselves away—but we just stepped out and began swinging. Boy!—his lunch pail went one way, his hat another and he went on his tail, sitting up, of all things. He

[181]

began to yell, just one yell, though. One of my boys stepped up and kicked him in the mouth so hard he had to pull his foot to get it out. And after that there was no more yelling. He just lay there and we put the boots to him. I really didn't mind it, either. To think of that so-and-so trying to get away from us by moving to that district. We could have done him up brown, too, but his kids must have heard him yell that one time, because they came running down there, calling, 'Pop! Pop! Hey, what's the matter, Pop?' And we had to beat it."

"You really earned your position, all right, Burke," J. Martin said.

"Damned right, I earned it," Burke said. "I remember seeing Sir Maurice right after he had been made a Knight of St. Gregory, and he told me: 'Burke, I feel that you and all the young men of my organization share in this honor. Because without your aid I could never have got where I am.' So that when Judge Moore or anyone else thinks I'm marrying Patricia for her money, they've got another think coming. I've earned my way and got where I am strictly on my own."

"Damn right, Burke, old man," Peter said. "You work for me from now on, though. I'll help with collections, too, by gosh. Got little persuader here." He fumbled at his back and brought out a .32 automatic pistol.

"Say, isn't that a beauty," Burke said.

"It certainly is," J. Martin said. His voice had risen perceptibly. "I suppose, Peter, it's one of the perquisites of your office?"

"Well, I bought it, myself," Peter said. "The badge allows me to carry it, though." He fumbled at a vest pocket and brought out the gold badge.

"I suppose it's loaded, old man," Burke said, turning the gun over delicately.

"Damned right, it's loaded," Peter said. "What you think I am?"

"Well, that isn't exactly what I meant," Burke said. "I mean, the service revolver is usually a .38, isn't it?"

"That's no reason for me to carry gun like ordinary cop," Peter said. "Don't you go worrying about whether this gun can stop them or not. You hit 'em in the right place, it'll stop 'em, all right. I been practicing." He took the gun back from Burke and, squinting one eye, aimed it at the near wall.

"Careful now," J. Martin said. "I hope the safety's on."

"Don't you go worrying about old Peter and any gun," Peter said. "I'm an expert with gun." He put it back in its holster.

"I think we all need another drink," Burke said. He felt keyed up and bright, the afternoon's letdown almost forgotten. Something, he didn't know just what, had set him up.

It was still early. There was nothing, J. Martin often told himself and now told the others, absolutely nothing that set him up like an evening in good male company. "In fact," he went on with a peculiar but jocular smile, "I don't see why you fellows have to be going and getting married. Here, I'm three or four years older than either of you, and I'm in no hurry to tie myself down to some girl." He laughed, one hand on Peter's arm.

"You've got something there, Martin, old fellow," Burke said. "But sooner or later a man has to get married and when a girl of good family, like Patricia, comes along—"

"Way it is with me," Peter interrupted, "I feel marriage will do me lot of good. Not merely physical side. Other things, too." He shook his head slowly and kept on shaking it until all meaning departed from the gesture.

The other two were silent while this went on, accustomed as they were to hanging on Peter's words. In the silence, far-borne, they heard the thin wail of a fire siren. It came first from one quarter of the city, then another.

Peter raised his head. "Sounds like big fire."

"Why don't we go to it?" Burke said. "Your car will get us through the lines."

"Good idea," Peter said. "You want to go, too, Martin?"

"Why, why, I guess so," Martin said. He felt disappointed that their cozy little evening was going to be broken up, but it would be better than nothing to have this company in the car for a while longer. He and Burke dutifully waited while Peter paid the check, then Burke led them outside.

The damp wind still blew, making them shiver. There was a glare in the sky downtown on the west side. It was decided that Burke should drive. The three of them crowded into the front seat and Burke, the commissioner's shield front and back, let her out down Park Avenue.

Police from squad cars had surrounded the building which stood on a quarter of a city block, three sides of it adjacent to sidewalks. When they started to enter it, two of them had been shot and wounded by the thief, before he fled up to the third floor. A call was sent in for reserves. Later on it was said that the police had set fire to the place to smoke their quarry out, but what had happened was that the thief, lighting a cigarette in the darkness and below the window sill, had thrown a match away without extinguishing it. The flames, spreading through the trash along the wooden floor, licked upward and the thief was forced to descend to the second floor. In his fear and bewilderment he showed for a moment against the light, and a detective standing in the street shot through a window and wounded him. From the way he cried out, the police knew he was wounded, and encouraged or stimulated by this, the cops and detectives posted around the building, began to take shots at any window behind which they thought they detected movement. Since the flames, still contained, burned with an uncertain light, the shooting was almost con-

[184]

tinual and the thief replied to it as long as his ammunition lasted, but no one else was hurt.

A large crowd had collected and the reserves arrived just in time to hem it in and gradually force it back until on all sides it was a block away. It was while the reserves were doing this that the first fire trucks began to arrive and a way had to be made for them through the solid, hundred-yard-deep mass of the crowd.

The flames had got a good start and had moved through the third and fourth floors of the building. The thief, with next to his last cartridge, shot and wounded the first fireman to enter and Fire Commissioner Danaher, arriving, ordered his men to stay out of the building. From the outside they played hose into it and so held the fire in check, while the cops continued sporadically to shoot their revolvers.

It became evident that their quarry was dead, badly hurt or out of ammunition. A small group of police and detectives entered the building accompanied by a squad of firemen dragging a hose and led by Commissioner Danaher. A few moments after they had entered, Fire Commissioner Gaffney arrived in his car driven by Mike Boland. Moon, who often came on such missions with his father, was not along; he was drunk in LaGatta's at the moment.

Patrick Gaffney looked at the fire and was not alarmed by it. The wind had almost died and while there was no hope of saving the building it was evident that the men had kept the flames from spreading and that, barring a rise of wind, the surrounding buildings were safe. Accordingly, he said a Hail Mary to himself, and then gave his thought to a private not to say secret concern. This was for Commissioner Danaher, who three times to Commissioner Gaffney's knowledge, had shown a disturbing reluctance to come out of a burning building. Particularly, Patrick Gaffney remembered a time when Danaher, his face working strangely, had struck away the hands

[185]

that had tried to lead him to safety and Gaffney had had to order the men to forcibly take Danaher out. There had persisted in Gaffney the feeling that something either more or less than blind devotion to duty made Danaher do this, but it was hardly a thing, he felt, you could ask a man about in cold blood.

So Commissioner Gaffney stood now for a moment in the street, the light making his face seem younger, but also indicating what some might have called his ineffectuality. He decided to go in and turned to tell Mike Boland to follow him. The shooting had ceased.

"For Christ sake, no, Commissioner," Mike said. "You got orders—"

"Who is running this thing?" the commissioner asked, which was his way of indicating he was the ranking official present.

"Oh, Jesus," Mike said and ran to a near-by truck to get the helmets.

While they entered, following the hose line—as in Galway their fathers the hill trail—and were lost to view in the darkness at that end of the building, two things happened. The car containing Peter and his friends finally got through the crowd and came up between the fire trucks. At the other end of the building the thief, cornered, fired his last cartridge at the approaching police and firemen and missed. So many slugs hit him in return that when they picked him up later his face was unrecognizable. Some of those outside fired, too, half a dozen shots, sporadic and careful, that the police sergeants and lieutenants, cursing, finally stopped. Peter, too, in the excitement, leaped from the car and standing near the darkened and partly gutted corner where the entrance was, gleefully pointed his gun at the second story and held the trigger until it was empty.

"At a boy, Peter, old kid," Burke cried, running up behind him.

"Hey, you dope," a sergeant called to Peter, "there's a lot of people in there."

"I'll have you broken, goddam you," Peter said. "Do you know who I am?"

Seeing for the first time the commissioner's badge, the sergeant turned away so that Peter couldn't see the number of his shield.

"Why, that impertinent bastard," Burke said. "Let me get his number."

"Never mind, Burke, old boy," Peter said, frightened. "We've done our duty. Let's go." They returned to the car in which Martin sat, glassy-eyed, and Burke turned and eased it back through the lines.

Mike Boland, helmeted, ax in hand more for reassurance than need, moved steadily before the commissioner, feeling his way by scraping his foot along the hose line, praying that the floors above them would not collapse. There was more smoke than Mike liked or thought there would have been. He kept talking to the commissioner as they moved but could understand few of the answers as the commissioner had tied a handkerchief over his face.

"We should of brought masks," Mike said. "I had no idea it would be like this. What do you say, I go back for the masks?"

It was just then that the burst of shooting occurred. It seemed all around them and Mike dropped to the floor. "You all right, Commissioner?" he yelled.

He couldn't hear the answer and he got up and began to move forward again slowly. The smoke striking him as he rose, he remembered there had been no answer about the masks. "What do you say about those masks?" he said. This time there was no answer. "Hey, Commissioner!" Mike yelled, turning. But there was only the near silence and the farther shouting. The smoke, Mike thought, the smoke's got the old man. He began to feel his way back along the hose, crawling on his belly in the foot or so of clear air on the floor. As he had suspected, the commissioner was out cold. He lay there, prone, the helmet knocked off as he had fallen to the floor.

Whimpering, Mike picked up the commissioner and started back along the line. The rubber of the old man's coat had charred and melted in places from contact with the floor and the sticky rubber scalded Mike's hands. He met a party of cops and firemen coming in. "They got the bastard," someone said.

"Here," Mike said, still whimpering. "The smoke's got the old man. Get him outside."

Two of them took the commissioner from Mike and when Mike fell on his hands and knees, another raised him and by one blistered hand led him outside.

They laid the commissioner in the emergency truck and taking off some of his clothing tried to revive him with the prone pressure method. Then when that wasn't effective, they became alarmed and thought they'd maybe better use the mechanical resuscitator, although with a man the commissioner's age it might hurt his lungs. It was while they were adjusting the mask of the resuscitator over his face that an intern noticed where a bullet had nicked the back of the skull, and suddenly deciding to put a stethoscope on the commissioner, they found the old man was dead.

11

*"Full fathom five thy father lies,*
*Of his bones are coral made . . ."*

THERE WAS, of course, the scent of lilies and the scent of carnations, the smells of garlic and of whisky. The floral pieces or "tributes," as McGinnis the undertaker preferred to call them, filled every room and overflowed into the halls on both floors. But still they kept coming with no place, absolutely no place to put them. Sleepless, Moon was driven into a kind of inchoate rage by their profusion, their bulk, by their all but meaningless significance. Or rather they were the precipitant of the rage that was in him. They were in his bedroom, in Mary's, in the one in which for thirty years their father had slept with their mother and in which she still slept or tried to sleep. They were in the kitchen and the dining room, while in the living room where the casket was and in the halls they were banked solid, crammed, crushed and smashed as McGinnis's elegant goons tried to fit those from one great name after another into places where they might be seen.

Moon thought of putting some in the back yard, but only so exposed himself to McGinnis's long exposition of how would people like to find their tributes out in the cold, that he felt foolish and hated McGinnis more than ever. "Of course," McGinnis conceded, worried over Moon's unspoken rage, "we could quietly take some of them away, now."

Turning from the man, Moon turned back. "For God's sake, yes," he said. But McGinnis didn't take any away.

It was the last night and secretly each member of the family was glad. Mary and her mother had found it necessary to alternate in accepting condolences from the line of people: there were just too many of them. They filed up the narrow stairs, they waited in queues outside in the cold, and there was no way of recognizing protocol and admitting the great before the others unless Moon knew when they would arrive and waited at the vestibule to take them up past the line on the stairs. And each of the family had thought, although none of them had said, that it might have been better if the commissioner had been laid out in a funeral parlor for the people of the district to see, while the big shots, the friends, and the district captains came to the house. But that was impossible, for as everyone knows the eagles gather only where the body is.

Moon had stopped drinking. He found it offered no consolation, nor yet any refuge except unconsciousness and that he did not want right now. By that last afternoon he had even recognized clearly that McGinnis and his bumbling were not the cause of the rage but only its object and suddenly he felt sorry for McGinnis. Two or three friends managed to see that Moon was rarely alone: Kavanagh, McGuffey, and to Moon's surprise, Schneider. Yet when it became evident that Moon had definitely stopped drinking, they left him alone.

That was the day Galvin first came to the house after his illness, and Moon, in a kind of wonder, found that far from being annoyed with Galvin, he had apparently no feeling at all about the man. Galvin appeared in the line of ordinary people as it filed by Moon and his mother, then past the casket. "Sorry for your trouble." "Sorry for your trouble." Sorry, sorry, indeed. The Italians, most of them, had to revert to their native tongue to say what they felt was necessary, and Moon found it a relief to listen to the liquid, meaningless words, whose tone seemed to indicate a grief he felt was not contained in the words of those he understood.

"I'm very sorry, Moon," Galvin said and Moon looked up.

"Glad to see you," he said. "I didn't know you'd be here. You didn't have to get in the line, though."

Galvin smothered that peculiar and annoying smile. "Why not?"

Moon smiled back. "Mary's asleep. Go in the kitchen. I'll be right in there with you. My aunts'll give you something to eat if you want."

Turning away, Galvin colored slightly. Or perhaps Moon only imagined he did. But it added to Moon's complex burden.

It was nearing suppertime and the line was thinning. Moon left his mother and moved toward the kitchen. The flowers brushing him as he walked seemed hands or hindrances and reminded him of the hatred he carried in him. Galvin was seated at the kitchen table and two of Moon's maiden aunts served him, fixing him with oblique glances of curiosity and uneasiness. One was a schoolteacher and the other a secretary in civil service; both had pondered often why, if Mary had to enter the risk and degradation of marriage, it must be with someone like Galvin who many doubted was even in the Church. Of course, there was the connection with Judge Galvin, but everyone knew what the judge thought of this nephew.

These two stoutish ladies turned in relief to Moon as he entered. For decades, he had been their joy, and for three days now they had eased their own grief by trying to smother Moon's in food, drink, and bosomy embraces. "Ah, here's the boy now," said Martha, the secretary. "And what'll you be having?"

"Not a thing, Aunt Martha, not a thing," Moon said. "I just wanted to see if you were taking good care of my friend here."

That gave them pause and they busied themselves, one at the electric stove, the other at the little potbellied coal stove on which a gallon coffeepot stood. Moon pulled one of the white kitchen chairs under him and rested his arms on the table. There was a half-eaten ham on it, store bread and a loaf of cheese. Moon reached absently for a sliver of the cheese. "You want a whisky or some brandy with that coffee?"

"I don't think so," Galvin said. "But don't let me stop you."

"I'm not drinking," Moon said. "I stopped two days ago. Feel like a new man." He faked a cough.

Galvin smiled. "I'd think you'd need a drink now and then with this mob pouring through the place."

"If I'd kept drinking, I'd have killed someone," Moon said. "I got a terrible hate on."

Galvin chewed a moment before answering. "At who, God?" Seeing how startled Moon was by this, he added, "I mean it's

[191]

not unusual to hate God after you lose someone close to you."

"No," Moon said. "A man's got to die. Something else."

"I don't know," Galvin said. He sounded as he had before Mary sent him to Jersey. The tone was in such contrast to the way he had been a few minutes past that Moon was struck by it.

The aunts went out of the room carrying sandwiches and the coffeepot. Although they had been talking so the aunts could not easily hear them, Moon was moved by their departure to make a kind of confession. "I hate politics. I hate every bastardly son of a bitch in politics. And most of all I hate—" His hatred, however, was not enough to force the name or names from his lips.

"You'll get over that," Galvin said. "You'll get over it good. And come November you'll be an assemblyman and maybe even be able to stop that cop coming into the Worker and brandishing his gun."

"Guns, all right," Moon said. "I used to think when I didn't like someone's guts or the way he tied his tie, that that was hating, but now I know. This thing—this thing—" pausing, he had to gasp for his comparison—"this thing is like, as strong as wanting some woman, only the opposite."

Galvin nodded, still chewing, and did not seem disturbed. "I know. I used to feel that way toward the people in the Church like that monsignor in the chancery." He paused and chewed. "I'll tell you, though. Until we become at least as ashamed of our hate as we are of our lust, we Catholics are going to be in a bad way."

Moon was distracted by someone engaged to his sister talking about lust. The old resentment of Galvin returned and with it a regret for his own frankness. Galvin went on. "You can't go into a Catholic church in the city on Sunday, particularly in Brooklyn, but what they're talking about collections or fornication or having more children. I can't remember the

[192]

last time I heard a sermon on charity, and charity is the key-
stone, the touchstone of Christianity."

"You don't mean you're in favor of birth control?" Moon
said.

"No," Galvin said wearily. "I think what I mind is the relish
with which the clergy, many of whom do not understand the
meaning of their own chastity, tell their people they must fill
their three-room flats with children on their twenty-eight dollars a week. The relish, you understand, that's what I object
to. A very small thing, perhaps."

"How did we ever get on this?" Moon said. Then, more
loudly, "I think you're all wet on this charity thing, though.
Hardly a week goes by but what there isn't a charity appeal for
some sort of funds in our own church." Watching Galvin, he
saw there was no reaction in the man. A placidity or even
serenity Moon had never associated with Galvin was newly
there.

"Giving money to other people or to the Church constitutes
about one per cent of what the Church originally meant by
charity," Galvin said. "It's only a minor, obvious, and personally gratifying manifestation of charity. It's some indication
of how we've perverted the Church's teaching, that we think of
charity solely in terms of almsgiving."

"What else is it?" Moon said.

Galvin almost smiled. "The Brothers at Manhattan would
be disappointed in you, Moon."

There were voices and the sound of feet crowding near the
kitchen door, and Moon, turning to rise, heard Galvin say:
"Essentially it's love, but when you start talking about that
it's confusing, because the radio and the pamphlet priests and
two or three other things have managed to convince us that
love is a dirty word, so—"

The noise came from the aunts standing aside and insisting
that James Kavanagh and Kate precede them into the kitchen.

Moon felt doubly lightened as he rose, for Kav he still felt to be his friend and also he was escaping Galvin or Galvin's words.

The newcomers greeted Galvin with surprising warmth. The assurance in Kav, Moon knew, came from Kav's having succeeded McGuffey at the union, but the warmth toward Galvin he could not account for. Kate sat in Moon's chair at the table and Kav drew Moon off into a corner. The aunts returned to their stoves.

"What do they tell you?" Kav said.

Moon felt the hate begin to shake in him again and knew then that for an amazing moment he had been free of it. "I wish to Christ you hadn't brought it up," he said.

"That's all right with me," Kav said. "Forget it. Let's go outside and talk to the politicians." His face remained unmoved.

"No," Moon said. "You want to know, I'll tell you. Only it's not for anyone else."

Kav looked at him.

"The ballistics men made a formal report today," Moon said. "He got killed by a .32."

"The ballistics men are full of cold tea," Kav said. "The cops all carry .38 specials and that guy they killed had a .45."

"He got killed with a .32." Moon's face pulled down in the effort to achieve and hold quietness. There was a moment of silence or hesitation, perhaps consciously willed, before Moon went on. In it, he knew more of himself than ever before in his life: how the fear and hesitation of the first two days after his father's death had been related to the baseless hatred for McGinnis, had themselves, indeed, been hatred . . . and how, with the news today, they had ceased to appear as anything but what they truly were; and he could see how some function of his being, the very perversion of prudence, had directed the rage toward McGinnis's clumsiness instead of its real object.

For he had heard about the early findings of the ballistics men and had himself looked at the listing of the guns police officials carried. He went on: "And there's only one man in the whole department enough of a pisswillie to carry a .32."

"Who?"

Moon looked at his friend almost defiantly. "Young Calahan. Peter Calahan."

Kav wilted. "Holy Christ!"

Even now Moon took pleasure in the effect of his own spoken words on another. "How do you like it?"

Broken, Kav turned toward the wall, as if in pain. Then catching himself quickly, he turned back to Moon. "Are you sure? I mean was he there? After all, he's just a kind of honorary—"

"Some say yes, some say they don't know or say no," Moon said. He caught at his breath once more. "The story apparently is that the guy they killed had two guns and one of them, a .32, got lost in the fire. They're going to have the ashes searched."

After a moment, Kav said, "Probably find one, too."

"I wouldn't be surprised." Moon moved to put a hand against the wall and accidentally knocked over a large, round floral piece. As he bent to pick it up, he read the gilt letters of the chiffon scroll: 431st Assembly District Democratic Club.

As Moon straightened, Kav said, "Why couldn't the boy reporter do something about it?"

"Oh, sure." Moon laughed at himself, and Kav grew embarrassed. "No one wants him or anyone else putting it in the paper. But I will say he's been all right. Twice now, he's sat up with me."

Galvin and Kate came over to where they stood and Kate, seeing her lover's emotion, grew troubled. The aunts had gone out again with more sandwiches and now Mary came into the room. The black dress accented the pale face with its freckles;

[195]

she became happy at the sight of Galvin; coming over to him, she gave him both her hands, then thinking better of it, leaned and kissed him, swiftly and intensely. Moon scuffed his feet and made the gestures of embarrassment but found he was not embarrassed.

"I'm glad you were able to get some sleep," Kate said.

"Oh, I'm all right," Mary said. "I hear you two have set a date."

"She couldn't do it fast enough," Kav said, "the minute she knew I had a few dollars in my pocket."

"Exactly," Kate said, looking at Mary. "I mean a girl can't afford to take any chances today when she comes across a man with a job."

One of McGinnis's men tapped Moon's shoulder. Stout, florid, bursting from a morning suit, the messenger looked like someone from the other side of the looking glass, and Moon found that he was amused by the man's appearance. "What goes?"

"Sure, Moon, your mother wants you."

"Right away," Moon said. Without turning or speaking to the others, he went out through the dining room, attended by the messenger. In the living room, his mother, very tired, in neat black, was at the line again. Agnes, the teacher aunt, attended her and, viewing blandly the casket, while smoking a cigarette, was Moon's cousin, seventeen-year-old Mickey Devlin from the Bronx.

Agnes came to meet Moon. "Now, Aloysius," she said, "your mother thinks you'd better go down to the vestibule again so that the friends won't have to wait. It's getting to be time for them."

"I was just on my way," Moon said. "Do you think you could get that Mickey Devlin away from his cigarette before I kick his teeth in?"

"Now, you go along, Aloysius," Agnes said, "and I will tend

to Mickey. I don't know what sort of upbringing that child has gotten."

Passing his mother Moon touched her arm with his hand, but neither of them spoke. He went down the single flight of stairs as quickly as he could so that no one would stop him or say more than hello. Although it was not seven o'clock, the line already went down the stone stoop and onto the sidewalk. As it moved, the people swayed slightly and Moon was uneasily reminded of the bread line at the Worker. And there flashed in mind with great vividness the figure of the black saint, so that Moon was moved to pray for the saint's intercession for his father or perhaps even for himself. He never knew . . . for he could not bring himself to pray for that saint's intercession.

He had been none too early. Hardly five minutes after he had taken his station, Billy Ryan and Leora arrived, and Moon stepped from the shadow of the vestibule to greet them. There were no condolences now as both had been to the house once already since the death. "How you feeling, Moon?" Billy asked. There seemed no change in the man, Moon noticed with relief. But Leora, like all children and the simple, could not dissemble so well as her elders. There was change in Leora, Moon reflected as he followed them up the stairs; but just what the change was or the exact meaning of it, he did not know. Striving for exactitudes, he could say only that Leora no longer seemed quite so anxious to please him as for the past two years she had invariably been.

Moon followed them into the parlor and stood by while Billy talked to his mother. He tried to talk to Leora but she seemed anxious to get to the kitchen where she had learned Mary was. Gradually, the crowd began to watch Billy until finally only a single crone knelt mumbling over the casket. Ordinarily, having escorted a politico up the stairs, Moon, after a suitable interval of five minutes or so, would return to the vestibule. But Billy seemed working up to something and Moon waited and was rewarded. Leora had disappeared toward the kitchen and the line continued to move slowly through the door into the perfume and the light. Less slowly now it passed out through the other hall door. Billy's voice rose: "And I want to go on the record now, Mrs. Gaffney, as saying that the commissioner's passing will make no difference to Billy Ryan so far as the Gaffney family goes. The Gaffneys will not only be my friends but one of my great concerns. And young Moon here is still *my* candidate for assemblyman." There was a murmur in the crowded parlor and one damned fool started to clap.

"That's very nice of you to feel that way, Billy," Mrs. Gaffney said. "You've always been a good friend to us." She gave the assemblyman a limp hand; taking it, he leaned back so that the porcine profile showed clear (as for the photographers crouched at the edge of the platform). Moon, the sudden rush of jubilation in him, turned to the hallway. It wasn't until he was halfway down the stairs that regret and shame came to him. His pace slowed, the flashes of insight which he had come to fear rather than welcome renewed their peculiar and spastic progression: in the chemistry of the emotions he found the hate had disappeared. And where the fine rage at the Calahans, at all politicians, at the many and induced silences? Where, indeed, he asked himself; where, you bastard?

Came now Judge Cloney of the Court of Appeals, Mr. and Mrs. George Hennessey of Brooklyn, Neal Hartigan—away downtown for him, Moon thought, but was grateful—Congressman Kelly and, of course, a delegation from the local K. of C., armed with rosary beads. All of these, Moon dutifully squired above. Came, too, Assemblyman Levy and Magistrate Mahoney, together; and, after a pause, a whole delegation from the Italian-American Democratic Club. Came messengers with still more flowers and friends bearing bottles. The line stretched now as far as the corner.

McGinnis's men had managed to turn the tide above in spite of the Ryan oratory, and a stream of mourners, less steady than the incoming ones, moved out past Moon in the vestibule. Quiet, smelling of whisky or tobacco, they went past him in the dimness and most of them didn't see him. He came to feel an affection for them, faceless, chastened as they were by his father's death. There were gaps in the departing line, its people seemed to move more in groups than those arriving, and it was in one of these gaps that a cursing figure bounded down the stairs and hurled itself into the vestibule. Moon put out a partly restraining, partly guarding hand and the figure turned to him a face full of hatred, that of his cousin, Mickey Devlin.

"What's the matter with you?" Moon said.

The boy was almost incoherent. "What the hell kind of a joint you running here?" he gasped. "Whole goddam place full of kikes."

Moon held him by the sleeves of his coat and looked down at him. He himself had no feeling at all, Moon thought, yet immediately knew there was a feeling and it was fear. "Get the hell out of here," Moon said. "You're nothing but a punk kid."

"Goddam Jew-lover," Mickey said. He whirled from Moon and ran down the steps.

That was a hell of a thing to happen at his father's wake, Moon told himself. He wondered if his cousin had done anything upstairs that would hurt anyone's feelings.

The arrival of the McGuffeys distracted him. McGuffey was sardonic or somber to an extent Moon did not remember, and he was sure was not due to the commissioner's death. Marie seemed to have mellowed. She hung on her husband's arm and somehow, Moon was relieved to find, her attraction for

[199]

himself had passed. "Would you mind going on up without me?" he said to them. "I have to stay here and wait for Father Malone to come for the prayers."

"You mean we'll have to listen to him tonight?" McGuffey said.

"Only the Rosary," Moon said.

Marie preceded her husband toward the stairs and Moon spontaneously leaned and plucked McGuffey's coat. "What you doing these days?"

McGuffey widened his eyes owlishly and winked one of them. "Got my first receivership. I'll be rich one of these days if I kiss enough judges' asses."

There was no need for McGuffey to talk like that, Moon thought, especially tonight. He resumed his vigil, wondering if the Calahans would show up. If they did, he didn't know what he would do. This was a rare condition for him, he knew, unable to know what his words or actions would be in a given situation. At times today he had wanted to kill Peter Calahan, but now he found himself only wondering—as from a professional standpoint—who might have been sent to take the word to Peter's father and exactly what the messenger might have said. Ironically, he thought in something like panic, he himself would probably have been the messenger if it had been someone else's father who had been killed. He remembered other, similar occasions when he had been the messenger, so that eventually he thought of what it was he had brought to Him that day and the clumsiness of Father O'Driscoll. But clumsy wasn't the word. He, Moon thought, would not be here tonight; He was still in Bermuda. Father O'Driscoll had been here the previous night when Moon had been out for a walk with Kav and his girl; and that had been just as well, Moon knew.

At last Father Malone arrived, accompanied by, of all people, Bernie Brosnan, the labor leader. Bernie was not well known to Moon except by reputation, but Moon felt more pleased than not, and when he accompanied them upstairs, this time decided to remain awhile.

The line on the stairs had stopped moving, for that part of it which had reached the top was confined to the hall by the glut of the good and the great who had wedged themselves into the parlor, the adjoining bedroom and the hall. Space was made somehow for Moon and his two companions and the stale and quiet greetings fluttered again in the room like leaves. At the moment Father Malone was the only priest present, and a little free circle was made for him, so that he rather than the corpse became the center of the room. He was a man about sixty years old, heavy-boned, stocky, with blunt, regular features and a bald head. At the moment he was neither sorrowful nor smiling, as befitted a man who existed beyond such trivialities as life and death; like some minor king, he held court for judge and bricklayer and took the gathering as his due.

Frantically McGinnis fought his way through the pack to whisper in the priest's ear would he please start the rosary now so they could begin to do something about moving the people. Majestically and with a vague reluctance, the priest nodded and reaching into his pocket drew out a rosary. There followed a dry rattle of beads all over the room and futile attempts to kneel. Fingers poised on the tiny crucifixes for the Creed to begin, breaths were gathered in throats, suitable expressions of piety contrived or brought forth. But the time was not yet: this priest was not one to let pass lightly such an opportunity. In the heavily breathed silence, in the odor of lilies, he girded himself one more time to attack his ancient enemy. "It is not my purpose," he began, with the light, deliberate shadow of a brogue, "to deliver a eulogy for our departed friend. There is a separate time and place for such things and the time is not yet nor is this the place. I came here tonight to do a very simple thing, an humble thing, to lead Patrick Gaffney's friends in a last rosary, a devotion of which he himself was very fond. Nor had I any idea that there would be quite such a gathering, although as we all know the departed had no enemies. Yet even as I began to say the rosary, the thought occurred to me that this was not an opportunity to be missed, that Patrick Gaffney himself would not have wanted such a gathering of the great and intelligent to pass without having addressed to it a few words upon the fearful menace of our times, a menace Patrick Gaffney himself often attacked like the true militant Catholic he was. I refer, of course, to atheistic Communism, that hideous blot, that furious enemy of Our Faith." He paused, as so often for applause, but quickly remembering where he was, went on in the fruity silence. "There is little need for me to detail again the immoral and aggressive features of this enemy of Holy Mother the Church. Even the degraded and pinkish secular press has not been able to conceal all of them from your eyes. My purpose in this brief talk is to let you know that Communism's enemies not only exist but are themselves militant, not only in Europe where the great Mussolini has cast down the gauntlet, but in this very country. . . . Not only have we fine, militant individuals like Bernie Brosnan here beside me now, fresh from a victory over Communism at the polls—a peaceful, gentle victory, I might add—but there are other Catholics only waiting the word to attack Communism and its Jewish janizaries with their own weapons, if need be. Bear this in mind, bear it in mind, all of you, so that when approached at the proper moment there need be neither ignorance or hesitation on your part. Now, a blessing I wish you all in the Name of the Father and of the Son and of the Holy Ghost, amen, and we will begin the Five Sorrowful Mysteries for the repose of the soul of Patrick Gaffney."

His eyes closed, as with the others he made the responses,

Moon tried to understand the nature and the sources of his unrest, whether Father Malone's words themselves were the cause or whether the words had merely stirred again the feelings of the past three days. He didn't like Father talking in quite that way at a wake, but after all a priest must certainly know what he was doing; still, he could have been a little more careful with Jews present. Moon found that he had begun to sweat. Opening his eyes, he could see, glimpsed only, the faces of Schneider and of Linford Thomas. Like Galvin, Moon thought, they must have come up in the line of ordinary people.

The clear voice of the priest was loud in that place, each pause setting off the dull turbulence of hundreds of other voices. Their susurrations reached down the stairs and into the street, the sluggish pullings of the tide in an icebound river. The voice ceased, the answering voices died away in a last Gloria, and finally the ice broke and the river began again to flow. Slowly space began to appear between the banked flowers, and for anyone interested, Patrick Gaffney's waxen face and newly prominent nose could be seen.

Talking or trying to talk to the Hennesseys, Mrs. Gaffney at last fainted. Moon, Galvin, and McGinnis's men carried her upstairs to the darkened, unoccupied part of their home, and after she had revived and was resting in her bed, Moon came down again into the light. Only some dozens of people remained and the line had thinned until it hardly deserved a name. Mary alone could handle it, Moon decided, and went back to the kitchen. Schneider and Thomas were there, as Moon had thought they might be. McGuffey, for whom he was more specifically looking, was not in sight. But the aunts were there, and Fire Chief Kelly, a friend of the commissioner's. It appeared that the fire in the wood stove had gone out and that none of them had been able to make a new one.

[ 203 ]

They appealed to Moon as he came in, but he said it was years since he had made a fire in that stove.

"You ought to be able to make a fire, Chief," Moon said.

"My business," said Chief Kelly, "is not making fires, but putting them out."

"A true specialist, you see," Thomas said.

"Exactly," Chief Kelly said. He seemed very content, leaning back against the wall in his blue uniform, and Moon, remembering the chief was a bachelor, wondered if Kelly could possibly be interested in one of his aunts.

"Well," Schneider said, "Padre Malone doesn't let any little chance go by, does he?"

"He had damned little to do," the chief agreed, "spouting like that at a wake."

"I disagree," said Aunt Agnes. "Where else would he have such an opportunity?"

"Where else, indeed," Schneider said. Moon saw that he had been drinking.

"The least he might have done," Thomas said, "was to have had some consideration for the Jews present."

"Oh, that," said Aunt Martha; "those here were good Jews. I know most of them, myself. They knew he wasn't talking about them. You don't think people like Magistrate Kahaner and Assemblyman Levy are Communists, do you?"

"There is, of course, no answer to that one," Schneider said.

"Exactly," said Aunt Agnes.

"Oh, don't be so smart," Moon said to Schneider. His undertone carried to most of the others, but no one seemed to have heard it; there was only a fresh unrest in the aunts: they knew of Schneider and classed him with Galvin or perhaps, because of the name, lower.

Chief Kelly said, "What's this talk about a great victory for Bernie Brosnan? The only thing I ever knew Brosnan to win a victory over was a pint of whisky."

The aunts, as though a team, busied themselves indignantly at the stoves. "No," Thomas said. "He won a victory over us, my union."

Aunt Martha gave a little scream and turned, a minute horror on her face. "Oh, God save us, who would ever have thought we'd have Communists at poor Patrick's wake!"

Schneider mumbled to himself and Thomas colored. Moon found he himself was ineffectual: he wished Thomas hadn't come here.

"Be at peace," Thomas said. "I'm not a Communist. There are a few in my union, but I am not one."

"Then where were your rosary beads during the prayers?" Aunt Martha said.

"She's got you there," Schneider said. "No novenas, no nothing."

"I'm sorry," Thomas said. "I followed the rosary on my fingers."

"It may be," Aunt Martha said, turning again to the stove. "But as my father always said, the one sure sign of a Catholic is whether or not he carries his rosary on him."

Moon began to want a drink. It was the first time in three days he had wanted one and it reminded him that somewhere in the welter of trivialities and misunderstandings the hate had indeed been lost. At least, his private and intense hatred had: there remained, he saw with a clarity new to him, other and vaguer hatreds, diluted oftentimes beyond recognition, which flowed in these rooms as lymph in the body. He pictured his father as seen under and through that clear ichor, yet beyond its poisons, its incredible misunderstandings. It gave him a relative and disturbing joy, and in that joy he lost the thread of thought which might have taken him to that place or entrance, fathom-deep indeed, where even he, crossing, would have to ask hate's reasons or again, as with the others, turn away.

[205]

Chief Kelly was saying, "What you need, Martha, is a husband. Then you wouldn't need to be worrying about affairs of state."

"Heaven forbid!" Martha said with a little yelp. "What a thing to be talking about at a wake."

Across the current of chatter between his aunts and the chief, Moon asked the others if they wanted a drink and when they said yes, he made it the excuse for getting them out of the room. They passed through the dining room and the bedroom-sitting room. Both were still comfortably filled with people, many of whom spoke to Moon, who had begun to feel faintly embarrassed by his companions. He started to pass through the parlor, his eye taking in any newcomers there, when he saw Rosemary and Whitey talking to his sister; perversely the old—he had for a time truly lost it—feeling for Rosemary returned. Like his aunt he felt it was not the time for such emotions and accordingly made a limping attempt to go through the room without noticing Rosemary and Whitey. But Rosemary saw him.

It was the first time she and Whitey had been there, although Commissioner Danaher and his wife had come the previous day and would again appear at the funeral tomorrow morning. "Old Moon," Rosemary said, after the usual condolences, "you've certainly had your troubles." Safe under the circumstances, she patted Moon's cheek and softly drew her gloved hand across it.

Moon felt his skin warm. "I guess we all got to go through it," he said. "You know Lin Thomas?"

Rosemary did not know Thomas, but Whitey had known him at school. Rosemary glanced away, as though to gather courage, and stung by the respect the men seemed to have for Thomas, she said: "Weren't you in jail or something recently? I mean—"

"Why, yes," Thomas said. He, too, colored, and Moon had

the feeling that such an indication in Thomas was less appropriate than in other people. "Only overnight. They moved me there from the hospital when they saw I was all right."

"Why bring that up, Rosemary?" Schneider said.

Why, indeed? Her eyes widened, her mouth opened at such obtuseness. "But I mean it's so unusual. And then to find him here. I mean Marie McGuffey mentioned it at The Sewing. She said the first thing her husband did when he got out of the hospital after falling in the water was to get Mr. Thomas here out of jail. And then Jim went right to the union and told them he was through with them. I mean, it was only out of curiosity and—"

She paused, seeing she had managed to make even Whitey uncomfortable. Schneider had found one of the undertaker's folding chairs and seated himself in it, elbows on his spread knees, his face in his hands. As usual in such moments, he thought of Concepción, wondering whether, if he followed her to Europe, he would be "frequenting the occasion of sin." Of course you can always marry the girl, he told himself, and again the thin sweat came: even that much Negro blood, he thought, and felt his twofold shame. He wondered if the sin were diminished by the lack of pleasure in it that one time. And in his manner, he was led to wonder what the jokers who passed as moral theologians would have to say about the women and men practicing birth control who, for one reason or another, were also unable to take pleasure in their intercourse.

He raised his head in a kind of spiritual nausea. Moon was smiling at last and Rosemary very pleased over something. Even Thomas seemed brighter. But then Thomas was never displeased with anyone but Thomas. As Schneider saw his own intellectual growth the fruit of a constant doubt of his own intention, now he saw Thomas's spiritual growth or actual achievement coming from Thomas's constant negation of self. McGuffey, coming with Thomas's bond, had found him pacing a cell full of petty criminals, reading a breviary and no one seeming to mind it. It was perhaps the strangest of all the things he himself had learned, Schneider speculated, that the very good and the very poor and the outcasts could always recognize some part of goodness in a man or woman, but the people like Rosemary just asked her kind of questions or stared at them as at Gideon.

"If you'll wait a minute, I'll have drinks for all of you," Moon told them.

"Moon's anxious for someone to take a drink, so he can have one," Mary said.

"That's a lie," Moon said. "I haven't had a drink in three days."

"A minor miracle," Mary said. "It took his father's death."

"That's unkind, Mary," Thomas said and Moon had the disquieting feeling that Thomas knew the real reason for his abstention. He started to speak sharply to Mary about her intention to marry Galvin, but caught himself. The thought made him look about for Galvin and he saw the man sitting quietly in a corner talking to some of the mourners. Moon turned away from the others and toward the door to get glasses and a bottle, only to confront a stocky figure standing unsurely in the doorway. Its high, stiff collar and handle-bar mustaches were singular enough in this gathering to attract anyone's attention, but Moon they froze to stillness, even before the conscious mind recognized the Italian, Giuseppe Buonaventura. Nor was it the memory of humiliation and rout that day in the chancery that now came to mind to paralyze and dismay Moon; it was simply that the four of them who had been at the chancery that day were now gathered here also. The mind, perhaps because it was dulled with grief, could not achieve meaning although it groped fearfully for it. Pain had united them once or at least hailed them together and now death had again, but only a fool, Moon knew, could see anything in that. Giuseppe misread Moon's face and waited uncertainly in the doorway, and in that moment Moon glanced at the other two, perhaps in their change to read his own. Galvin still talked quietly in the corner and Schneider sat on the folding chair, his face in his hands. Galvin alone seemed to have achieved some measure of tranquillity while Schneider had apparently lost what little his glibness might have wrought him. And about Giuseppe, Moon could not tell, although about his own change there was no doubt. To give it not only name, he thought, but direction. Gasping once, as in pain, he advanced to meet the Italian.

"You' fad'," Giuseppe said. "I very sorry."

"I know," Moon said. "You knew him?"

"Once. Once he talked at-a my club."

"And you remembered," Moon said. "That's very nice. Here, sit down. Maybe you'd like a drink?"

"If you got-a anything," the Italian said.

"Now that's a hell of a thing to say at an Irishman's wake."

"Okay, whatever you say." Giuseppe laughed uncertainly.

"Say," Moon went on, "whatever happened about that moving business?"

Giuseppe glanced at him slyly and shrugged. "What-a you think happen? We all move quick. One good thing, though, I move across the line now and I'm in you district."

"Well, that's fine," Moon said. "You wait here. I'll be right back." He went out the parlor door, walked a few steps down the hall and came back by the bedroom door. That way he could avoid Mary. There was a liquor cabinet in the dining room and he went toward it. Forgetting his reason for moving by way of the hall, he told himself that he was going in circles.

When he got back to the parlor, Galvin and Schneider were with the Italian and the three seemed amused over something, while Mary still managed the few newcomers, and Whitey and

Rosemary had seated themselves with some Gaffney cousins. "What's the joke?" Moon said to the three men.

"Oh, we were just feeling mellow about our old tiff with the chancery," Schneider said. "Kind of an alumni meeting."

"I know you'll all be happy to hear," Galvin said, "that that monsignor has been made a bishop."

"And why not?" Schneider said. "Would you say he had no head for business? That he was not a good organization man? That he was not prudent and farsighted? After all, what more could you ask of a bishop?"

"You've got something there, all right," Galvin said. Nervously he moistened his lips. "I'll tell you, though, what you could expect of a bishop." He paused again. "He would live among the poor instead of the rich. And he would fast—every day. Instead of worrying whether his parishes were big enough to pay the mortgage on their churches, he would be concerned about whether they were small enough for his pastors to know their parishioners. And instead of pietistic shysters to handle the diocesan real estate, he would employ people to move among the poor, feeding and instructing them. If he really wants his people to have more children to know God in Heaven, and not just to have the numerically largest church in his country, he would see to it that there was good maternal care provided for very little and not streamline rest cures at seventeen dollars a day. He would be in manner humble . . . and besides the ring of his office he would wear another and plainer ring to remind him that when he dresses in his purple and when people kneel to kiss his ring and when the unco good leave him with presents, it is not he who is being honored. Every day, every hour he should be reminded of this. Because it is not only others who are in danger but himself. He—"

"What's this talk about bishops?" Thomas said, coming up to them.

"You go home, Lin," Schneider said. "You go down to the Worker. This talk'll shock you."

"Oh, sure," Thomas said. "I shock easy."

Whitey Travis, his overcoat on, paused by them. "I'll see you guys in a little while. I'm going out for a minute."

"Aren't you afraid to leave Rosemary here all alone?" Schneider said.

"I guess Rosemary can take care of herself," Whitey said.

Moon poured each of them a shot of rye, the best his father had had in the house, but when he started to pour one for himself, he again decided not to, although he was not sure why; perhaps because he would remember he had been drunk while the commissioner died.

The aunts came in yet another time with coffee and sandwiches, but no one seemed hungry and they retired to the kitchen, defeated. Chief Kelly followed them back. Schneider said, "Galvin's going to write a book. About the Church in the United States. Or rather about the monsignori. Which leads me to ask, is there a difference? Anyhow, Ed, tell them what you're going to call it."

"I've thought better of it," Galvin said. "I only want to write it when I'm angry and I'm not angry any more."

"Anyhow, the title is what was important," Schneider said. *Under the Bingo Banners.* Isn't that a beauty?"

Moon started to laugh and couldn't stop. When he began to attract attention he handed the bottle to Schneider and went into the hall. It was not until Mary followed him into the hall and angrily told him he was a disgrace, that Moon stopped laughing. He had been sitting on the stairs that led to the floor above, and looking up at Mary he saw in the light across her face its weariness, its pity and its concern. Even her anger, always superficial, he knew, could not hide these other things. Rosemary stood with her in the light, but Moon could not know most of the things in Rosemary's face, for indeed

[ 211 ]

what were the realities in his sister were only their shadows in Rosemary. Vanity and a kind of fear were all he could name. And he knew that his love for her—if that was its name—was gone.

"As soon as you can begin to act like a Christian again," Mary said, "you can take Rosemary up to see your mother."

"Take her up yourself," Moon said.

"I would if I dared trust you down here with the people coming in."

"Okay," Moon said. With a hand on the banister he pulled himself to his feet. "Nothing personal intended, Rosemary." He supposed Mary was right and he shouldn't have laughed, at least not as much as he had. Yet following Rosemary upstairs he still could not understand the wildness and duration of his laughter. He felt better, though, and he thought idly of the imitation of Al Smith which he had not given in some months. *My friends, let's take a look at the record.*

"Where is she, Moon?" Rosemary paused on the landing.

"Right here." The door showed a crack of dim light and he pushed it slowly open. In the radiance from a night lamp his mother lay sleeping, exhausted, as her open mouth and limp, covered figure indicated. As much because she was not sightly as for any other reason, Moon closed the door again. "She's dead asleep," he whispered. "And she's had so little sleep in the last few days I'd just as soon not wake her."

"That's right," Rosemary whispered back. Her head nodded, her lips came out to give force and assurance. "Let her sleep."

For a moment they paused in the dimness. Both the light and the voices from below came to them as shadows. And themselves shadowed, the two of them paused and did not know quite what to do. Turning toward the stairs, Rosemary seemed tentative and unsure, and Moon reached and took her arm, turning her. Not only to Moon's surprise but her own, she came up to him silently and surely and he held her very hard and kissed her for what seemed a long time. Then there was the shame again and he loosed his hands and let them drop to her hips, where for an instant they lightly rested.

"Heavens," Rosemary said. "How did that happen?" She turned and started down the stairs, Moon following her. They slowed, then parted, Rosemary because she thought of her lipstick, and Moon for his own reasons. She went along the hall alone on the lower floor while he went into the parlor again after carefully wiping his lips.

Even in the few minutes they had been gone, the rooms had changed people and their patterns. Moon could tell only vaguely what ordinary people had come and gone, but Chief Kelly was going and Giuseppe and three of the cousins had disappeared. Schneider talked earnestly to Mary, who had finally sat down, and Galvin had been cornered by an aunt. Thomas, too, had gone, but to Moon's surprise, Dorothy, the young priest and the Italian girl had appeared. For some reason their presence heartened him. It seemed to him that it was perhaps because he was convinced of their goodness, as of no one else's. Thomas's, too, he thought then, but his mind grew wary here: these people, he felt, moved on his own level, or at least on one whose climate he might in time endure. But Thomas, he knew suddenly and in dismay, walked in places far beyond himself or Schneider.

It was odd, this pairing of himself with Schneider, and he wondered at it. Was it because they both drank, because they both liked girls and suffered in their chastity? Or something else, a common stumbling, perhaps, a reluctant homage to good, a clinging to the edge of the precipice. In his uncertainty Moon was glad to listen to Dorothy, to press a drink upon the young priest.

"There aren't so many here now, are there?" she said.

"My lord," Moon said, "you should have been here an hour ago. They were knocking each other down coming in." And where Assemblyman Ryan now and niece, Leora? Where the good and great? They really had not stayed very long, he thought. "I bet there's been a thousand here today, alone. Let me get you a drink, Father?"

The young priest said he would take a drink. Moon felt more troubled in his presence than when he had been with the same man on Mott Street. For now, seeing his quietness and deep assurance, that other time when the man had wept seemed as though it could never have been. And Galvin, too. Disturbed, Moon turned away to get the bottle.

Whitey Travis came back through the parlor door and Moon brushed hurriedly past him. Returning to the room, he found a late burst of people there and Mary again on her feet. Four election district captains had come in a body and Moon had to tend to them. Kav and Kate Bannon had re-appeared from the kitchen. The lights seemed dimmer, the flower scents heavier and cloying. He would be damned glad when this was over, Moon thought. But he mustered the grin, the heartiness and the bluster for his own reassurance and the captains' delight, telling them the suitably grim story about the Scotch woman who, upon receiving a packet containing her dead husband's ashes, asked where her "drippings" were.

One of the captains, an Italian, was obviously disappointed that, by arriving late, he had missed the big boys.

"I don't know why, but they were mostly here early," Moon said. Finding himself grateful that neither Galvin nor Schneider had heard the captain, he wondered why he him-self accepted the remark with even interior quiet and answered it as calmly as he had. Habit did not seem to be the full answer.

The captains did not stay long. After their departure, Moon found himself quieter than at any time since the death. He found also that he did not want to be with anyone at all, neither relatives nor earnest asses like Galvin and Schneider.

[214]

So he went out in the hallway again and sat on the stairs. Characteristically he wondered whether kissing Rosemary as he had involved anything more serious than disrespect for his father or a betrayal of Whitey. The fact that he could still think this way reminded him again of how far hatred had gone from him and he wondered whether it would return. Neither would the peculiar disturbance the captains had induced depart, and he knew finally that the lack of hatred—here, now, for this—could be a political asset. So that even his charity was perverted. The knowledge shamed him and he sat there dully on the steps, sensing how the half-light shed a proper radiance for his mood—the shames, the dimness, and the confusion.

The parlor's sound changed its note, became vaguely higher and obscurely troubled. There was a fresh stirring, a new and strange anxiety. Moon stood up, knowing it must be someone important arriving late. Then through the doorway he saw them, the Calahans, father and son—and knew not the shock of hate but of dismay: he had been sure they would not come and had abandoned any planning of his action if they should. He decided he would not go out to them: he would go upstairs until they left. Yet he stood there, watching from the doorway. Mary was talking to them and seemed pleased that they were there: Moon wished he had told her what he knew. He had been trying to spare her and their mother . . . but now he wondered if that had been the reason. To get away from the thought he moved out again into the flowers, the confusion, and the light.

Together the Calahans advanced upon him; in each man's eagerness to shake Moon's hand, their actions had the ridiculous similarity of a vaudeville team. Moon, looking at their faces, did not hear their words. The father's was troubled, furtive and the lips seemed to cling to the teeth. Peter looked duller than ever and resentful, although Moon could tell he was stone sober. Moon knew the father felt the injury done, but that Peter not only didn't feel it but couldn't. And finally Moon let himself think of what neither he nor Kav had dared to speak of: how he and his own father had brought the word of Peter's appointment to the Calahans that Sunday afternoon.

"Your father was a great man, Moon," Mr. Calahan said.

"I guess he was, in his way," Moon said.

"It was—it was a pleasure to know him," Peter said. His voice squeaked like a boy's.

You only met him once, Moon thought. "Sit down," he said. "I'll get a drink for you."

"Oh, no," Mr. Calahan said. "It's getting late and you people must certainly want to get some sleep. We'll just pay our respects to the commissioner." With his son he turned and knelt heavily on the double prie-dieu before the casket. From a little distance Moon watched them carefully. He felt that Peter was pretending to be stupider than he was—another refuge. They all had their refuge: drink had been his, as with so many Irish, and Rosemary's her pathetic brightness. Schneider's was similar to Rosemary's, cutting perhaps a little deeper. But what was Kav's and what his own father's? Galvin's new and Thomas's old one were the same. And now that it seemed he might not drink again, what would be his? A few hours ago he would have thought it to be hatred and now watching Peter he waited and even willed hatred to again arise. But there was nothing, only a kind of scorn, so thin it reminded him of some light and bitter aftertaste on his lips.

As gradually one becomes aware of a lamp or picture at the edge of one's vision, though the gaze is elsewhere, so Moon became conscious of Kavanagh's face, pale and severe, watching—and he remembered that of all those he knew well, only Kav had as much knowledge of this thing as himself. And what was Kav thinking, what did Kav expect him to do? Moon

[ 2 1 6 ]

realized how little he knew of his friend, of the man's intensity, and memory went back to that night in Brooklyn when Kav had walked beside the car. And yet not all happening then had been clear until now—so that Moon at last knew with clarity this phenomenon of delay in knowledge, and wondered if always tragedy would be required to bring these things to himself. It was a fearful and a somber thought, and in a kind of spiritual gasp he realized that he was not willing to pay that price. He had never been willing to pay it . . . even when he had not known these things by their right names.

The Calahans rose from the prie-dieu and moved stiffly and unsurely a little distance off. The last of the ordinary people stared at the Calahans in awe and Mary had remained touched and pleased that they had come. The families had not known each other and Mary could not quite understand why the Calahans had come so far downtown, especially when neither of them was or had to be greatly interested in politics.

Kav, Moon noticed, had not moved from his chair since the Calahans had arrived; nor had Kate moved from her love's side. There was something wrong with Kate, all of her more tense than he could remember her being.

The Calahans moved and turned in a kind of slow fretting and Moon found that he was not disposed to go toward them. They began to say good-by to Mary, who urged them to stay. Whether Moon saw it so or whether memory only later made it so, or whether the mood of the room did change and become electric, no one could have said; but for that instant of their turning and departure some force or pulsing filled the place, made hazy all faces but Kavanagh's, white and narrow, as it came up to his full height and moved toward the doorway where already Mr. Calahan had passed through and Peter was about to.

It seemed to Moon that he could have acted, as Kav, his words incoherent, taller and thinner than Peter Calahan,

[ 217 ]

swung viciously, struck the suddenly hunched shoulder, then the lintel as the other man passed into the doorway. Galvin moved to hold Kav, whose face contorted behind his eyeglasses, and finally Moon also moved toward them.

Mary confronted Kavanagh. "Are you crazy, James? Disgracing us like that. What did those people ever do—" Her voice broke.

Now Moon's fear was that Kav might tell her. Touching Kav's arm, he saw that Kate had the other arm. "Let's get some air," Moon said.

Kav stood ashamed in the hallway while they got his overcoat and hat. Moon dressed, too, although in the vestibule he found that he did not want to go further; but he walked with them to the subway. There was, they all discovered, nothing to say. His own feeling toward Kav, Moon found, was one of gratitude, now that the fear had gone. Not knowing what Kav might have said to Kate, Moon felt he could not risk saying anything. "Take care of him," Moon said to Kate at the subway entrance.

"Don't worry," she said, "someone's got to."

Moon watched them disappear down the steps, Kav's head last, not unlike some gawky animal's becoming extinct through lack of adaptability.

Turning, Moon met Schneider hurrying after them. "What got into Kav?"

"Damned if I know," Moon said. "You and the union and your ideas about the proletariat have probably got him so coked up he goes around swinging on the nearest capitalist."

"Oh, sure," the other man said. With Moon he walked silently back to the house, from which a few people still emerged. He wouldn't go up again, though. Moon watched him go off down the shadowed street, shoulders hunched against his invisible enemies. As Kav, Moon remembered descending often into subways, so Schneider he remembered most clearly moving off alone at night down streets of shadow. Each was irreconcilable, yet for the first time Moon felt less disturbed by Schneider than by Kav.

Again—as so many thousands of times—Moon ascended the dim stairway. Violence had cleared their home as it had come to seem nothing else could. There was only Mary, the aunts preparing to go upstairs where they had slept since the death, and one or two last mourners, already departing. Two of McGinnis's men folded and stacked chairs, and moving past them, Moon found he was grateful to McGinnis, whom he saw now as an ally . . . although against what he did not know, perhaps only the night.

In the kitchen Moon made himself a sandwich and ate it, drank some milk, sitting dully at the table. Then, through dimness, silence and the flowers' importunate arms—231st District Democratic Club; Irish-American Marching Club—he returned to the parlor.

He was alone in it, he found, with the body and the vigil lights. In their uncertain radiance he approached his father's casket, realizing he had made nothing resembling a meditation over it nor even prayed much for his father and knowing that tomorrow he could not. It was many years since Moon had wept, and he had come to think of himself, dry-eyed since the death, as also hard of heart. Even now he found himself so. There was nothing new or special to think about his father: an earnest, intelligent, half-educated man, his experience, his bravery and his political connections had advanced him. A good provider. So far as Moon knew, his father had done nothing crooked, although he had been a faithful organization man who would make political speeches at Holy Name breakfasts and never think there was anything amiss. Still, Moon thought, there was nothing so wrong in that, and it wasn't like Father Malone tonight.

He wondered if grief would be delayed as knowledge had

been, and if so would it last always, a source of vague regret, of unreasonable sorrow? Or would it, untimely, emerge to confuse and embarrass him and others on some entirely inappropriate occasion, say, as with Kav tonight? It was, he thought, not the death for which he mourned, but its manner and time. Nor yet only those, but something still to come, the mute evidence of some inadequacy, the vague perversion of a noble thing. Kneeling there in dimness he saw it finally, not the thing itself with its complexities, its incredible frustrations, its blind and confused, confusing yammerings; but the whole made into a symbol, and one he could in no way avoid, whether now in thought or tomorrow morning in reality when he must follow his father into the church while above them both the bingo banners flapped.

So that Moon did weep.

## 12

THE MASS seemed empty to Moon. What it had ever contained for him, he could not have said, but now he felt it meaningless. For two or three weeks after the funeral Moon went to church almost every morning and found that the sight of Father Malone celebrating Mass disturbed him so deeply that he could not give the feeling a name. When he realized that there might be some relation between the emptiness of the Mass for himself and the sight of Father Malone on the altar, he decided to try going to an earlier Mass celebrated by one of the curates. There was a difference; some tension eased; despair lost its edge. In time, and after going to Confession he received Communion.

After that, Moon went once or twice a week to early Mass. Leaving the church one morning, he paused in the vestibule to settle his hat, and looking up encountered Marie McGuffey and Ellen Doarn entering. Marie carried an infant and Moon could guess why she was there.

"It's a long way downtown for you, Ellen?" he said. He was nettled that she had not come to the wake.

"Oh, Ellen knows so much about babies from the hospital," Marie said, "that I thought I'd ask her to come with us this morning for me and the baby to get cleaned."

"Churched, you mean, Marie," Ellen said. She seemed pale, Moon thought, but still pretty.

"It's the same thing,'' Moon said.

"Why don't you come in," Marie said. "It doesn't take long. I remember from the first baby."

"All right, I will," Moon said. There had been a hesitation as he thought probably Father Malone would do the churching.

"I think you're wrong about this cleaning," Ellen said. "I have an idea it's supposed to be a kind of blessing on the mother and newly born child."

"Oh, no," Marie said. "It's to clean you."

"But from what?" Ellen said.

Marie colored. "Why—why, from having the baby. Come on, let's go in."

Moon followed the two young women down the center aisle. The church was almost empty and the first sunlight touched through stained glass the usual androgynous statues. Father Malone was expecting the mother and her baby, for no sooner was Moon settled in a front pew while the two young women knelt by the altar rail, than the priest emerged from the sacristy vested for Mass except for a chasuble and accompanied by an altar boy carrying the aspergillum. A conventional smile illumined the wintry countenance. "Glad to see you coming so prompt," Moon heard him say to Marie. He began to intone Latin and Moon's attention wandered. One of the young curates, whose name Moon could not remember, came across the church's transept and over to him. Touching his shoulder, he whispered, "Glad to see you coming to Mass, Moon." Then when Moon flushed with pleasure: "I suppose these young women are getting cleaned up?" He gave an approving pout and was gone up the aisle, swaggering.

The ceremony was brief and after some debate as to whether the young women should stay for the next Mass, they decided not to as Marie was only a few days out of the hospital. Outside, Moon asked them to have breakfast with him, but Marie said she had to go home and get breakfast for Jim, and Ellen also had to return to her home. Leaving them, Moon quickly forgot the whole incident as he began to wonder about the peculiar attitude of his secretary, Miss Clancy, who lately didn't seem to care to do his work for him.

Ellen found no one home but the nurse and the two youngest children. She came in through the high stoop door, so strong was the pattern of habit in her, although she knew the morning's mail lay in the areaway behind the grilled basement door. Taking off hat and spring coat, she went down to the basement and passed along the hallway. It still held its morning darkness and even in April the morning chill. In the little vestibule between it and the areaway, sunlight had pierced the grilling and lay like water, faintly warm and golden on the stone. Stooping to pick up the mail, Ellen stayed bent for a moment, letting her hands remain in the golden light, feeling the faint warmth on them as the beginning of a fulfillment, the promise that Lent would soon be over and the spring begun.

Returning to the kitchen along the hallway she felt self-conscious and a little foolish at the small indulgence; she could think of no one she knew who would have done it. In a way, she thought, it was the measure of her lack of consolation, of the need for some kind of support. In the kitchen, bright with white paint and electric light, she looked at the mail. There was nothing for her except the bimonthly newsletter Mount Murphy sent its alumnae. Although Ellen usually found it dull, she sat down to read it now while the coffee heated. The older children had gone to school and her mother had followed her father downtown to a sale.

This issue of the *Mount Murphy Alumnae Bulletin* was like all the others. The usual genteel and unenthusiastic appeal for funds for a new gymnasium, the successes and failures of the basketball team, the date of the next alumnae meeting, and a few news items about alumnae who had become buyers for department stores or "clothes consultants" or junior executives of a radio chain. Even so, there was a lesser sterility than that emerging from the ordinary secular girls' college, for those Mount Murphy girls who married had a few more children. These vital statistics were duly recorded on the last page of the bulletin along with occasional deaths. This last page was usually one of the first Ellen looked at, for most of her classmates were getting married and no issue went by without a record of some of them. She had even thought until a week or so ago of how her own name would look there.

There was one death in this issue, recorded as In Your Charity You Are Asked to Pray for the Repose of the Souls of the Following Alumnae Departed:

Monica (Brady) Laverty, 193—

Memory dropped back in a slow loop. Its elliptical course was clear to Ellen but not the reason for it. Coldness, a certain fear, shapeless and without name, came to her. And although she actually tried not to, she could not help but wonder if Monica had died having her third child: and the story of Father O'Driscoll's famous advice, which she had never wanted to believe although she knew it to be true. Tears of anger formed in her eyes, but because anger was rare in her she mistook them for evidence of grief. And yet she had not known Monica well. So that gradually she knew what her emotion was and like the carefully trained young Catholic woman that she was, she began a process of rationalization designed to clear Father O'Driscoll of any blame. After all Monica would have died having her third child no matter when, and besides Ellen wasn't sure that it was that which had caused Monica's death. And certainly by that time Monica and her husband should have known how inaccurate Father O'Driscoll's advice was. The process went on in Ellen, repetitively, while she busied herself with some sewing. She twice pricked her finger and stained the child's nightgown she was making. It was no good, she knew, nothing she thought about it was any good: always there were the years Monica might have had if her pregnancies had been delayed, always the two children motherless. Ellen was aware of the providence of God, but now the knowledge of it seemed to lack power, and the wantonness of Father O'Driscoll alone seemed to hold it.

In a sense and perversely, the thought gave her a feeble consolation for breaking her own engagement: at least the time of her own childbearing would be delayed. This she knew to be a curious thought for her, as even before her puberty she had wanted intensely to have children. She even knew from her work at the clinic that she was beautifully and safely made for having them as Monica had not been. And that, she decided, was why she had broken her engagement to Peter, because she had not wanted to have children by him. It was a relief to know definitely her reasons for the compulsion that had led her to tell Peter she could not marry him. It was nothing she could freely talk about with Father Rhatigan.

He was coming here to see her this morning, summoned from his Jersey stronghold, Ellen knew, by the Calahans to see if he could persuade her to change her mind. She had felt both flattered and disturbed when he had telephoned, but had no course but to agree to see him. She supposed she could tell him it was because Peter drank, but then all the young men drank, though not like Peter. And besides that any number of people, including Peter and Father Rhatigan himself, had told her that marriage would solve Peter's drinking. It was not clear to Ellen just how this would be accomplished, but she knew it would be brought up if she gave Peter's drinking as her reason.

It was odd, she thought, that she had no dislike for Peter although he had gone into a rage when she had told him. It seemed she had known of his pettiness and lack of control, but had ignored them until his rage had brought them to memory. And it was strange how that rage could go along with his control of himself otherwise, for he had never attempted passes at her as had one or two other boys. Peter had told her it was no more than he could have expected of her, for he knew about her kissing Schneider in the hospital. Idly, she wondered who had told him; probably Rosemary, in some fashion.

She had not been asked to Patricia's gathering the following Sunday, nor to the cocktail party at the O'Reillys' last Sunday. She wondered if they could be trying to indicate displeasure. She remembered Rosemary's true horror when she had first told her the news. "But my God, Ellen," Rosemary had said, "that's like throwing a million dollars in the gutter. I mean, Peter is such a fine person, too."

If she hadn't been able to explain to Rosemary, how could she explain to Father Rhatigan? It would have been better not to have agreed to see him this morning. Noticing again the small blood stains on the white cloth, she told herself she must wash them before they dried. At the white sink, with the warm water running between her fingers, she came closest to understanding: she feared childbirth undertaken for Peter. Monica Brady's death had only reminded her of it. Yet she had never

[ 225 ]

thought of herself as fearing it. But that was before she had had any idea who her children's father might be. Was the fear then something to be ignored, defied, or assimilated in or by a transcending love? Why had she been so sure her love would be so? There was no one she could imagine loving that way. Her marriage to Peter would have been another of those marriages of convenience all their friends made, and Peter's money alone would have made theirs an enviable one. But if that were so, why her cold distaste or even revulsion for Patricia and Burke Riley's? Was it because Burke at college had always said he would marry a rich girl? She supposed it was his coldness about it. Then she thought of Burke rather frighteningly as a small, blond and ingratiating reptile whom no one dared ever quite defy. Already, she heard, he had furiously denied Peter had ever been engaged to her. . . .

It was ten-thirty and Ellen decided she had better go upstairs and see how she looked, perhaps put on an afternoon dress. When the bell rang she told the nurse she would answer it. There were two figures outside the door; seeing them through the curtain Ellen found herself hoping it was not Father Rhatigan. But it was and with him was his good friend, Father O'Driscoll.

Smiling, beaming, merry, the two priests followed Ellen into the living room. They had taken off their hats and coats but Father O'Driscoll retained his white scarf about his neck, perhaps against the cold, like a stole.

"Well, Ellen," Father Rhatigan said, "this is a fine, comfortable house."

"Yes," Ellen said. "We've been in it since I was a child."

"There is nothing like a house that has been lived in by a family and its children," Father Rhatigan went on.

"Indeed, yes," Father O'Driscoll said.

"We've always been happy here," Ellen said. "I'm sorry mother's not here to meet you."

[ 226 ]

"Sure and I've met your mother," said Father O'Driscoll, with an expression of great sagacity on his face. "Down at St. Linus's. And didn't you use to go there yourself for The Sewing?"

"Yes," Ellen said, "and—"

"And sure why haven't you been there lately?" said he.

"I work in the maternity clinic downstairs at St. Linus's."

"Oh, I see, I see," said Father O'Driscoll, who didn't see at all. The girl must be even more of a fool than he thought she was, down there handling Ginny babies when she could be up at The Sewing with nice, clean bandages. And God knows what she might be catching from the Ginnies. Maybe young Calahan was lucky to be rid of her.

But Father Rhatigan nodded judiciously. Having a bigger stake to lose than his confrere, he guarded thought as well as word. "That is a good work, Ellen. I didn't know you were in it."

"Well, it's more interesting, and—" She caught herself, felt the faint color rise and knew they must have seen it.

"And it gives you some knowledge for future use with your own children," Father Rhatigan finished for her.

"Yes," Ellen said. "It was so good to see the sun today, wasn't it?"

"It was," said Father O'Driscoll. He was anxious to begin the attack, but allowed himself to be diverted. "Let me tell you, this was a bitter winter for me. I had but two weeks in Miami, what with one thing and another calling me back here."

"That was a shame," Ellen said.

"I wish I had had as much," Father Rhatigan said. "If anyone thinks northern New Jersey is a comfortable place to spend the winter."

They laughed at that and after a moment of silence, Father

[227]

Rhatigan said, "Well, Ellen, you know why we're here, of course."

She leaned back stiffly in the overstuffed chair and smiled, but before she could speak, Father O'Driscoll said, "Leaving our parishes and all. It must give you some notion, Ellen, of how important we consider this entire business."

"It isn't as if it were a couple of ordinary people," Father Rhatigan said. "After all, it is not every day that a girl like yourself decides she will not marry the son of a Knight of St. Gregory." He had meant to save that for later.

"I'm sorry it seems to have upset so many people," Ellen said. "I had no idea it would be made such an issue. I mean, I thought it was something between Peter and myself. At least, mostly."

"Ah, that's where you are mistaken," Father O'Driscoll said. "That's where you are mistaken, my dear young woman. The marriage of a Calahan is an important thing to Holy Mother the Church. Who a Calahan is to marry is important to her. Just as the cardinals and archbishops are princes of the Church, so are the Knights of St. Gregory, just what their name implies, knights of the Church. Ellen, I have wondered if you fully know what you are doing when you take this step? I mean, I wonder if you realize everything that is involved?"

"Why, I don't know. Apparently not." She hesitated. "But I mean marriage is such a personal thing, at least it is for the principals, that one might overlook its effects on others. That isn't very well put, but—"

"I think the thing that bothers Mr. and Mrs. Calahan," Father Rhatigan said, "the thing that bothers them the most, at least the most after Peter losing such a fine girl as yourself, is your lack of any definite reason for breaking the engagement." The priest spoke in the measured tones of a reasonable person. "And I must say that I share their bewilderment."

"I suppose what I wanted was time," Ellen said. "And I

[228]

wouldn't be truthful if I didn't say that Peter's drinking had something to do with it."

"Ah, that," said Father O'Driscoll. "What are a few drinks? Do you know any young man who doesn't drink?"

"I can't say that I do," Ellen said. "But Peter has been drunk too often for it not to be disturbing to me."

She was surprised to have silenced them, even by her frankness.

"I think, Ellen," Father Rhatigan said slowly, "that there are certain things carefully brought up girls like yourself are not aware of. I would confidently predict," he went on even more slowly, "that Peter's drinking would be considerably lessened after his marriage."

While they waited for an answer, Ellen found she was heartened. "And if it isn't?" she heard herself say.

The violence of their reactions startled her. Father Rhatigan opened his mouth to speak, but only a sort of gasp came from it, while he ran a finger inside his collar as for relief. Father O'Driscoll's face contorted but in no way that conveyed meaning. "My dear young woman," he burst forth, pointing a finger at her, "I think you miss the point and miss it most badly. Most distressingly, I might say. The main point is that you have broken a promise, one might almost say a sacred promise. A promise to marry Peter Calahan, and you have given no really valid reason for it." He took his finger down, but continued to stare at Ellen.

"I hardly thought of it as a sacred promise," Ellen said after a pause. "I didn't know the Church had any particularly well-defined ideas on engagements. I thought it was just a period, of trial, one that could be ended by either party without any moral harm done."

Father O'Driscoll shook his head sorrowfully. "Very specious reasoning, indeed, Ellen. Very specious. The good nuns at Mount Murphy would be disappointed in you."

[229]

"I would say doubly disappointed," Father Rhatigan said. "After all, think how overjoyed they would feel at a girl from the Mount marrying a Calahan, a son of a Knight of St. Gregory. Think of the publicity for their school! And as for myself," he said, "my disappointment would be greater than theirs. For whereas you are no longer actively associated with their school, you would be a member of our parish in Oakmoors. As I told you, my hope is to gather there a select group of young Catholic married couples who would be a kind of colony, something exemplary to the godless people of the country club set. And I had further hoped that with you and Peter coming out there to live, others would be attracted, with the two of you as a center or nucleus for the group. I mean young couples like Patricia Moore and Burke Riley. Perhaps even your friend, Rosemary, and her fiancé, who I understand is already taking instructions to enter the Church." He paused for breath.

"You don't say," said Father O'Driscoll. That was one he had missed, all right; and it would have been so easy for him to have had young Travis as a convert, with him a member of the athletic club.

The sun came into the room and lay in geometrical shapes on the patterned rug. Ellen looked at it in relief, but could think of nothing to say. There was an amazing temptation to tell them she would marry Peter and so be free of them. In the silence she heard the children crying upstairs and wondered if the nurse were with them. "I really don't know what to say," she said. "You both make the whole thing seem so much more important than I thought it."

"Ellen," said Father O'Driscoll, "let me ask you to do just one thing. Reconsider. Don't give us your answer now. Just tell us that you will reconsider, so that we can bear such word to Mr. and Mrs. Calahan. You have no idea how stricken they have been by the happening. In their way as much as poor Peter."

Poor Peter, she thought; poor, indeed. Her lower lip was between her teeth. That was it, all right, she just didn't want Peter as the children's father. Yet who else and she was twenty-four? She shook her head, not so much in negation as in an attempt to be rid of her tormentors.

"And Ellen, mercenary as it may sound," Father Rhatigan said, "it is not every young woman who can marry in the assurance that in time she will help to administer many hundred thousands of dollars."

"I've thought of that," she said. "I suppose it's one of the things that has made it all as confused as it is. Even when I thought I loved Peter, I couldn't help at times doubting my own intention."

Rubbish and poppycock, Father O'Driscoll thought. He said, "Everything you say, Ellen, is beside the point. But as you have also said, you've been confused, so the best thing is to take more time."

When Ellen made no reply, Father Rhatigan said, "Time is not of the essence in this matter, Ellen. I don't think either of us expected you to change your mind while we were here. But I do wish you would tell us you will reconsider."

"If I did, it would be only a kind of delay. A kind of dishonesty, even. I don't think I could ever marry Peter."

Neither priest spoke for a moment. Father O'Driscoll indicated controlled or concealed anger, and Father Rhatigan a concealed amusement or perhaps even scorn.

"Tilting at windmills," Father O'Driscoll said. "My dear young woman, perhaps it is just as well if you do not marry if you think taking a few drinks is an insuperable barrier in a husband."

"Perhaps you're right," she said. She was dismayed to find her rare anger stirring again and she wished the priests would go.

"I'll tell you what I'll do, Ellen," Father Rhatigan said. He

[ 231 ]

paused to lean forward, his elbows on his knees. His face had a faint, too eager smile on it as if patronizing some earnest, sensitive but dull child. "I will have a talk with Peter about his drinking. Now, in return, will you allow us to take word to Mr. and Mrs. Calahan that you will reconsider?"

She likened it to a nightmare. There was the unreality: the light shed upon the scene emanated from or perhaps was their incredible insistence. There were qualities in it, too, which though not escaping her, she could not name. The light was water and in it she gasped once for air.

Apparently they took it for some sort of assent, for their faces relaxed, grew cheerful again. She had said, "All right," for relief, she remembered, and now, in regret, did not know what to do. For it was a lie: she could never marry Peter.

They shook her hand at the inner door of the vestibule; warm, cheerful and ruddy they took their leave. Peter, too, would be delighted, they told her.

*Peter, too,* she thought, closing the door slowly upon them. She supposed that was part of it, also, but how to tell anyone, let alone the priests, that in marrying Peter she felt she would be marrying all his relatives. It was not a valid explanation to anyone that she knew; what was valid was the money, and of course one naturally put up with anything to get at that. There was that perversion again: the Church, seeking order and the fulfillment of the word of God, had bade them in charity endure one another, and in time they could and did endure anything, but almost always for the wrong reasons.

Ellen went up to the room she shared with the next to the youngest child and lay down exhausted on the bed. While the nurse prepared lunch, Ellen tried to sleep. A sense of guilt, entirely unreasonable, permeated her: after all, just what was she looking for? Everyone drank and marrying someone like Moon Gaffney or even Bart Schneider would be the same as marrying Peter, but with less security. If there was someone she could talk it over with, someone disinterested or at least unimpressed by the Calahan money. Ellen had no specific confessor. At Mount Murphy she had felt more free to speak face to face with certain of the nuns than to Father O'Driscoll behind the screen of the confessional. Mother Thomas More was still there, although no longer president, and Ellen decided she would go to see her. And go today if she could, before Peter joyously called her on the phone.

The nun received Ellen in one of the smaller parlors of the school's main building. Like all the institution it was neatly furnished, with just a hint of richness in rug and curtains. Ellen kissed the nun's wrinkled cheek. Coming up the graveled walk she had felt assurance returning, and now in the little parlor it seemed that she was strong again. As an undergraduate there, she had often felt restrained, but now some of the conventual freedom, of ease within boundaries manifested itself in her.

They talked, over tea, about teachers who had come and gone, about girls contemporary with Ellen, and twice Ellen caught herself in time to keep from mentioning Monica Brady's name. The early spring twilight came on them unaware but it was not until the nun's face was shadowed by her coif and wimple, so that only the lips and the tip of the nose showed, that Ellen was moved to speak of why she had come.

"I've broken my engagement, you know," she said.

"No, I hadn't heard," the nun said. Her mouth, moving evenly, showed, and now one of the lines that bracketed the lips. Her tone did not change.

"It's mainly why I wanted to see you today," Ellen said. "I suppose I should be ashamed of myself, waiting until a personal crisis before paying a visit."

"I don't know. It's more flattering than not."

[233]

"You see, I broke my engagement to Peter Calahan and now everyone seems so upset about it."

"That you feel guilty?"

Ellen laughed nervously. "I suppose that's it."

"It's one of the unpleasant things about engagements," the nun said. "Especially where a family like the Calahans is concerned. Friends and relatives or their sense of values are variously outraged, and so much tension and pressure is generated that the principals often do things they regret. If you don't want to marry the man, you don't want to marry him, and that's an end to it."

"It's such a relief to have you not ask me why."

"I don't think a stated reason is necessary or even good," the nun said. "It seems to me the unstated or rather the unstatable ones are the more valid. Words don't get in their way. If you don't want to marry someone now, the chances are you won't want to live with him the rest of your life."

Ease and relief flowed over Ellen like water. She laughed. In the sudden happiness she forgot about the Calahans and their allies waiting her answer in New York. She raised the cup to her lips; the tea had become cold and the change reminded her of them in the city waiting. "I suppose I knew that," she said, "but was afraid to state it or couldn't clearly." She paused. "They sent two priests to the house this morning to talk to me."

"They had little to do," the nun said.

"One of them was Father O'Driscoll."

"I wouldn't doubt it," the nun said. "We had him here for a while and since then he's been chaplain of an athletic club, a professional addresser of communion breakfasts and I don't know what else. I wonder he ever gets around to saying Mass."

"He seemed pretty impatient with me this morning," Ellen said. "And it was rather puzzling. Father Rhatigan is the pastor in Oakmoors where Mr. and Mrs. Calahan have their country place. I could understand his interest. But Father O'Driscoll seemed more upset about it than I thought he should have been and even talked about how disappointing it would be to the nuns here."

"How disappointing what would be?"

"Breaking my engagement. At least, breaking my engagement to a son of a Knight of St. Gregory, as Father put it."

"Heavens!" the nun said. "That man. Most of the Knights of St. Gregory I know are that only because of their money and with some of them it's money gotten in pretty unspeakable ways."

"He thought you'd be disappointed because the publicity would help the school."

After a moment the nun said, "We have too many girls come here for the wrong reasons as it is. Too many of them coming to all our colleges for the wrong reasons." She gave a sigh. "I think we even teach sometimes for the wrong reasons. I know there are the Benedictines and the Jesuits that have been teaching orders for a long time and are in general qualified for it. But there are too many communities that decide to teach simply as the most likely or the easiest or the most genteel way of supporting themselves—and that simply aren't qualified. I just don't see the point in having too many overstaffed Catholic colleges when Catholic hospitals and missions are so shorthanded."

"I know that down at St. Linus's Hospital, there aren't enough nuns to go around," Ellen said. "I've been going there once or twice a week as a nurse's aid and there just aren't enough."

"That's where they have the new maternity pavilion with rooms at seventeen dollars a day," the nun said.

"Isn't it silly?" Ellen said.

"Silly and terrible," the nun said.

"And they seem to resent so people's coming in. I'd hate to

have to go there with a miscarriage. They have a policy apparently of treating all miscarriages as though they were induced."

"Yes," the nun said wearily. "It's to be sure not to let any guilty ones escape their feeling of guilt."

"I suppose the sullenness and the abuse is bad enough," Ellen said, "but they delay operating an awfully long time. One girl came in about two weeks ago with her husband. She had had two children and had started to bleed with her third pregnancy. They let her lie there for one solid week, still bleeding before they'd do anything. Then I was there in the room that morning and heard Dr. O'Doulihan say to his assistant, 'Well, there's a definite odor now, I guess we can operate.' "

"Mother of God!" the nun said. "The filthy butcher."

"So they did and found there was nothing left but the placenta. She'd lost the fetus heaven knows when, but the placenta was enough to give a positive result with the Asheim-Zondick test and she went to all that trouble trying to save nothing."

"I wonder she didn't infect, with the delay."

"She came out of it all right, but they say her husband called Dr. O'Doulihan some awful names."

"I wouldn't blame her husband," the nun said. Regretting her frankness, she changed the subject. "But this thing about our schools—it's a kind of vicious circle. A community starts to teach to support itself, not because it wants to teach or is qualified to do so, and it begins to build after a while and acquires a debt. And the publicity department or the football team or the swimming pools keep bringing more students who need more buildings, which make more debt. Why, we can't even give people that want an education a reasonably priced one. It costs a girl's family twelve to fifteen hundred dollars to send her here for a year. And about all we offer more than the more reasonably priced Catholic schools is a laboratory."

"But, that's a necessity in these times."

"I suppose it is," the nun said, "but you couldn't prove it by the girls who have taken a B.S. here. The only one that actually uses her training works in the laboratory of a cosmetic factory."

It was dark now and the nun's triangular shape leaned to switch on a lamp. In its radiance her eyes showed, half-closed in the tired face. The change startled Ellen, and the nun, recollecting herself, pulled the mouth straight again, opened fully her eyes.

To save the nun embarrassment, Ellen thought to humble herself, and said: "I suppose having told you about the hospital, you'll think it had something to do with breaking my engagement."

"I hadn't thought of it," the nun said. "I suppose it could have. You would know, I think, since you're aware of the possibility."

"It's bad to not know," Ellen said. "I've been telling people I broke the engagement because of Peter's drinking, but actually it's something else. I just don't want to have children by him."

The nun didn't speak for a moment. "Not have children, or not have them by him?"

"Oh, I know about that," Ellen said. "Not have them by him. It sounds silly, I know—"

"The best reason in the world," the nun said. "A woman's reason though it be." She paused. "I suppose it's a man's world. Even our girls are trying to think like men when they haven't got the equipment to do so. I'm full of clichés tonight."

"You've been a great help to me," Ellen said.

"I don't see how."

"In definitely making up my mind."

"I thought you'd already done that."

"I did, too. Then this morning they made me say I'd recon-sider."

"Oh, for Heaven's sake. Well, what *are* you going to do, Ellen?"

"I'm not going to marry Peter."

"Good. But you will get married sometime?"

"I suppose so. I can't imagine to whom though. So I suppose it'll be a year or two."

"But not another interminable Irish engagement, I hope?"

Ellen laughed. "They do last forever, don't they. I wonder why?"

"I really don't know," the nun said. "For the wrong reason, though, that's the only thing one can be sure about. . . ."

Something struck Ellen like a wind: here was the last place to encounter despair. And she thought of Mary Gaffney's fiancé, Ed Galvin, and of Bart Schneider. In the silence the supper bell sounded and there were girls' voices in the hall, the rustle of serge, the distant closing of doors. "Well," the nun said, "we've missed vespers. Stay for supper. We'll have you taken to the station."

In spite of the somber closing note of their meeting, Ellen felt more heartened than at any time in weeks; it almost seemed as though here alone she was sure of herself. Returning to the city on the local, she tried to account for the feeling. Nostalgia and Mother Thomas's easy approval of what she had done could not account for its depth. She wondered if it could be the incidental knowledge of the nun's humanity: her verging on despair. As undergraduates they had never thought of nuns as subject to their own frailties. She supposed it might be a defense, unconsciously raised in Mother Thomas, as was— Well, as was what? Her own mildness, all their various accept-ances? Patricia's acceptance of Burke Riley's pragmatism and worse, herself of Peter's drinking, or Mary Gaffney of Ed Galvin's radicalism? She was disturbed to find that Mary's relation to Galvin seemed least artificial of all. Conform, conform—the word tolled in all of them like a wooden bell. And the letter of the law had blown over them, a freezing wind.

The train stopped and she saw alongside her the station platform at Grand Central. In thin yellow light the dirty concrete lay, a miniature desert, a symbol she felt of her own life, of virtually all the lives she knew. Not accustomed to thinking in such terms, she grew alarmed and supposed the cause lay in the nun's words. But that was only the catalytic, the immediate cause; actually she had known these things a long time. Trying to know for how long, she could not determine the beginning of them in her. Nor their ending. She grew frightened and wondered about her life—and so wondering was moved to concede that Galvin's alone of all the men she knew seemed to possess meaning. And she wondered why she was so uneasy about the loan business that Burke Riley, and now Peter, was in. Why did all of them, even Patricia, deliberately avoid talking about it?

The heresy still in her, a disease that stimulated and enlightened while it destroyed, she came up into the light of the station and walked across it toward the Vanderbilt Avenue stairs. Someone was calling her name in the many noises of the place, but the first time she did not turn, thinking it one more manifestation of her mood. She heard it again—"Ellen"—and now turned. A figure ran toward her, topcoat flapping ridiculously, and it took her a moment to recognize Schneider's face, sardonic and grateful. "Remember me?" He gasped as he came up to her. "I, too, was once affluent, wealthy, cultured. Then—"

"Don't be a fool, Bart."

"Ah," he said, "if only I could refrain from being one. Imagine finding you here alone."

"Alone with two or three thousand others."

[239]

"Oh, you know what I mean." He took her elbow and walked with her. "Are you departing or returning? Or merely passing by?"

"Call it passing by." Waiting for the old unease he had always brought to her, she was puzzled it did not come.

"Hurrying to your love?"

"Well, no." It struck her as funny.

"Then perhaps I could at last get you to sit down and have a drink with me?"

"Perhaps you could," she said. "I'd like to call my home first, though."

"As a precaution?" He turned her and led her back to the phone booths across the station. Through the booth's door she saw him waiting with, for him, curious patience. He had lit a pipe and was walking back and forth, the ridiculous top-coat still flapping. She wondered why his tension, his harassed air, real or fake, no longer made her uneasy and thought perhaps now if she did not altogether share it with him, at least it resembled her own state.

She asked her mother if she were needed at home and was told she wasn't. Also, her mother told her, Mrs. Calahan had phoned twice and Peter once. They both wanted Ellen to call when she could. Hanging up, Ellen started to leave the booth, then thought it might be better to get the Calahan call over with. Dismay quickened in her when Peter answered. "Oh, dear girl," Peter said. "I knew you'd call. Father Rhatigan has told us the news. I do hope you'll be able to come right down and talk with Mother and the rest of us. I'll come over for you."

"I'm not home, Peter," she said. "And it won't be necessary to call for me. I'm sorry about Father Rhatigan telling you, because I really haven't changed my mind. I—"

"You mean—" Peter's voice rose—"that you still want the engagement broken?"

"Yes. There's—"

"Oh, you bitch," Peter said. "You—"

Ellen hung up. She found her breathing had to be done as by a conscious effort. Leaving the booth, she wondered if she were a bitch. She had never been called one before. And then she wondered if it were Peter's change that had affected her, that anyone could change so abruptly.

"Hey," Schneider said, "what's happened to you?"

She shook her head without speaking; then took his arm and walked again toward the stairs. "Where do you want to go?" he said.

"I don't know. Maybe just walk."

"If we go downtown we'll run into Moon or Jim Kavanagh."

"I wouldn't mind that."

"I would," he said. "Don't want to let you get away from me."

"Oh, come, come. I thought you had a girl in Europe?"

"I have them all over," he said. "One for every mood."

"I see. And which am I for?"

"I've been thinking about that. I think you're for my noble but frustrated one."

"Is that so? You make me feel like a statue."

"Oh, you're no statue. Although sometimes I think you'd like to be."

"I don't catch," she said.

"You'd like to be on a pedestal and so forth."

"No," she said slowly. "I think you're wrong. Anyhow, I've just been called a bitch."

The violent reaction she had expected from him did not occur. After a moment he said, "By whom?"

"Peter Calahan."

"That lush. Jim Kavanagh took a swing at him a couple weeks ago."

"I didn't know. I wonder why?"

[241]

"I don't know. Just general principles, I guess."

They were out in the air and paused. "Where do you want to go?"

"It's still Lent," Ellen said. "Maybe I'd better go home."

"You don't like to drink well enough for abstaining from it to be a penance. And besides you need a drink."

"You think of just everything, don't you?" she said. "But I still think I'd better go home."

"All right. So I'll take you home."

"If you like. Maybe my father will give you a drink."

He started to say something as he helped her into a cab, but cut it off. "I have a reputation as a lush, too, apparently," he said, sitting next to her.

"Oh, not quite."

"Thanks for them kind words."

They rode in silence for a few blocks and then Schneider put his arm across her shoulders.

"Just like in the movies," Ellen said.

"Uh-huh. Here, look this way." His fingers tilted her chin, but when he bent to kiss her, she ducked away. "Just like that statue. A very agile one, though."

"Oh, all right," she said. He kissed her a long time with tight lips. He had not been drinking. When he raised his lips, she put her head on his shoulder.

"You're very nice, Ellen."

"I suppose I need someone to tell me that."

"Oh, I always rise to such occasions." His voice changed, some dark, sneering note came into it.

"I see," she said. "I'm just an occasion for your charity."

"Well, no," he said. Neither spoke as the lights flicked across their faces. He turned to her and put a hand inside her coat, cupping it firmly over one breast. Surprisingly, she thought only of how devious the others had been attempting the same thing.

[242]

"I wish you wouldn't," she said.

"Do you still think it's charity?"

She shook her head. "No . . . but I still wish you wouldn't."

"Because like all well-brought-up Catholic girls, you think it's dirty?"

She shook her head again. "No. Not any more. At least, I don't know if I ever did. Let's say it's good but not for us."

He laughed once and took his hand away. "You're a fine girl, Ellen."

The cab stopped in front of her home. As they went up the brownstone stoop, she said, "Maybe I should warn you. There'll be brothers and sisters all over the place."

"Oh, it's Lent," he said. "I'll offer my frustration or my deprivation or whatever it is, as a penance."

"I see. Now I am merely an instrument of your penance."

"What else?" he said. "What else are all of us?"

The light from the opening door fell full upon them and the two of them passed through it as into a new country.

13

THERE WERE CHANGES but it was two or three weeks after the death before Moon began to notice them, and longer before he gave them meaning. Grief continued to cloud some perceptions and sharpen others. There was, to everyone's surprise, even Mrs. Gaffney's, not much of an estate. The flat they lived in, five thousand dollars of K. of C. insurance, the departmental pension and a surprisingly small amount of cash. Safe deposit boxes were common enough among the politicos to be a joke, but when Moon opened his father's there were in it only some papers and five hundred dollars in old, large bills. Yet in his disappointment there was a masked, faint stir of pride.

It was decided to stay on in the flat, and Moon found that unconsciously years ago he had determined not to marry. Now he found his justification: with death he must care for his mother. It gave him satisfaction, marred only by the knowledge that actually she needed no financial support from him; a woman of simple tastes, she had more than enough from the pension, living in the rent-free house.

So with one thing and another it was weeks before Moon began to notice the changes. There were little pressures, like the note from the chief clerk asking Moon to account for certain days spent outside the office. There was the change in greetings, in facial expressions at the club, a technique of avoidance—Moon thought of it as such—practiced by Billy Ryan and one or two others. And finally the deviously traveled but authentic rumor that Moon was not going to get the nomination for assemblyman. It was, Moon knew, hardly a matter he could discuss with just any district captain, the more so since this early in the year theoretically no such choice had been made; and no one but himself perhaps, Moon realized, could have taken Ryan very seriously the last night of the wake. But too many smaller things had occurred along with the rumor. Still, he went the remainder of Lent without doing anything about it, until he noticed he was no longer used on the small, confidential missions. For the first two or three weeks after the death, reason enough could be found for this, but now, during Holy Week, Moon knew there was no longer an excuse. Reluctantly and for his mind's ease he decided to call Ryan. It took him several days to decide to do this, for he had found he could ask advice of no one, not even Kavanagh, and he thought the reason might be pride. On Holy Thursday he called Ryan and found him as brisk as ever on the phone but with a lack of enthusiasm. He could see Moon at the club the following afternoon.

"What's the matter with seeing you at the house tonight?"

"For one thing," Ryan said, "I'm busy, and for another I don't see why you can't come to the club to see me the same as anyone else."

So then Moon knew how it was, but the next day, even while he stood through three hours at a strange church, he still was unable to find reasons for what had apparently happened. Although he reproached himself for not paying attention to the priest's explanation of the Seven Last Words, and even thought of leaving the church because of his lack of attention, he did not leave. When the three hours were over and he was on his way downtown to the club, his personal concern, the subdued anger could not quite do away with the feeling of guilt. He wondered why Billy had picked Good Friday for their meeting and supposed it just happened to be the next day, the first opportunity Billy really had to meet him. In a way this was a heartening thought.

There was no one in sight at the club but the caretaker, a sad and emaciated alcoholic named Joey Scanlon. His feverishly blue eyes looked at Moon with a mixture of hope and concern, in which charity or its shadow was delicately balanced.

"Who's here, Joey?"

"Sure, no one but the boss, Moon. He's in the back."

"No one with him?"

"Not yet. I think he expects two or three of the boys."

Moon walked back over the uncarpeted floor, noticing, not so much the plainness of the rooms as their institutional quality, the cane-seated chairs, the posters and banners on the wall, the heavy curtains. At the end of the hall, next the toilet, was the office where once his father had sat until he no longer wanted to be district leader. Billy Ryan sat there now behind the large flat desk, its top bare. His elbows rested on the wood and his round face had a freshly lit cigar stuck in it. "You're early," he said.

"Didn't know we'd set a time," Moon said. Deliberately, he took off his overcoat and laid it on a chair, then pulled another chair up to the desk across from Billy and sat down. Moon wondered at the outward calm he seemed so suddenly to possess and he saw that Billy wondered, too. The contrast between the eager and ingratiating youngster Moon had been, with the gift of gab and a powerful father, and the Moon here, wary and quiet, was something even Billy couldn't miss.

"What's on your mind?" he said.

"Not too much," Moon said. "There's a story going around that I'm not getting the nomination this fall."

Billy puffed his cigar two or three times before answering. His small eyes moved to the window, the door, back to Moon, a move for each puff. "What made you ever think you were going to get it?"

"A little bird told me," Moon said. "A little bird named Billy Ryan. Remember?"

"I don't remember nothing."

"Look," Moon said. "I don't want the nomination. See? I don't want it. All I want to know is why the sudden change? That's all. Why the sudden change? Couldn't be the commissioner's death had anything to do with it?"

Billy took the cigar out of his mouth, blinked half a dozen times, then lowering his head a little, looked earnestly at Moon. "You surprise me, Moon Gaffney. Thinking like that, that your father's death could make any difference to Billy Ryan. Why, the commissioner was like a relative to me, like a father. And when I had to make up my mind about you, it broke my heart. See?" Here Billy placed one hand over his heart. "What's happened so far as you're concerned would have happened no matter what. The plain truth is that you are a pretty irresponsible feller."

"How do you figure that one out?"

Heartened, Billy pounded his fist on the desk. "In fact, you are a goddam clumsy fool."

"All right, all right. Get to the point. You were going to tell me why."

"You and your goddam Communist friends," Billy said. "Embarrassing me, embarrassing the organization, embarrassing the Church."

"If you don't mind me saying so," Moon said, "you're full of bullshit. I have no Communist friends. And as for embarrassing the Church, you just don't know what you're talking about."

"So I don't know what I'm talking about? So I don't know what I'm talking about? That's it, eh?" He leaned forward. "Let me tell you, Moon Gaffney, I know everything. See, everything? Right back to the day you lied to me and took your Communist friends into the chancery. And used *my* name to do it. You think I don't know. I know everything, Moon Gaffney, everything." Intoxicated by his position, he slapped both hands down on the desk and looked at Moon with small, bright eyes.

"That," Moon said quietly, "was something for which no one could be blamed. When I phoned you about that, I had no idea it was anything for anyone to get excited about. And none of the men who came with me were Communists."

"Then why did they act like Communists? Going after Monsignor Claffey like he was just anybody instead of a holy priest!"

"To tell you the truth," Moon said, "I wouldn't say the monsignor acted like one that day."

"Oh, you wouldn't? And with Communists coming right into his office, at his throat as it were, who would blame him? Who would blame him if he had taken out a pistol and shot them?"

"Communists, my ass."

[247]

"And what else is this Edward Galvin? This filthy turncoat of an Irishman!"

"He's a better Catholic than you or I," Moon said. "Furthermore, he's going to marry my sister."

"I wouldn't doubt it," Billy said. "Not for a minute. Why couldn't she marry some fine, clean young Irish lad from the district?"

"That's none of my business and less of yours."

"And you," Billy said. "Leading my niece, Leora, on, and then not doing anything about it. Why—"

"That is a damned lie," Moon said. He had flushed red. "Leora had no reason to think my intention was serious. Why, I never even kissed Leora."

Now Billy colored. "I didn't ask for details. I'm just telling you of an impression gathered by more than one person."

"Sure, by two persons," Moon said. "You've got funny ideas. I've taken maybe twenty girls to dances, but none of them except Leora thought I was going to marry her."

Billy nodded in complete knowledge. "You're as slippery as they come. But even that I wouldn't mind. It's your damned clumsiness along with all the rest."

"I told you the business at the chancery couldn't be helped. And—"

"What about your bringing this Father O'Driscoll onto the boat that day to see Him? I suppose you don't think that made trouble?"

"Now, let's get this straight," Moon said. "I brought no one on any boat to see Him. I drove my car onto the dock purposely to avoid meeting anyone. And it wasn't until I was on the boat that I ran into Father O'Driscoll."

"Anyway, that's your story," Billy said. "Father O'Driscoll's is that he was on the dock to see some friends off and he met you and you urged him to come and say good-by to the big boy."

Moon shook his head. "That's not so."

"I suppose you want us to think Father O'Driscoll is a liar?"

Moon shrugged. "Someone's a liar. Not necessarily Father O'Driscoll."

"Maybe you mean me?"

"I don't know who I mean," Moon said. "I know where I met Father O'Driscoll and I know I couldn't get rid of him."

"That's a fine way to talk about a priest," Billy said.

"I've heard you call him a flannel-mouth yourself."

"You are a goddamned liar, Moon Gaffney." Some change in the assemblyman's eye and tone made Moon turn his head. It seemed to him that he had known what he would see, the Lenihan brothers, Eddie and Pat. They greeted Moon sheepishly and Billy not at all. For the first time fear mixed with Moon's anger. Horse-faced, raw-boned and tall, the brothers had been for years the club's bouncers. Moon turned back to Billy. "I thought this talk was going to be private?"

"It was," Billy said. "And now it's finished." After a moment he added, "Like you," and for the first time a smile creased the round face.

"So I see," Moon said. For a moment the fear dominated the anger. "And what are people going to say, the people who heard you shoot your mouth off at the commissioner's wake?"

"When they know the facts," Billy said, "they'll understand. I said I would take care of the Gaffney family if need should arise, but that doesn't include putting you into office. Don't think for a moment that Father Malone doesn't know of your activities."

"My mother doesn't need any help from you," Moon said. "She could buy and sell you three times, you punk."

"So now you're getting abusive," Billy said. "And you know how Eddie and Pat here dispose of abusive people in this gentlemen's club."

[249]

"I'd like to see them or you do something like that," Moon said. The fear was still there, but it wasn't strong enough to stop. him.

"Oh, you would?" Billy said. "Boys, put this young jackass out of here."

Moon whirled rising to meet them, but only Eddie moved at him. His fists half-raised, Moon saw Eddie hesitate; then all of them looked at Pat, who had not moved. "Come on, Patsy," Eddie said, rather plaintively. Pat's face had clouded and the lips were drawn tight over the horse teeth. They could hardly hear what he said. "I will not lay a hand on any of the commissioner's people," he said in a thick brogue. In wonder, Moon saw the man was ashamed of himself, ashamed not to obey Billy.

"You dirty, yellow bastard, Patsy!" Billy screamed. On his feet now, his hands remained on the desk. "I'll have you broke!"

Pat's face contorted horribly. "Even so," he said.

Moon had dropped his hands and now turned back to Billy. "Don't worry. I'll go. Only I want you to know where I'm going—right to Father Malone's to call your bluff."

"My bluff!" Spit flew from Billy's mouth in a fine spray. "My bluff, you call it? Why, it was Father Malone that first knew how the Commies were taking advantage of your thickness."

"About that we'll see," Moon said. Deliberately, he put on his topcoat—the hat he had not removed since coming into the room—turning his back on Billy. As he left the room the Lenihans stood one to either side of the door and each of them looked down.

In the cool, wet air, Moon shook his head. Only now, it seemed, did he know the depth of his confusion. In the moment before some clarity returned to him, he saw his confusion as related to and even part of a larger one, a babel-like vision strange in his mind, of many faces calling, some known, some never before seen, and over and through and among them and superimposed on them, figures of crosses and wheels and platforms, beams and giant strings of rosary beads. "I am going nuts," he thought. But the confused images vanished and he was himself again, striding westward toward the water front. The anger seemed to go, too, as he walked, and he wondered at the new feeling of relief, as if he had been freed of a burden. But when he tried to think what the burden had been, he could not.

The brick rectory stood next to the church. Both looked deserted in the gray light; only the bingo banners moved in the wind and now Moon hardly noticed them. The center door of the church yawned dark and Moon wondered if he should first go in and make a "visit." He found that he didn't want to—although he had been to Mass there that morning—and going up the rectory steps he pushed the bell button. Maggie Sullivan, Father Malone's housekeeper, let him in. Bony and frowsy, carefully chosen as such, she was pleasant enough to Moon; he clutched at that pleasantness as drowning he might at a straw. She told him she was sorry about the commissioner and she'd see if Father was in. She pushed a call button twice and Moon could hear the ring above. Sitting in the little reception room, Moon could see through open double doors into Father Malone's office. The phone was on his desk and, with Father upstairs, Moon was reasonably sure Billy had not called while he was walking over. Then there was Father's regular, heavy tread on the stairs and presently the priest appeared, smiling and affable under the bald head. He held out his hand as Moon rose and shook Moon's heartily. "How are things, Moon?" he said. "Sit down. Your mother taking things well?"

"Oh, yes," Moon said. "She's all right now. We wanted to

send her South for a while, but she wouldn't go alone and neither Mary nor I could get off to go with her."

"Understandably," the priest said. "Understandably. A fine woman, your mother."

"Father," Moon said, "I've come here on what I suppose could be called a delicate matter. I've just come from a talk with Billy Ryan and I'm afraid I've broken with him and the organization. But that's not what bothers me so much as a statement he made to the effect that you think I'm a Communist or at least a tool of theirs."

"*I* think you're a Communist?" Father said quietly. "That's a surprising statement to come from Billy. I wonder what made him say that?"

"Then you didn't say it?"

"Why, no. What I did say was that I thought you'd been unwise on one or two occasions, as when you took that group to the chancery office. But—"

"That was a pretty mixed-up affair," Moon said. "I had no idea it would turn out the way it did. What happened was—"

"Oh, I know you didn't do it deliberately, Moon," the priest said, holding up a restraining hand. "It was an impolitic thing to do, that was all, the sort of thing that might embarrass the associates of a young politician. That might give them pause as to his future reliability."

Moon felt the slow flush come to his face. "But there was no chance to explain. When no one mentioned it at the time, I thought it was unimportant. I thought of it that way myself. And now to have it brought up and made an issue of is pretty confusing."

"Oh, I don't think it was entirely that," the priest said levelly. "There's that matter of the new labor union and your sending lawyers to it. A definitely Communist-inspired group."

Moon looked at the floor. "I don't know. I know at least one Catholic who's an official in it and besides, McGuffey, who

[ 252 ]

worked with them, told me that of the union's seven officials only two were Commies. And I didn't even know that at the time."

The priest nodded slowly, deliberately. "But that's the point. You didn't know but you went ahead and barged in. I can hardly blame Billy or the organization for feeling as they do."

"I see what you mean," Moon said. "But it still seems to me I didn't get a hearing. They just went ahead and acted. If I wanted to make an issue of this thing I could go to the Hall. The commissioner being dead won't make any difference there as it seems to in this district."

Almost the priest smiled, a smile with gentleness and pity in it, or at least their mockery. "Not with your sister going to marry Judge Galvin's nephew. Everyone knows what the judge thinks of that nephew. You see, Moon," he went on, his avuncular manner increasing, "there were just too many of those things. No one of them would be sufficient by itself, but the sum total of them was something to give your friends pause."

"I could still go to the Hall and make an issue of it."

"And risk ruining your career completely?"

"It's pretty well ruined as it is," Moon said. "Such as it was." They had him, he knew. He wondered why he had had to come here and sit in this room, before fully knowing his defeat.

There was a moment of silence in which the priest seemed to weigh something. "I don't see why you should be concerned too greatly over your position in the Hall, anyhow," he said. "It will be outmoded soon as an organization of influence."

"You mean this talk about a reform movement? Why, that kind of thing hasn't a prayer in New York."

The priest was shaking his head. "No, that isn't what I mean. I mean something newer, more modern, stronger. It's hardly begun here in Manhattan but in Brooklyn it's not only started but is growing stronger every day."

"I don't catch," Moon said.

Again the priest seemed to calculate his hesitation. "I mean, if you really want to redeem yourself? Not so much with Billy or the organization as with the Church and all true Irishmen. . . . I mean that if you truly do, there is a way."

Moon thought that over. He found that he didn't much give a damn about redeeming himself, if only because he still felt he had done nothing wrong. But he said, "What is it?"

The priest's face grew solemn, what some might have called dedicated. "Join the organization fighting atheistic Communism and its Jewish allies. What are needed now are men like yourself, of executive caliber, young lawyers and businessmen."

"I didn't know there was such an organization," Moon said.

Again the wintry smile, the mockery of compassion. "That shows how far you are from reality, Moon. . . . Supposing I told you it was part of a world-wide organization, one already highly successful in parts of Europe? You know of Mussolini?"

Moon shrugged. "I don't know much about him. He's an awful flannel-mouth, that's all I've ever thought about him."

The priest looked at Moon without expression. "I can't say I have too much sympathy with you in your quarrel with Billy."

"I'm sorry about that," Moon said. He lowered his head, thinking again how he had certainly made a fine mess of things.

"But it shouldn't take any special intelligence," the priest went on, "to see the way the Jews have come to dominate American life."

"I don't know," Moon said. "There's good Jews and bad Jews, the same as with the Irish or the Italians or anyone else.

[254]

The only people I get bothered by are niggers and I don't know why."

"You certainly aren't very careful," Father Malone said, "about the names you associate with the Irish. Niggers and Jews."

Moon looked at the floor. He wondered if he should say it and then heard himself saying it. "To tell the truth, I've had a bellyful of the Irish today and I'm pretty sick of them."

"Then this is no place for you," Father Malone said. "No one can sit in my rectory and malign the greatest race God ever put on earth, His own true chosen people and the great repository of the Holy Catholic Faith on earth. You can go now."

Moon rose and walked toward the hall. For an instant he hesitated at the doorway and considered turning back and making an apology, but didn't; it wasn't clear to him just what he could apologize for.

In the street a paralysis seemed to have overtaken part of him, similar to that sometimes caused by fright. His legs moved, his arms swung, his body leaned in the gestures of walking, but his guts seemed to have frozen tight, his chest and belly pressing on them in some true winter of the spirit. Gray was its color and went into all things. He breathed in deeper gulps and slowly the air restored him. By the time he was able to notice his surroundings it was dark and he found himself near LaGatta's. Since his father's death he had not drunk, but he knew he was going to break that long abstinence. Still, he hesitated in the street, thinking that he should go home to supper, that today was no time to be in a bar. Nor was LaGatta's the place. But none of the boys would be there tonight: of that he could be reasonably sure: he went down the two steps and pushed open the door.

Under the lights the square whiteness of each table showed clear: sterile and exact. There were no diners yet. The Italian

[255]

bartender was behind the bar and two waiters loitered at one end of it. Breadsticks pointed stiffly upward from their glasses, like the stalks of some gross flower from which the blooms had been hacked. The bartender seemed pleased to see Moon, but after taking a step or two toward the bar, Moon thought it would be better to go into the back room, and carried his coat in with him across his arm.

The back room was like most back rooms, bare tables, dark wood walls, the smell of men and cigar butts. A waiter followed Moon in and said they hadn't seen him in a long time. "I know," Moon said. But they would see him tonight, all right, they would see him good. When his highball came, he let it stand while he looked at the bubbles rising in it. Some of them moved in chains. Still he would not touch the drink, and at last decided it was because he did not want to drink alone. Going to the phone booth he called Kav. Kav was reluctant to come over but said he would call Kate and probably be over with her after supper.

"I'm here alone," Moon said. "And I don't want to drink alone."

"I thought you weren't drinking," Kav said..

"I started again today."

"You picked a good day for it, didn't you?" Kav seemed amused, and Moon winced.

"It's been a hell of a day. I'm all washed up."

"Washed up how?"

"With the organization, the Church and everything else."

"You're sure you're not drunk already?"

"I wish I was."

"All right," Kav said. "I'll be there but I can't come now. If you want, I'll try to get hold of Schneider or McGuffey and send one of them over."

"Send someone," Moon said. "I don't want to drink alone." He went back to the table and decided it would be all right to drink alone because someone would be here soon. The flat highball went down like water. Moon told himself McGuffey wouldn't come here; Marie would see to that. He tried to dismiss them from mind, but couldn't. He thought of the last night of the wake, of McGuffey tossing a derby hat around at a dance, and again of McGuffey grave and stricken on the hospital cot. And Moon thought again of Marie's breasts and the way she had come out into the hall that night at her parents' home as if he were a new boy friend. The more Moon tried to rid himself of the McGuffeys, the more vividly they returned in memory; so that some relation of them to his present mood or condition seemed clear, and Moon tried to know what it was; yet while he saw it existed, its nature remained obscure.

He was on his fourth drink when Schneider came in, grave and tired looking. "I hear you've been excommunicated," he said, sitting across from Moon.

"Very funny," Moon said. "Very funny." Schneider was one of the last people he wanted to see. "Who told you that?"

"Why, it's all over the papers."

Moon looked at him. "What did Kav tell you?"

"Apparently what you told him."

"I didn't tell him much of anything," Moon said. Bitterly he remembered how he had been going to have Schneider write his speeches for him . . . even get his advice on social legislation.

"Enough to have him call and send me down here."

Moon looked at the table. "I didn't want to drink alone. Besides, it's no hardship for you to come to a bar."

"You've got something there, all right. What are you drinking? Aren't you going to eat?"

"I hadn't thought about it," Moon said. "And I'm drinking rye."

"Good. I'll drink Scotch."

[257]

"Just to be different?"

"Just because I like it."

They sat there, waiting for Schneider's drink, and not looking at each other. After a while, Moon said, "You're beginning to look respectable. New suit and everything. What's happening?"

"I'm going to Europe for the paper. Got to look the part."

"Being sent to Europe," Moon said scornfully. "I know why you're going to Europe."

"Could be, could be," Schneider said.

"Why don't you marry some respectable girl here?" Moon said. "Instead of chasing that dancer all over Europe?"

"I don't know whether I could get a respectable girl to marry me. Besides, I don't know how much chasing I'll get to do. I expect to be stationed in Lisbon although I'm to report to our Paris office first."

"Say," Moon said, "just how much colored blood has that girl got anyway?"

"Just about as much as weak characters like you and me can stand in our women at this stage of our fine Christian civilization. A sixteenth."

"I guess it's all right so long as you're not going to marry her."

Schneider colored for the first time in Moon's memory. "I don't know," he said. "We could marry and live in Europe or in South America."

"And what about your kids?" Moon said. "You want to bring kids like that into the world?"

"I hadn't thought too much about it," Schneider said. "Anyhow, intellectuals don't have children."

"You mean birth control?" Moon said. "Intellectuals!"

"No, I mean bitching. What the hell's happened to you?"

The sudden shift caught Moon unawares. "They just gave me the boot out of the party."

[258]

Schneider nodded. "What's this you said to Kav about the Church?"

"I got thrown out of the rectory, too."

"To be thrown out of some rectories these days would be an honor."

"Christ, I know," Moon said. "But to have everything happen at once and today of all days."

"What did you think they'd do today—give you a prize?"

"You know, I never figured it like that."

"Maybe I shouldn't have said it," Schneider said. "A man could get to take himself too seriously."

"If you're going to eat, you better eat," Moon said. "I'm not hungry, so don't wait for me."

While Schneider ate, Moon told him about Billy Ryan. He drew it out, finding in himself a reluctance to speak to Schneider about Father Malone. When Kav and Kate Bannon came in, Moon found himself suddenly almost happy. Indeed, he noticed after a while that he was the only one of the four cheerful. He talked, he even presently ate, but did not mention his troubles until Kav asked about them. "I've just told Bart," Moon said. "I don't want to bore him."

"I don't bore easy," Schneider said. "I even get a perverse pleasure in hearing how God's chosen race knifed one of their own in the back."

Moon thought about that for a moment. "That's not quite fair," he said. "In fact, it was a cheap remark."

"Never mind," Kav said. "Get to the point. When you phoned I thought you were going nuts or something."

Moon looked at the table, aware of their eyes on him. "I guess I was in pretty bad shape. After all, they did a terrible job on me." He told Kav about Ryan and when he had finished, Kav said, "Well, what did you expect?"

"Don't give me that," Moon said. "The whole thing was a

[259]

put-up job. Prearranged, as soon as they knew the commissioner was dead."

Kav shook his head. "No, it wasn't. Everything Billy said is true. If you're going to fool around with unions and so on, you're going to have to expect what you got."

"All I wanted to do was get McGuffey a job," Moon said. "And what about yourself?"

"I'm all right," Kav said. "I know I've got to work with all kinds of people. No one's kidding me. My mother doesn't like my working for a union, but she's old-fashioned. Kate likes it and that's what matters."

Moon looked at Kate and half-smiled. "But what about this Father O'Driscoll thing?" he said. "I—"

"Somebody's protecting somebody, that's all," Kav said.

"Sure—O'Driscoll is protecting O'Driscoll." Schneider's voice, clear, bitter and sneering, silenced them.

"You know," Kate said after a moment, "I agree with you. But I think someone ought to tell you you're in danger of becoming an anticlerical."

"And the rest of you are in danger of not becoming anticlerical," he said. "Let the theologians decide which is the graver danger."

His vehemence made them uncomfortable, but he went on. "You could make out a case for St. Bernard being anticlerical or Teresa of Avila when she said that the Vatican stank."

"But you don't really think you have their purity of intention, do you?" Kate said.

Schneider wilted. "You've got something there."

"What about your being thrown out of the Church?" Kav said to Moon.

"Oh, that," Moon said. "That was a slight exaggeration."

"You didn't sound like it was when you phoned."

"I guess I was feeling sorry for myself," Moon said.

"Don't give me that," Kav said. "What happened?"

"Well, I'll tell you." Almost, but not quite, he faked a Jewish dialect. "I went to see Father Malone because Ryan said he hadn't liked some of the things I'd done."

"Who hadn't liked them?" Kav said.

"Father Malone. He wound up giving me a spiel on Communism and the Jews and how the Irish were the greatest race on earth. So I told him that even if I was Irish I'd had a bellyful of them today; and so he threw me out of the rectory." He hadn't expected to make them laugh, certainly not as much as they did.

"I'd like to have seen him," Schneider said.

"And I," Kate said.

"I thought that was a lousy thing he did at the commissioner's wake," Kav said.

Again their silence. Moon looked at the table and wondered why he didn't speak.

"I thought so, too," Kate said quietly.

Well, say it, Moon told himself, but nothing happened. He felt them watching him again.

"I wish to heaven someone had guts enough to report that kind of thing to the chancery office," Kav said.

"And what do you think you'd get for your pains?" Schneider said.

"Oh, the threat of excommunication, probably," Kav said.

"The thing that puzzles me," Kate said, "is how people, priests if you will, can do that sort of thing and still call themselves Christian."

"Now, who's anticlerical?" Schneider said.

"All right, bum," Kav said.

"We had a bewildered young priest from one of the missionary orders," Kate went on, "come into the chancery in Brooklyn. He'd been sent around by his order to collect funds in Brooklyn churches, one parish each Sunday. He went to one out in Flatbush and the pastor threw him out, actually

[ 261 ]

pushed him through the door. You know why? A Jew had written a book about that particular missionary order and this pastor told the young priest that he wanted none of him if a Jew was the best his order could get to write a book about them."

"So what did the chancery say?" Moon asked.

"They told him to say three Hail Marys, turn around twice and run once around the block for a penance," Schneider said.

"Not quite," Kate said. "The bishop will probably do something, but what Father McTiernan said was that he wouldn't mind so much if these men weren't celebrating Mass every day. How can a man celebrate Mass each day and still go around with his heart full of hate?"

No one answered her. Schneider drank and said, "Jansenism, thy name is great. You know, the old Jansenist crucifixes had Christ with his arms stretched up at a forty-five-degree angle instead of straight out because Jansenism taught that He died for only some men instead of all. The beginning of snobbery— or anyhow the beginning of it in the Church."

"What has that got to do with us?" Moon said.

"Everything," Schneider said. "Jansenism hung on in France a long time after Rome condemned it. And when Ireland had to educate its priests in France during the English persecution, the seminarians all got loaded to the eyeballs with Jansenism and brought it back to that fair green land, whence it came over here."

"Then blame the English," Moon said.

"No more. Their responsibility ended so long ago that only God can assess it now. Our concern is with the immediate effects of Jansenism in our time. The way it's bitched up the Church's teaching so that the average Catholic thinks sex is filthy and hates or is suspicious of anyone not a Catholic. Why doesn't the hierarchy do something about it instead of sitting around on their tails and telling each other what a great race the Irish are? I'm half Irish and I hate the way they've bitched up the Church, perverting her doctrines and twisting her teachings and then patting themselves on the back. I hate their insane pride of race and of religion and their incredible fatuousness. But then fatuousness is just another form of pride. And—" He stopped, seeing Kate had begun to weep. "Oh, hell," he said.

"But if you know why they're that way," she said, "why do you hate them? Why do you let their hatred affect you?"

"I don't know," he mumbled, looking down. "That's the way things are. I don't hate the Irish," he said more clearly. "What I hate is a priesthood that lacks both charity and humility and has misled and confused its people until they mistake black for white, hate for love and darkness for light. A priesthood that has substituted chastity for charity and frequently a chastity so warped and misinformed that its ultimate fruits compare with those of lust. St. Bernard said, 'Hell is paved with the bald heads of priests.' Will someone of you tell me what he meant? Or was he full of cold tea, too?"

"I don't know what he meant," Kav said. His long face was turned downward.

"He meant that their responsibility is greater than ours, their temptations more subtle and their judgment by God harsher."

"Why don't you leave the Church and be done with it?" Moon said. He had been drinking glass for glass with Schneider although neither Kav nor Kate had drunk.

"I wish I could," Schneider said. "Did you like what they did to you today, Moon?"

"Naturally, I didn't. But I know enough to realize it wasn't typical of either the Irish or the Church."

"Even when you add a thousand similar instances? Even when you see pictures in the photogravure section of the cannon-blessing bishops in Italy?"

[ 263 ]

"I wouldn't know about any thousand times," Moon said. "And you wouldn't either."

"I know of maybe a hundred," Kate said, "just from the correspondence in the chancery."

"You never see Irish priests over here living with women," Moon said, "like some of those priests in Europe."

"No, nothing so simple as that," Schneider said. "Nothing so direct and pitiful. No, indeed. Here their secret is hate and avidity. Sins of the mind. And the whole New Testament tells us that the sins of the mind are more grievous than the sins of the flesh. Do you actually think it's worse for a priest to break his vow of chastity than for him to stand in his pulpit and preach hatred? Tell me—I'd like to know. And I'd like to know which does greater harm to other·people?"

No one answered, but Kate's tears had stopped.

"It's the confusion that's so terrible," Schneider went on, "and apparently even God won't save us yet. When France went through times like ours, it had great saints come to it, close to the people. It had the Curé d'Ars and Bernadette. But what have we got?—a priest spilling hate into a microphone. That's the kind of saint we get."

"I wish you'd stop," Kav said. "I wish to *Christ* you'd stop, Bart!" He shook his head pathetically.

"All right," Schneider said. "I'll stop. I wish I hadn't started." His voice broke. In the silence none of them looked at another. With one hand James Kavanagh shaded his eyes, while his other held Kate's fingers under the table. But there was nothing for Moon or Schneider to hold.

The record player in the other room began to play a jig. Schneider's face changed. "That's it," he said. "That's the whole thing." He sprang up and began to dance clumsily to the music while the others watched, each in his own horror. Schneider began to chant to the music:

[ 2 6 4 ]

*"Biddy O'Boulihan, Patsy O'Toolihan, Nicky O'Noulihan—
these are their names—"*

"Stop it!" Moon said.

*"Mickey O'Mulihan, Frigid O'Foolihan, Georgie O'Goulihan—
these are their fames—"*

"Goddam you, stop it!" Moon screamed. He rose and when
Schneider kept on, picked up an empty glass and flung it at
him. It missed his head and shattered against the dark wall.
Schneider kept on: *"Larky O'Loulihan, Tricky O'Troolihan—"*
and Moon charged at him.

Schneider turned to meet him, the face bright, even eager
and now lacking hatred, the body crouched for a tackle; so
that the head went under Moon's wildly swinging fist, as
Moon aiming one knee of his charge felt it thud warmly home
against the temple, saw the blood spurt before the shoulder
rising in the clean tackle took Moon's legs away and his head,
driven forward, slammed heavily against the wall. . . .

So that each man fell separately into that same darkness
where God spoke to them with the voice of an Irish Catholic
priest.

### 14

It was no surprise to Moon when he lost his clerk's job,
although he acted as though it were and complained accordingly. He told himself he had expected it, but there remained
the feeling that if so, he should have resigned. He also told
himself it was probably a good thing, as he would be forced
to practice the law, he who had never tried a case, who had
gone to law school in the conscious knowledge that he never
would practice. But he remained disturbed, knew at last that
he was troubled partly because his friends were marrying. Now

that Lent was over, not only Kav and Kate but Mary and Galvin, too, only a few days after the others. Even Rosemary had finally consented to a June date with her Whitey.

Moon was twenty-nine now. Always he had taken unconscious pride and conscious pleasure in knowing that he, so young, had gone as far as he had in politics. Now that failure had come, he saw himself as old beyond his years, of his acquaintances the only one unmarried and unengaged. He was, of course, not the only one unemployed. Never having saved anything, he found himself reduced to asking his mother for spending money. As this pleased her in a way, she never protested until Moon asked for fifty dollars to buy Kate and Kav a wedding gift.

"Aloysius," his mother said, "I can't be giving you money like that. It seems to me you ought to be able to get some kind of law work."

"I've tried," Moon said. "I can't just go and set up an office with no money. And nobody's taking on any young lawyers."

"I should think some of your father's old friends—"

"You saw what some of his old friends have done," Moon said. There was a strong desire to tell her of Peter Calahan; he discovered in quiet horror a desire to hurt her: she had not been sufficiently outraged at what Ryan had done; it was as if she felt Ryan had been justified, if not by circumstance, at least by custom.

"I bet Father Malone could do something for you," she said.

Moon turned away, the words choking him. He had been thinking about Malone lately, nor was it clear why he did not return to the priest. Nor yet attend his Mass. He looked back on their interview in a kind of shame, gradually knowing that this priest did not represent the Church; so that Moon wondered why he had felt exiled and cursed at the time, why he had not known then that the priest spoke in no large or legitimate sense for the Church. He came to know what it was for

[266]

someone like Giuseppe to oppose even an individual cleric, and of how Galvin had become ill doing so. He tried to convince himself he had known these things before seeing the priest on Good Friday, but realized it wasn't so. And he wondered again about his rage with Schneider. His feelings about the fight had never become clear to him; there was only chagrin and a kind of shame, the persistent feeling that no one was right, neither Schneider nor those whom Schneider thought the enemy. And if they were wrong, who was right? It seemed to Moon that the people of the Worker came closest to being Christians, but he knew that was an exaggeration. And he remembered the cop who came in to the Worker, patting his gun. He had been going to have that cop broken, but he had been broken instead. Christ, Moon thought, one Catholic going to kill another. Why had he never thought that before? And then he saw it repeated in many forms, so often he grew frightened: himself and Schneider; Kav and Peter Calahan; McGuffey in the water with Brosnan's men; Galvin and the monsignor. Galvin's sneering words came to him from a time before Galvin's illness: "We call ourselves Catholics—why, we not only don't love other people, we can't even love our own." Moon would have liked to believe such thoughts merely the product of his own ill fortune. But he knew differently, knew these things existed and occurred, in the same way he knew there was air or sun. Yet since they were that obvious, why had it taken him so many years to see them, how was it people like his mother, to say nothing of the Hennesseys, died without knowing they existed?

"Aloysius," his mother said, "I asked you about Father Malone."

"He couldn't do anything," Moon said. His gestures had become quick, almost erratic. "He'd have to go to the Hall and the Hall hasn't got much use for me since Pop died."

"I don't believe that," his mother said. "They're gentlemen and they wouldn't change like that overnight."

"I don't know about that," Moon said.

"If they were not, what would Al Smith be doing with them? Answer me that."

"You know," Moon said, walking back and forth, in the ambience of new and erratic motions of head and arm; "I've begun to wonder about that. Sometimes I think there's a man now and then can be like him in spite of his associates." He supposed he had wanted to be like that himself: carrying pitch and not smeared: remembering with slow shame what he had brought to Him that day on the boat. "Besides," he went on, "you don't think Mary's marrying Ed is going to do us any good at the Hall? If you must know, Judge Galvin has said that if his nephew ever came up in court before him, he'd jail him for as long as the law allows."

When his mother didn't answer, Moon turned and saw she was crying, her head shaking as the tears dropped onto the sewing in her lap. "Aw, don't cry, Mom," Moon said. He went and sat on the arm of the Morris chair and put his arm around her. She kept stitching and he saw it was on a slip for Mary.

"I don't know what's going to happen to any of us," she said. "Everything seems to go wrong since your father's death."

"I wouldn't say that," Moon said. "I wouldn't say that at all. You have money and a house. And I'll stay around so you won't be lonely."

"I know you will, Aloysius. You're a good boy."

She had stopped crying and her stitching, faster now and skillful, held Moon's eye. He stayed close to her, thinking idly that whatever he was, he was not a good boy: neither good nor a boy. And he saw how, until a few weeks ago, he *had* thought of himself as a boy. The boy wonder, the boy assemblyman, the boy politician, the youngest mayor New York ever had. . . . All the dreams had gone and with them the boyishness.

What had taken their place he was not yet sure, but part of it was hate. It had returned. He had thought himself purged of it that last night of the wake, but it had returned, more gradual than lust and as strong. And he felt himself much more helpless before it: all his life he had been taught that lust was wrong, its instrument evil; yet who except fools like Galvin and Thomas had ever thought hate was evil? The Franciscans hadn't taught him so in prep school nor the brothers at his college. So now hate lay in Moon and there was nothing he could do to rid himself of it, nothing he particularly wanted to do. There were whole techniques to rid oneself of lust: play ball, pray all, take walks, swim, get out of bed promptly, don't kiss girls, don't: the brothers had known them all. But how did a man rid himself of hate? Moon didn't know and he took pleasure in thinking Father Malone couldn't tell him. Hate took various forms in his mind, some of them pleasurable: smashing Peter Calahan in the face next time they met, knocking him down and kicking him; kicking also Billy Ryan's fat tail; telling Galvin off in no uncertain terms; telling Kav he would not be his best man; even—although this *was* wrong, Moon knew—going to McGuffey's when McGuffey was away and laying Marie. Telling Rosemary off, she and her society boy. Really going to work on Schneider sometime, when he wasn't drunk and could punch straight.

"Aloysius," his mother said, "I'll give you the money. I know you need it for the wedding. Only do try to get some work. Not that we need the money, but I think it would be good for you."

"Thanks, Mom. I guess you're right." He still sat on the arm of her chair. He had known she would give him the money. He wondered why the hatred for Schneider was less than the hatred for some of the others? Because Schneider, too, hated? Yet what Schneider seemed to hate were ideas, or rather he tried to hate ideas but ended in hating more. Moon supposed

Galvin alone among them could hate ideas only. He wondered if he himself were trying to hate ideas. The Hall was an idea, although what the idea was he could not have clearly said. It was not a very good idea. In hating Billy Ryan and Peter Calahan, could he be trying to hate the idea the Hall stood for? And if so, what about Father O'Driscoll? Here, Moon felt himself on ground trebly dangerous and stood up to break the thought. "I think I'll go for a walk, Mom."

"All right, Aloysius, but be sure to get back for supper."

"Don't worry. I got to go over to Brooklyn later anyhow, for the wedding rehearsal."

So walking Moon came one more time and now at dusk to the place where the black saint stood. Outside the store window he felt more alone than ever in his life. Children ran by him and pushcarts, laden with food and cheap clothing, lined the street. The smells of chestnuts roasting and of squid and peppers were those of a strange land. He wondered why he came here. This week he not only was unable to attend Father Malone's Mass but even to enter the man's church. He had gone to another. He did not know why. Nor yet why he came here. Then he knew that only in his home and here were people whom, knowing, he did not hate—and in sudden terror he entered the place.

Kate Bannon and James Kavanagh were married on the Saturday that Schneider sailed for Europe. It was a small, formal wedding and for the brief time of the reception Moon was his old self again, giving toasts, greeting guests, consoling Kav's mother, who wept frequently. She was a stout, handsome Irish woman with steel-gray hair and a great bosom that heaved when she wept. Her husband had been a policeman before his death and she a police matron.

Schneider was not there and Moon felt his own presence was responsible. But Kav said Schneider had too much to do that morning. He and Kate were going down to see Schneider off at noon.

"I suppose I'd maybe better go with you," Moon said. "I've got nothing against the guy. We were both drinking too much that night."

"Suit yourself," Kav said. "He's not sore at you."

"He shouldn't be." Moon put a hand to his head. "My head rang like a bell for two days."

"He was laid up himself," Kav said.

"I guess that makes us even," Moon said. "I'll bring him a bottle or something."

"He'd like it," Kav said. He went off to where his bride was surrounded by relatives and admirers, and Moon, seeing that Mrs. Kavanagh's bosom was heaving again, went over and sat on a chair next to her. "Look, Mrs. K.," he said, "if you could only see it this way—instead of losing a son, you gain a daughter. You don't think you're losing Jim, do you? Why, they'll be living right here in the neighborhood and where could Jim have possibly got a nicer girl?"

"Oh, it ain't that, Aloysius," Mrs. Kavanagh said, dabbing at her eyes. "It ain't that at all. It's the kind of work he's in. Low-grade like. Here when I worked myself to the bone helping put him through law school after his father died, I never thought he'd grow up to be a labor lawyer. Oh, my God." She began to weep again, then stopped. "Why, it's—it's like I don't know what. I remember those women pickets when they'd be brought into jail, their clothes half-torn off them, fighting and screaming like cats. Eyetalians, Jews, and the low-grade Irish. And to think of my Jimmy working with such people. And all so he could get married."

There was not much to say, Moon realized. Yet after a moment, he said, "I wouldn't look at it like that. There's something to what you say, but actually what Jim is doing is helping poor people to get a living wage. In a sense he's doing what the Church wants done. It's a sin to pay low wages and—"

"Oh, I suppose it is," Mrs. Kavanagh said. "But there'd be no need for such things as strikes and unions and the like if people would take a decent civil service job. There's that Galvin your poor sister is infatuated with, and there's that Thomas that I don't know what to make of, and there's even worse. And poor Jimmy working with them. And for what? I wish to the good God in Heaven he'd never met such people as them or this Bart Schneider. Bart we've known since he was a baby. Why, a nicer boy you'd never want to see. An altar boy and we all thought he'd study for the priesthood and all and Father McGlone talking about his chastity and all and how he'd go into the seminary. And now look at him. Of course, he's only part Irish or he'd never have gone back on the priest. The Irish always go into the seminary when they're intended for it. Sometimes, I think it's him put poor Jimmy up to this, and other times I think it's Kate. God knows, though, her family is decent, God-fearing people, though, and so I don't know except to say it's a queer time we're living in."

It was, indeed, Moon thought, with families divided against themselves. He felt no scorn for Mrs. Kavanagh, only a kind of pity, a terrible yet formless concern. Across the parlor, Linford Thomas was trying to catch his eye and Moon excused himself and went over to him.

Moon had thought of Thomas as a disturber, but knew in time that that was too simple. What the word to associate with Thomas was, Moon didn't know, but he did think of him as someone who could not be hurt. Which was doubly odd, for McGuffey had told him what he could of the fight in the water.

"What goes with you?" Thomas said.

"Not much," Moon said. "I am reduced to the status of

[ 272 ]

being a professional best man. James and Kate today, my sister next week."

Thomas smiled. "And we to that of wedding guests. . . . Are you working, Moon? I mean—"

"Why, no, to give you a plain answer. If the truth were known, I'm on my ass. Driven to bumming cigarette money from my mother. I should be a lesson to all politicians."

"It's not that special," Thomas said. "I wish we could do something for you. Jim is taking a couple of weeks off for his honeymoon. What I was wondering was if you would be available while he was gone if we needed someone?"

"Someone for *what?*" Moon said.

"To go to court for us if need be."

"Listen," Moon said, "I have never tried a case in my life. See? Not once in my life. Why, I'd get my brains beaten out by some of these big corporation lawyers."

"I didn't mean anything like that," Thomas said. "Small stuff, maybe nothing more than a magistrates' court."

Moon looked out a window from under his brows. "I used to know most of the magistrates. . . . But I'll tell you, you wouldn't want someone like me. I do the wrong thing by instinct. And even when I do the right thing, it's wrong. . . . I'd gum things up good."

"No one could say you were lacking in humility," Thomas said. "A rare enough virtue in anyone, especially a politician."

"Take it easy. I'm not a politician any more."

"So that perhaps the humility becomes despair," Thomas said. "While you were subject to the pressure of politics the doubts were humility: with the constraint removed the humility becomes despair. A kind of pressure physics of the spirit."

"I don't know what you mean," Moon said. "But what's so wrong with despair?"

[273]

"It's a sin of the mind," Thomas said. "Some people think it's the unforgivable sin."

"Christ," Moon said, "it's not a sin at all. I just take it in stride."

"In a sense it's not believing in God."

"Oh, I believe in God all right," Moon said. He wished Thomas hadn't started this.

"We can get hold of you then, in case we need someone?"

"Oh, sure," Moon said. He was anxious to get away. "But you'll be sorry as hell. I do the wrong thing naturally."

"Maybe you're one of those people St. Bernard speaks of— whom God pursues and eats up."

"That's a fine thought," Moon said, turning away. "Someone is always throwing St. Bernard at me." Moving toward Kate he thought about that. For his senior year in Christian doctrine, he had been required to do a paper on a saint and had read a book on St. Bernard, but remembered from it none of what Thomas and Schneider had said of the man. The only phrases Moon could think of were one having to do with bees and another about the saint being a defender of the Church. Defense, defense, Moon thought, we are always defending something.

"We've been looking for you," Kate said to him. "If we're going to get over to the boat, we'd better leave."

"I was thinking the same thing," Moon said.

While Kate was changing her clothes, Moon went out and spent his last five dollars on a bottle of whisky. When he got back to the house, Kate, James, and Thomas were waiting for him in a cab. During the ride over the Brooklyn Bridge Moon was quiet, thinking of the night he had driven Schneider and Concepción across the same bridge. Glancing around he saw he was the only one still in a morning suit. At the dock, the cab wasn't allowed past the entrance and Moon felt a twinge of impatience. Along the dock the smell of raw sugar and

of rope reminded him of Father O'Driscoll, and if he had
hoped the hate might be gone, it was in vain.

"I wish we were going," Kate said.

"You should have married a rich boy or a newspaperman,"
Kav said.

"I guess I didn't know any better," she said.

There was a good-sized crowd on the dock beside the boat
and most of the crowd was in a single group. Over the heads
of this group showed the white-plumed hats of two uniformed
men. "Holy Heaven," Moon said. "Knights of St. Gregory.
You don't suppose they're down here to see Schneider off?"

"Sure," Kav said. "They've made him a Knight of St.
Gregory."

As they came closer to the group, they saw it was gathered
around a figure in a wheel chair, and Moon began to recognize
people he knew. One of the two uniformed men was John
Calahan, Peter's father; Father O'Driscoll was also there and
at least two monsignors, in purple-piped cassocks and white
surplices.

"Whatever it is," Kate said, "it's not for Bart."

"You can say that again," Moon said.

As they passed the group to approach the gangplank along
its right flank, two or three people greeted Moon. "Ah, there
you are, old man," Burke Riley said to him. "It's really heartening to see you, too, turn out."

Moon's companions kept walking, but Moon felt himself
held, perhaps by habit. "What goes, Burke?" he said.

"You mean you don't know, old man?" Burke said. "Knobby
Brannigan is sailing to France. Going to Lourdes, you know,
to be cured. Quite a turnout, isn't it?"

"It sure is," Moon said. "I have a friend sailing on the same
boat. Sorry I can't stay."

"Sorry, too, old man. But you can watch from the dock. I'm
sort of acting as master of ceremonies."

"Say," Moon asked, "who's the other Knight of St. Gregory besides old man Calahan?"

"Why, that's Knobby's father, my employer, Sir Maurice Brannigan."

"Oh, I see," Moon said. He hunched his shoulders, as against the cold, and went up the gangplank. The others had found Schneider alone, overlooking the scene on the dock. Joining them, Moon found they not only had a fine view, but could hear what went on. Yet Moon made first his peace with Schneider, who had turned to him, a thin strip of white bandage above his cheekbone. "Say," Moon said, "I'm sorry about that night. Here's something to keep you warm." He held the bottle out tentatively.

"Thanks," Schneider said. "It's not as good as a blonde, but it'll do. I must have shot my mouth off pretty bad. . . . Come on now and see the circus."

Burke Riley stood on a packing case. "Folks," he was saying, "there isn't much more to say. We all know what a great fellow Knobby is and we all know that a month or two from now we will be right here at this same dock watching him walk down this same gangplank and him knowing we will be right here to give him the old Georgetown yell as he comes back. The old Notre Dame yell, too, I might add, for I see as many N.D. faces in this crowd as there are Hoyas. And it is a wonderful thing to think that even if Knobby didn't go to school in the shadow of the Golden Dome, nevertheless many of you boys here are from there and have come to see him off and to wish him well. And he knows that your prayers will go with him, too. Now, before the good padres here give Knobby their blessing, I call on his father, Sir Maurice Brannigan, for a few words."

Everybody clapped as the Knight of St. Gregory mounted the rostrum. Then spoke he thusly, the usurer, Sir Maurice Brannigan: "Me friends, I am deeply touched at this turnout.

For a simple, uneducated man like meself to be made a Knight of St. Gregory the Great is a wonderful thing. But to have so many of the holy and the great come out to see me boy Knobby off, is almost too much for me to bear. When a short time ago I was knighted, the thought came to me that if such a divine blessing could come to a simple man like meself, why could not a similar one come to me boy? If Holy Mother the Church could come to me with such unsought honors, I figgered that there must be some special quality in me blood that attracts holiness, something obtained now solely in Ireland, let us say, and that it must also be in me boy. And this being the case, I figger he must stand a good, an even certain chance of being cured at Lourdes."

Having indicated his humility and piety, the usurer, Sir Maurice Brannigan, K.S.G., now turned to humor. "I figger," he went on, "if all them Frenchies can go to Lourdes and come away cured, how much more so a son of old Ireland, a boy in whose veins runs nothing but the purest Irish blood, even though he was born here."

Pausing for the delicate laughter, Sir Maurice now turned, also delicately, to the subject of grace. "For we all know that when God Almighty showered down his blessings on this earth, He sent his choicest ones on that grand, green land beyond the seas. So much so that no one who has a drop of that blood in his veins cannot but be regarded as especially favored in the matter of Grace and virtually saved forever.

"And so, me friends, I will conclude. The time grows short and all I can say is that just as in Pittsburgh I built one of the finest churches in the world, so here in this very parish that the dock stands in, I will build still another church when me boy Knobby comes home whole and well."

So saying, his white plume nodding gallantly in the sun, e'en as with the knights of eld, Sir Maurice sware a favor to his Lord and stepped down into the applause, the tears running past his nose. And now lightly, his squire and sometime to be young knight, Burke Riley, leaped lightly to take his place on the rostrum. And now at his bidding advanced in serried ranks, the monsignori and attendants, swinging censors, chanting hymns, brandishing aspergilla. With bell, book, and candle they blessed the thin-faced figure in the chair, its head bowed and partly shielded by a hand, and then in turn they, too, retreated.

And still again young Burke Riley, slender, blond and assured, leaped to prominence. "So that's all, folks," he said, "except I don't think any of us should be ashamed to say a Hail Mary in public for Knobby. So I call now on our good friend, Father O'Driscoll, to lead us in a Hail Mary." Which the good padre did.

"And now, folks," Burke said, "Knobby is going aboard. And I don't think there is a more fitting way to finish our good-by than to sing *Sons of Georgetown*."

So while a male nurse pushed the wheel chair up the gang-plank, the words of the famous old song rose on the spring air, sung by all present, who always knew each other's college songs. Before the song was finished, the boat's whistle blew, drowning out the closing words, descending on all of them in a fine spray like rain.

The small group on the deck had not spoken much during the ceremony. The sight of Sir John Calahan in uniform made Moon a little guilty about his feelings toward the man, but he knew his feeling included more than that.

"Well," Schneider said when the whistle stopped blowing, "there's still half an hour before we sail. I'd like to buy lunch for all of you."

"You mean you could eat after that?" Kate said.

"Sure," Schneider said, "I can rise to any occasion. There's a built-in vomitorium on all passenger ships for just such times."

No one spoke, no one even looked at anyone else. Then Kav turned to Thomas. "All right, Lin, what's the answer? You're the only one I know that maybe has the answer."

"I don't know any answer," Thomas said. "I can't think of anything except to pray for such people."

"They've poisoned the wellsprings of prayer," Schneider said.

"The wellsprings of it are within," Thomas said.

"For you, maybe," Kav said, "but what about the rest of us that have to rely on not only the Church's sacraments but go to Mass with those people? I received Communion this morning at our nuptial Mass. But if I'd seen this first I never could have received it."

"Perhaps God will send a saint," Thomas said. "The Little Flower was a bourgeoise. That's her principal meaning, some think, that even the bourgeois can be saintly."

"Tell me, Lin, was her father a moneylender?" Schneider said.

From below on the dock, Rosemary Danaher had seen them and yoo-hooed. "I'm coming right up," she called. When she arrived with Whitey, she said, "Wasn't it wonderful?"

No one answered her. "Well, what's the matter?" she said. "You all look like you've been to a funeral."

"We have," Schneider said.

"Whose?" she asked.

"Christ's," Kav said.

Rosemary gave her little yelp. "Now don't talk like that. Here Whitey's getting ready to come into the Church and you talk like that."

They all looked at Whitey, who smiled foolishly. "What did you think of it?" Kav said.

"I don't know," Whitey said.

"See?" Rosemary said. "You just leave him alone."

[279]

"Did Rosemary tell you she wouldn't marry you," Schneider said, "unless you came into the Church?"

Rosemary's sallow face darkened. "I think that's a terrible thing to say. I wish I hadn't come up here. Come on, Whitey, they're all pagans." She took his arm and pulled him off after her.

"Aren't you glad you're not marrying her?" Kav said to Moon.

"Oh, I'd discipline her," Moon said.

"I bet," Schneider said.

Steam blew off from the ship's boilers. "What's that?" Moon said.

"That," Kav said, "that funny whirring sound, is St. Gregory turning over in his grave."

"Very funny," Moon said. "Very funny." The words came automatically; he was distracted by the thought that maybe Whitey didn't go to whorehouses: if Whitey did, he wouldn't be coming into the Church, at least not with such a foolish look on his face. This relation of cause and effect, at least of this kind of cause with this kind of effect, was new to Moon. Now that he knew it functioned in himself, he saw its possibilities, for good, for evil, but saw mostly its ability to confuse himself and again, as so often, turned away.

"I guess we'd better go," Kate said. She turned to give Schneider her hand. "Good luck, Bart. I don't know whether I envy you or not. Europe seems so sick, even the Church there."

"Europe?" he said. "I suppose it's the difference between dry rot and wet rot. In Europe it's wet rot, more spectacular, that's all."

Impulsively, in quick pity, Kate leaned and kissed him, just to one side of the lips. "Oh, hell," he said, "you don't have to feel sorry for me."

"Say hello to your friend for me," Kate said.

"She's not particularly mine," he mumbled, shaking Kav's hand. "Have a good time, Shamus."

"And you." Kav's narrow face clouded with emotion. "Take it easy." He turned away.

"And, Moon," Schneider said. "Don't let that lousy deal they gave you get you down."

"Oh, I'll get along," Moon said.

Thomas stood there, last, and Schneider realized that even now he knew little about the man. Yet certain things, known or at least apprehended before, returned now in memory: Thomas who never spoke ill of anyone, who suffered violence, who without effort seemed to knit, to unite others. He wondered foolishly if Thomas might just possibly be, not the saint, but the forerunner of the American saint. He wondered what they would do to Thomas or to the man or woman Thomas might precede. What the official Church had done to so many of its saints, jail, burn or damn him? Or just ignore him while it sat by the radio?

And Thomas, seeing clearly in that moment Schneider in the concentration camp in Holland, could scarcely speak. Trying to, as they shook hands, his lips twisted into a foolish grin so that Schneider was sure then that Thomas was not the saint.

Schneider stayed in his cabin most of the afternoon. He had opened Moon's bottle, but with the second drink the whisky lost its taste. He didn't want to get drunk. He wondered why such spectacles as they had witnessed on the dock drove him to fury or despair. A kind of intellectual arrogance or pride in himself? His own sins were various: fornication, hatred, pride, and despair. Even now he placed the last of them first: he supposed his reason for doing so was the same as for hating those who had taught him to do so. That was hating human error or original sin: a pastime for fools. If you hated the living people who still fostered the ancient error and so twisted the lives of those they were to save, the hatred was one more thing they could be blamed for: the hatred, the homosexuality, the fearful puritanism—the whole overlaid with that insane and fatuous pride. He wondered if certain prohibitions secreted in some people elements more deadly than those they were intended to suppress. God knows, he thought, there are enough unchaste people also haters, but theirs seems to lack edge. Maybe it was the kind of chastity the clergy imposed or tried to impose: an abstention from a thing called evil instead of good. Much easier for the average mind the way they had conditioned it. For so long had the clerics given the letter precedence over the spirit that now none of them could jabber about anything but the letter and the usurer's apprentice governed over them. . . .

He began to whistle *The Sorcerer's Apprentice,* then stopped and decided it was better to go out on deck. It was growing dark as he walked around the vessel. Only parts of things showed or manifested themselves. The two girls he noticed on one round of the ship were no more than a faint scent of Chanel when he passed them again. The taffrail log he could no longer see and, in a kind of alarm, he stopped and ran his hand along the rail. The log was still there, still turning. The rope moved in his hand and for a moment there was the illusion that the frail cord itself drove the ship . . . or at least essentially communicated with the sustaining element. He felt better when he found this was so.

Thinking then about the girls, he supposed he could meet them at dinner. He smiled: he had thought of himself as following Concepción to Europe. At least, she had been one of the reasons for going. The last faint shame about his feeling for her had gone, but some of the urgency had vanished with it. He wondered about Ellen Doarn, if she were responsible, if somehow his devotion to Concepción had been diluted by the new, colder one to Ellen. Yet it seemed he could not love either fully. Nor was his departure a leaving of Ellen and a going to

Concepción. It was neither abnegation nor devotion, neither love nor lust nor their refusals; its name was despair—so that he could wonder now if the voyage were a mortal sin, his fullest and most complete act of despair. He had not wanted to be a foreign correspondent, he did not even possess a second language other than the few words of college French; and he had seen the change in the men he had known who had become European correspondents, and feared it in himself.

The landward light alone remained. Walking toward the stern, against the light he saw the skeletal shape of the wheel chair and the boy's thin, wrapped figure. Closer, Schneider saw the chair was fastened near by and that the boy had been lifted out and placed in a deck chair. Puzzled by the illusion, Schneider hesitated and the boy said, "Hello, Bart."

"Hello. I didn't think you could see in this light. Didn't think you remembered me." They had met only once or twice to speak.

"I read your stuff all the time."

"You mustn't have much to do with yourself."

"As you see."

"I know," Schneider said. "I get clumsier all the time."

"I wouldn't say that."

"Why not?"

"I just wouldn't."

For some reason Schneider found he couldn't continue walking. The boy's voice was thin, clear and what Schneider reluctantly could think of only as gentle. "That was quite a rally they had for you on the pier."

"It was pretty bad, all right," the boy said.

After a pause, Schneider said, "Why did you let them do it?"

"I suppose because it pleases my father. There isn't too much I can do."

Again the silence before Schneider said, "Do you think— I mean do you believe going to Lourdes will help?"

[ 283 ]

Now the boy was silent. "If you mean," he said after a moment, "whether I believe I *can* be helped there—yes. If you mean do I think I *will* be helped there—no."

"Then why are you going?"

"I suppose to please my father."

"But why don't you think you can be helped?"

"I think I can be. But I've asked God not to heal me."

"Oh, for Christ sake," Schneider said, and turning moved brokenly down the deck.

## 15

MOON FINALLY DID GO to a Mass celebrated by Father Malone, for the priest officiated at Mary's wedding. It took place so soon after their father's death that no reception could be held. And for several reasons, Mary wanted to be married at an early Mass to avoid being seen by too many neighbors. She and Galvin were going to live on Mott Street and she had had a last-minute feeling of shame. Moon stopped talking about the wedding some days before it took place. And when he stopped talking about it, gradually it came to seem less outrageous. He found that he could not wish for Mary an existence such as that of the McGuffeys, nor for her to marry someone like Burke Riley or Peter Calahan or himself. He supposed that of all the men they knew, Galvin might be the most solid. And yet Mary was going to live in voluntary poverty with him, while he would work part time at the docks as a concession of sorts to Moon and Mrs. Gaffney.

A cousin named Eleanor Gaffney was the maid of honor. Mary had wanted Ellen Doarn, if only because Ellen seemed the only one of her acquaintances besides Kate who was not shocked by the marriage; but Ellen had gone away to teach at her old school. At the church there were only the principals,

Mrs. Gaffney, Moon, Eleanor, and Linford Thomas. The previous day, Thomas had phoned Moon and asked him to represent in court three union members who had been arrested for picketing. Thomas had overcome Moon's reluctance by promising he would have a more experienced lawyer to go with him.

The church was gray for the six-thirty Mass. Shadows stood in every corner. Moon had expected to be uneasy when placed as close as he must be to Father Malone on the altar, yet he found himself fascinated by the priest's graven face, so that Moon was puzzled by the man, who now performed meticulously all the movements of the ceremony, yet as though he had never seen any of the people before. It was this exactitude of word and gesture that made Moon change his mind. He had been determined not to receive Holy Communion from the priest, but when the man moved and spoke with that kind of impersonal respect, Moon was shamed. If Father Malone could recognize himself, even periodically, as merely the bearer of the sacraments, even to people he might dislike, Moon felt he himself could also see the priest as such, a transmitting agent, a servant of God—and so Moon did receive the Host.

Leaving the Church, he found himself preoccupied with how someone like Father Malone could touch and be every day informed by the sacraments and yet be as he was. The thought made Moon somber, something he had not wanted to be today, but he felt there was no despair in it. Yet despair had been with him for weeks like a shadow.

The party returned to the house in two cabs, Moon and the bride and groom alone in one of them. "Well, we were married under the bingo banners after all," Galvin said, "and liked it."

"I didn't like it," Mary said. "I took it as a penance."

"That's the way she'll probably feel about me after a while," Galvin said.

"Not unless you beat me."

"That depends," Galvin said.

[285]

"A fine thing to be talking about now," Moon said.

Their breakfast was happy. The cousin was puzzled by Thomas and Galvin, but not enough to refuse Thomas's offer to take her home after breakfast. Before he left with her, Thomas told Moon that the lawyer who would go with him to court was Neal Hartigan.

"This is a long way downtown for Neal," Moon said, putting it mildly. "How did you get hold of him?"

"He came in one day and said he'd work for us part time. He and his wife."

"His wife? I didn't know he was married."

"He married some Jewish girl a month or two ago."

Moon decided to say nothing: he must have missed hearing that in his concern with his own troubles. "That makes me feel better," he said. "I'm all set. I even bought a brief case."

Thomas smiled. "Neal will pick you up here in his car at nine-thirty."

"I'll be waiting," Moon said.

Mary went with her mother into the kitchen and Moon was left alone with Galvin in the parlor. The morning had remained gray, and outside they could hear the traffic of Canal Street beginning.

"I hope everything goes all right with the two of you."

"We'll get on," Galvin said.

"How did you feel about that old turkey marrying you this morning after damning both you and me?"

"I didn't know he'd damned me," Galvin said, "although I'm not surprised."

"How can a man like that go on as he does," Moon said, "and him receiving the sacrament every day?"

"I don't know," Galvin said. "Invincible ignorance is an explanation, although not a very good one."

"I'll tell you a funny thing," Moon said. "I got to thinking something I thought I'd never think. I got to thinking I'd

[286]

maybe leave the Church. Not that I would, but I just thought of it."

"That's nothing. We all think it sometime or other."

"Yes, I know." Moon was annoyed by Galvin's casual acceptance of the revelation. "But this is a serious thing with me. I used to think you and Schneider were crazy. But now I know what you mean and I don't know what to do."

Galvin lit a cigarette and looked out the window. He almost smiled as he said, "I don't think it's that bad. . . . There are hopeful signs."

"As what?"

"I suppose the fact that there are still people willing to work with the poor, specifically someone like Mary willing to marry me. There's Thomas—even one man with charity. And the young priests seem better. You find them in places the older ones would never go near, places like picket lines and Mott Street. At least when they're fresh from the seminary and before they're assigned to a parish with some old curate killer for a pastor. There's even someone like Schneider. Isn't it something for one of us to go so far for a girl who's part Negro?"

"I'd feel better if I was sure he'd marry her. Or I mean if I was sure that what he wanted was to marry her." Moon immediately regretted his words. Today just didn't seem the day for them.

"Even so," Galvin said. "Even if he doesn't. His going to Europe after her would still be an advance over—over what we were."

"I never thought of it like that," Moon said.

"And Kav going into the work he is. Even you."

"Don't worry about me," Moon said. "I'm not going to court because I want to. I'm doing it to help Kav out and for the fifteen bucks. Just like that story of his about the lawyer that had the fifteen-dollar case, the ten-dollar case and the two

[287]

small cases. I'm starting out good, a real magistrate's court shyster."

"I don't think your doing it against your inclination is as rare as you think," Galvin said. "We'd all do nothing, left to our own devices."

They were silent for a moment before Moon said bitterly, "Only one thing can move me now."

"Sure . . . and in time you might do it without hate. . . . But hate can be a starter. St. Augustine says God uses even sins to work in time his good. And it's obvious to anyone how he uses defeat."

Moon darkened. Galvin, he thought, was a wise guy. "I don't know," he mumbled. The doorbell rang. "That must be Hartigan for me," Moon said. He felt an unpleasant tension begin in him. "You and Mary will be all right." Putting on gloves and topcoat, Moon talked without looking at Galvin. He picked up the empty brief case. "I guess. Anyhow, we'll see you in a few days."

"Good luck," Galvin said. "Be as uncontemptuous of the court as you can."

Downstairs, Moon found Hartigan waiting in the vestibule, quiet, expensively dressed. "Glad to see you, Moon," he said.

"This is a long way downtown for you."

"I guess it is." Hartigan laughed uneasily. They got into the car and Hartigan began to drive uptown.

"I don't know whether you've been warned or not," Moon said, "but I never tried a case in my life."

"You've got to begin sometime."

"What about the poor clients?"

"Oh, they'll settle for anyone," Hartigan said. "Look at me. Today, we just enter a plea and ask for a postponement."

"They must be in a damned bad way, then," Moon said. "I wish Kav was back. What's the charge?"

"Alleged violence while picketing. I think an *agent provocateur* was used. It's hard to tell where Commies are involved."

"Where what?" Moon said.

"One of the three defendants is a Commie and known as such in the union. And—" Hartigan paused.

"And what?"

"I suppose you'd better know. Apparently Thomas didn't tell you."

"He didn't tell me anything."

"All three are Negroes."

Moon slowly rolled down the car window. "You know," he said, "I knew that was coming. Sooner or later."

www.ingramcontent.com/pod-product-compliance
Lightning Source LLC
Chambersburg PA
CBHW020541020726
47494CB00006B/1871